B53 089 534 3

KT-144-860

PASHA

JULIAN STOCKWIN

PASHA

HODDER &
STOUGHTON

First published in Great Britain in 2014
by Hodder & Stoughton
An Hachette UK company

1

Copyright © Julian Stockwin 2014

The right of Julian Stockwin to be identified as the Author of the Work has been asserted by him in accordance with the Copyright, Designs and Patents Act 1988.

All rights reserved. No part of this publication may be reproduced, stored in a retrieval system, or transmitted, in any form or by any means without the prior written permission of the publisher, nor be otherwise circulated in any form of binding or cover other than that in which it is published and without a similar condition being imposed on the subsequent purchaser.

All characters in this publication are fictitious and any resemblance to real persons, living or dead, is purely coincidental.

A CIP catalogue record for this title is available from the British Library

Hardback ISBN 978 1 444 78538 8
Trade Paperback ISBN 978 1 444 78539 5

Typeset in Garamond MT by Palimpsest Book Production Limited,
Falkirk, Stirlingshire

Printed and bound by Clays Ltd, St Ives plc

Hodder & Stoughton policy is to use papers that are natural, renewable and recyclable products and made from wood grown in sustainable forests. The logging and manufacturing processes are expected to conform to the environmental regulations of the country of origin.

Hodder & Stoughton Ltd
338 Euston Road
London NW1 3BH

www.hodder.co.uk

ر گل می وار بو گلشن عالمده خارسز .

Bir gül mü var bu gülşen-i 'âlemde hârsız

('Does any bloom, in this rose-garden world, lack thorns?')

Divan poetry from the court of Sultan Selim III

ROTHERHAM LIBRARY SERVICE	
B53089534	
Bertrams	13/10/2014
AF	£18.99
CLS	HIS

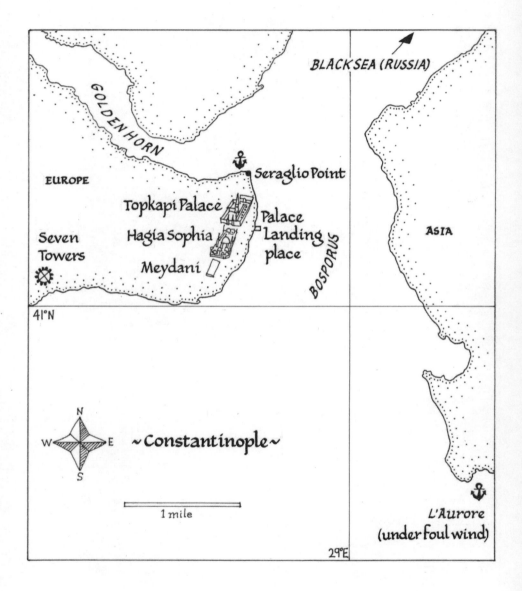

BLACK SEA (RUSSIA)

GOLDEN HORN

EUROPE

ASIA

Seraglio Point

Topkapi Palace

Palace
Landing
place

Hagia Sophia

Seven
Towers

BOSPORUS

Meydani

41°N

N

W   E

S

~Constantinople~

1 mile

29°E

L'Aurore
(under foul wind)

~The Mediterranean~

HUNGARY

DALMATIA

OTTOMAN
EMPIRE

BLACK
SEA

Constantinople

Naples

MOREA
(GREECE)

Entrance to the Dardanelles

ANATOLIA

Smyrna

37°N

SICILY

Malta

MEDITERRANEAN SEA

N
W — E
S

EGYPT

0   100   200   300   400   500
miles

20°E

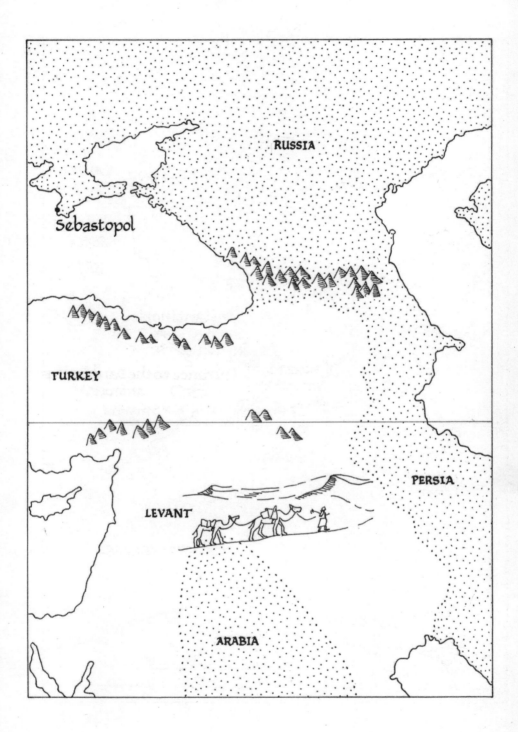

RUSSIA

Sebastopol

TURKEY

PERSIA

LEVANT

ARABIA

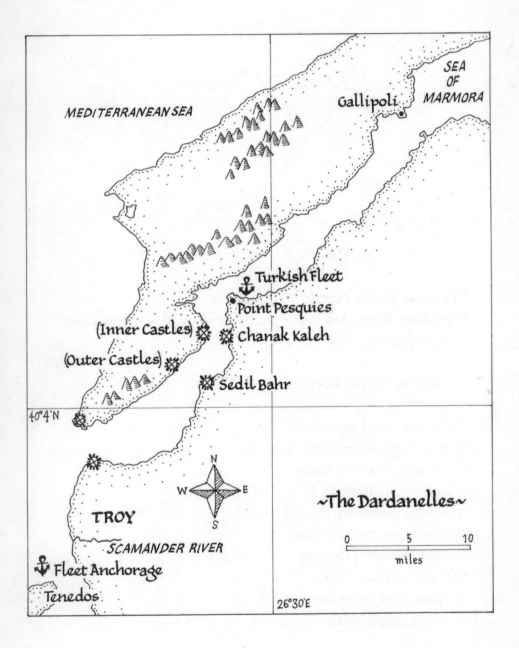

MEDITERRANEAN SEA

SEA
OF
MARMORA

Gallipoli

Turkish Fleet

Point Pesquies

(Inner Castles)

Chanak Kaleh

(Outer Castles)

Sedil Bahr

40°4'N

N
W   E
S

~The Dardanelles~

0   5   10
miles

TROY

SCAMANDER RIVER

Fleet Anchorage

Tenedos

26°30'E

Dramatis Personae

(*indicates fictitious character)

*Thomas Kydd, captain of *L'Aurore*
*Nicholas Renzi, his friend and confidential secretary, later Lord Farndon

L'Aurore, ship's company

*Bowden, third lieutenant
*Brice, officer appointed into *L'Aurore*
*Calloway, master's mate
*Clinch, midshipman
*Clinton, lieutenant of marines
*Curzon, second lieutenant
*Dodd, marine sergeant
*Doud, seaman
*Gilbey, first lieutenant
*Goffin, ship's clerk

*Kendall, sailing master
*Oakley, boatswain
*Owen, purser
*Peyton, surgeon
*Poulden, captain's coxswain
*Redmond, gunner
*Saxton, master's mate
*Stirk, gunner's mate
*Tysoe, Kydd's valet
*Willock, midshipman

Officers, other ships

Admiral Cuthbert Collingwood
Vice Admiral Duckworth
Rear Admiral Sir Thomas Louis
Rear Admiral Sidney Smith

Captain Blackwood, *Ajax*
Captain Bolton, *Fisgard*
Captain Boyles, *Windsor Castle*
Captain Brisbane, *Arethusa*
Captain Lydiard, *Anson*
Captain Moubray, *Active*

*Lawson, lieutenant in command, *Weazel*

Dmitry Senyavin, Russian Navy admiral
Aleksey Ochakov, lieutenant of *Tverdyî*

Others

Alexander Ball, governor of Malta
King George III
John Murray, publisher

*Congalton, Foreign Office
*Dillon, under-secretary, Eskdale Hall
*Emily, Kydd family's maid
*Fortescue, confidential secretary
*Jago, under-steward, Eskdale Hall
*Cecilia Kydd
*Fanny Kydd
*Walter Kydd
*Marquess of Bloomsbury
*Hetty Panton, friend of Cecilia Kydd
*Perrot, Kydd school boatswain

Constantinople

Ahmed, secretary to Selim III
Arbuthnot, British ambassador
Crown Prince Mustafa
Haji Samatar, grand mufti of Constantinople
İbrahim Hilmi Pasha, grand vizier
Isaac Bey, Ottoman envoy
Italinski, Russian ambassador
Kabakji Mustafa, Janissary official
Kaptan Pasha, port captain of Constantinople
Köse Musa, deputy grand vizier
Mahmut, chief of eunuchs of harem

Mehmed Ataullah Efendi, leader of Ulema
Memish Efendi, Selim supporter
Nezir Ağa, eunuch of the harem
Pakize, favourite concubine of Selim
Sébastiani, French ambassador
Selim III, sultan Shakir Efendi, Selim supporter

*Doruk Zorlu, British ambassador's aide
*Dunn, merchant
*Mustafa Tayyar Efendi, foreign ministry official

Chapter 1

It was as if the handsome frigate knew that she and her two-hundred-odd company were going home. After leaving the Caribbean she had quickly picked up a reliable westerly and now hitched up her skirt and flew, overtaking the broad Atlantic waves one by one in an eager swooping that had even old hands moving cautiously about the deck.

Channel fever was aboard and it gripped every soul. Soon after the chaos and drama of Trafalgar, HMS *L'Aurore* had been sent to join an expedition to wrest Cape Town from the Dutch. Success there had not been matched by the following ill-starred attempt at the South American colonies of Spain, and after capturing the capital, Buenos Aires, they had been forced to an ignominious surrender. Their later few months of service in the Caribbean had been abruptly terminated in an Admiralty summons to return to England. No doubt her captain was wanted at the vengeful court-martial to follow. But at last the handsome frigate and her crew were homeward bound.

Standing braced on the quarterdeck, Captain Thomas Kydd tried to take pleasure in the seething onrush of his fine command but he couldn't shake a feeling of foreboding.

A snatch of song floated aft. The men were in good heart. They had served nobly in all three actions and could rely on liberty and prize-money to spend while *L'Aurore* received overdue attentions from the dockyard. Her captain, however, could only look forward to—

'How now, old horse! Do I see you the only one aboard downcast at the prospect of England?'

His old friend and confidential secretary, Nicholas Renzi, had come on deck to join him. They'd shared countless adventures since they'd met as common seamen so long ago and had no secrets between them.

'England? Why, not at all – it's rather what's lying in wait there that troubles me.'

'The court-martial.'

'Quite. We gave it our best against the Spanish but lost. And our leader to be crucified for quitting station – if we'd prevailed it would have been overlooked, but the Admiralty will never forgive us now.' Kydd gave a bitter smile. 'There's above half a dozen captains who'll bear witness that I was in league with the commodore. It's beyond believing that they'll stop at only a single one to pay.'

'Possibly. But *L'Aurore* has done valiantly since, which should ease their lordships' wrath a trifle.'

'You think so? They won't yet have learned of our putting down the sugar-trade threat, and while we did stoutly at Curaçao, who's ever heard of the island, let alone Marie Galante? No, m' friend, after Trafalgar the country expects nothing less than victory, every time!'

2

'It might not be as bad as—'

'Don't top it the comforter, Nicholas. I'll take it, whatever comes. It's . . . it's just that it would grieve me beyond telling should I lose *L'Aurore*.'

'That would put us both in a pickle, I'm persuaded,' Renzi said. 'For at this particular time I'm obliged to say there are no shining prospects in store for me at all. I'll not hide that I'm disappointed my novel was not received more warmly. It did seem to me a sprightly little volume, but the public's taste is never to be commanded.'

'Well, I thought it a rattling good yarn, Nicholas! Are you sure?'

'It's been over a year and I've heard not a thing.' Renzi's head dropped. It was no use pining, though: he had to accept he was clearly not destined to be a novelist.

'But there's one thing you can look forward to.'

'Oh?'

'Nicholas, sometimes you try the patience of a saint! You seem to have forgotten your promise!'

'My . . . ?'

'Yes, your promise that when we touched port in England,' he ground out, 'you would that day post to Guildford and lay your heart before Cecilia.'

Nothing would please Kydd more than to see the long attachment between his sister and his particular friend brought to a satisfactory conclusion.

'Yes, of course,' Renzi said awkwardly. 'I'd not forgotten. But . . .'

'Yes?' Kydd said, his voice rising.

'Well, in the absence of prospects, I rather thought—'

'Nicholas, dear fellow,' he barked, 'if you're not on a Guildford coach within one hour of our casting lines ashore

3

I'll ask Mr Clinton for a file of marines who will personally escort you there. Am I being clear enough?'

It was the age-old excitement of landfall. A screamed hail from the volunteer masthead lookout, whose height-of-eye was more than that of the legitimate watch-keeper in the fore-top, sent pulses racing. The man would later claim his reward from the tots of his shipmates.

The pace of their homecoming quickened: now England would be in sight constantly, the well-known seamarks passing in succession until they reached the great anchorage at Portsmouth – Spithead.

The Needles, white and stark against the winter grey, were Kydd's reminder that within hours all would be made clear. The order that had reached out to him in the Caribbean would have been followed by another, now waiting in the port admiral's office. Relieved of his command pending court-martial? Open arrest?

Gulping, he realised that these last few sea-miles might very well be the last he would make under the ensign he had served since his youth.

Rounding Bembridge Point would bring Spithead into view and, if the fleet was in, he must make his report to the admiral afloat. If they were at sea, it would be to the port admiral in the dockyard. Gun salutes, of course, would be needed in either case.

The deck was crowded with men gazing at the passing shoreline, some thoughtful and silent, others babbling excitedly and laughing. It seemed the entire crew was on deck.

'Mr Oakley!' Kydd threw at the boatswain. 'Is this a pleasure cruise? Get those men to work this instant!'

L'Aurore had long since been willingly prettified to

satisfaction but she was a king's ship and had her standards. And he knew the real reason for his outburst and was sorry for it. Would the crew remember him fondly or . . . ?

The point soon yielded its view of the fleet anchorage – but four ships only and bare of any admiral's flag. Thus it would be the port admiral to whom he would make his number.

Her distinguishing pennants snapping at the mizzen halyards in an impeccable show, *L'Aurore* rounded to and her anchor plunged into the grey-green water.

Everyone knew what must follow but Kydd told them nevertheless. 'I shall report and return with orders, Mr Gilbey. No guardo tricks from the men while I'm gone or there'll be no liberty for any. Secure from sea and I want to see a good harbour stow. Carry on, please.'

With a tight stomach he boarded his barge, taking his place in the sternsheets and determined not to show any hint of anxiety.

'Bear off,' he growled at his coxswain, Poulden.

The boat's crew seemed to sense the tension and concentrated on their strokes even as they passed close by the raucous jollity of Portsmouth Point.

Reaching the familiar jetty oars were tossed in a faultless display and the boat glided in.

'Lay off, Poulden,' Kydd ordered, and stepped on to English soil for the first time in what had seemed so long. It had been nearly two years.

There was no point in delaying: he turned and strode briskly up the stone steps. At the top, unease gripped him as he saw a line of armed marines ahead.

Orders screamed out, muskets clashed, and an officer began marching smartly across.

'Captain Kydd. Sah!'

'I am he.'

'Sah!'

The port admiral, accompanied by his flag-lieutenant and other officers, appeared from behind the rigid line of red coats. 'Kydd, old fellow! Welcome to England! How are you?'

He held out his hand. 'We've been expecting you this age.'

The flag-lieutenant stood to one side in open admiration. 'Sah!'

'Oh, do inspect Cullin's guard, there's a good chap.'

There was nothing for it, and with a senior admiral at his side, Kydd did the honours, pacing down the line of marines wearing an expression of being suitably impressed, stopping with a word to one or two. At the end there was a flourish of swords and the party was released to go to the admiral's reception room.

'Sherry?'

A sense of unreality was creeping in: had they mistaken him for someone else? 'Sir. I thank you for your welcome, very pleasing to me. But might I enquire why . . . ?'

A small frown creased the port admiral's forehead. 'Do you think me a shab not to recognise a hero of the hour? Let me tell you, sir, since Boney set off his bombshell the public have sore need of same!'

'Hero?' Kydd said weakly.

'The papers have been in a frenzy for weeks. Curaçao – as dashing an exploit as any in our history! Throwing a few frigates against the might of a Dutchy naval base, sailing right into their harbour in the teeth of moored ships, forts and armies. Then every last captain takes boat, waves his sword amain and storms ashore to carry the day! How can it not thrill the hearts of the entire nation?'

'Well, it was a furious enough occasion, I'll grant you, but—'

'Nonsense! A smart action – and deserving of your prize-money,' he added, with a touch of envy.

'Sir.' Kydd paused. 'Are there orders for *L'Aurore* at all?'

The port admiral turned to his flag-lieutenant.

'Yes, sir. I'll get them instanter.'

He was back but not with a pack of detailed orders, just one, folded and sealed with the Admiralty cipher. Kydd signed for it, with only the slightest tremor to his hand.

'Do excuse me, sir,' he said, as he stepped aside to read.

It was short, almost to the point of rudeness. He was to place his ship under the temporary command of the port admiral forthwith pending refit while he should lose no time in presenting himself in person to the first lord of the Admiralty.

His heart bumped. There was a world of difference between a public hero and a naval delinquent and, without doubt, this was going to be the true reckoning.

'I'm to report to the first lord without delay. Do pardon me if I take my leave, sir. *L'Aurore* is to come under your flag until further orders – Lieutenant Gilbey, my premier, will be in command.'

'You know the routine, Mr Gilbey. I'm . . . not sure of future events but ship goes to harbour routine, full liberty to both watches. Don't be too harsh on 'em.' His first lieutenant touched his hat and left.

Renzi watched his friend gravely. 'In truth, it doesn't appear you're to expect a welcome from their lordships.'

'That's my concern. Get your gear together – we leave in an hour.'

'You want me to—'

7

'I'm posting to London. You're coming with me as far as Guildford, Nicholas.'

'You have my promise,' Renzi said, in an injured tone.

'Yes. And I have you for a shy cove. You'll do the deed or I'll know why!'

There was little conversation in the swaying, rattling coach. A cold winter rain beat at the windows and the countryside blurred into anonymity.

Past the little town of Petersfield, Renzi said stiffly, 'There's nothing I can bring to mind that makes my matter the easier to say.'

'Fire away nevertheless, Nicholas.'

'It's that . . . should Cecilia accept me . . . then, to be brutally frank, I have very little means to support her as a wife, as I keep telling you. Is it morally right then to—'

'If she agrees to marry you, I shall settle something on you both – tell her it's your prize-money portion, if you like.'

'That's very hard to accept, Tom, but nobly offered.'

'You'll take it for *her* sake, Nicholas.'

'Very well.'

'And none of your tricks o' logic. No telling me you'll marry her right enough, but the wedding day's only to be when you find the time.'

They continued on in companionable silence. Some time later Hindhead appeared out of the driving rain. Renzi turned to Kydd and said, in a low voice, 'Whatever is ahead for us both I know not – but the friendship in my heart I will value for all of time.'

The whip cracked over the tired horses as they toiled up the steep hill in Guildford Town. The Angel posting-house was halfway up and the coach swung through the arch. The driver cursed as he descended, tearing off his dripping cloak and keeping out of the way of the ostlers.

Renzi turned to his friend. 'You'll . . . ?'

'No, Nicholas. I have to get to the Admiralty without a moment lost. I don't want to disturb my folks only to be off again. After they change horses I'll be away. Now, you're going through with—'

'You have my solemn word on it.'

'Then . . .'

'I wish you well, dear friend. It's my prayer you'll still be in possession of a ship at the end of it.'

'I never took you for the praying sort, Nicholas, but thank you. And I do wish you every happiness, you and Cecilia both.'

They clasped hands, then parted.

Renzi turned and left the Angel, crossing the road and taking the short cut through the Tunsgate to the Kydd naval school.

His mind raced – even now it was not too late to slink away, avoid the issue entirely, for there was every chance that Cecilia had given up on him, had married another. Or perhaps she was out somewhere in the far reaches of the world with her employer, that diplomat of mysterious assignments, the Marquess of Bloomsbury.

Or she might be at home.

Hammering at him was one overriding question: was it right to propose marriage dependent on a settlement from his friend? A delicate ethical dilemma: on the one hand there was every moral imperative to decline to pursue his suit but on the other he had given his word to Kydd.

He looked up from the rain that drove in his face and

9

found that he was close to the school. He must make up his mind quickly. So much hung on—

A hand touched his arm. Startled, he swung around to see the rosy face of Emily, the Kydds' maid.

'It is! Mr Renzi, as I stand!' she blurted, with a broad smile. 'Come t' visit. Right welcome you are too, sir.'

'Do let me assist, my dear,' he said, taking the basket of vegetables she was carrying.

'Why, thank you, sir. They'll be main pleased t' see you, what with no news about Mr Thomas and such. Have you had tidings a-tall?'

There could be no retreating now and he let her prattle wash over him until they reached the door.

Unexpectedly, a calm settled. He would go through with it: he would formally propose to Miss Cecilia Kydd.

'Why, Mr Renzi!' Mrs Kydd cried. 'Do come in out o' that rain. I'm so pleased to see you – have you any word o' young Thomas?' she added anxiously.

'He's hale and hearty, Mrs Kydd, let me assure you. He's important business in London but desires me to convey to you his filial devoirs and promises to visit at the earliest opportunity.'

'You're so wet, Mr Renzi. Emily, run and get a towel for Mr Renzi – quickly now!'

'Who's that, Fanny?' quavered a voice from within.

'Why, Mr Renzi, Walter, that's who,' she replied.

'Come into the parlour, Mr Renzi. Sit y'self down while we find you something to warm the cockles.' She ushered him into the small front room, so well known from times before.

'You are in good health, Mrs Kydd?'

'So-so. I always gets chilblains in this blashy weather, but never you mind.'

'And Cecilia?' he asked carefully.

'Oh? Yes, she's fine. Now do tell us where you've gone to these last – bless my soul, it must be coming on for two years now.'

'A long story, and I'd much rather it were Thomas in the telling.' He paused, 'Might I enquire, what does Cecilia these days?'

'Poor lamb. She had a fine position, as y' know, with the marquess an' lady, but now they can't travel so she's been let go with an encomium. Spends her days about the house moping – she should get out and find herself a man, if y' pardon my speaking so direct.'

'Is she here? I'd like to pay my respects.'

'She was. Gone out to see a friend – she'll be back soon, I'll not wonder.'

Renzi's heart skipped a beat.

'Emily!' Mrs Kydd called in exasperation. 'Where's that posset? Mr Renzi here is a-dyin' from the cold an' wet. I'll give you a hand.'

She bustled out, leaving Renzi alone.

He looked about: was there anything that spoke of Cecilia's presence, that was hers? He was now about to face the one who had captured his heart, and a sudden wave of emotion engulfed him. He loved the woman: he adored her, was hopelessly lost to her. And he would propose, go on bended knee – but what if she turned him down?

Desolation clamped in. Refusal was a very real chance: this was a hard world where marriages were largely contracted on the basis of income expectations and a lady would be considered a fool to marry beneath her station. Even were Cecilia still to bear him an affection, she had her future to consider and . . .

A lump rose in his throat. It wouldn't be long and he would know her answer – and if it was unfavourable, his heart would surely be broken.

In a frenzy of apprehension he looked again to see if there was anything of her in the room. She must spend hours here, sitting – needlework? Not Cecilia, her mind was too active. What did other young ladies do in her circumstances? Drawing? Piano? There was neither here. He knew so little of her at home . . .

What was that, peeping out from under the cushion? A book, shoved under in haste to conceal it, almost certainly what she'd been reading.

Guiltily Renzi pulled it out. It was a novel of sorts, the cover gold-embossed with a romantic manly figure standing atop a rock. He felt a tinge of disappointment that it was a work of fiction she was reading rather than an improving classical tome. He flicked the pages to see what had attracted her to it, some with dark Gothic pictures, the text closely spaced.

He picked a paragraph at random and began reading – he had seen those very words before. They were his *own*, damn it!

Nearly dropping the book, he flicked hastily to the title page. *Portrait of an Adventurer* by Il Giramondo. *The peregrinations of a gentleman rogue who loses his soul to dissipation and finds it again in far wandering.*

He feverishly searched for the publisher's name: yes, it was John Murray.

The implications slammed in on him. He was a published author! And therefore he had an income!

He choked back a sob, undone by the sudden reversal of Fate.

Then a cooler voice intervened. To tell Cecilia that he had

an income as an author would be to reveal that he must necessarily be this wastrel. How could he?

Thinking furiously, he realised he must go immediately to John Murray to ensure his identity was kept secret.

Yes! It was what he must do – but he knew nothing of authors and royalties. Supposing the amount was a pittance only?

Standing about would solve nothing. Only action!

'Oh, Mrs Kydd?'

She came in, hurriedly wiping her hands on a cloth. 'Mr Renzi?'

'I'm devastated to find I forgot to attend to an urgent matter. I must deal with it – I pray you tell Cecilia that I called and that I will return. A day or two at the most.'

'Mr Renzi!' Mrs Kydd said, shocked. 'You're not going out in all that rain again? It's cold and—'

'I must, dear lady. I'll take my leave now, if I may.'

The rain continued relentlessly as the coach ground and clattered over the cobbles towards the London road at the top of the hill. Kydd hunkered down, glowering under the press of dark thoughts that crowded in. As each rose in his consciousness, he met it with a savage riposte: there was nothing he could do about it now so he must let events take their course. A logic that would undoubtedly have met with Renzi's approval – if he had still been by his side.

Renzi, a friend of times past. Those long-ago years tugged at him with their elemental simplicity, their careless vitality. Now his bosom friend was to be wed, settle down, have his being on the land, no more to wander. They would meet again, of course: he would be married to Kydd's sister and she would keep in touch. But at this point their lives had irrevocably diverged.

In a pall of depression and aching from the ride, Kydd morosely sat through the final miles into the capital, grey and bleak in rain-swept gloom. He directed the driver to his accustomed lodgings at the White Hart in Charles Street and answered the vacuous civilities of the innkeeper with monosyllables. Tomorrow he would learn his fate.

Kydd hadn't slept well. He dressed slowly, defiantly hanging on to the fact that to the world he was still Captain Kydd, commander of His Majesty's Ship *L'Aurore*, and dared any to say otherwise.

His orders had been to present himself immediately at the Admiralty and it would only tell against him if he did not, so at nine precisely he was deposited outside the grim façade of the home of their lordships. He knew the way: the Captains' Room was in its accustomed crowded squalor; the usual supplicants for a ship, petitioners and those summoned to explain themselves.

He handed his card to the clerk. 'To see the first lord per orders,' he muttered, and found a seat among the others. Curious at a new face, several tried to start a conversation but were discouraged by Kydd's expression.

The minutes turned to an hour. It was here in this very room that he'd found out he'd been made post. That was in the days of the granite-faced sailor Earl St Vincent. Now the office of first lord of the Admiralty was occupied by a civilian, Grenville, younger brother of the prime minister. It had been he who had summoned him so peremptorily.

Then why was he waiting? He hailed the clerk. 'Captain Kydd. As I told you, I've orders from the first lord that demand my immediate presenting in person. Why have you not acted?'

He knew the reason: it was the custom to grease the palm of the man to ensure an early appointment. But this was different: he was not a supplicant. He had been ordered to attend, and woe betide a lowly clerk who thought to delay him.

'Orders? From Mr Grenville?'

'Yes,' Kydd said heavily.

'Very well,' he responded, with a sniff. 'I'll inform him of your presence.'

'Thank you,' Kydd replied, trying to keep back the sarcasm.

He settled in his chair in a black mood. If he was not ushered into the presence within the hour he'd make damn sure that—

At the top of the steps a genial aristocratic-faced man burst into view. 'Ah! Captain Kydd! So pleased you could come.' It was the first lord himself.

Naval officers shot to their feet, confused and deferential. Several bowed low.

He hurried down the steps and came to greet Kydd with outstretched hand. 'We've been expecting you this age. So good of you to, ahem, "clap on all canvas" to be with us.'

Shaking Kydd's hand vigorously, he ushered him up the steps in the shocked silence.

In the hallowed office Grenville threw at his assistant, 'Not to be disturbed,' and sat Kydd down.

'Now, what can I offer in refreshment? Sherry? No, too early, of course. So sorry to keep you waiting – that villainous clerk will hear from me, you can be assured of it.'

'Sir – you wished me here at the earliest . . . ?' Kydd began.

If this was the preamble to disciplinary proceedings he was at a loss to know where it was leading.

'Yes, yes! You're the last of the Curaçao captains come to town. And now we're all complete. My, I've never known the public to be in such a taking! Raving about your gallantry and so forth. It's done the government no end of good, coming as it does in these dog days after Trafalgar.'

Kydd smiled tightly. So the whims of popular opinion had decided they were heroes not of the ordinary sort. If they only knew it had been an attempt to uncover a deeper plot against British interests in the Caribbean that had, in fact, failed in its object.

'Pardon me, sir. Am I to understand that this is why I've been recalled?'

Grenville blinked. 'Why, if I had not, the people would have howled for my head.'

'Ah. Sir, I had thought it was possibly in connection with the forthcoming court-martial of Commodore Popham,' he said carefully, shifting in his seat.

'Oh, that. Not at all, dear fellow. I can't see it happening for a good while yet. In any case, as I read it, the merchantry love him because he opened up the river Plate trade to our goods as can't find a market after Boney's decree, and would never stand to see him pilloried. And it's nothing to do with you, a Curaçao idol.'

As it sank in, the tension slowly drained from Kydd.

'The Curaçao captains – there's to be a public procession or some such?' If there was, this was an odd reason to recall a valuable frigate and her crew from across the ocean.

'Naturally. And – well, you're going to have to move speedily, I'm persuaded. The occasion is set for very soon – we didn't know when you'd arrive.'

'Move speedily, sir?'

'Yes. Know that your recall was never my doing. My dear

Kydd, it came from the palace – His Majesty wishes in person cordially to felicitate the principals in the affair. By his royal command I'm to direct you to attend on him the instant you land.'

'The King!' Kydd stuttered.

'Indeed. In view of the imminence of arrangements I would have thought it not too precipitate to seek an audience this very afternoon. Does this suit?'

He gulped. 'Y-yes, sir.'

'Very well, I'll set it in train. His Nibs's business will be concluded by three, so shall we say four? I'll send my carriage – to Windsor is tiresome in this weather.'

'That's very kind in you, sir.'

'Oh, and you'll find it more convenient should you choose to return here afterwards, you still in full fig and such. There's a reception to be hosted by the prime minister for the heroes of the hour but it shouldn't go on too long, he having pressing business in the Commons.'

It had happened! It was every naval officer's ardent desire to gain distinction, to rise above the common herd – to gain notice from on high. And there was no greater such in the land than the King of England. He had arrived – it was breathtaking! It was marvellous!

Kydd took extreme care with his full dress uniform, the snowy neck-cloth and fine linen shirt that he had thought would last be worn before a hostile Board of Admiralty. His sword was in impeccable order, the scabbard rubbed with horn and blacking to a lustrous gleam by his loyal valet, Tysoe, his gold lace glittering after careful application of potato juice, and his court shoes in a discreet shimmer of polish and gold buckle.

In a fever of tension and exhilaration, it seemed for ever

17

before there was an excited knock at the door. It was a near-swooning innkeeper who wrung his hands in emotion.

'Y-your carriage is – is here, Captain,' he stammered.

When he reached the door he saw the reason for the man's excitement – it was the first lord of the Admiralty's personal carriage: spacious, gleaming black with scarlet and gold trim, his cipher blazoned on the side, built for the express purpose of public display of the occupant. Four white horses and two footmen in blue and gold – and in front matching black steeds of an escort of four of the King's Troop, with sabre and cuirass, looking stolidly to the front with a further two bringing up the rear.

A liveried footman was standing at attention by the coach steps, the other perched aloof behind.

A crowd quickly gathered, thrilled to be so close to what must be a very important personage, and as Kydd appeared, there was a ripple of excitement and muffled cheers. He doffed his cocked hat to them and couldn't resist calling loudly to the innkeeper, 'I'm off to attend on His Majesty, my man – I shall not be dining tonight.'

It brought gratifying gasps and chatter as he allowed himself to be handed up, to sit in lonely splendour as the resplendent sergeant on the lead horse barked orders to set them smartly on their way.

Fortunately, although the sky was dull and grey, the rain was holding off. The cavalcade had no difficulty with the notorious London traffic and they bowled along westwards at a steady clip, the massed clatter of hoofs drawing admiring attention as people stopped to gape. Kydd kept a stony expression, looking only to the front, ignoring cheers and catcalls from urchins but deigning to lift his hat to gentlemen who troubled to remove theirs as he passed.

The King's residence, Windsor Castle, hove into view, all stern battlements and round towers, and Kydd's heart thumped. In a twist of irony he remembered it was not the first time he had been directly addressed by his sovereign. That had been long ago when he was a young seaman in *Artemis*, a man-of-war the same size as *L'Aurore* in which he had fought in the first big frigate action of the Revolutionary War. He recalled a kindly face, bemused blue eyes and a comment about Surrey Cross sheep. Would he . . .?

In a practised show they swung about to clatter in through the ancient archways, proceeding to the solemn entrance the other side of the vast courtyard. Kydd glimpsed the mast above the great round tower. It did not fly the Union flag of Great Britain: instead the lions and leopards of the Royal Standard of King George III floated there imperiously. The sovereign was at home.

As Kydd rose to alight, he looked around. It was so unreal, so impossible, that this day Tom Kydd of Guildford was about to be received by the monarch that his vision dissolved into a series of dazed impressions.

Here he was, standing in a castle first occupied by William the Conqueror after 1066, and witness to the stately panoply of the centuries since that was England's past – and which he had first learned about in dame school. If crabby Miss Bowling could only see him now . . .

An equerry and royal footmen in blue and gold edged with red emerged to greet him. It seemed he was expected, and that His Majesty had expressed a desire that he should be presented at once.

He was ushered inside to a quiet magnificence, passing through majestic rooms hung with vast ancestral portraits, then across a hall of blinding splendour before reaching the state apartments, set about with lordly bewigged footmen.

An elderly gentleman of infinite dignity was waiting before high closed doors. The equerry murmured Kydd's name to him and he was introduced to the lord chamberlain.

A quiet briefing was given: Kydd should bow as he was introduced but a short bow rather than the elaborate affair fashionable in drawing rooms. He should not speak until spoken to and he should remain standing until bidden otherwise. This being an informal audience without others present, full expressions of fealty were not to be expected and, indeed, His Majesty was known for his kindness and interest in meeting his subjects.

With his cocked hat firmly under his arm, stiffly at attention, Kydd took a deep breath and nodded.

The lord chamberlain smiled encouragingly and knocked discreetly. The door was opened wide from the inside and Kydd nervously followed him into the Presence.

Oblivious to the subdued grandeur of the room, Kydd had eyes for one thing only.

George III, by the Grace of God, King of the United Kingdom of Great Britain and Ireland, Defender of the Faith, sat at a table spread with a silver tea service, his queen standing next to him, a lady-in-waiting behind.

'Your Majesty, may I present Captain Thomas Kydd of the Royal Navy?'

Kydd bowed jerkily, his heart in his mouth.

'Thank you, Dartmouth. Well, now, Kydd, and you'll be relishing a dash of peace and quiet after your mortal perils in Curacoa, hey?'

He became aware of a heavy face but kindly eyes, albeit rheumy and filmed.

'Your Majesty, to return to this realm is a pleasure indeed.'

It would probably not be done to tell a king that his pronunciation of Curaçao was somewhat awry.

'As it should be, young man.' The King harrumphed. 'It's our pleasure to take a dish of tea at this hour and we're not minded to alter our custom. Do join us, will you? Charlotte, my dear . . .'

Kydd had a moment of panic – should he sweep his coat-tails elegantly behind as he sat or keep his sword from twisting under him? But, of course, unlike those of army officers, a naval sword hung loosely, the better to sit in boats, and he concentrated on a flourish with the tails. The sword obediently conformed and in relief he accepted an elegant, tiny porcelain cup from the Queen, who smiled winningly at him.

'So, Kydd. The Hollanders were all before you and the battle not yet won. What did you say to your men that they followed you into the cannon's fury? Tell away, young fellow!'

Kydd's mind froze as he tried desperately to remember exactly what he had shouted in those mad moments as he'd thrown himself and his crew against the forts. Then he realised that exactitude was not what was being asked and he replied gravely, 'Sire, I remember it as, "Come, my lads, to the fore and the day is ours!"'

'Ah! A true son of the sea speaks! Would that we had more of your ilk, Kydd!'

There was then nothing for it but to deliver a detailed account of the action, the obvious interest and enthusiasm of the King easing his fears.

'Capital! In the best traditions of the Navy, of Nelson himself, I shouldn't wonder.'

Kydd flushed, overwhelmed at such praise from his sovereign.

'Now you'll want to be on your way, we fancy,' the King said, rising. Kydd scrambled to his feet.

'But before you go, if we might detain you a little longer . . .'

On cue a court official entered noiselessly, bearing something on a satin cushion.

The King lifted a glittering object on a white and blue riband from it and turned to Kydd. 'Captain, in the name of England we bestow upon you this, in distinction of the valour you displayed upon the field of Curacoa.'

Kydd knelt and bent his head, feeling it pass over his neck, then rose, overcome.

'We wish you good fortune, Captain, and God preserve you until next we meet.'

'I do thank you for the great honour you have done me, Your Majesty,' Kydd managed, with a bow.

Dazed by events, Kydd descended from the carriage at the back of the Admiralty. He had taken tea with the King of England and now wore his honour. He looked down on it yet again: a pure gold medal on a riband as put there by the hands of His Majesty. It nobly bore a representation of Victory placing a wreath upon the head of Britannia, standing proudly on the prow of a ship with her shield and spear.

It was beyond imagining – what more could life bring?

He was met by an unctuous flag-captain, who ushered him into a room where the reception was well under way, the candlelight glittering on gold lace and stars – and dramatic with the splash of colour in sashes and uniform.

'Sir, may I present Captain Kydd of *L'Aurore* frigate?'

The prime minister smiled with every evidence of delight. 'Glad you could make it, old fellow. Wouldn't be the same without we had all the heroes of Curaçao.'

'My honour entirely, sir.'

'We'll talk presently, I'm sure. Do find yourself some refreshment.'

Kydd turned to see a familiar face beaming at him. It was Captain Brisbane, whom he'd last seen in the Caribbean near hidden in the smoke of guns.

'What ho, Kydd! We'd just about given up on you.'

'Ah, Charles, we were detained by the little matter of relieving the French of yet another island.'

'Stout chap, always knew we'd find you where the action was thickest. My, what a fuss they're making over us. You'd think we'd sent Boney himself to Hades.' He leaned forward conspiratorially. 'We never did get to lay those privateers by the tail. Did you hear if . . . ?'

'We found 'em on Marie Galante and collared the lot,' Kydd answered. 'Couldn't say much about it for fear of scarifying the planters.'

'Well, that's good to hear. So you're only just arrived? Not heard the news?'

'Orders to report here without losing a moment, no reason given.'

Brisbane frowned. 'That's not the way to treat a hero of Curaçao.' He brightened. 'Look, I know what we'll do – over here.'

They threaded through the throng until they reached the back of the room. Copies of the *Gazette* were stacked neatly on a small table under a mirror. Brisbane took one. 'Nip in there for a minute and read all about why you're here,' he said, gesturing at a side room.

Kydd did so and soon found a dignified headline announcing the capture of Curaçao.

He read avidly – it was a fair account, detailing all the acts of individual courage and dash shown that day. He went pink with pleasure to see his own part lauded in measured, stately prose, his name there in print to be read by any in the kingdom.

He moved on to the last paragraphs, which detailed the honours and reward of the actions.

A naval gold medal was to be awarded to every captain, His Majesty insistent that he present the honour himself.

Then in a cold wash of shock he saw his name – right there, in a list of those . . . to be further honoured with a . . . knighthood. These several captains to be elevated to the style and dignity of a Knight of the Bath. The investiture at St James's Palace . . . installation into the Order . . . Thursday next at Westminster Abbey.

His hand trembled as he gripped the paper and his eyes misted with emotion. He was very soon to be . . . Sir Thomas Kydd, KB, knight of the realm.

Honours and fame were now indisputably his.

In a trance he entered the main room again, carefully placing the paper back where he had found it.

Brisbane gave a soft smile. 'Now you can see how you've been cutting it so fine. The accolade – where you get your step to knight from the King – there, your sea gear is more to be expected. But your installation into an order of chivalry, you have to be in the right rig for that or they won't have you. Clap on all sail – I'll give you the address of the court costumier fellow.'

Kydd took in some of the others in the room. Over there was Lydiard of *Anson*, whom he hadn't seen since the frightful drama of a chase together in the depths of a hurricane; Bolton of *Fisgard,* out of his depth, stuttering at a half-deaf statesman . . . He could have hugged them all.

The day had changed so drastically – like a weathercock in a storm. The morning, with its dread and worry, to this, this . . .

With a stab of feeling, his thoughts went to Renzi. He wished he knew what was happening in Guildford.

But he had his duties, and he turned to the chancellor of the exchequer with the wittiest quip he could find.

It had been just four days. In a blaze of honour, pageantry and the ancient rites of chivalry, he'd become a man of unassailable consequence in the world. He would never again fear any social occasion and could expect deference and respect wherever in life he found himself.

Kydd fought down a jet of elation as he looked about him. Here he was, in attendance at the Court of St James's by right, at a levee in company with statesmen and dukes, diplomats and ambassadors, admirals and generals as the King moved about the throng on the highest affairs of state.

He'd never forget the actual moment when King George had, in company with his fellow captains in the Throne Room of this very palace, granted the accolade, dubbing him knight with a tap on each shoulder from the Sword of State and bestowing the riband and star he now wore.

And that had not been the end of the pomp and ceremony. The accolade had been a private occasion between his sovereign and himself; the public expression had been the installation. It was all now a blur of images. Richly dressed in the order's crimson mantle, lined with white and fastened with gold tassels, its great star on his left, sword and spurs, black velvet cap with a plume of white feathers. The knights moving in solemn procession to Westminster Abbey, two by two in their regalia, with awed crowds on either side. Met by Bath King of Arms, with tabard collar and escutcheon, then ushered into the beautiful fan-vaulted splendour of the Henry VII chapel and gravely welcomed by the Great Master of the Order. Passing within, the walls overhung with crests and banners of great antiquity, helms and achievements in stern display. At the bidding of the Gentleman Usher of the Scarlet Rod, taking his place in the knights' stalls. There before him the stall plates of others who had preceded him: Clive, Rodney, Howe . . . and Horatio Nelson.

In solemn splendour he had been inducted, from the hands of the King receiving his knightly honours: an enamelled badge of crowns suspended from a glittering gold collar of interlinked crowns and knots.

The hallowed proceedings held the weight of history. In ages past knights would have spent the night before their ennobling in vigil, then were ceremonially bathed and purified, but since the time of the first King George much of the medieval pomp had been discarded; although on the statutes there was still the requirement of a new knight that he provide and support four men-at-arms to serve in Great Britain whenever called upon. Not to be taken too literally, he had been hastily assured.

Kydd had joined the pantheon of heroes who had been honoured thus by their country, their fame assured in perpetuity. He was entitled, as Nelson was, to a coat-of-arms, his crest and heraldic banner, which would be laid up here on his passing and would be blazoned on the side of his carriage to tell all the world that he had been touched by greatness.

Now, at this august levee, he tried not to be too obvious as he snatched another glimpse of the resplendence of his knightly honours as he bowed and greeted in a haze of unreality.

'Well, Sir Thomas, pray tell, how does it move you, your illustrious translation?'

It was the first lord of the Admiralty, Grenville, smiling broadly.

'Why, sir, it is the most wonderful thing,' Kydd said sincerely. 'As I do hold to my heart.'

The smile slipped a little. 'As you should, of course. You deserve well of your country and may rejoice in your honouring.'

Was that a tinge of envy?

Yes! There was no sash and star, no collar and badge – even the first lord of the Admiralty had not attained the heights of chivalry that Kydd had.

It set the seal on his happiness. All he wanted to do now was to fly to his family and lay his triumph before them . . . and sink into blessed rest until it had all been digested.

It seemed to Kydd that it had not stopped raining since he had left Guildford in a very different mood. Now there was no possible danger to his continued sea career: the Admiralty would never risk the wrath of the public by failing to employ a frigate captain of such fame. Where could it all end?

At the Angel, he'd had to hire a pony and trap for his baggage was so great, but his heart was full as he tapped on the door.

'Son! Welcome back, m' dear. Let's get you out o' them wet clothes. Emily – here, girl!'

He allowed himself to be fussed over, hugging his news to him.

'How long will ye be staying this time, a-tall?' Mrs Kydd asked casually.

'Until the Admiralty sees fit to send me orders. There is a war on, Ma.'

'Goodness gracious – is this all your baggage arriving, Thomas?' she said, with a frown at the carter's knock.

'I need to keep a few things safe. My room is still . . . ?'

'O' course it is, son! As long as y' want it, you bein' unmarried an' all.'

'Is that you, Thomas?' Cecilia said in delight, coming into the room. 'My, you *are* wet.'

'Cec,' Kydd demanded immediately. 'Has Renzi talked to you at all?'

'Nicholas? Well, no, he called a few days ago but I was out, and then he found he had business to do and I haven't seen him since.'

'That black-hearted scoundrel!' Kydd spluttered. 'I knew he'd skulk off if I left him.'

'Thomas, what do you mean? He said he'd return shortly,' she said frowning.

'Never mind! Just keep a weather eye open for the shyster.'

But nothing could spoil the swelling happiness he felt. Should he tell them now or save it for when he'd changed? He knew he couldn't keep it to himself indefinitely so he compromised. 'I'm just going off to shift out o' these wet togs – don't go away, anybody. I've a surprise for you all . . .'

In his room he opened the big leather trunk – and there it was, not a crazed fantasy but a reality, and his by right. The glittering splendour of the accoutrements of a knight of the realm.

He stripped, towelling vigorously, then began to dress. There was an aged full-length mirror in the corner with a crack across its middle. He inspected himself in all his finery. The crimson mantle with its gold tassels, the star and riband, white leather shoes, spurs of gold and, of course, his sword. The cap with its flare of feathers he couldn't wear in the low-ceilinged room so he carried it carefully as he stepped out.

He paused outside the little drawing room and settled the cap firmly on, then flung the doors wide.

'Lawks a-mercy!' squealed Mrs Kydd. 'Whatever are you doin' in them clothes, Thomas? Take 'em off afore someone sees you!'

Cecilia's eyes widened in dawning comprehension. 'T-Tom, is it that you're . . . you're a . . . ?'

'Ma, Cecilia,' he said proudly, 'meet . . . Sir Thomas Kydd, Knight o' the Most Honourable Order of the Bath.'

'You are!' his sister breathed, her eyes shining. 'You really are!'

'Aye, sis. Just these two days. By the hand of His Majesty himself, as I'm a hero of Curaçao.' He chuckled. 'And this is my gold medal – he gave it me when we had tea together. That's with Queen Charlotte as well, o' course.'

'Tea! With the King!'

'Oh, Tom dear, I wish ye wouldn't scare us so,' Mrs Kydd said faintly, having had to sit suddenly. 'Now, you're not flamming us, are you?'

'No, Ma. If you don't believe me, you can read about it in the *London Gazette*, like all the world does.'

Cecilia took in his full court dress in awe. 'Then you've been to the investiture?' she whispered. 'At Westminster Abbey, and all? I nearly went to one with the marquess but he wanted us to remain outside for the procession. Did you . . . ?'

'I did, Cec! In the abbey among all that tackle from long ago. It's where Nelson himself got his knighting and you can still see his stall plate with the common sailor on his crest.'

This time it was she who had to sit, looking up at him with a hero-worship that was agreeably gratifying for an older brother.

'You're famous, then,' she said, in hushed tones. 'Mama, Thomas is a hero. He's going to be talked about and – and . . .'

She stopped, at a loss to put into words that now there was a Kydd who would tread an inconceivably larger stage.

Chapter 2

Crossing Blackfriars Bridge and walking on to Fleet Street, Renzi brought to mind the outcome of his previous interview with the publisher John Murray: the summary destruction of his hopes of publication of his ethnical treatise. It had been done in the politest and most gentlemanly way, yet with finality, along with the offhand suggestion of an alternative course – a novel.

The office was further along, the polished brass plate still on the door.

This was now a matter of the gravest import. If the book had met with success . . . If, however, what he had seen was a scandalously copied version . . .

He hesitated, then knocked firmly.

The door was opened by the same old gentleman in half-spectacles who had wished him well before. 'Why, sir! How kind of you to call again. Do come in. I'll tell Mr Murray you're here – I won't be a moment.' He hurried up the stairs, leaving the lowly clerks glancing at Renzi with curiosity.

Shortly a call came from the next floor. 'He bids you join him, sir, and you are welcome!'

Renzi entered the book-lined office.

'Come in, come in! Sit yourself down, man,' Mr John Murray said, showing every evidence of interest and politeness.

Renzi perched on a carved chair of another age.

The publisher leaned forward. 'What's your tipple?'

'Thank you, no.'

'Well. We've things to discuss, I believe, as bear on your future with us, sir.'

'My future?' Renzi responded carefully.

'Why, yes, as an author of the first rank, sir.'

Renzi held back a surge of hope. 'Oh? Pray do enlighten me,' he said politely. 'I've been out of the kingdom for some years now and am unaware of any . . . developments.'

He managed to remain cool.

'Of course! Mr Renzi, let me be the first to tell you, your excellent Il Giramondo tale has captured the hearts of the nation. We have booksellers crying for stock faster than we can print it.'

'That is gratifying, of course, Mr Murray. Might I be so indelicate as to enquire if there are proceeds from this that might, shall we say, accrue to myself?'

'Royalties? Why, of course, dear sir! Should you wish to sight a statement of account?' He rang a silver bell on his desk and the clerk appeared suspiciously quickly.

'Mr Renzi's ledger, if you please.'

It was produced with equal promptness. 'Let me see now,' Murray said, peering down the columns. 'To the last quarter I find we have a most respectable sum in your name. I rather fancy you will not wish to maintain your present employment situation for very much longer.'

He passed across the ledger, pointing to a column total.

Renzi looked down – and it took his breath away. 'May I be clear on this? The figure I see is in credit to myself?'

'Mr Renzi, you have earned this entirely on merit. It is yours, and should you desire it, I shall present you this very hour with a draft on our bank to that amount and you shall walk out of these offices a man of consequence.'

His mind reeled. 'B-but it's so . . .'

'On the other hand, you may understand public taste is fickle and the work may drop from fashion as rapidly. Nothing is sure in publishing, sir.'

Renzi slumped back, dazed. A vision of Cecilia, his cherished love, flooded in. His eyes pricked while the publisher prattled on.

'This is why we must settle matters at this point, the chief of which is agreeing a date for the delivery of the manuscript of your second piece.'

He would post back to Guildford and lay his heart before her and—

Murray continued, 'It is of the first importance to keep your good self in the public eye to sustain sales of the first and at the same time establish your reputation as an author of worth.'

If she was reluctant he now had the means to dazzle her with prospects, even if she must never know their origin.

'Mr Renzi? Can you not see this, sir?' Murray said, looking at him with concern.

'Oh? Yes, of course.'

'Then you'll be looking to something along the lines of a sequel, no doubt. The same characters the public have come to take to their hearts? Or is it to be a darker treatment, a cautionary tale, which—'

'I will think on it, Mr Murray.'

Then he suddenly recalled what he had come to secure. 'But be aware, sir, that I value my privacy above all things. I would wish that you keep my true name in this entirely confidential. If it should find its way into public knowledge then I'm obliged to say, sir, that I would look upon it as a final breach in our relationship.'

'Oh, of course we will, be assured it will be done,' Murray hastened to say. 'All your works will be published under what we call a "pen name" – Il Giramondo is an excellent device.'

He leaned back and smiled. 'And it has its advantages. Who is the man of mystery behind the sobriquet? Just who was it around us who wrote these revealing tales – this beggar on the street brought low by his debauchery or that noble lord who is now anxious to conceal his sordid past? Or—'

'Mr Murray,' said Renzi, dangerously, 'you may not sport with the world as to my origins. Merely refrain from releasing my name, if you will.'

'Yes, yes, it will be so, Mr Giramondo.'

'Thank you, sir. Now in a related matter, might I enquire this of you – is there a form of transaction whereby the proceeds may be remitted into an account anonymously?'

Outside, Renzi blinked in the wan sunlight. Every instinct screamed at him to fly to Guildford and seek Cecilia's hand that very day.

For him everything had changed – his future was as a gentleman of comfortable circumstances, and if Cecilia accepted him, he was about to be made the happiest man alive. But what of Kydd? He remembered his friend's drawn face, the piteous attempt at normality in the face of the worst. After Trafalgar the public had become accustomed to victory

34

and nothing less. A humiliating defeat would demand scape-goats, whom an uneasy government would surely find.

Would his friend be cast into exile from the sea he so adored?

It was so unfair – but life had to go on and he had arrangements to make. As he hurried to his cheap lodgings, he tried to unscramble the racing thoughts.

So, if he was to be married the usual course was for the new wife to cleave to her husband and his establishment – but he had none.

Item: get one.

He had no decent attire, certainly none that could be considered seemly for a proposal of marriage.

Item: find a tailor, expeditiously.

His financial standing did not run to a bank account, let alone an amicable relationship with a bank manager for the establishing of standing and credit and so forth.

Item: use the cash draft nestling in his waistcoat to start one.

He was not a regular attender at any church – how could banns be called, a wedding arranged?

Item: er, ask Cecilia.

Then there would be whom to invite and . . .

But a dark pall slowly gathered, dominated by the image of his father. The Earl of Farndon.

For an eldest son a marriage contract in the aristocracy was the stuff of lawyers, of negotiation, of delicacy in the settlement with the bride's noble family. But a moral confrontation with his father had resulted in a titanic rage and the threat of his disinheriting.

His brother in Jamaica had sorrowfully confirmed that his father had taken the legal steps necessary. Although he could not prevent the title passing to Renzi, Eskdale Hall and the large estate would now go to his younger brother, Henry.

His title would be therefore an empty mockery, and he would never put Cecilia to the humiliation of maintaining a sham. She would never know, and would be Mrs Renzi to the day she died.

Yet he owed it to his father to inform him of his intentions. There was no question of seeking his blessing, for had he not been disinherited? By his own act, therefore, his father no longer had power over him.

Any interview would be nasty, brutish and short.

But then it would be finished. He could turn his back for ever on Eskdale: he would never ask anything for himself of the smug and supercilious Henry. And the darkness would then lift and disappear.

Yes! He would get it over with, then let sunshine flood his life.

A post-chaise to Wiltshire? It was not unheard of, but would cost a pretty penny. Would Sir prefer an open or closed carriage? Where was his baggage at all?

Impatiently, Renzi climbed in and settled back with a dark frown. It was going to be hardest on his mother, who had been helpless to prevent his vengeful father going through with the shameful deed. Now she would never meet the woman he was marrying and he knew she loved her first-born dearly.

A lump formed in his throat: Eskdale Hall had been, after all, his birthplace and the scene of his youth. To turn his back on it completely was a hard thing to contemplate.

It was some eight years since he had last been there, his visit culminating in the ferocious argument and ultimatum that had ended everything for him at Eskdale. His father had even gone so far as to forbid his eldest son's name spoken in his presence.

The horses were being whipped unmercifully – he had promised a shilling for every hour they made up. The sooner the distasteful business was over the better.

They reached Noakes Poyle in the early afternoon of the next day.

Renzi directed the driver to the inn where he had stayed previously before sending word of his arrival, but this time it was different. He told the post-chaise to prepare to return – but the destination this time would be Guildford. Their astonishment turned to avarice when he handed over an earnest of his intention that would see them comfortably ensconced with an ale before the fire for the hour or two while they waited.

A local diligence was hired – he had no wish to answer questions as to why he had posted down instead of the more usual stagecoach. It smelt of horse-hair stuffing and dust, and had small, grubby windows, but as they swung into the long drive to Eskdale Hall it suited his mood.

The sweeping light-grey immensity of the building looked as stately as ever, but today it seemed to harbour an air of menace, of pent-up malevolence, that chilled him.

On either side gardeners tended the ornate hedges and lawns, or clipped rosebushes, and horses were being led to the stables as the business of a great estate went on.

The cab took the smaller roadway to the side that led to the tradesmen's door. Renzi knocked sharply at the roof until an upside-down face appeared. 'To the main entrance, if you please.'

With a look of resignation the man obeyed. He had to

stop the vehicle and lead the horses around but soon it had come to a halt at the foot of the grand steps leading to the massive door.

Renzi got out, paid the driver and sent him on his way.

He was committed.

As he turned towards the house, he saw the head footman descending importantly to deal with the impertinence. But when he drew near, the man's expression turned to surprise and then confusion.

'Master Nicholas! We thought . . .'

'Take me to my father,' Renzi snapped, and seeing him hesitate, added, 'This instant, whatever his instructions to the contrary.'

'Lord Farndon is . . . not available, sir,' the man said awkwardly. 'The countess will be at home, I believe.'

'Very well.' If his father was posturing he would send a message in and leave without seeing him.

He followed the man through the tall oak doors into the entrance hall. 'I will inform her ladyship of your arrival, sir.'

Keyed up for a confrontation that had festered over the years, Renzi was taken aback by what he saw before him.

His mother stood in the far doorway. Her eyes glittered with tears as recognition came. Then, impulsively, she ran towards him.

She was wearing a black veil and shawl.

Clinging to him, she shook with paroxysms of sobs while he held her. Eventually she drew away, dabbing her eyes.

What did the black veil mean?

'Father?' Renzi asked quietly.

She nodded, looking into his face. 'Two months hence. Of an apoplexy.'

'Mother, I'm so grieved for you.' The words came

automatically as he tried to grapple with the fact that his demon father was no longer in existence.

'Nicholas. We must talk. Please!'

He crushed his raging thoughts and tried to focus.

If she was going to try to mediate between himself and his brother Henry, now master of Eskdale, in order to beg an allowance and quarters that would see him take up residence here with her, she was sadly mistaken.

'Very well, Mother.' He would hear her out.

They went to the blue drawing room. The footman closed the doors quietly and left.

'Please sit, Nicholas,' she said, with a brave smile, patting a place next to her on the chaise-longue. 'We've tried to get word to you, but they had no idea where . . .'

'We were occupied in South America, Mother,' he said quietly. 'And then the Caribbean.'

'You never received the letter,' she said.

'If I had to learn of it,' he murmured, 'I'd rather it were from my own dear mother.'

She squeezed him tightly for a long time, then held him at arm's length. 'You're not eating well, Nicholas. You should take more care of yourself!'

'Mama, I came here to see Father to—'

'He is no more, my dear. This is a new beginning.'

'It was to—'

'Nicholas. If you came here to contest your rightful inheritance, then rest easy. It is secured for you. I allowed him to be gulled of a hundred guineas by a scheming lawyer to produce a worthless bill of disinheriting. It seemed to answer.'

'Then . . .'

'Yes, my dear. I can tell you that the vile paper was quickly determined invalid and that you are now indisputably the Earl

39

of Farndon and master of Eskdale Hall both. No one in the land may disinherit a noble lord.'

He went pale. All those years, those times of moral questioning, the vows of distancing, the bitter reflections . . . Where did this news leave him?

Getting to his feet he crossed to the window and looked out on the sculpted greenery, the formal gardens, the dark woods in the distance.

'My dear Nicholas, you must return home to take up your birthright. Do you understand me?'

He said nothing, the thoughts like a torrent too great to stop.

She got up and went to him, stroking his hair, as if he were still a child. 'My dear boy, you've had such adventures on the sea as would put even Tobias Smollett to the blush. Isn't it time to set it behind you at last?'

He couldn't find the words in him to answer: the poverty but freedom, the scent of danger but the deepest satisfaction of true friendship won in hardship and peril. Could he ever . . . ?

'Should you decline,' she continued in a pleading tone, 'it will undoubtedly provoke a scandal that will have the newspapers of all England in a frenzy. Do pity us, Nicholas. To be the subject of every careless wagging tongue, on penny broadsheets, in theatre dramas, it's really not to be borne. And the estate. Without a sitting lord there will be none to sign the rolls, to—'

'Yes, Mama, I do understand. Pray grant me a space to consider it.'

Renzi felt confined, unable to think, to reason. It was stifling him – the past was bearing down on him, distorting his vision, his perceptions.

He threw open the french windows. 'I – I need to be by myself,' he said hoarsely, and thrust out into the fresh air.

A gardener with a wheelbarrow stopped to gape at him but he was past appearances. He threw one glance back – his mother's face was at the window, white and strained.

Determined, he stepped out strongly, passing beyond the tall, immaculate hedge and into the grounds. As far as the eye could see in every direction, this was the Farndon estate.

Tenants and farmers, gamekeepers and ostlers. The ancient village beyond the gates. In a timeless mutual reliance based on two things above all others – trust and stability.

It was their ancient feudal right, and in their conceiving he was the earl, the fount of all grace and bounty.

He had grown used to the freedoms he had enjoyed in the open fellowship of the sea, his snug place aboard Kydd's ship wherever it had taken them both, on deeds of daring or desperation, to adventures inconceivable, of far places in the world where none might visit save they were borne there in a man-o'-war.

Could he give this up for ever?

He had at last secured an income by his own endeavours and could deploy it in any way he chose. His studies of an ethnical nature could now proceed . . .

He strode to a field that had a single gnarled oak at its centre. Here he had faced his father in that fateful confrontation that had led to the break. A clash of wills that he had resolved by galloping away, leaving his enraged father to take his revenge.

It had failed. And with it the power to hurt him.

In that moment something passed on: he saw his father more to be pitied than hated, as the memory of what he had done began to fade. There was now nothing that he had to react against, to withstand . . . to justify his exile.

In that realisation his emotions ebbed. They were replaced by calm.

And he began to reason. If this was his present situation other moral imperatives must come to the fore. He knew he had a clear duty: to his family first and to society second. To turn on them both for selfish motives was not an act he could easily live with.

Therefore, whether he desired it or no, it had to be accepted that, with his inheritance secure, there was no conceivable reason to decline the honour.

And so, irrespective of every other consideration, the decision was out of his hands.

Turning slowly on his heel, he paced back, letting the logic work its healing on his soul.

A light-headed relief suffused him. It was all settled: there could be no more disputing with his conscience or any more vain reasonings.

He would do his duty.

His mother stood alone, tense and watchful.

He smiled softly at her. 'You are right as always, Mother dear. Perhaps it is time. I will return and do my duty.'

She stared at him, then dissolved into tears, hugging him to her until they eased. Then she gently disengaged herself and returned to the chaise-longue, her eyes never leaving him.

'There's much to do, my son. But first we will have a welcome banquet for my dear Nicholas, returned to his place of honour in the bosom of his family.'

'Thank you, Mama.'

'Henry will be much put out, for his father promised him Eskdale, but take no heed – he's impetuous and yet to be fully acquainted with the world.'

'I will not take offence, Mama.'

'And then we will throw a ball for all the world to take sight of the new earl. A grand affair – I shall invite noble families from up and down the kingdom. You'll go to London for the season, of course, and there—'

'Mother. There's first a matter I must deal with, as we must say, in my former life. It should not take long.'

'Oh. Cannot it wait, Nicholas?'

'I rather think not, Mama. I desire to quit such an existence without detail to be dealt with later.'

'Then do go, my son. I can understand you wish to leave nothing that can cause awkwardness later. When do you think . . . ?'

Renzi twitched his neck-cloth and settled the sleeves of his plain brown coat: there hadn't been time to get the tailor to work but he'd managed a pair of more formal breeches and stockings in place of his faded pantaloons. It would have to do: time pressed.

He stepped out of the Angel into the street. No one noticed him as he strode through the Tunsgate market up to School Lane, so named by the citizens of Guildford in honour of the successful establishment run on naval lines by the Kydd family.

It came into view but it was different now. This time he was controlled, calm and knew what he must do.

At the door he drew himself erect, took a breath – and knocked three times.

'Oh! Mr Renzi,' the maid said faintly. 'Ma'am,' she called anxiously. 'It's Mr Renzi. Are you at home?'

There was movement and voices – then Kydd himself came to the door.

'Nicholas!' he spluttered. 'Where in Hades have you been?'

'I am here, as you may observe. Am I to be allowed to come in at all?'

'Damn it, and you've some explaining to do.'

'Inside?'

They went to the drawing room. Cecilia rose guardedly. 'Why, Nicholas! It's been such a horribly long time . . .'

She tailed off at his stiff bow.

Kydd bristled and threw Renzi a dark look.

Cecilia looked at both men in turn: what was passing between them? They'd always been such true friends.

Renzi's face was set as he turned to Kydd. 'There is something that Cecilia should know. I would be obliged if you would allow us the privacy.'

Kydd hesitated. Then, throwing a warning glance at Renzi, he left the room.

Cecilia sat rigid, her eyes wide.

'I should tell you, Miss Kydd, that my business in London proceeded well.'

She went pale at the distancing. Had she been wrong to hope all these years?

'You will know that my situation and fortunes have until now not been favourable.'

'Yes, Mr Renzi,' she murmured, picking up on his formality. 'But it does not—'

'Now they have improved to the point where I believe that decisions must be made.'

'I see . . .'

'That bear so on the future. Miss Kydd, I have to tell you that I'm now in a position some would describe as of consequence. I would therefore not wish you to be under any misapprehensions as to the reasons for what I have to say.'

44

'Nicholas . . . ?' she blurted pitiably.

'Miss Kydd. There has been before an . . . an understanding, a measure of assumption – of presumption, if I may. However, as I recall, I did write you a letter of release from any implied obligation in this tenor, I believe.'

Her eyes filled.

'Which obliges me to choose my words with care.'

'Nicholas – Mr Renzi – I beg, do know I've never felt bound by our . . .'

He dropped his gaze and when he looked up again there was resolution, and the serenity of a dilemma solved.

With the utmost dignity he fell to one knee. 'Miss Kydd. If your situation does permit, then with the most unutterable feelings of tenderness and love I do this day propose marriage to you.'

Her hands flew to her mouth as she stared down at him for a long moment. Then she burst into tears and, with anguished sobs, ran from the room.

Almost immediately Kydd flung in. 'Renzi – what the devil did you say to her? I demand to know!'

'I proposed to her, is all,' he said quietly. 'It would seem, however, that there is another . . .'

Kydd took a ragged breath and hurried out after her.

She was in her room, lying on her bed weeping inconsolably.

'Cecilia – sis!' he said, with concern. 'Is it that you've fallen for someone else? I can understand that, the beggar dithering on for so long.'

'No!' she sobbed. 'A thousand times no!'

'I – sis, I don't understand.'

'I do l-love o-only Nicholas!' she wept.

'Then why . . . ?'

'I've waited and waited for him and now . . .' She burst out anew with anguished sobbing.

'Ah. Well, if I were you I'd clap on all sail and go back to him before he changes his mind.'

He produced a handkerchief and waited while she composed herself. 'Now then, sis, you go to him and say – well, say what you need to.'

They left the bedroom but Mrs Kydd and the maid were standing white-faced outside.

'Whatever is the matter, m' dear?'

'Ma, Cecilia has something she wants to say to Mr Renzi.'

'If he's been upsettin' my darlin', then—'

'We wait outside, Ma.'

It was not long: the door opened and the pair stood before them, hand in hand.

'Mama, we're to be wed!' Cecilia breathed, eyes sparkling.

'Oh! My dear, I never guessed – at all! We're so happy for you an' Mr Renzi, you've no idea. Why, I thought—'

In a formal tone Renzi addressed the mother of his intended. 'Mrs Kydd. I'd be obliged to Mr Kydd for a few words in private, should he be at leisure.'

'Y-yes, o' course. Um, Walter's upstairs restin', but what with all this to-do, I'm sure he'll be awake by now. I'll call him down for ye.'

'No, no. I do not wish to inconvenience. I shall go up to him.'

In a short while there were voices, and Renzi came down, guiding the sightless Mr Kydd into the drawing room, the others eagerly following.

'My dear Fanny,' he said, his voice quavering. 'I have given Mr Renzi my blessing on the union of himself and young Cecilia.'

This time it was Mrs Kydd who broke down in floods of tears and could only be consoled by much hugging from her daughter.

Kydd gazed at his friend with affection and respect. 'I never thought I'd live to see the day, Nicholas, this I swear.'

Renzi gave Cecilia a look of such warmth and rapture it reduced the whole room to silence. 'My love, we are now to be married. In token of this I would have you accept this gift, which comes from my heart.'

He drew out a small pouch of crimson velvet.

She took it reverently and opened it to find a shining gold ring.

'Nicholas! My darling!' She bravely held back the tears as she held it up to admire. 'Oh, this is a posy ring! There's something written inside . . . What does it say?'

'This is the noble Seneca, observing the human condition. "*Quos amor verus tenuit, tenebit.*" By which he means "True love will ever abide in those whom it does seize." And this is to say I'm sanguine we could never have escaped our fate, my dearest Cecilia.'

She clutched him tightly, then kissed him with passion, oblivious to the audience.

He held her away, tears starting in his own eyes. 'Need we delay in our wedding, my dearest?'

'Never a moment!' Cecilia whispered. 'I shall have the banns called for this very Sunday.'

'Then there's but one thing left to complete our betrothal. My love, I want to present you to my family, if you will.'

'Oh, Nicholas, in all the excitement, we haven't told you Thomas's news.'

*   *   *

'And Mrs Foster being so disagreeable about William, it was all I could do to hold my tongue, my dear.'

Cecilia smiled sweetly. 'I do feel for you, Hetty. I vow, it's more than a saint could endure, that odious woman.'

Her old school-friend adjusted her bonnet and looked at her affectionately. Not everyone was sympathetic to the lot of a governess in an aspiring household. 'That's kind in you to say so, Cecilia. Tell me, have you any news at all?'

'Why, yes, I suppose I have,' Cecilia said, hugging the moment to herself.

'I'm to be married, Hetty.'

'Married?' she squealed, so loudly that other customers in the tea-house looked over curiously at them. 'Who – that is, may I know who the fortunate man is to win your heart?'

'No one you've met, Hetty dear. He's from Wiltshire, an old country family. A gentleman of travels, we might say.'

She daintily removed her ring. 'His name's Nicholas – and, Hetty, look what he gave me at our betrothal.'

Her friend exclaimed in delight. 'How lovely! All set about with acanthus leaves – this is a fine piece, Cecilia,' she said shrewdly. 'And inside – there's writing. It's all in Latin.

'How romantic!' She sighed, trying the ring on and admiring it wistfully as Cecilia translated the inscription. Hetty had no immediate hopes; an intelligent and practical woman but of lowly family, she could not bring herself to consider advances by the callow youths in her social circle. In any case, next to beauties such as Cecilia, with her handsome strong, dark looks, she knew she could only be accounted a pleasant soul.

'You'd never credit it, Hetty. Nicholas had been away for so long in strange parts of the world and then he calls on me without warning, and I'm not in, and he goes away again!'

She giggled. 'And all the time I had my hopes of him and

never a word except to say he absolves me from any under-standings. After years of . . . But then he returns from his business and in that very hour goes to his knees and makes his proposal.'

'Oh, Cecilia! How you must have stared! Did you make him wait?' she asked eagerly.

'Nicholas is not the man to be trifled with I'm persuaded, Hetty. I accepted him and we're to be wed without delay.

'Now, Hetty, this is not why I asked you here. There's a favour I'd beg that would gratify me extremely were you able to grant it.'

'Why, of course, my dear.'

'Well, it's this. I know it's scandalous short notice, but Nicholas wants me to meet his family. We'll take the stage to Wiltshire where they live but naturally it would be improper to be seen alone together. Is it at all possible that you could take leave from Mrs Barlow for a day or two and come with us? I'd be so grateful for your company, Hetty.'

'How exciting! Yes! I was saving my days up for the summer, but this is much more fun.' She glowed with animation. 'Oh, but – I've nothing to wear that will answer.'

'I'll lend you something.' Cecilia squeezed her friend's arm. 'Oh, my dear! I'm so nervous – what if they don't like me? I'm so glad you'll be there.'

The three met at the Angel. Hetty curtsied shyly as she was introduced.

Renzi bowed elegantly. 'A friend of Cecilia's is my friend as well, Miss Panton.'

A four-horse post-chaise was led out to the little group with their baggage, the horses nodding and snorting impatiently.

'For us?' Cecilia cried, in consternation. 'All the way to

Wiltshire? Nicholas, it would be much more economical by coach, and with you travelling outside we could save—'

'My dear, allow that my means do in fact permit me this indulgence for my bride-to-be and her companion. Shall we now board?'

The chaise lurched into motion and clattered off over the cobblestones of High Street. Quite soon they were in the deep green Surrey countryside.

'I'm so excited, Nicholas. And very nervous to meet your family. You've never spoken about them much.'

'All in good time, my love.'

The carriage made its way through the country, the weather remaining merciful. At the stops the two friends chatted happily together. Cecilia was informed at length of Hetty's considered opinion that her betrothed was a vastly superior catch, a man of manners and consideration, and with a pleasing air of romantic mystery.

In return Hetty was regaled with a detailed account of the ups and downs of their affair, which each time kept her agog until the next halt.

Renzi was annoyingly quiet, seemingly content to contemplate the passing country.

They stayed the night in Trowbridge but at the evening repast Renzi would say nothing of what the next day would bring.

Early the next morning they set out at a brisk clip, the soft chalk downlands passing agreeably by.

'How far now, Nicholas?'

'Above an hour, I believe.'

They went on in silence until they drew up at a modest inn. 'We'll rest here a space before the last stage,' Renzi announced.

The ladies took their leave to make themselves respectable

while a discreet note was passed to the innkeeper, who hurried away.

They boarded once more, and in a short while, they swung into a long, curving drive.

'Oh, Nicholas!' Cecilia cried. 'A noble's mansion! Is this why you haven't told me about your family? You silly billy – to be in service to one as high as this is a great honour indeed. You've no need to hide it from me.'

She watched breathlessly from the window of the coach, then suddenly spotted what was going on. 'Nicholas – quick! They're expecting someone. All the staff, they're coming out and lining up. Oh, dear, we're going to be in the way. Tell the coachman to go back!'

Renzi didn't answer, gazing absently as they drew nearer until the carriage ground grittily to a halt at the foot of the steps before the grand entrance.

'Nicholas!' she hissed, in anguish. 'We can't . . . *Please*, we'll be making a spectacle of ourselves.'

A bewigged footman in green and gold arrived to assist them down. Cecilia stood helpless, gazing anxiously at the long line of staff in front of the stately magnificence.

And in the centre a lone figure, waiting.

Renzi moved forward, and as one, the line curtsied and bowed. 'Nicholas!' she gasped in consternation. 'They think we're someone else.'

He still said nothing, leading them on towards the figure at the top of the steps, watched in silence by a hundred or more.

Struck dumb with confusion, Cecilia followed until they reached the top.

Renzi bowed. 'May I present Miss Cecilia Kydd and Miss Hetty Panton?'

Cecilia curtsied with as much grace as she could find, unable to face the keen glance of the great lady standing there.

'Miss Kydd,' Renzi said quietly, 'this is the Dowager Countess Farndon of Eskdale Hall. My mother.'

She looked up suddenly, struck dumb. Then the significance of the black veil and shawl penetrated her numbed mind.

'If her ladyship is . . .'

'Yes,' Renzi said gently. 'You see, I am now the Right Honourable Lord Farndon, and this is my seat.'

After the shocked ladies had been ushered away to rest after their journey, Renzi walked with his mother into the blue drawing room.

'Dear Nicholas, it is so good to see you. May we indeed believe you are now returned to us?'

'You may, Mama.'

'To take up your title and inheritance – to assume your duties and ancient obligations in line of succession?'

He straightened and faced her gravely. 'This I will do, Mother – you have my solemn promise.'

She took his hands, and there was a glitter in her eyes as she murmured, 'You have no idea how happy you have made me, my son.'

They stood for a long moment together until she let go his hands and said, with just a hint of curiosity in her voice as they took their chairs, 'I do hope your guests enjoy their stay.'

There was no point in delaying the inevitable and Renzi braced himself. 'Mother, Miss Cecilia Kydd has accepted my proposal of marriage. I bring her here for your blessing.'

At first he feared she hadn't heard but then she spoke, calmly but with determination. 'My child, I find this difficult to follow. Am I to understand you have given a form of betrothal to a – a commoner? With all the noble families of England more than happy to make a connection with ours? Others may well reckon it a rash and imprudent act – but fortunately it is not too late.'

'Mama, I pledged my troth.'

'Yes, dear. And now we have to do what we must to remedy the situation.'

'I've given her my word, Mama.'

'I'm sure you meant it, dear. Now, not to drag it on unnecessarily, what amount would you say would satisfy, that would see her departure in good grace?'

'Mama, I told you, we are engaged to be married.'

'You are saying she is in a certain condition that requires a hasty arrangement.' The countess sighed. 'This brings complications, it's true, but nothing that cannot be attended to with a favourable outcome to both parties. It is not unknown that—'

'Mama,' Renzi said, with increasing feeling. 'Listen to me!'

He waited until he had her full attention, then spoke with a forcefulness and intensity that was unstoppable. 'Know that my heart is entirely lost to the woman. There is no one – none – in this mortal existence that I would otherwise contemplate in a life's union.

'I love her, Mama. I love Cecilia with all my heart and soul, and before God I say I will marry her!'

The dowager stood up with great dignity and moved to the mantelpiece, fingering its ornate marble carvings. 'I see,' she replied, after some moments, clearly taken aback by the fervour and sincerity of his declaration. 'Yet I cannot believe you have reflected fully on the consequences.'

Renzi stood, but said nothing, returning her gaze with defiance.

'A belted earl marrying beneath him to such a degree – it will be a scandal. All will ask why this must be, and will not fail to suggest good reasons to this end.'

'I care not for—'

'But you must in your position, my dear. What if—'

'Mother, it is done. I will not retract. It must be Cecilia or none. Do you not see this?'

A faint smile eventually came. 'I believe that indeed you truly love her.'

The smile warmed. 'And for that how can I not give my blessing? Marry your Cecilia and I will rejoice for you both.'

Renzi took her hand and kissed it. 'Thank you, Mama – thank you.'

'Society will howl, but what is that against the joining of two lovers in blessed happiness?'

'You will love her, too, Mama. She has qualities of . . . gentility and politeness above her station, and her practicality in matters . . .'

They finally reached the woods at the edge of the estate. Walking together as in a dream, the two stopped and held hands, looking into each other's eyes. 'Cecilia, my darling love. There's something I must know,' he said tenderly, but with an edge of seriousness.

'Nicholas?' she answered softly.

'It will affect our marriage, our life together, and I must have an answer.'

She hesitated. 'What is it, my dearest?'

He looked at her with an odd expression. 'You gave your

heart to one Nicholas Renzi. Can you find it in you to love the Lord Farndon at all?'

She smiled playfully. 'Nicholas, I fell in love with Mr Renzi and he it is who has secured my entire devotion. If Lord Farndon lays siege to my affections he will have to woo me with yet greater ardour.'

They kissed, long and tenderly.

'My darling, there is—'

'Sweetheart, I—'

'You first, my dear Cecilia.'

'You have precedence, my lord.'

'Then in the matter of our nuptials, dear love. At our station even St Paul's Cathedral is available to us in a great affair of moment and ceremony. Yet I feel it . . . improper to indulge in pomp and display while the family is in mourning. Can you . . . ?'

'Nicholas, it is what I would wish. My father is old and frail and could not possibly endure the strain. And my mother would . . .'

Unspoken was the fact that the Kydds would be wildly out of their depth in such grandeur and would know it. Cecilia, after years as lady companion to a marchioness, was not unfamiliar with society – but there could be no question of exposing her family to ridicule.

'In Guildford, perhaps?' she asked doubtfully.

'So be it, my love.'

'I've asked that the banns be read beginning this Sunday.' She smiled impishly. 'We shall be wed in a month. I hope you don't think me forward, my lord.'

Renzi stopped. 'Ah . . .'

Her smile faded. 'Nicholas, what is it?'

'Peers of the realm have certain privileges, my dear.'

'Oh?'

'I rather thought for us – a special licence from Doctors Commons attested by the Archbishop of Canterbury. It will serve to have us married within this very week, setting aside the need for banns and similar.'

'Nicholas! You darling man! Yes – yes!'

'As I trust you will forgive my precipitate behaviour, occasioned, may I point out, only by my earnest wish to secure the presence, before he returns to the sea, of my particular friend at our happy event.'

She melted, and clung to him while their passions surged. Then they turned and walked slowly back.

'Mother?' Renzi said softly.

She was waiting on the steps for them, but she turned first to the woman on his arm. 'Cecilia, my dear. Did you enjoy your walk?'

'I did, my lady, very much.'

'You will have some notion now of the duties that await my son as lord of Eskdale Hall.'

'Yes, indeed – and we saw only a part of the whole.'

It seemed to please, and the countess went on, 'You have yet to make a tour of the house. At above a hundred rooms it is no easy task in the managing. And soon you will be chatelaine, my dear. Do you feel equal to it?'

Renzi intervened smoothly: 'Miss Kydd has for some years been in an intimate situation in the household of the Marquess of Bloomsbury, Mama, and is no stranger to society. I have every expectation that she will be an ornament to our establishment.'

'Of course. Then shall we pass on to the wedding plans? In view of the . . . irregular nature of proceedings it were best, I feel, if the customary great ceremonials be exchanged for something a little less . . . formal, so to speak.'

'Quite so, Mama.'

'The gutter press will have their sport on this occasion, no doubt,' she said acidly. 'There's no reason to flaunt it in their faces.'

'As we both agree, Mama. We rather thought in Guildford, the Kydd family town?'

It was settled, and with a pronouncement that the evening would see a grand banquet in their honour, she left them.

They wandered on through fine rooms and cloisters, banqueting halls and drawing rooms until they came to the library.

'And here is where I will have my being, dear Cecilia.'

He looked fondly at the endless shelves, the familiar volumes showing no sign of use since his departure those long years before. And there was the broad desk that dated from the first George with its leather inlay and ink-stains, positioned to take the light from the tall french windows that looked out over the formal gardens.

The peace and tranquillity, the fragrance of books and learning, the centuries of time that the room had seen, all reached out to him. Here it would be that his ethnical studies would attain their fruition, a labour of pride and diligence.

He sighed in anticipation. But before he could resume it would be necessary to take up the reins as lord and master of Eskdale. And for that—

A slight cough sounded from the door. He looked up: it was Jago, the dark-jowled under-steward.

'Does m' lord desire I should instruct the footmen?'

In the hierarchy of a noble estate, every bit as rigid as aboard ship, Jago ranked very near the top. The valets-de-chambre, butler, footmen, cook and gardeners, all were regulated and administered by himself and the steward. He was now asking if he should put into motion the delicate business of assigning attendants to wait upon the new earl wherever he might be at any hour, day or night.

'We'll leave it until later, I think, Jago.'

Renzi was aware that his father had been up to all manner of sly tricks to further his interests and prejudices, and it was beyond belief that Jago, at his eminence, had not been party to the whole sordid process. Especially as the estate steward himself would make very certain he was not involved directly. Jago's appearing now was, without doubt, an anxious testing of the waters; he stood to lose his place and prospects if Renzi decided to make a break with the past.

'Thank you, for now,' he added neutrally.

'Very good, m' lord,' the man said, expressionless, and withdrew.

At the door there was a soft knock. 'Ah, come in, Mr Fortescue.'

Renzi turned to Cecilia. 'My dear, my confidential secretary.'

He had every trust and liking for the old man who had striven all he could to moderate between his father and the estate tenants.

'I shall endeavour to give satisfaction, my lord. And might I present Mr Edward Dillon, under-secretary and assistant to myself?'

An intense young man came forward and bowed. 'My lord Farndon. Allow me to express how delighted I am at your arrival at Eskdale.'

'Thank you, Dillon. I can assure both you gentlemen of a lively employment to come.'

'My lord. Do forgive my presumption but it was spoken of that before your translation you have had travels and adventures about the world yet untold. Is it in your conceiving to make good record of the same?'

'We shall see. Do you yourself yearn for adventure, perchance?'

'Saving Mr Fortescue's presence, I should say I am truly envious of your lordship's peregrinations – a world to discover, to delight in.'

Renzi gave a half-smile. 'Quite so, Dillon. However, do bear with your lot for now, there's a good fellow.'

By evening the entire household was abuzz with conjecture and excitement. A banquet had been set and the kitchen and staff had striven hard. A superb occasion promised.

Renzi found dinner attire left by his brother Richard, who was back in the Caribbean, while Cecilia was arrayed in finery borrowed from his younger sister Beatrice, even if it clung overly snug in places. She wore a dazzling display of pearls and diamonds selected from the parure, a family heirloom set of jewellery presented to her by the countess.

The candles were lit, the guests arrived. An orchestra in the minstrels' gallery played delicate airs, and scores of footmen stood poised.

Outside the closed doors Cecilia gulped, 'Nicholas – I'm so nervous. What if—'

'If they laugh at you? Then I'll tell the noble executioner to chop off their heads, in course!'

The dowager countess joined them. 'How lovely you look, my dear.' She primped her cheeks, then prompted gently, 'Shall we go in?'

'Mother?' Renzi said, trying to take position behind her.

'No, my son. You are the earl now and take precedence. I must follow.'

With Cecilia on his arm he nodded to the footmen.

The doors swung wide and instantly Cecilia's senses were overwhelmed by the blaze of light in a vast hall glittering with jewels, men's stars and decorations and great quantities of silver tableware, the light intensifying the crimson and gold of sashes, the fine silk dresses of the noble ladies and, all around, the handsome livery of the footmen of Eskdale.

The orchestra fell suddenly silent. There was a massed scraping of chairs as hundreds of the great and good of the county rose and stood respectfully, their faces turned to take sight of Lord Farndon and his bride-to-be.

They processed in with great dignity – and on that day Cecilia felt she could bear no greater happiness.

'Dear Nicholas – it will come as a great shock to them. You remain here at the Angel, and I'll go and tell them.'

'Very well, my dearest.'

Alone, Cecilia set out for home. It was a strange, eerie sensation, almost like floating on nothingness in a world that was so familiar but now about to be lost for ever. Would she make a good Lady Farndon, mistress of Eskdale? For the sake of her future husband, she would give it her all . . .

She smiled at Mrs Simkins hurrying down the road and stepped hastily out of the way of the uncouth baker's boy with his basket of bread. They'd barely noticed her in their bustling daily round – but most surely this was the very last time it would be so. When the news got out that a daughter of Guildford was marrying a peer of the realm there would be no more of the simple, unaffected life she knew.

Hetty had been shocked, dazed, and had sat like a

frightened mouse all the way back; she was herself only now recovering from that earthquake revelation.

Shy Mr Partington, the Kydd school headmaster, saw her and fell into step. 'Miss Cecilia? Do the gossips have it true, that you are to be—'

'I am to be married shortly, that is right in the particulars.'

She kept it at that and bade him a good day at her door.

'Well?' prompted her mother, before she had even taken off her bonnet. 'Were they nice, a-tall? Did you—'

Cecilia bit her lip. This was not going to be easy.

'Mama, I've something to tell you – and Papa too. It's very important: shall we go into the parlour?'

'Oh, dear, I hope this won't take long. I've a rabbit pie as I'm . . .' She saw something in her daughter's face and without another word hurried off to find her husband.

'Why, Cec – what's to do?' Kydd wanted to know.

'Not now, Thomas. There's . . . I have to speak to them both.'

'Oh, well—'

'Not with you, Tom. This is serious.'

Her mother returned, leading her father. Cecilia followed them in and, with an apologetic smile, left Kydd outside to wait.

Ten minutes later his parents came out – and they were as white as a sheet, passing him silently without noticing he was there.

'Cec – what's this mean, for God's sake?' he blurted.

'Thomas, I think we should take a walk in the garden.'

They returned slowly, Kydd shaking his head in disbelief.

'Dear Tom. If you're surprised, think how I felt. In the

61

morning I'm Cecilia Kydd and in the evening I'm . . . well, I'm to be a countess.'

'Where's he now, sis?'

'At the Angel until we send for him.'

'Well, we'd better do that now. There's a gallows lot to hoist in.'

The maid was told to fetch Mr Renzi while Kydd gazed in awe at his younger sister.

'Have you set a date yet?'

'Nicholas needs to have a consort by his side when he takes his place as an earl, he says. And so it will be an early wedding.'

'This year? Or six months only, you shameless devils?'

'Tom, we thought this week.'

'*Whaaaat?*' he gasped. 'You can't just—'

'He's a noble lord now, Thomas. He will have leave from the Archbishop of Canterbury himself to wed by special licence.'

Kydd sat down suddenly, lost for words.

Emily bobbed at the door. 'Miss, it's Mr Renzi here.'

'Oh, do show him in, please.'

Scrambling to his feet, Kydd saw his friend of years come in, his countenance serious.

'You've heard the tidings.'

'I have, you wicked dog. Frightening the womenfolk like that, you villain!'

But Cecilia had noticed her brother's tense watchfulness, his unease. 'Thomas!' she scolded. 'And that's no way to speak to the Earl of Farndon.'

'Oh? Then how am I . . . What's his tally now, can I ask?'

'This is the Right Honourable the Lord Farndon of Eskdale Hall in Wiltshire. He's to be addressed as "my lord" or "your lordship" and never on your life "you villain", Tom.'

'Then it's "your lordship", if it serves,' Kydd said, in an odd voice, and gave an exaggerated bow, but when he looked again Renzi's grave expression had not altered.

'This is harder than ever you will know, dear friend,' he said, in a low voice. 'I see before me the sea hero I respect and admire above all men, and society demands he bends the knee to me. I would be gratified beyond measure should you hold to "Nicholas", dear fellow – or even "wicked dog" would answer.'

They clasped hands.

Kydd turned to his sister. 'Now, how about you, Cec? What do I hail you as?'

'Why, I'm sure the Countess of Farndon would be content with "my lady" or "your ladyship" but never in this world "sis", good Sir Thomas.'

'As it shall be, Your Worship. Now if we're to be squared away and all a-taunto for a right true wedding in this week, we'd better bend on more sail. Where do we start, Cec?'

It was quickly settled that the cosy familiarity of St Mary's Church would be best suited for the Kydds, and Renzi hastened to make clear that it would suffice also on his side. Its small capacity dictated a family wedding only with a strict limit on guests. This brought a measure of relief in other arrangements, particularly when it was learned that the groom's family would certainly be invited to Hatchlands, the county seat of Lord Onslow, a distant relative, who might be depended upon in the matter of carriages.

Kydd assumed charge, sending Cecilia off to fit for a bridal gown and reassuring his parents that they could remain indoors quietly while he took care of all the arrangements.

The delighted tailors of Guildford went to double tides, Kydd and Renzi both to be as resplendent as it was possible to be, and after judicious choices the needles flew.

Canon Chaddlewood of St Mary's allowed he was more than happy to conduct a marriage: who were the blessed couple? When told of the quality of the celebrants and congregation he nearly swooned, and on learning of the Archbishop of Canterbury's intercessionary licence, he shrank in fright. It took all of a threat to lose the honour to rival Holy Trinity to move him to accept, with the offer of an organist from Hatchlands and a choir from the school.

The wedding was therefore set for Friday next at ten.

Kydd had his own preparations to make. Orders under his name were sent on the Portsmouth stage to the officer-of-the-day of *L'Aurore*. It desired him to send a party of trusties by return for special service, their rig to be their best as for captain's inspection.

He then instructed Boatswain Perrott of the school to transform his assembly hall into a temporary mess-deck, and left the gleeful peg-legged sailor teaching his eager boys how to rig header tricing knittles for hammocks.

It was all shaping up in a most satisfying way.

'So you're not nervous at all, old horse?' Kydd said lightly, helping Renzi with his snowy cravat.

'Only that this may in fact all be a vain imagining to vanish at any moment with a loud pop. Thomas, days ago I was a lowly secretary – however honourable the post,' he hastened to add. 'And now the world may see me as the espoused of the loveliest creature in existence.'

'Hold still, Nicholas. How can I get a decent tie if you move?'

'Dear fellow,' Renzi said softly. 'You've said that before.'

'What? And I never did!'

'I'm desolated to contradict my best man, but do you not recall in *Artemis* frigate we were most certainly tie-mates?'

Kydd stopped. The memories flooded back of a young man with a cherished deep-sea mariner's long pigtail being combed and plaited by his friend, the favour to be returned afterwards.

'Aye, I do, Nicholas.' A stab of feeling came as he realised that not only were those times so distant in the past, but the continued friendship, which saw them that morning performing exactly the same favours for each other, was now about to be concluded.

'I . . . I'm going to miss you in *L'Aurore*, m' friend,' he said quietly. 'It won't be the same without I have a learned cove scratching away for me somewhere.'

'You may believe that I too shall miss . . . deeply . . . the freedoms and sights of the sea life.'

He paused, then brightened. 'Yet there is perhaps a final service I can do my good captain. It crosses my mind that, should you continue to require a confidential secretary, may I recommend for your consideration a young man of shining qualities whose discretion I can vouch for personally?'

'Oh? Who then is this splendid fellow?'

'An under-secretary on the estate, Dillon the name. He has notions of one day travelling the world, as I have done, and it seems to me that were you to oblige him in this manner then his loyalty would be unbounded.'

'Life in a man-o'-war is not for the faint-hearted, Nicholas.'

'Is that so, dear chap? You might give him fair trial and see if he measures up to the profession.'

'Very well. Send him to *L'Aurore* and we'll take a look at him.'

A fore-top bellow sounded outside. 'Ah. That's Toby Stirk rousing our carriage alongside. I fear it's time to face your destiny, Nicholas.'

They were not prepared for the sight that greeted them at St Mary's.

'Be damned! There's half Guildford Town here!' spluttered Kydd, red-faced with pleasure.

Surrounding the church was an overflowing, joyous crowd of chattering, delighted men, women and children in their best dress, bedecked with flowers and ribbons. They were not going to miss the wedding of the age.

Harassed church functionaries managed to keep a lane to the entrance free but the people were impatient to catch a glimpse of the principals and pressed them sorely.

Kydd stepped down and bowed to them pleasantly. It brought a ripple of excitement and scattered awed applause. This was Sir Thomas Kydd, a son of the town and now a famous frigate captain; there in his gold and blue with a crimson sash and star, looking every inch the sea hero.

The tongues clucked. Look at that gold medal and riband! The tall cocked hat with all the gold lace! Was it true he once laboured in the wig-shop that used to be up High Street past the clock?

No! Never! It couldn't be!

Then the Earl of Farndon descended. There was a respectful hush and a spreading sigh as he formally greeted an awestruck Canon Chaddlewood.

Such a vision had not been seen at St Mary's within living memory: a white waistcoat and silk stockings with knee breeches and discreetly jewelled shoes – this was your genuine article, an earl of an ancient family of England, come to do the greatest honour to their little town.

Once more Kydd felt unreality creep in. This couldn't be happening to him, young Tom Kydd as was. It must be a dream. Here in this church, which had stood on this spot for a thousand years and had seen christenings, weddings and funerals of the good people of Guildford in an endless succession. And on this day . . .

As they entered the packed church a sea of faces turned to watch them take their place at the altar. There was his mother, blubbing into a handkerchief, his father struck dumb with the occasion – and Lord Onslow, whom he'd been summoned to see in *Monarch*'s great cabin after the great battle of Camperdown when he'd been set on the quarterdeck and his path to glory.

And the dowager countess, cool and aloof, others he could only guess were members of Nicholas's family, with nobles, gentry and notables beyond counting. His vision swam with colour and circumstance.

The organ stopped suddenly, then began a grander air. He twisted round: it was his sister entering in an exquisite white gown, supported by a tremulous Hetty Panton.

She reached the altar and gave Kydd a look for him alone, of the utmost softness and love.

A lump formed. He had always hoped it would happen – but this was the reality.

The organ stopped and time-hallowed words fell into the silence.

'Dearly beloved, we are gathered together here in the sight of God . . .'

The wan sunlight of winter streamed through the

stained-glass windows, bright motes of dust held in motionless thrall to the words.

'. . . to join together this man and this woman in holy matrimony . . .'

That was the Cecilia who, as barely more than a child, had travelled alone to Portsmouth to plead with him to return to the wig-shop and leave the sea. The practical good sense, but then the tears of understanding as she saw the desolation of Fate closing in on his carefree existence.

'. . . signifying unto us the mystical union that is betwixt Christ and His Church . . .'

And the man now in the glittering pomp of a peer of the realm: he had seen him stand with bloodied sword at the gates of Acre, denying Napoleon Bonaparte himself his victory. The one who, in only months past, had, single-handed, brought down the devilish plot to destroy England's precious Caribbean trade – and who could ironically never claim the credit, while he himself was proclaimed glorious victor of a lesser triumph.

'The ring!' hissed his mother from her pew.

He had been oblivious and scrabbled for it in his pocket. Pink-faced, he handed it to his one true friend, who slipped the ring on to his bride's finger.

The rector joined their hands and solemnly pronounced to all the world, 'Those whom God hath joined together let no man put asunder.'

It was done.

Bells pealed out overhead in a glorious, joyful din as the newly married couple went to the sacristy for their formal signing.

Then they reappeared, joined in blissful, self-conscious union.

The congregation rose and waited as they processed along the aisle to emerge at the arched entrance, to a muffled roar of ecstasy from the crowd outside.

Kydd followed them out and stood blinking as wheat grains were showered on the couple. Traditional wedding gifts were pressed on the guests and coins thrown high into the crowd.

Joining with others in expressing their wishes to the couple for a long and fruitful marriage, he was taken aback when Cecilia leaned forward and whispered fiercely, 'The carriage! Thomas, you forgot to send for it!'

He hid a smile and shook his head in sorrow. 'Sorry, Cec – no carriage, I'm afraid.'

She looked at him, speechless.

Then he clapped on his cocked hat with a flourish. It was the signal.

From around the corner came a frightening bellow. 'Billy Roarers – forward!'

The crowd fell into a stunned silence – and into view came a boat.

It ran on wheels and was pulled by a dozen Jack Tars as large as life, tailing on to ropes, driven by a roaring Stirk.

'Handsomely, y' lubbers,' he bawled. 'Star'b'd a touch forrard, there.'

It was gaily ornamented from stem to stern and had huge imitation anchors and mermaids, ribbons streaming everywhere and on its stumpy mast it flew an enormous Union flag. On the centre thwart, a pair of dainty cushions.

The people were delighted. It was very seldom that the Navy, so popular after its recent victories, could show itself so far inland and they immediately gave a raucous appreciation.

Stirk, in an exaggerated sea roll, went to Renzi and snatched off his cap. 'An' yer boat's alongside, y' lordship.'

'Thank you, Mr Stirk. You and your Billy Roarers all. My dear?'

They sat in state, waving regally as the boat set off to the sudden skirl of fife and drums of the Surrey Militia, which had magically appeared and was now marching behind.

Grinding up the steep High Street, the din and revelry were deafening. They brought shopkeepers and customers on to the street and children screaming and running by the incredible sight.

Under the projecting clock of the town hall, past the Tunsgate, and followed in procession by the lords, nobles and honest townsfolk of Guildford in an unstoppable show of happiness and pride.

Then, at the top of the hill where the old Elizabethan grammar school stood, and the road out of town ran, they stopped.

There, with liveried footmen attending, was Lord Farndon's four-horse open landau. Its gleaming black with the scarlet, gold and green swirl of its crest spoke of another world, unattainable to the mortals who looked on.

The merriment ebbed while the newly married earl and his bride disembarked.

And then, in the short distance between the boat and the carriage, Kydd saw Cecilia transmogrified from his young sister into a countess – from a laughing girl into a noble lady.

The landau glided away. Cecilia turned to wave, blowing him a kiss, and then they were off into their future together.

He watched them disappear and his eyes misted.

In that moment he had lost both his sister and his best friend.

Chapter 3

Portsmouth was the same: somewhat grubby and showing not a little wartime drab – but there was magic, too, and as he peered from the window of the stagecoach Kydd could just make out the distant sight of slender masts and yards soaring above the mean roofs. Among them would be *L'Aurore*, his command and his love – his true home.

The orders that had come so soon after the wedding had been blunt about the need for dispatch. Kydd wasted no time in calling upon the port admiral and received his pack for the coming voyage, as well as yet more letters and messages imploring a place on his quarterdeck as midshipman for a son, a nephew, others – all begging for a chance to ship with the now famous frigate captain.

It wasn't so very long ago, in dear old *Teazer*, that he'd been snubbed by those who believed a captain who'd come aft the hard way not really the thing but now, it seemed, it was quite another situation.

Kydd had his views about a lean and hungry frigate being

overrun with youngsters, and although he could ship up to six midshipmen, he'd settled for just another two.

One was William Clinch. Kydd had received a dignified letter from a Mr Jarman, sailing master of *Ramillies* 74 of the North Sea Squadron. Even before he had begun to read he remembered the lowly merchant-service sailing master of *Seaflower* cutter who had taken Able Seaman Tom Kydd and taught him his figuring, as well as how to use a sextant and work up a position. It had been his first step to the glory of the quarterdeck and he still had the man's worn octant, presented to him in admiration after a difficult open-boat voyage.

Jarman had written on behalf of the only son of his sister, who desperately wanted to go to sea, like his uncle, but unless interest could be found he would necessarily have to ship before the mast. In painfully crafted phrases it was implied that Kydd's sound grounding in seamanship that he'd learned in *Seaflower* would ensure his nephew received a prime nautical education.

The wording of the other request that he'd acceded to could not have been more different. It had come from Boyd, the urbane and patrician flag-captain, now a retired admiral, who had taken Kydd, the raw sloop captain, aside in the fearful days of Bonaparte's plans for invasion before Trafalgar, to give him his first lessons in strategics for a naval officer. In mellifluous prose, Boyd warmly complimented Kydd on his honours and begged he might oblige him extremely by taking up his godson, Josiah Willock, his own circumstances being a family of daughters only.

L'Aurore had completed her refit, not a lengthy one as it was still less than two years since she had left dock in this very place just before Trafalgar. She now lay at anchor in

Spithead and Kydd begged a dockyard launch to go out to her.

As always, it was a deep satisfaction to approach her from seaward and admire her elegant lines.

The boatman's hail back was practised and sure. It sparked instant activity on deck and Kydd feigned not to notice as a full side-party was assembled and the boatswain summoned from below, the officer-of-the-watch with his telescope watching anxiously.

The launch curved round, oars tossed smartly, and the bowman hooked on at the main-chains.

L'Aurore's captain had arrived to resume his command.

After the peal of the boatswain's call had died away, Curzon stepped forward and removed his hat. 'Sir Thomas – and I know I speak for the entire ship's company of *L'Aurore* – welcome back aboard!'

Kydd had taken in the trim appearance of his vessel, the spotless decks with not a line from aloft out of place. Considering that he was not yet expected, this spoke volumes for the care she had been given.

'The first lieutenant?' he prompted.

'Not aboard, sir,' Curzon said, adding respectfully, 'Do we have orders for sea, Sir Thomas?'

'As shall be made known to you all, just as soon as my dunnage is struck aboard.'

The sound of the call had brought others on deck. Bowden came up and gave a bow of respect. 'My deepest sensibility of your elevation, Sir Thomas,' he said warmly. 'And I—'

He was interrupted by a sudden noise from forward. The fo'c'slemen, stealthily lined up on the fore-deck with their caps in their hands, broke into a masculine roar with 'See the Conquering Hero Comes!'

From these old sailors it was a deeply affecting honour and Kydd removed his hat and waited while they finished.

Going below, the peace and orderliness of his quarters reached out to him. Tysoe, his valet, came up to remove his boat-cloak and accoutrements.

'A right handsome job you've done here, Tysoe.'

'Thank you, Sir Thomas. I'm happy to be of service to you.'

There was a faint fragrance of lavender and beeswax and the cabin spaces were spotless.

Kydd suppressed a sigh. In their relatively short commission he had been fortunate in his ship's company. Originally pressed from an inward-bound frigate just arrived back in England, they had overcome their sullen resistance in the fires of Trafalgar and the two supporting actions following, and now were a tried and true weapon forged from the very best.

'Pass the word. Officers and warrant officers in my cabin in one bell.'

They arrived with suspicious promptness.

'Before I begin, I'll have your reports. Mr Curzon, if you please?'

It was all very satisfactory: the ship had left dock six days ago and had readied for sea. Not under sailing orders, she was under watch for liberty, and omitting stragglers – those locally adrift from leave less than three days – there had been only two desertions. Storing and victualling must await orders before a line of expenditure could be opened, but in all other respects *L'Aurore* was trim and taut in her particulars.

'Thank you, Mr Curzon. The first lieutenant still not aboard?'

'Ah.' Curzon smothered a grin as he glanced at the others. 'Soon after you left for London he received news he was promoted commander into *Fly*, sloop o' war. He begged to be remembered to you but thought it proper to take up his command directly.'

There were knowing looks about the table.

Kydd guessed what had happened. 'So it was a right glee-some frolic he had that night?'

'As required the watch to be turned out to carry him ashore, Sir Thomas.'

Kydd chuckled. His tarpaulin first lieutenant had at last achieved his greatest wish – command. It was, of course, a gesture to Kydd, promotion out of the ship of his first lieutenant, but Gilbey wouldn't care about why: he could now eventually retire from the service a sea captain, not a lowly lieutenant, and with all the honour and veneration that that description commanded ashore.

'So we're short a first lieutenant.'

There was an instant quiet: what followed could be either the introduction of a tyrannous new first lieutenant imposed from the outside or the wholesale promotion of the existing officer complement – or anything in between.

'Before we go on, I'd like to make something clear. I thank you all for your warm wishes on my . . . good fortune. Yet I'm an old-fashioned sort and I'd rather you keep the "Sir Thomas" for shore-side. Aboard *L'Aurore* I'd be satisfied with being addressed in the usual sea-kindly fashion.'

'Aye aye, sir.'

'Then we'll proceed. Without we have a first, we cannot put to sea, and in course I've petitioned the Admiralty to provide one. And they have.'

He watched their faces. He'd only known their lordships'

75

pleasure in the orders he'd picked up from the flag-lieutenant earlier that morning.

'You should know that our new premier will be taking up his duties this very day, I'm told.'

There were significant glances about the table.

'What's his name, sir?' asked Curzon, carefully. Hard characters were legendary and life could suddenly turn very difficult.

'His name? Why, Curzon is his name.'

'You mean . . . ?'

'I do, sir. You are now the first of *L'Aurore*.'

Curzon's widening smile told it all. If the frigate was fortunate in action, and *L'Aurore* invariably was, he, too, could look to a promotion out of her – at the least to a substantial sloop command or possibly to a flagship directly under the eye of a commander-in-chief.

'Then . . .' the third lieutenant dared.

'Yes, Mr Bowden. You are now second lieutenant.'

There was relief, satisfaction and exulting all round.

'And for our new third, it will be a Mr Brice, whom I'd like you to welcome in the usual way.'

'Have you word of our deploying, sir?'

Kydd hesitated. They would know soon enough and there was no easy way to break it to them. The far-ranging frigate of Cape Town and Caribbean fame was headed to a much different place.

He'd treasured the oblique offer from the first lord to remove from *L'Aurore* into another, larger, command but had felt reluctant to leave his pretty little frigate. He had to concede, however, that she was looking increasingly old-fashioned, and her slight twelve-pounder main armament was the lightest in the establishment.

But she was *L'Aurore* – his first ship as a post-captain, a frigate command, whose dainty and sometimes whimsical ways he had come to know and respect.

'We're to join Admiral Collingwood in the blockade of Cádiz.'

'Blockade?' Curzon's groan was echoed around the table.

'Yes! And an honour for all that,' Kydd said sharply. 'The Mediterranean squadron, Nelson's own command. And we, a light frigate, can count on action a-plenty, I'd wager. The closest inshore reconnaissance, and as the fastest ship, we'll not lack for interesting voyages with the most important dispatches, I'll remind you.'

'So . . . not much chance of—'

'And if you think yourselves hard done by, then as you bask in our southern sunshine, Mr Curzon, do take thought for our brothers keeping the seas off Brest in damnably ugly winter Atlantic blows.'

There could be no answer to that.

'Very well. We've orders to put to sea without delay. Mr Curzon will ready his watch and station bill and we'll begin storing against these orders in the forenoon tomorrow.

'Yes, Mr Kendall?'

The sailing master rubbed his chin. 'Charts f'r where, sir?'

'Iberian coast, Gib, western Med – I don't fancy we'll be elsewhere in a hurry.'

The meeting broke up in a buzz of expectation. Resting peacefully at anchor off the fleshpots of Portsmouth was all very well, but there was a war to win and distinction to be gained out where *L'Aurore* belonged – at sea.

'Do sit down, Mr Brice,' Kydd said mildly, regarding his new third lieutenant.

He was young but of a very different stamp from Bowden.

There was no trace of the social refinements, the confident ease of the well-born. Not with those hard lines about his mouth, the controlled tension. The look he returned was guarded but direct.

'What then was your last ship?'

'*Raven*, brig-sloop. Sir.' He had a northern burr, and there was no relaxing of the watchful gaze.

'Oh?'

'Leith, east-coast patrols, some Baltic convoys.' Kydd nodded: a small ship perpetually at sea in the often ferocious conditions of the North Sea, a thankless and dangerous existence but a priceless schooling in seamanship. That the man had not tried to make something of it to his new captain was curious, though.

Was this the taciturn attitude to be seen in some tarpaulin officers, those whose origins were from before the mast, like Gilbey, who felt the need to assert a salty distinction to set them apart from the usual well-born officer class?

'Do you have experience as a common seaman at all?' Kydd enquired carefully.

'I beg pardon, sir?'

'That is to say, did you come aft through the hawse, so to speak?'

'I did not.' The reply was instant and defensive.

'As I did myself,' Kydd added casually, before asking, 'Your service previous to that?'

'Midshipman, *Triumph*, North American station. Master's mate and lieutenant in *Boadicea*, the same, sir.'

'So this is your first frigate.'

'Sir.'

There was something unsettling about his manner, which

raised a niggling question. Just how had one from such an undistinguished background landed one of what must be the most sought-after lieutenancies in the service? He had seen no major battles, had served no top-flight admirals. It must therefore have been the workings of 'interest', the favour of a higher power who had exercised preferment on his behalf.

'You've done well, if I might remark it, Mr Brice. Tell me, is there any who do take a special concern in your career? Who—'

'Would you wish to see my commission, Sir Thomas?' Brice said tightly.

'No, no. I merely wished to get some idea of your background. Time presses – I believe for now I will second you to Mr Bowden until we are more sure of you.'

Kydd leaned back, considering. Why was his new third lieutenant not more anxious to please? This was a plum appointment: why was he not more . . . joyful?

'Will that be all, sir?' The tone was even and polite, but it was unsmiling, tense.

'Mr Brice. This is a happy ship and we've had adventures aboard together that must satisfy any. If you desire it, your place in our band will be professionally rewarding and personally gratifying – if you make it so by a whole-hearted commitment to *L'Aurore*, your ship and her company.'

'Yes, sir.'

'Have you any questions?'

'No, sir.'

'Then I do welcome you aboard, Mr Brice.'

There were two others joining *L'Aurore*. He was very busy but the least he could do was cast an eye over them.

'Pass the word for Midshipmen Clinch and Willock.'

79

It was some time before they appeared, breathless and wide-eyed.

'So. My two young gentlemen. Which one is Clinch?'

They were both so young – mere children in fancy-dress.

'S-sir.' The boy clutched his absurdly large cocked hat under his arm and stood awkwardly in his brand-new uniform. His eyes were a startling blue and seemed so innocent.

'Welcome aboard, Mr Clinch. Your sea service, sir.'

There was hasty fumbling inside his waistcoat and a paper was produced. It was a certificate of service for two years as a first-class volunteer in an Irish Sea dispatch cutter.

'Well, unusual sea-time but acceptable for all that. What were your ports-of-call generally?'

The boy stood in mute horror until it dawned on Kydd. 'Ah, this is book-time, not sea-time, I gather.'

The lad nodded miserably, unable to speak, for at that moment his sea career could well be brought to an end. Regulations were that none could be rated midshipman without two years prior sea service. It was commonly flouted by the device of having the child's name entered on a ship's book while still at school, a course so widespread that Nelson himself had thought nothing of practising it. The crime was not so much in the false muster of the books, but in the venality of drawing pay for a fictitious boy.

'So you'll need to try double-tides to earn your place on my quarterdeck,' Kydd said gruffly.

'Sir,' he whispered. Touchingly, the child's relief had nearly brought him to tears.

Kydd turned to the other. 'Right. Well, you must be Willock.'

'I am, Sir Thomas.' The cultured accent would endear him to Curzon but would be a sad liability to him in the gun-room.

'And your sea service?'

The boy blushed. 'Um, none that would stand with a frigate.'

'Well, what ship, then?'

'*Squirrel*, sir.'

'I can't say I can bring her to mind. What rate is she?'

The boy hesitated, then blurted, red-faced, 'Tender to *Royal William*, s-sir.'

'Tender to a guardship?' Kydd said, aghast. It would be unlikely that the little craft would even have left Portsmouth harbour, tied to such a virtual hulk. He then realised that this was his admiral godfather, doing just the same thing as Jarman.

'Then no sea-time for you either, younker?'

The boy hung his head.

'Clinch – how old are you? Say up, and no stretchers!'

'Oh, fourteen, sir.'

With that childish voice?

Kydd snapped back, 'What year were you born in, pray?'

'Th-that would be seventeen and ninety-three,' he stammered, after a pause.

'The year they did for King Louis?'

'Oh, did they?'

They were caught out and he found himself facing a child of eleven and another of twelve.

He had to make up his mind: a midshipman was rated as a petty officer and had a place on both the watch bill and at quarters and was expected to pull his weight with the men. These were under-age for a midshipman, even if it was only by a year or two, but that counted when in a position of authority, taking charge of a crew of hardened man-o'-war's men.

But then he recalled the slow-talking but meticulous Jarman patiently explaining the requisite tables to the eager young seaman he had once been. Without doubt he and his sister were anxiously waiting for word – and he hadn't the heart to send the boy back. Besides, he had the look of a sailor and – who knew? – he might do well in a happy ship like *L'Aurore*.

And if he accepted one and turned away the other . . .

'I'm not pleased you've flammed me this way,' he harrumphed. 'We're a crack frigate, not a nursery. I should turn you both down, send you back to your mothers, do you hear?'

They stood rigid, their childish faces pale.

He let it sink in, then said sternly, 'But I'm minded to give you a chance. Should you faithfully promise to me that you'll bend your best efforts, night and day, to hoist inboard the elements of your profession in double-quick time, then there's a berth as midshipman for each of you in *L'Aurore*.'

'We promise, sir!' they chorused ecstatically.

'So get your dunnage below, then report to master's mate Calloway. Smartly now!'

They scurried away.

A wartime frigate on active service could see them without any warning in fearfully dangerous waters or under savage fire from the enemy. Was it fair to thrust a child into such peril when their school-friends were still at their books and games?

It was the way of the Navy. There were ship's boys aboard *L'Aurore* who were still younger, one nine years old, who had been a whole voyage in her. They had found, among other things, that there was nowhere to hide in a ship-of-war but they had taken to the life – these lads, no doubt, would too.

He turned back to his work.

The next morning, amid all the bustle of storing ship, it was time to take stock. He was more than satisfied with the way

L'Aurore was readying herself for sea. At this rate he could look to a departure the day after next, presuming the powder barges were alongside at the time promised.

'How's the watch and station bill proceeding, Mr Curzon?' he asked the distracted first lieutenant.

The evolution of turning to the entire ship's company for the task of victualling would be taxing enough for any brand new first lieutenant, without the added burden of the careful assignment of stations to every man. Each must know what was required of him, not only at quarters in battle but in all-hands exercises like coming to anchor – as well as his routine part-of-ship and station for watch-keeping.

It needed fine judgement to ensure there was an equal balance of skill in both watches but Curzon was starting with a crew he knew intimately and a ship that was already in commission, and if it cost him midnight oil, well, that had ever been the lot of a first lieutenant.

Later in the morning *L'Aurore* was visited by a respectful young officer. He was piped aboard by Boatswain Oakley, for he was the captain of his own ship.

'Lawson, Sir Thomas. Lieutenant-in-command *Weazel*, brig-o'-war.'

In the privacy of his cabin Kydd found out the reason for his coming. 'We've a Mediterranean convoy scheduled to sail, sir. I'm senior officer escorts, and I've just been advised by the admiral that you'll be accompanying us to Gibraltar.'

'Oh? I've yet to decide our sailing date, let alone our dispositions for the voyage.'

'The admiral assures us that should we await your pleasure our escort will be greatly increased by your presence.'

'When did he tell you this?'

83

The young man had the grace to blush. 'Perhaps an hour ago, sir.'

He had obviously found out *L'Aurore*'s deploying and had had the initiative to go to the admiral with a request. Just as he would have done, Kydd had to admit.

'What's your number?'

'Ourselves, two cutters and a schooner. In the convoy, thirty-eight merchantmen.'

No wonder the lad had jumped at the chance: this was what it was to have prevailed at Trafalgar. Convoys worth millions were now being sent into the open ocean with the flimsiest protection, for had not the French been driven from the seas? It was a dangerous presumption and might one day cost the Treasury far more than any additional escorts.

'Very well. We'll sail together.'

Kydd knew what was coming next, and waited for it.

'You being much the senior, Sir Thomas, you will, of course, have the honour of commanding the convoy.'

'Not at all,' Kydd came back. 'The honour remains with *Weazel* and your own good self.' There was no way he would take on the onerous task of maintaining the convoy paper-work – signals, identification vanes, sailing diagrams and the like – the inevitable consequence of having issued his own orders.

'Thank you, sir.'

'At sea I shall be under your orders, Mr Lawson, and if we fall in with an enemy you will dispose of this frigate as you see fit.'

'Why, sir, if—'

'The convoy is your responsibility. And responsibility without command is an impossibility, don't you agree?'

'Yes, sir.'

'You'll be employing the Channel Squadron's signal book?'

'Sir.'

'Then we're in agreement. Kindly send across a copy of your convoy sailing-order folder, if you please, and I'll undertake to give you twelve hours' notice of our readiness to proceed.'

'That would be appreciated, Sir Thomas.'

It would be even more so by the merchant captains whose ships would be consuming stores while they idled at anchor.

'I've a notion we'll be at sea the day after tomorrow. Good day to you, Mr Lawson.'

Storing complete, the powder barges were summoned and, with very great care, the copper-banded barrels were swayed aboard and stowed snugly in the magazines in the bowels of the ship.

That evening Kydd saw fit to declare himself at twelve hours' notice to sail.

The last hours of a ship in her home port were always bittersweet. In the excitement of the outward bound every man in her also realised that, once anchor was weighed and sail set abroad, there was no longer any chance to provide for himself for the months – or years – to come within the wooden bounds of his sea world.

Small comforts in the misery of stormy night watches made all the difference: seal-fur warmers to slip under tarpaulin jackets, patent nostrums for chilblains, neat little sewing kits, an illegal Crown and Anchor throwing mat and dice, and other distractions, all eased a hard sea life.

Officers needed to ensure they were well stocked in reading matter, spare dress uniform accoutrements, perhaps a pistol, a pack of cards, a pocket spy-glass, sketching gear or a private journal.

For Kydd it was also the laying in of cabin stores, having on hand pickled or canned delicacies and tracklements for entertaining important visitors aboard. A married officer would come well provided with touches a woman's practical sense could produce: a lovingly embroidered cot quilt, an extra-long muffler, a dozen hand-stitched shirts. Fortunately Kydd's valet, Tysoe, had spent most of his adult life at sea and could be relied upon in the article of personal comforts.

Their last night was an active time for those who could get ashore, but by nine the following morning the last boat was returning with newspapers, a small sack of mail – and a new addition to the frigate's company.

Dillon pulled his cloak more tightly around him – it was so unexpectedly raw and blustery out here on the open water, away from the shelter of hedgerows and buildings. Here the wind ran wild and unconstrained, a metaphor perhaps for the freedom of the high seas.

It was really only a short pull from the Sally Port to the anchored frigate *L'Aurore* across the legendary stretch of water called Spithead, but he was already shivering; whether from the excitement that gripped him or the keen cold, he couldn't say.

It really was exhilarating: here he was, in a ship's longboat, hard-faced seamen at the oars glancing at him curiously, the young officer at the tiller barking orders, like a captain. And they were on their way to go aboard the crack frigate that had been so recently in the newspapers, with its famous captain, Sir Thomas Kydd.

He couldn't take his eyes off the trim ship, sitting low in the water but with a pent-up grace that told of speed and aggression, much like a panther. The lofty rigging and spars were of an impossible complexity but for some reason added a sense of mission, of purpose, and the blue, white and gold of the figurehead under the bow gave a pleasing touch of humanity. And at the end of the ship a large flag, the ensign of Great Britain's Royal Navy.

They drew nearer; there were figures on deck moving, the glitter of gold lace on one, and suddenly they were alongside the black, varnished ship's side. Orders rapped out and they hooked on next to a set of steps and he was helped up to land staggering on the open deck.

Men were hurrying everywhere but here and there groups were conversing and watching others. He spotted gold stripes and an important cocked hat on one and went over.

'Captain Sir Thomas Kydd? May I introduce myself—'

'Who's this idiot?' spluttered the harassed first lieutenant. 'We're putting to sea! Get him off my deck until we've time to deal with him.'

The mate-of-the-watch hurried over. 'You there! What's your business, then?'

'Oh, well, I'm expected. The captain,' he answered, leaping out of the way of a line of seamen clapping on to a rope in a hearty pull.

'What do you mean, fellow? You're volunteering for this ship?'

'Why, yes. You didn't really think that in my place I'm taken by the press-gang against my will?' He felt pleased that he seemed to be holding his own among these old shellbacks.

'Why didn't you say so in the first place?

'Simmonds!' he called over to one of the seamen. 'Take him below to your mess and sit him down. He's not to move until we're at sea and stood down from stations. We'll see if anyone's got time for him then.'

'And my baggage, if you please.'

'Baggage?' said the mate-of-the-watch in amazement.

'Aye, sir. Still in the boat,' the coxswain intervened, with a twisted smile. Few volunteers had anything beyond a small bundle.

'Very well, get it in,' Bowden said impatiently. 'We'll sort it all out later.'

Dillon was hurried below, sat at a mess-table and told firmly to stay there.

In the gloom, hearing the anonymous thuds, rumbles and squeaks as the ship prepared to meet the sea once again, for the first time he felt doubt. Had he done the right thing to exchange the security and comfort of his position at Eskdale Hall for this?

L'Aurore's pulse quickened. Boats were stowed on their skids, lines laid for running, and the age-old mingled exhilaration and apprehension of the outward bound mounted.

Signal flags rose and snapped in the stiff breeze and stations for unmooring were piped.

Captain Kydd came on deck and sniffed the wind appreciatively. 'Nor'-easterly, Mr Kendall. Fair for the Channel for once.'

'It is, Sir Thomas,' said the sailing master. 'Yet I have it in my bones it could freshen a mite.'

'How's the convoy?' he demanded of Bowden.

'Fair, sir. Still sorting themselves by the look of it.' Off Shag Rock there was a cloud of sail, as usual in a hopeless tangle. Once in the open sea, the chaos would diminish as it always did.

'Then I believe we'll not delay further. Carry on, Mr Curzon – take her out.'

The new first lieutenant licked his lips nervously. 'Aye aye, sir,' he managed.

There was the anchor to be won, sail to be spread at just the proper moment – and the correct quartermaster at the wheel, topmen in place, fo'c'sle party under the right petty officers to cat and fish the anchor in time, all the outworking of his painful hours at the watch and station bill, which would now be tested to the full.

At the side of the quarterdeck stood the two new midshipmen trying to look important but clearly nervous and excited. Kydd hardened his heart – they'd better not let him down.

Under eye from his captain, the sailing master and a prudent boatswain, Curzon's manoeuvre was successfully completed and the frigate stood away. She passed the milling sail and, in a fine show, leaned to the wind for the open sea where, as agreed, she would deter by her presence any lurking predators watching for a chance.

The wind was keen and fair and Kydd saw no reason why they shouldn't make good time in the voyage south. He glanced up at the expanse of curving sail, his pennant streaming away to leeward, and felt a lifting of the heart – he was back where he belonged.

Eight bells sounded forward: the forenoon watch closed up and the morning watch went to breakfast. Sea routine had begun.

Reluctantly he quit the deck and went below for his own meal. As he ate alone he was suddenly touched by melancholy. Before, Renzi and he had started their day together with intelligent conversation between equals, friends. Now he was as most other captains were, solitary grandee at the pinnacle of the hierarchy where, by definition, he had no equal to unburden himself to or seek opinion from on a course of action.

He had long since not needed Renzi's guidance and advice in the social graces. While his friend's erudite observations

89

on the world's condition had always been appreciated, he had now to make his own discovery of how higher matters were concluded, take his decisions unaided.

But, more than anything, he was putting to sea without his dear friend and he felt a twist poignant twist.

Life had to go on, but he gave a small smile at the thought that at this very moment Renzi – the Earl of Farndon – would be sitting down to a lordly breakfast with Cecilia. An even bigger life-change for him, no doubt.

He finished his coffee and resumed the deck. The convoy had nearly completed forming up, four columns with nine merchantmen in each, backing and filling while the last found their place, shepherded by the distraught antics of the escort.

At last the head marker ships let fly their pennants and the convoy got under way – down Channel.

'Station astern of the convoy, Mr Bowden. Eyes on *Weazel*, any trouble let me know instantly.'

'Station astern, *Weazel* senior, aye aye, sir.'

He turned to go but was stopped by Curzon. 'Sir Thomas, I—'

'Belay that, if you please.'

'Sir? Oh, yes. Well, sir, there's one of the volunteers insisting he's to see you. I do apologise, but he was most insistent. Unusual sort of chap.'

'Very well. In my cabin in ten minutes.'

Dillon was shown in briskly. In trepidation he looked about him. It was a spacious but neat cabin, stretching right across the deck, with a fine set of ornamental windows at the end. A handsome escritoire stood up against the opposite end, and the domestic touches were masculine and spare.

'Leave him with you, sir?'

'Yes, carry on.

'You're a volunteer. What is your objection to service in this vessel?' Kydd snapped.

Dillon straightened. 'You are the captain, sir?' The officer had a taut, unforgiving air, with more gold lace than the others, albeit somewhat sea-tarnished, and dark, strong looks. He had to be the famous and recently elevated hero of Curaçao – and Dillon was daring to put himself forward as his personal secretary?

'I am.'

'Sir Thomas Kydd?'

'Yes.'

'Then I beg to introduce myself. Edward Dillon, lately in the employ of the Earl of Farndon.'

He essayed a bow – but this was no drawing-room introduction; the hard lines in the captain's features indicated he was not one to waste time on vanities.

'Sir, I have a letter from the earl.'

Dillon handed it across. There was no change in the flinty expression as it was read. He knew what was in it: with pronouncements of complete trust, there was a mild suggestion that in his character were the attributes to be expected of a confidential secretary sufficient to render him a suitable candidate for the post.

He found it hard to take his eyes from the man who had been knighted not for courtly toadying but for a battle won with blood and courage. This was a man of a kind he had never in his life met before and it was intimidating.

Kydd put the letter down and looked at him. 'You know his lordship was the previous occupant of this post?'

'He did tell me something of it, yes, sir.'

'What makes you think that you can fill his shoes, hey?'

'Sir, only the undoubted fact that he himself did so put me forward for the position.'

Kydd's expression eased fractionally at the reply.

'You were confidential secretary at Eskdale, then?'

'Under-secretary, Sir Thomas.'

'Did Renzi . . . that is, did Lord Farndon inform you that service at sea is quite another thing? No soft shore-side ways, damned uncomfortable at times and always a job of work to do to annoy the enemy. No passengers in a king's ship, Mr Dillon.'

'His lordship was also at pains to point out to me that the deck of a man-o'-war is a sovereign perspective from which to learn of the world, Sir Thomas.'

'That's as may be,' Kydd snapped. 'Now, a confidential secretary to the captain of a warship has to learn many novel things – it takes time. What assurance do I have that you'll stay the course?'

Dillon paused. 'May I then tell you something of myself?'

'Go on, but make it brief.'

'My father is a lawyer at some eminence in the Inns of Court and desired me to go up to Oxford to pursue law, which was not altogether in my reckoning. After my bachelor degree we agreed that I needed time to consider the matter while experiencing something of the world. My post at Eskdale seemed to answer, touching as it does on matters both confidential and complex in law, satisfying my father and at the same time allowing me to pursue my first interest, which is modern languages.'

'I cannot see how—'

'Sir, bear with me. For its convenience to myself I agreed to serve for a period of some years, which the present Lord Farndon was kind enough to remit, providing my service and loyalty remained with his old ship. Sir, if you'll take me, I will stay.'

'Hmm. So you have a good round hand at the pen, can hoist in the meaning of a paragraph of legal cant, express yourself clearly?'

The glare was unsettling but Dillon came back strongly. 'That you may rely upon, Sir Thomas.'

Kydd hesitated, then leaned back, regarding him for a space. 'This is a hard thing for me, Dillon. The post of confidential secretary to the commander of a man-o'-war, especially one of the significance of *L'Aurore*, is considerable. It's to be made privy to confidences affecting the lives of those aboard my vessel and possibly those of national importance. I must be sure you're the man for it.'

Dillon waited politely as Kydd considered.

'Very well. I've a mind to take you on. Temporary acting rate as it were, subject to stout performance at the pen and so forth.'

'Thank you, Sir Thomas. I'll endeavour to give full satisfaction.'

'Good.' He suddenly gave a quizzical smile. 'And I've another duty as will see you well occupied while you shape up in your role.

'As you're acting secretary only, as it were, there's a post aboard you're eminently suited to fill. That of schoolmaster to the young gentlemen. They'll muster daily to receive your lessons in figuring, history and French, that sort of thing. I'll not have 'em leading a heathen existence while there's a learned cove aboard to teach 'em otherwise.'

'Very well, Sir Thomas.'

'So – you're on my staff as of this moment, subject to review. You're on the ship's muster roll as schoolmaster and you'll mess in the gun-room with the officers. Your duties will be explained to you later.'

The hard expression returned. 'Mr Dillon, you've a lot to take in, and a short time to do it. Settle into your cabin now. Tomorrow morning Mr Calloway will stand by as you learn your larboard from your starboard. In the afternoon we'll have the ship's clerk, Mr Goffin, explain how we conduct our affairs.'

Almost absent-mindedly, he added, 'And on the first night at sea we generally have dinner together, a get-to-know-you sort of thing.'

Then he looked up grimly. 'You'll stand with the warrant officers, share a servant with the purser. Your duties will be explained to you later. Should you fail to satisfy you'll be landed at Gibraltar for shipping back. Clear?'

Dillon swallowed nervously. There were those at Eskdale who would take great satisfaction in an inglorious return.

'Yes, Sir Thomas.'

He summoned Tysoe. 'Kindly conduct this gentleman below and inform Mr Curzon that I'm now possessed of a new confidential secretary and the ship has a schoolmaster.'

At his curt dismissal Dillon left awkwardly, following the valet down a hatchway to a bewildering world of polished doors and a long table; this was apparently the gun-room where he would sleep and mess. His luggage was piled outside his cabin, which was impossibly small.

The convoy sailed on uneventfully westward, and as the last dog-watch mustered and darkness fell, canvas was shortened to topsails, and leading lights began twinkling in every ship's rigging. *Weazel* surged alongside to hail a goodnight.

Kydd entered his great cabin when all had assembled at the table. His officers scrambled to their feet.

'It's right good to see you, Sir Thomas!' Bowden said,

with unaffected pleasure. 'On this our first night of the commission.'

'Hear him,' others echoed.

Kydd took his place at the head, looking down with unfeigned pleasure at the familiar faces – and those of Brice to his left, and at the junior end, Dillon, sitting apprehensively with the boatswain and gunner.

'Mr Curzon is not . . . ?'

'He wishes to express his disappointment at not being able to attend but feels it his duty to remain on deck at this time.'

It left Bowden and Brice free to take pleasure in their evening.

Tysoe moved forward unobtrusively to fill Kydd's wine glass, the servants behind each chair taking their cue.

'Then let us rejoice in our good fortune,' Kydd said loudly. 'A well-found ship, good company and the Dons to provide for our entertainment later!'

Glasses were raised amid happy shouts of approval.

'And here's to our new shipmates,' he added. 'Mr Brice! To your good health and fortune in *L'Aurore*!'

The man's tense expression barely eased as he raised his own glass in answer and sipped sparingly, his eyes watchful.

'Do relate something of your sea service,' Kydd prompted. This was a chance to unbend, to regale his new mess-mates with well-polished yarns and emerge as an individual.

'As I told you, sir. Out of Leith in *Raven*, brig-sloop. North Sea, the Baltic.'

'Come, come, sir. You're much too modest. We here know a trifle of what it is to be in the North Sea in dirty weather. And your Baltic convoy – I've heard numbers of above two hundred mentioned. How is this possible with so few escorts?'

'You may believe we did our duty, sir.'

95

'You've smelt powder on occasion, surely.'

'Some action, sir, yes.' He took another sip of his wine.

'Good God! You're with friends now, Mr Brice. Can you not speak of your service to us?'

'Three French corvettes on Dogger Bank and we with a forty-sail convoy. We saw them off over three days.'

The man's wariness was unsettling.

''Pon my soul, but you're a tight fellow with your words,' Kydd said, in mock exasperation. 'Yet we'll have it out of you before long.'

He looked directly down the table. 'And here we have Mr Edward Dillon, my *pro tem* confidential secretary following the elevation of Mr Renzi and about to take up his duties. Here's to you, sir, and may your time in *L'Aurore* be a happy one!'

'Th-thank you, Sir Thomas. I'll strive to win your approval.'

'And that'll be a hard beat t' windward, I'm thinking,' the sailing master, Kendall, muttered, addressing his glass.

'How so?' Clinton, the Royal Marine lieutenant, asked mildly.

'In course he's a-following in Mr Renzi's footsteps.'

'Ah. That I can see,' he answered, nodding wisely.

'Aye, and a rare hand, him, wi' his learning an' such.'

'Not forgetting his undoubted talents in the article of intelligence ashore,' Bowden added respectfully.

'Always to be relied on t' tip us the griff on any foreign moil.'

'And a taut hand wi' a blade an' all.'

'Remember 'im in Corfu? Coming it the Russky, then gets the Frogs to hand over their papers?' Oakley chortled. 'Heard they's all a-tremble as he tells 'em to!'

'And there was Curaçao,' Bowden said, in admiration. 'And Marie-Galante. I don't rightly know what he was about, but the admiral seemed mightily pleased at the end of it all.'

96

Dillon blinked nervously. 'I – I really can't say that—'

'Pay no mind to them, Mr Dillon,' Kydd said kindly. 'Your duties will not include adventures such as Mr Renzi had, have no fear about that.'

The morning dawned cold and damp but the dark shapes of the convoy columns continued to lumber on ahead, a quick reckoning telling that none had strayed during the night. Familiar routine had the watch on deck about their duties and looking forward to their burgoo.

'Mr Calloway?'

'Sir?'

'You aren't planning on making Mr Dillon's day more confusing than it already is for him, are you?'

'What, me, sir?' the crestfallen young man answered.

'Yes, you, sir. I've a need for that gentleman's services in the shortest possible time and it's your job to see he takes inboard his nauticals at the gallop. None o' your tricks with finding the key to the starboard watch or how to swing a sky hook, you rascal. Just show him the ship's main particulars and have him speaking some sea lingo that makes sense. Compree?'

'Aye aye, sir.'

'And our newest reefers?'

'A useless pair, sir, but they'll shape up, or I'll know the reason why.' Calloway had himself started sea life as a runaway waif and clearly had his views about mollycoddled young gentlemen.

'Piping the eye, homesick both. They're together in Mr Bowden's watch. I dare say he knows how to teach 'em their duty,' Calloway added.

Dillon arrived, clutching a large notebook and pencil, and wearing a suitably studious expression.

'This is master's mate Calloway, Mr Dillon. He's to teach you the essentials, which I trust you'll absorb in quick time.'

'You'll not find me wanting in application, Sir Thomas. Mr Calloway?'

Kydd found quickly that he did indeed have a call for a secretary – in fact, a sore need.

Barely into their voyage there were so many papers at his desk clamouring for his attention. In the course of things, Renzi would discreetly have sorted them for priority and importance before ever he saw them, flagging those needing thought and deliberation as opposed to the 'requiring signature' rained on him by an officious ship's clerk.

It was too much to expect of his new man at this stage, and as well there were confidential matters that he'd have to handle himself until there was sufficient trust. He was becoming acutely aware that the task, with its complexity and delicacy, was not one for a temporary jobbing secretary. He needed one who would grow into the job and see it as a long-term prospect.

Was Dillon the man to take it on? His talk of seeing the world might be satisfied in full by the time they reached Gibraltar and Kydd would have to look for another. With Dillon's romantic notions it was not an impossible prospect.

Moodily, he gazed down the deck forward where the watch was bending on a fore-topgallant. A routine procedure, furling and sending down the old sail for repair first, it still required skill and timing. It was Brice in charge at the foot of the mast and Kydd stopped to watch.

The boatswain had immediate control of the men on the yard and Brice was standing impassive, letting Oakley and the topmen get on with it. This was a good sign, demonstrating his understanding of the intermeshing authority of petty officers and men, whose trusting interdependence could so easily be perturbed by interference from the outside.

Once, he had spotted a fouled clew-line block out of sight of the boatswain; with crisp, efficient orders he had dealt with it and returned authority to the boatswain immediately. The officer's seamanship was faultless, no doubt the result of the close-quarter responsibilities he'd have encountered in his small brig in stormy waters. Given a good report from Bowden, he'd have him take full officer-of-the-watch duties earlier rather than later.

A hail from the masthead told of landfall.

Ushant. The strategic hinge point of France where ships for the Mediterranean and further south turned sharply left; those to the New World set out on the long beat into the broad Atlantic.

It was a point of convergence for ships of every nation leaving Europe or inward-bound from overseas to the great ports of the north – and therefore a prime target for privateers of all flags.

In a well-escorted convoy, they had little to fear from those vermin but such a concentration of wealth was a tempting prize. Any stragglers would be set upon without mercy and, as if knowing this, the convoy seemed to huddle even closer.

'Yes, Mr Dillon, that's France, and on that little grey island are some of Napoleon's finest, with cannon and muskets enough to fire into us and do us harm.'

The young man had come up and was staring across the sea with an intense fascination at the first foreign shore he had seen, and that of the enemy to boot.

The wind still in the north, it couldn't have been fairer for

99

the long stretch across the Bay of Biscay to Spain and around to Gibraltar.

The far-off grey island was momentarily hidden by the white of a line-squall of rain, and when it reappeared it was appreciably further along as they passed it.

Since those days long past when, in *Teazer*, these were home waters, Kydd had always felt unease at passing through this foremost hunting ground for sea predators anywhere in the world. The sooner they made the open sea of the deeply indented Bay of Biscay the better he'd like it.

It was not to be.

With the craggy island abeam, a trap was sprung. From the sheltered lobster-claw-shaped inlet of Lampaul Bay sail was sighted emerging – and more, still more – on a direct course to intercept.

Kydd snatched Curzon's telescope and steadied on the sight. Still some five miles away but in a perfect situation were at least two corvettes and a cloud of lesser craft, possibly privateers, and any number of the inshore vessels the French were employing in ever-increasing numbers to take the war to the British.

It was well conceived: the same north-easterly that was bearing the convoy southward was being used against it, for as it passed the island the crowding hunters would fall in astern of it – to windward, where they could harry the slower merchantmen at will.

And two corvettes: these were ship-rigged, like a frigate, and although smaller, a pair together could take on one, certainly of lighter register like *L'Aurore*. And while the smashing match was going on, the pack of smaller craft would overwhelm the few escorts and it would be a massacre.

'To quarters, Mr Curzon.'

It was plain what had happened: while the convoy was assembling in Portsmouth someone had carelessly mentioned its destination in a waterfront tavern and French agents had picked up on it, giving them plenty of time to mount their ambush.

Dillon's face was flushed with excitement. 'They're not our boats, then, Sir Thomas?'

'No, sir, they're not.'

'Then—'

Calloway interrupted. 'From *Weazel* – "assume the weather station".'

'Acknowledge.'

'Aye aye, sir.'

It was what he would have done, put the biggest ship between the enemy and the convoy. Lawson was thinking coolly. He, the two cutters and the schooner would stay with the merchantmen and rely on the frigate to deter.

Clinch and Willock came on deck in still-new cocked hats, each self-consciously fingering a dirk and watching Kydd gravely.

The winds were brisk and steady, the seas slight. There would be no escape in a weather change.

He took another sight: the two corvettes were standing on with all plain sail, and the faster of the lesser vessels were passing them, eager to be in the best position to take their pick of victims while the corvettes were engaged with *L'Aurore*.

'Sir, what will we do?' Dillon asked, in thrall.

'Do?' Kydd said sharply. 'We fight! The convoy is much more important than we, sir.'

He checked himself. 'This is a serious situation, Mr Dillon. You have a battle station and that is next to me. You'll take notes of everything of importance as will assist later in writing my dispatch after any action with the enemy.'

'Yes, Sir Thomas.' The intensity of his concentration was touching.

'There's no need to fret so. You're not expected to bear arms or face the enemy directly, or even to give any orders. Just be sure to keep a clear head and be accurate in your observations. Nothing else, you see.'

To add point to his words he raised the glass again and calmly dictated the strength of the enemy. Dillon wrote furiously and wisely refrained from asking for explanations.

As if for the comfort of his presence, the two young midshipmen sidled up to their captain.

'Where's your station at quarters?' he snapped.

'Well, we don't really—'

'Go to the gunner in the forward magazine and tell him I've sent you.' The last thing he wanted now was a distraction.

Kydd had noticed that the corvettes were separating, revealing that they intended to take *L'Aurore* under fire from two sides. It was likely that, while they'd received word of the convoy and its slight escort, they had not been prepared for an accompanying frigate and were now on the defensive.

An idea was forming. 'Mr Curzon – do attend on me for a moment.'

The officer approached and took off his hat.

'We've a good advantage, I'm persuaded.'

'Sir?'

'A fresh-fettled ship and a fine crew. I intend to make best use of this. I desire you to make known to the gun crews that what I have in mind requires they leave their guns for sail-handling and back to their guns several times. They're to obey orders at the rush, even in peril of their lives, Mr Curzon. All depends on speed and instant execution of the manoeuvre. Is that clear?'

'Understood, sir.'

The enemy was coming on at speed. There were several substantial vessels ahead of the corvettes – two with the characteristic three lug-sails of a Brittany privateer and three brig-rigged, foaming out under a taut press of sail.

Now was the time to move.

'Haul to the wind, Mr Kendall. Hard as she can lie.'

L'Aurore curved about and laid her bowsprit precisely in the centre of the two corvettes now a quarter-mile apart, racing ahead as only a thoroughbred frigate could do.

The effect was instant. The corvettes luffed up into the wind, warily closing together then staying in position and waiting for the onrushing frigate to join battle.

Which was not what Kydd did. Instead he threw up the helm and bore down on the astonished privateer passing to starboard. Too late, its captain saw what had happened and tried to slew around but all this did was to slow the vessel and present an unmissable target.

In a pitiless broadside *L'Aurore* blasted the craft into splintered fragments that, after the smoke had cleared, simply littered the sea.

At the instant the guns had fired Kydd began tacking the frigate about and took up on a course at right angles to the enemy. The leading brig was smashed to flinders by the guns on the opposite broadside, to become more floating wreckage.

The corvettes came to their senses and hardened in for a thrust together at *L'Aurore* but Kydd had anticipated this and wore around. A luckless privateer lugger took the frigate's carronades at close range and was out of the fight – and still with not a shot in anger against them.

Dillon, white-faced with shock at the blast of the guns and mad frenzy of seamen racing from tacks and braces to guns and back again, did his best to keep up. Kydd calmly interpreted the action for his noting down.

All the small craft had scrambled to escape the mayhem, putting back for the protection of the corvettes. The convoy had gained a respite; there would be no wholesale falling upon the helpless merchantmen until *L'Aurore* had been dealt with.

With *Weazel* shepherding them on, the convoy forged south, but now the enemy's force was entirely to windward and behind them and, once regrouped, could run them down as it chose.

Once past *L'Aurore*.

Their force was barely diminished: what Kydd had achieved was a moral victory of sorts but it would not last. The enemy was now under no illusions and would plot his moves carefully and with malice.

His frigate was considerably outnumbered and, in a fair fight against these, could not be expected to survive – but, damn it, this was not going to be fair.

He had one priceless advantage: this was the combat of a crack frigate of the Royal Navy ranged against a ragtag swarm of privateers, not a disciplined fleet.

This translated to many things: gunnery, sail-handling and, above all, command. The senior corvette captain had no means to communicate with his 'squadron' for they were not trained up to signal work, and Kydd's direct assault on the smaller craft had left them in retreat. There would be no co-ordinated simultaneous onslaught, which would certainly have finished *L'Aurore*.

Now it was the two corvettes. How could he take them on together?

As he pondered, he caught a glimpse of Brice at the forward

guns, standing with his feet on a carronade slide, his arms folded: the picture of calm and fearlessness. The man might be odd in his particulars but with his seamanship and coolness in action he could look to a welcome place in *L'Aurore*.

Kydd deliberated on the alternatives. He believed his frigate to be not only handier but faster so he could turn the tables if he was careful. The main thing was to avoid being trapped between the two.

He glanced back at the convoy. To his surprise it was shaping course inshore to France, not out into the anonymous expanse of ocean. Then he grinned in sudden understanding. A smart move by Lawson.

He knew what to do now.

'Put us about again.'

L'Aurore went around with a will and took up in a broad diagonal pass across the path of the oncoming corvettes.

The implication was stark: either they manoeuvred to avoid a raking broadside into their unresisting bows or they stood on into *L'Aurore's* fury of shot.

They broke and fell back, firing as they did so.

It was long range and most of the balls fell short and skipped. Several punched holes in the frigate's sails but Kydd had achieved what he needed to – delay to allow the convoy to escape.

He turned. 'Why, are you hit, Mr Dillon?' he asked in concern. The man was on all fours.

'Sir – one came near me, is all,' he stuttered, and picked up his fallen notebook. His hand trembled as he noted the time of the enemy's first salvo.

'Pay no mind to the fuss and noise. You've a job to do and it's an important one.'

Dillon nodded grimly.

'Ready about!' Kydd ordered. They would retain their position criss-crossing for as long as it took to allow the convoy to get away. It was working – out of respect for the frigate the lesser breed were staying behind the corvettes and the ships were safe, even now well on their way to safety over the horizon.

But for how long? Kydd knew there was one course he would take in their position that would in a stroke checkmate his strategy. He could only hope that it would be later rather than earlier that they tumbled to it.

And he knew they had when, after an hour of exchange of fire, the gap between the two corvettes began widening.

Still to windward and bows on to *L'Aurore* they diverged steadily until they were more than a mile apart.

'Doesn't look so good, sir,' Bowden said, watching them.

Kydd said nothing, hoping they would not take it further – but they did.

Sacrificing their superiority as a pair, they were now so widely apart that they presented Kydd with an insoluble conundrum: they were ready to make a strike – but separately. He could go after one but meanwhile the other would get past and lead the pack to fall on the convoy.

It was no use expecting to batter one into submission then return for the other – any captain worth his salt would bear away, leading him off on a chase while the carnage was being completed by the first.

So it was payback time; the last act.

The hero of Curaçao would be pointed out in the streets as the one who, in command of a famous frigate, had allowed inferior French warships to prevail over him and decimate a convoy under his protection. An outraged public would show no mercy.

There was little he could do now, but he would play it to the end.

Putting about once more, he was not committing to one or the other, but as they came up to pass him on either side he must choose and then it would be all but over.

They came on, under full sail and determined.

It was time.

'The starb'd one on this board, I think,' he said heavily.

But then salvation came. Lawson's inspired tactic had paid off.

In a glorious vision that brought wild cheers of relief from the gun crews, first one, then another massive shape firmed out of the grey winter haze. In stately line ahead, the battle-ships of Cornwallis's Brest blockade were proceeding on their occasions, not to be troubled by the convoy's insignificance, and only the weather escorting frigates were detached to investigate.

It was all over: the French had turned tail and were fleeing for their lives.

L'Aurore crept northward over a calm, glittering sea, a long swell from the west languidly rolling in as it had not a year and a half ago when these waters had echoed and resounded with the madness and ferocity of the greatest sea battle of all time. The desolate sand-spit, with, further inland, a line of cliffs and a modest tower, was gravely pointed out to gaping new hands as the very Cape Trafalgar that had given it the name.

And not much more than twenty miles further on was the great Spanish port of Cádiz – and Collingwood's fleet, which had a stranglehold on it.

They had left the convoy at Gibraltar, watered and stored,

then turned north to join the blockade and were now raising the fleet, which lay arrogantly at anchor across the port entrance.

'Flag, sir. *Ocean*, ninety-eight, Vice Admiral the Right Honourable the Lord Collingwood, commander-in-chief Mediterranean fleet,' Curzon intoned formally, reading from the Pennant Book.

'Thank you. My barge, if you please.'

He would pay a call and receive the standing orders that would mark the solemn accession of *L'Aurore* to the Mediterranean fleet. He would as well make his first acquaintance with the friend of Nelson's who had led the lee column into the enemy line as Kydd had watched from the deck of this very ship.

In full dress uniform, shyly conscious of the broad scarlet sash and glittering star of his knighthood, he mounted the side and came aboard through the carved and gilded entry-port.

The piping died away and there, past the side-party, was the admiral.

Kydd took off his cocked hat and bowed, careful to note the height of the deckhead as he straightened.

'Captain Thomas Kydd, *L'Aurore* frigate, my lord.'

'Do I not spy that it were rather "Sir Thomas"?' Collingwood said, with a twinkle, and held out his hand. 'My, but you've no idea how good it is to see a new face! Come below for a restorative and tell me all about it.'

As they went into the day cabin, a dog ran up to him, leaping and snuffling joyfully. 'Down, Bounce,' Collingwood said, in mock severity. 'Where are your manners, sir?'

The cabin was the homeliest Kydd had ever seen in a man-o'-war. Miniature portraits, knick-knacks and ornaments that could only have come from a woman's hand – it was touching in a great admiral.

'Now, sir. You've come to join our little band?'

'As *L'Aurore* and I were here in October of the year five,' Kydd said quietly.

'Yes. Well, I'm still here, you see.'

It was difficult to credit but Collingwood had stayed faithfully at this post after the great victory of Trafalgar, doing his duty by the nation, and had not once set foot on land, while others had returned to bathe in the delirium of public adulation that had followed their release from the mortal fear of invasion.

His genial face was careworn and old. It was said that while he yearned for peace and retirement the government had been too fearful to let him go for want of any with his formidable skills as a diplomat and strategist.

'Flags will give you your fill of orders, signals and so forth, so let me tell you something of how the larger situation has changed our position here.'

The dog curled up under his chair while he gathered his thoughts.

'The main purpose of the Mediterranean fleet remains the same. To deny the French the Mediterranean. To that end we've a close blockade of Toulon and the same at Cartagena. But there's complications as you'd expect of Boney.

'We've lost Naples but we must perforce keep Sicily or the eastern Med is denied us.

'In the west we have the Barbary Deys in Morocco and similar to be polite to, else we lose our beef and water, but further east it's much more troublesome. The Russians have ambitions to be a player upon the world stage and have thereby sadly affronted the Turks, who consider themselves to be the reigning power in the east. As they are our allies both, it makes for tiresome dealings.'

'My lord, what of Bonaparte's decree? What is its effect in these waters? And you are speaking to one only recently returned from the Caribbean.'

'His grand Continental System? Then it has to be said that it's a sore trial to our manufactories and traders in their northern markets but in these parts, while we suffer his ships to moulder in port, he cannot enforce it.'

He sighed and gave a sad smile. 'Here we sit, Kydd, in the full knowledge that it is in our power to lose the war for England in a single day. Yet in this peril we are given less force by far than a year ago. And all the time we are commanded at a distance by a landlubber first lord and a parcel of ninnies in government who have no conception of sea power and expect me to act upon their vapourings of the moment.'

Kydd murmured something but Collingwood hadn't finished. 'At times I wake up from a dream where I'm a circus whip, who prowls up and down to keep the wild beasts at bay, armed with nothing but a goad and a fierce look. All it needs . . .'

He stopped, then brightened. 'But let not my maunderings spoil the hour. You'll stay to dinner? And you shall send for your officers. Are there any performers at all? We have a very passable theatre troupe of amateurs, who display their talents upon the slightest provocation . . .'

Chapter 4

'Lord and Lady Barradale,' the master of ceremonies intoned.

A portly noble in crimson and gold with silk breeches and an old-fashioned wig brought his wife forward on his arm. He made an elegant leg to the Countess of Farndon and a polite bow to the dowager countess and the earl, while his wife sank down in a curtsy.

Cecilia bobbed with a smile. 'It was so good of you to come. And in this tiresome weather.'

The viscountess was sharp-faced and wore no less than seven strings of pearls over her elaborate gown. She answered in cool tones, 'Our pleasure to be here, Lady Farndon. I do hope you are settling in well. I find servants can be so trying at times, don't you?'

Cecilia recognised the look but she herself was a countess and had precedence over a mere viscountess.

'Farndon does not allow familiarity and will not brook insolence in any form,' she said sweetly, and allowed her gaze to slide to the next couple.

This was the neighbouring Earl Chervil, who seemed a jolly enough fellow, and Cecilia warmed to the prospect of a returned visit.

Her years with the Marquess of Bloomsbury, as companion to the marchioness, were paying off handsomely. She knew every bit of the code, all the artifices of snobbery and aspiration, and backstairs she had acquired a sound understanding of how things were actually contrived. She was thus perfectly able to cope, acting as hostess directly instead of at the bidding of others.

Beside her, Nicholas was performing his noble duty but she knew he took it too seriously for it to be a pleasure and it would be her mission to lighten his burden.

Chervil was earnestly holding forth to him about the soils of north Wiltshire. She fanned herself daintily, taking the opportunity for a discreet survey of the ballroom. It had been a good response to the invitations even if, she suspected, many had accepted only out of curiosity.

As her mother-in-law had predicted, the newspapers had seized on the occasion of a society wedding out of the ordinary and had speculated wildly. A young earl-in-waiting who had disappeared into the world, some said for eccentric scientifical pursuits, others for salacious wanderings in exotic parts, was recalled to his duties by his father's demise. And had taken for bride a nameless country girl in defiance of society.

Their conclusions, however, were generally the same. It was not unknown for an ageing noble to marry a compromised milkmaid, but this could not be the case here, for in the peerage Lord Farndon was a most eligible catch. There was no other explanation possible than that it had been a truly romantic match, the noble lord smitten by an unknown beauty.

It had made splendid copy, with Cecilia an object of intense interest.

The reception line ended. She caught the eye of the orchestra leader and nodded discreetly.

The music faded and a loud chord was struck.

The Earl of Farndon turned and stood attentively.

The dear fool. 'Nicholas!' she hissed. 'Come on – it's for us! They're waiting for us to start the ball.'

She swept him out into the centre of the floor for the minuet and they danced together under the magnificent chandeliers.

The canopy of the four-poster great bed was prettily patterned with interlocked heraldic flowers, holding in the candlelight a soft mystery of time and ancestry. Cecilia lay looking up at it, still coming to terms with what she had become – and the man she had married.

He was next to her, reading from a volume of verse, which she now knew he invariably did before sleep. She had learned other things: he was serious and thoughtful, reflective and calm, and it were better she allow him to reach a conclusion by his chain of logic than to interrupt with a stab of practical intuition.

But there was so much she didn't know about him, now, as they set out on their married life together.

She rolled over to face him. 'Nicholas, my love.'

'Oh, yes, my darling?' But his eyes were still on his book.

'Can we talk?'

'Oh?' he said, in concern, laying down the book and turning to her.

'Yes, do you mind?'

'What is it, Cecilia, my very dearest?'

'Nicholas, don't you agree that if we love each other and worry about things, we shouldn't keep it to ourselves, we should share them?'

'Why, I suppose so.'

'Then we shouldn't have secrets from each other?'

'Do we? What, then, should I tell you, dear?'

'Nicholas – one question only.'

'Certainly.'

'Who are you?'

'I . . . I beg your pardon?'

'I know nothing about you really, Nicholas. You've told me so little about yourself.'

'Oh.'

'Yes. I think you should tell me the story of your life so that I'll know just who it is I'm now joined to.'

'All of it? I really don't think—'

'All of it, Nicholas,' she said quietly.

'Well, I was born here at Eskdale Hall some many years ago and—'

'I'm serious, Nicholas. I want to know what in the past has made you . . . you.'

He looked at her with great tenderness, then turned and lay back, staring up into the blackness for so long she thought he was rebuffing her.

Finally he spoke. 'Yes, my dear. You are right – there will be no secrets between us and you have every right to know who I am – although this is a question I'm not sure I can answer.

'There will be those who find strange my obedience to logic, my refuge in the moral certainties. Still more the profundity of my interest in the human condition . . . and, most of all, my contentment upon the bosom of the deep and wheresoever it takes me.'

Her hand found his and he squeezed it. 'Please be prepared for a . . . strange and wistful tale.'

He began with his self-imposed exile for a compelling moral reason as a common seaman into the gun-deck of a man-o'-war, there to meet a young press-gang victim called Tom Kydd. How they had formed a friendship so deep it had sustained them over the years to follow until they had both won through to the quarterdeck.

He spared her nothing, in a flood of release telling of the dangers and exhilarations of the war at sea, breath-stopping adventures across the South Seas, fighting against Napoleon Bonaparte himself at the gates of Acre, battles of conquest and betrayal, feats of heroism and defeat.

And he told her, too, of his being swept into the maelstrom of deceit and treachery that was the failed uprising and assassination attempt against Bonaparte, how later he had travelled into the very heart of Paris to woo the American inventor Fulton, with his crazy plans for a submarine boat.

Then finally, only that very year in the Caribbean, his near-disastrous but ultimately successful penetration of a plot to bring Britain to its knees with a privateer fleet, which had nearly cost him his life.

She clung to him, held him, loved him: what she had heard was thrilling, marvellous and, ultimately . . . heartbreaking.

This was the death-knell of his life of danger and excitement, of companionship and fulfilment. Whatever he had been before he could be no longer. He was now to know life arrayed only in velvet and silk, cosseted and fawned upon.

What, in the name of their love for each other, could she find for him that could even begin to match the thrill and drama of what had gone before?

*   *   *

'I'm surprised his lordship has not yet advised you, Mr Bardoe,' she said, to the hovering bursar. 'He insists always that books of account should be rendered in proper form, double entry and traceable to the day-books. I see here that it's frankly impossible to determine how your figure is arrived at without it is correctly entered.'

'Yes, my lady. I'll see to the bookkeepers today.'

There were going to be changes at Eskdale.

'Do ask Mrs Grant to attend me, if you please.'

Cecilia now had her private sitting room, equipped with a desk and bookshelves, serving both for entertaining ladies to tea and as an interview room for the staff.

'Good morning, Mrs Grant. Do sit down. I wanted to speak to you about the condition of the public rooms in the east wing for which you have the charge. Do you not feel . . .'

The day wore on. At eleven she tiptoed to the door of the earl's study and listened.

He was dutifully attending to the tenant roll on this the first Monday of the month.

Inside, a grizzled farmer was telling a tale of woe about the season and the crops in a practised moan, and her husband was hearing him out politely, the estate steward standing by with an ill-tempered scowl.

She slipped back to her sitting room. This afternoon, she vowed, they would ride together over the winter-hard slopes to the woods, the wind in their hair, hearts beating fast. And then return happily to their home.

A tug on the tasselled bell-rope brought an awe-struck maidservant with a tray.

As she sipped her tea, she realised she was so happy with Nicholas that she had not noticed how alone she was. As if she was in a foreign country. No doubt she would make friends later but there was something she could do about it right now.

She reached for a pen and paper.

Dear Hetty,

I do hope you have got over your shock about the wedding, my dear, for here is another one.

I was just wondering if you can bear to leave your odious brood to take a position here as my companion. We shall have fun together and . . .

Renzi finished his breakfast. 'My dear, I feel I should show my face in London. I've a suspicion Father may not have left affairs in as regular a fashion as I'd like.'

He knew of his father's political cronies, the fast set at the races, the disgrace at Almack's and, no doubt, there would be other distasteful matters to deal with.

'Do we have a town house, Nicholas? I would so like to entertain!'

'We do, dearest, but I fancy now is not the time for you to be seen in Town. Let them get over their rude curiosities first, I beg.'

He would do all in his power to protect her from the tittering behind fans and ogling from the ill-bred that would be her lot if she went with him.

'I won't be offended, Nicholas dear – don't concern yourself on my account, please.'

'Sweetheart, I won't hear of it. I'll be gone only a short while to see how things are and I shall return at the gallop, I swear!'

There would be no shifting him so she took charge of the packing and saw him off in the carriage, waving forlornly as it ground away down the long drive.

Renzi shifted into the agreeable comfort of the padded seat and let his mind wander.

What would he find in Curzon Street? He had been there only once, long ago, when his mother had sent him to implore the earl to return to his neglected estate. He had found him in raucous squalor with his sycophants, deaf to pleading, sarcastic and threatening. Renzi felt a twist of sadness that his mother, in her arranged marriage, had never known the deep happiness that was now his.

Dear Cecilia – his heart went out to her. As long as he drew breath he would shield her and safeguard her from the savagery and hypocrisy he knew lay behind much of the façade of gentility and politeness at the pinnacle of society.

The town house was much as he remembered, a little shabbier, a little sadder. The butler was surprised to see him, and somewhat surly, and the rooms smelt stuffy and uncared-for although he could see they had been used recently.

Renzi went to the drawing room and hesitated for a moment before sitting in the grand high-backed leather chair his father had used. It felt stilted, awkward, and he found another. Damn, but there were ghosts here he couldn't shake off.

The front-door bell sounded and the butler came bearing a card on a tray.

Charles Grosvenor. The thin-faced wretch who'd been his father's electoral agent. He'd lost no time in making his number, but as he lived opposite he would have seen his arrival.

He strode in, dressed in the fashionable tight pantaloons and ridiculous high collar, then bowed, with a wide smile and a click of heels. 'Hail to you, sir, the new lord of Eskdale and the parliamentary seat of Noakes Minor!'

'Yes?' Renzi said flatly. He did not get up, or offer a chair.

The smile slipped a little. 'Why, my good lord, I came to enquire as to your plans for your installation in the House.'

'I haven't made any.'

'Sir, it is the season, Parliament does sit and there are those in the Party who are anxious concerning the fate of the upcoming Rents and Imposts Bill. The Tory Party that is – whose cause you will, of course, be warm to.'

Lord Farndon could take his seat in the House of Lords but also had the right of patronage of a local rotten borough. Votes in the upper and lower house both.

'Mr Grosvenor. Let me be clear: the entire practice of politics is distasteful to me. It is founded on the odd notion that all of nature and man, in all its diversity and wonder, might be compressed and then divided in twain – one or the other, none else. How then is it possible to reach an under- standing of a matter touching on the behaviour of all men, when one is obliged to regard it through the lens of one artificial polity?'

There was now no smile at all.

'Thank you for calling. I shall doubtless inform you should I feel a sudden urge to politick. Good day to you, sir.'

There would be other pressures. For a certainty he was now labelled awkward, and bigger guns would be brought up. He sighed and closed his eyes.

It would be better once Cecilia was here but in the mean- time there was so much to—

'Hello – who the devil are you?'

Renzi's eyes snapped open. A tousled, unsavoury man of years in a dressing-gown stood in the doorway, blinking.

'I'm Lord Farndon. And who the devil are you, sir?'

'Ah, of course. The old boy popped off and you're his whelp.'

Anger suddenly boiled and Renzi got to his feet. 'I demand an explanation from you, sir,' he barked, 'or I'll have you thrown on the street as you stand.'

The man sniffled, wiping his nose on his sleeve. 'You can't do that, it ain't allowed.'

'I can, and I—'

'I've got assured and legal occupation in this house for a peppercorn rental – your father was generous to those that were useful to him for . . . certain purposes. As you will be, when you know the lie, young fellow.'

The utter banality of a pointless, aimless existence for the rest of his life threatened to choke him. Head down, Renzi stormed out of the house.

The Mayfair streets were stirring. Calls were being made, assignations of the evening settled. Footmen hurried on their errands and tradesmen of the better sort were making their rounds.

As he turned the corner a black carriage taking the shorter path turned across and obliged him to flatten to the wall. It ground past and he caught a glimpse of an old, pale face. Their eyes met but then the coach was gone.

He set off in the opposite direction, in his black mood ignoring the faint shouting behind him.

Then he became aware of a commotion. It was the black carriage in a desperate tangle, trying against the irate flow of traffic to turn about and come back. Curses and cries from other carriages rang out as it finally trotted up to him.

The door was flung open and a man leaned out and cried, 'Dear fellow! Ren— that is to say, my lord Farndon! Well met, well met indeed! Are you in haste? Or would you do me the honour of a luncheon at my club?'

It was the Marquess of Bloomsbury, Cecilia's previous

employer, now retired from some discreet diplomatic post on account of health.

'Most willingly, sir,' Renzi said, brightening, and climbed in to sit beside him.

'I do beg your pardon most humbly,' the marquess said. 'I see from the *Gazette* you are now ennobled. I could scarcely credit the news. My earnest felicitations, of course.'

He had aged greatly, was frail and bent, but his eyes nevertheless held a keen humour.

'More deserved of your kind sentiments, sir, is my recent marriage to the woman of my heart – Miss Cecilia Kydd as was.'

'Splendid! Now, why do I believe the marchioness will not be surprised one whit?'

Time passed agreeably on the way to Boodles. They had first met in dramatic circumstances together in a shipwreck in the Caribbean and much had happened since.

After the rib of lamb they retired to the library for brandy.

'I can't pretend that I find our meeting other than fortuitous,' Bloomsbury said. 'I've been vexed for some time to think of an excuse to speak to you alone, as it were.'

'Sir?'

'In truth I'm in despair of my health. It has cruelly affected me. Particularly where it bears on my service to my country.'

'I'm sorry to hear it, sir.'

'Are you aware, dear chap, of just what it is that I've been engaged upon for these years in the country's cause?' he said quietly, glancing about.

'To be frank, no.'

'I will tell you. But only in the strictest confidence that you are able to conceive.'

'In that case, sir, I'd rather you—'

'Be certain, this is no trivial matter. You may believe I have my reasons for divulging it to you.'

'Very well.'

'Then you will hear it.' He waited until a club member clutching a newspaper had passed then began, speaking softly but with compelling force.

'When nations strive against each other – as they have always done and will ever do – there is a code of conduct between them that rises above their bitterest rivalries. It is the diplomatic code, to which all civilised nations subscribe. A country's nominated representatives, your ambassadors, plenipotentiaries and so forth, are empowered to treat, with the object of arriving at an understanding that ends expressed in the form of protocols, treaties and the like.

'This level of intercourse rises far above petty politicking, involving as it does the highest levels of state to which it is possible to go.

'I ask you to reflect upon this, if you will. The players are known to each other. They sit in their entrenched positions, which are also known, holding their cards to their chests and playing them to the greatest effect they can manage until the situation stabilises, whether in the form of a treaty or perchance a stalemate.'

He paused then continued with increased intensity: 'This is how it has always been done. And it has to be said to the dispassionate observer there is a major flaw. Since the positions are known they may not be modified by concession without possible loss of reputation and standing of the player and his principal. You may easily see how this can result in ruinous confrontations, to the desiring of neither side. How much better, then, that an unknown agency might, by judicious inter-vention, cause one or the other to yield covertly?'

'I'm not certain I follow you, sir. Are you suggesting a form of clandestine mediation?'

'Not at all. This agency operates with the sole intent of furthering the interests of its principal – in our case the Crown of Great Britain.'

'A form of espionage, then.'

'No, sir,' Bloomsbury said coldly. 'It is never that. The practices of gathering intelligence and acts of secret assassination have their place, but are beneath notice for this agency. It is in the realm of princes and governments that it has its calling.'

'Do be plain, sir, I beg. If this is your following, I honour you for it but its remit is not clear to me. Do you—'

'I will be plain, my dear Farndon. With distressing regularity there are situations in this world that loom suddenly to menace the interests of this country. If there is any possibility that I can be of value, that I perceive an opening, however slight in the crisis, I will hasten there to see what can be achieved.'

'Alone?'

'Quite. No one troubles an English milord, for they are patently harmless and useless, yet are known to have the priceless gift of the ear of the highest in the land. I am thereby well placed to listen sympathetically to grievances, be open to the radical and place dismaying information where it will have the most effective consequence.'

'Then I begin to see how—'

'But my enterprise goes beyond this, far beyond. What if a situation arises that demands, shall we say, a need to show resolution, commitment, even? In a cause sympathetic to England, perhaps, or a player too timid to act without he has a shadowy friend to reassure him? It is out of the hands of ambassadors and their ilk for they and their positions are open and known, but it is a very different matter for me, able to take any stance I desire with them.

'You see, I have been invested with secret competences, powers to commit England to any course of action I deem necessary and which may be trusted therefore by the recipient. In this way may be accomplished what the blunt weapon of a whole army division or your naval fleet may not.'

'This is extraordinary to hear, sir! You imply that the government of the day will allow you this latitude, and support you in it *ex post facto*?'

'These powers are used sparingly and as a last resort, but I have had occasion. Much the more common is the innocent subverting, the guileless deception, the empathetic audience and, still more, the vacuous entertaining.'

'You will have had your successes, I'm persuaded.'

'It is to be admitted. You'll recollect when we first met in 'ninety-four?'

'In difficult circumstances in the Caribbean.'

'Yes – that was when I carried in my bosom the knowledge of the treacherous plot of the Spaniards to fall upon our possessions there, in forward anticipation of a declaration of war. This was won from a disaffected Don, whom I suborned in the usual way. And, more recently, in the assassination of the Swedish prince, there were elements more than willing to be turned and . . . Well, I find I am an old man babbling, I do apologise.'

'Sir, do not, I pray! You have my most earnest admiration – as much for what you have not said as what you have revealed to me.'

'I knew you'd understand, my friend.'

For some reason the words touched Renzi greatly. He coughed self-consciously and said, with much feeling, 'And

I'd believe you'd be finding it hard to resign yourself to inactivity, sir.'

'Yet I have the consolation of my dear wife, who has been by my side over these years . . .'

'Sir, purely out of unforgivable curiosity, is the marchioness privy to what you've been undertaking?'

'There are no secrets between us,' he answered simply. 'Else what might she think?' he added, with a dry laugh.

There was an awkward pause.

'Sir, I have to thank you for your hospitality, and look to—'

'Capital brandy. Another?'

So there was to be a postscript.

'Certainly, sir.'

The marquess resettled himself in the high-backed chair, cradling his glass. 'You'll be wondering why I've told you this. It is for a purpose.'

'Sir?'

'The times are dolorous but I cannot respond any further to the call. I must needs pass on the banner to another.'

Renzi sat upright. 'Sir! If by that you mean—'

'I do. In all my dealings with humanity I cannot think to find another more nearly suited to my trade. You are upright, honourable and possessed of an acute moral sensibility. Unusually, this is coupled with a most complete experience of the world in your nautical travels and similar – and while I'm well aware of your views on covert activities, our Mr Congalton was at pains to laud your successes with the Duc d'Auvergne in Jersey, and may I point out, so recently as Curaçao and later.'

He smiled briefly. 'Your matchless performance in Paris was observed with envy by myself, who was powerless to act in the matter, and' – he held up a hand to stop the protests

— 'this can only demonstrate you are undoubtedly possessed of the prime requisites for a species of discreet diplomacy in every respect. And now, since your *élever* your qualifications are complete.

'Lord Farndon, I invite you to take my place as – shall we say? – an ambassador *extraordinaire* to serve your country as is seldom that a single individual can. The going will be onerous, the burden dire – but your reward is the sure knowledge that there will be very few indeed who can lay claim to have served Crown and country as lies within your power.

'What do you say, sir?'

How could he refuse the offer? It was a clarion call to purpose in his life, the noble cause of his country. Guiltily he knew that it would as well offer the danger and excitement he craved in exotic parts of the world – his wanderlust would be more than satisfied.

He knew he could do it: already his mind was seething with possibilities. His ethnical studies had given him a certain name in scientifical circles that was genuine and would open doors abroad. And he was virtually unknown to the French. The Mr Smith who had gone to Paris on cartel was untainted by discovery and would never be mistaken for the elegant Lord Farndon, while the activities of an obscure ship's secretary in the remote Caribbean would not be brought up in the glittering chancelleries of Europe.

And, above all, it was an honourable and decent occupation.

Natural caution, however, dictated he find out more before accepting.

He spent a restless night but there was never any question: if his queries were satisfied he would consent.

* * *

'Well, dear fellow, have you considered your position?'

'I have, sir. And I'm to say that I do accept, should certain queries I have be satisfied.'

'Good man! Well, fire away.'

They were quickly dealt with.

In the matter of his standing with the government of the day, he would be made a Lord Chamberlain's Gentleman of the Presence, to kiss hands with the King as his liege man of demonstrable privy loyalty, but his prime and only contact would be a certain Mr Congalton in the Foreign Office, the only one to know his true mission – and who was most keen to meet him.

Necessarily his actions, if revealed, would be repudiated by the authorities and no military or civil jurisdiction would have knowledge of him. While this left him completely alone, on the other hand it allowed him to act without orders, hindrance or the necessity to report to a superior.

It would become more complicated if he should need to invoke external forces. As a matter of routine each flagship in the Navy, wherever based in the world, would carry among its sealed orders a single envelope. He could demand its opening with a code phrase and it would contain an instruction to the effect that the name it contained was authorised to request a movement or action of a ship or squadron forthwith.

Communications would be sparing: he would be left alone to make decisions with the best information to hand and it would be understood that any action of his would have been made in the light of this.

In all, it was a relationship of complete discretion, immense trust and grave moral responsibilities. And precisely as he would want it.

'Sir, you have answered me in full. I do now accept the honour.'

The formalities were settled without delay. After his visit to the palace he was immediately taken to see Mr Congalton.

A spare, abstemious man of indeterminate years, he inhabited a windowless office at the rear of the grand building in Whitehall. In its hushed atmosphere Renzi was left to make acquaintance of the man who would know everything, whose reach spanned the planet and who would stand between him and those who would never know of him.

'The marquess has served us faithfully since the American war,' Congalton said drily. 'He will be a hard man to follow, sir.'

It was a long afternoon but he heard much more of the marquess's career, his many successes and rare defeats. It was a useful way to perceive how it had been done: the stratagems and intelligence, creative improvisation and inhuman patience that had achieved so much, always over extreme odds.

He saw how his position in the world was paradoxically both a perfect character for his work but, as well, made him a figure of prominence unable to step back into an anonymous background. Too important to overlook, too exalted to suspect.

He learned of the limitations of his office: the tyranny of time, of being unable to be in two places at once – the stark impossibility of some situations.

A post of great loneliness with none to applaud and none to grieve.

'You will want to be apprised of the state of the world as you would see it, my lord.'

He did, and his eyes were opened. This was no dry

reciting of the news of the day: this was a view from the centre of the web, informed by intelligence won from the heart of the opposing forces, which hid nothing of the desperate grappling of the two principals on the world stage and the scrambling of lesser powers to profit by their preoccupation.

He was exhilarated – and awed. How could he, a single man, conceivably alter the balance in this titanic struggle?

'What in your opinion is the greatest threat to us at this minute?' Renzi asked.

'For your answer, I ask you to recall our strategy at its core. That Bonaparte is imprisoned in Fortress Europe, and while he may strut up and down he is helpless in the larger arena. He needs to burst out into the world, either by crushing and eliminating us or finding a corridor out of the continent.'

'Yes, I grant this.'

'He has an opportunity.'

'The Levant?'

'He sees that our allies, Turkey and Russia, are poised for war against each other. If he is successful in an intrigue with Sultan Selim in Constantinople and detaches him from us he stands to gain an overland route direct to India and the world, not a fathom of salt water to send our fleet – and we are lost.'

'Quite. Are the French succeeding, do you think?'

'They began in 1802 at the armistice, and ever since have been steadily wooing him with advisers and soothing words and now, it's reported, with guns. Our ambassador there, Arbuthnot, is no match for the French in this game, especially ranged against their General Sébastiani, who is a close friend of Bonaparte. He's a fellow Corsican and was hand-picked to ingratiate himself to a commanding position, which now, we must grudgingly admit, he has achieved.'

A reluctant smile appeared. 'I have the distinct feeling that my first engagement will be among the pavilions and harem of the Topkapi Palace. Am I right?'

'It is always yours to refuse, my lord.'

'Very well. Shall we plan?'

There was remarkably little to discuss. The only operational objective that could in any way be defined was that the French intriguing and influence in Constantinople must at all costs be countered. The stakes were colossal: if they succeeded in taking Turkey from the British, Bonaparte would have his highway out of Europe, and falling on India from landward, the end of Britain and its empire would not be long behind.

It was now left to him to travel out as soon as it was possible to do so.

'Oh, Nicholas, darling! Please pay attention, I beg. I was talking about the arboretum. If we plant now, they'll blossom next summer and what a wonderful show they'll make. We have only to pull down that old barn and put up one of those new glass houses and—'

'I'm sorry, Cecilia, I was thinking on other things. Shall we go inside?'

It couldn't be postponed any longer. There was a dispatch cutter leaving from Plymouth for Gibraltar and he dared not miss the chance, not with its speed in the face of the urgency.

'Dearest, you'll never guess who I met in London.'

'Tell me!'

'The Marquess of Bloomsbury.'

'Oh, how wonderful! Did you tell him—'

'He extends to you every wish for happiness, my dear.'

'Did he—'

'Dear Cecilia,' he broke in. 'I don't know how to – to break this to you.'

'Nicholas?' she said uncertainly, her hand going to her mouth in concern.

'You know his work dealt with diplomatic matters of the highest degree of discretion?'

'Yes, but he never spoke of it.'

'He told me much, you may believe. Enough that I know now the frightful peril that England lies under at this moment.'

'Nicholas, why did he . . . ?'

'He knows me of old and has been told of Paris, Jersey and Curaçao. And since learning of my ennobling he has conceived that . . . that I am the one best placed to take up his work.'

'You – you mean to be like him, to go about the world and . . . and . . .' she said, breathless.

'That is what he desires me to do.'

'You mean to say, to be the new . . .' She laughed delightedly. 'Oh, darling! This is wonderful news! No – it's marvellous! You've no idea how worried I've been that you'd be so discontented with a quiet life. This is just what you need.'

She hugged him.

'Then you're not . . . ?'

'Oh, sweetheart, I'm happy for you, can't you see?'

'Even if it means that I must embark immediately?'

'If it's an urgent matter there is no question – we must leave without delay.'

'Cecilia. My love. There is no "we". I go alone. It's much too dangerous for you, believe me.'

'Nicholas – it has to be "we". I'm a strong woman and I want to be by your side.'

'Sweetheart, this is no place for the woman I love so dearly. I will not—'

'The marchioness went everywhere it took her husband – why not me? Am I less than she? Are you saying—'

'No. I will not have it, Cecilia. I cannot have my attention diverted with worry and anxiety on your account.'

'You've forgotten, Nicholas, that as lady companion I went everywhere with them both. And that included some odious and frightening places, believe me.'

'Oh? You've never told me—'

'Because I've not wanted to worry you, darling. Look, we'll be just like them, together we'll—'

'No. And that's my last word on it, Cecilia.'

Chapter 5

'They're out, sir!' Curzon said urgently. The first lieuten-ant's glass was on the opposite, northern, side of Bahia Cádiz.

L'Aurore was alone, deep in the bay. She had gone in on reconnaissance to steal past the sheltering peninsula of Isla de León and look direct into the inner harbour.

It was a very risky manoeuvre, usually done in boats.

Nelson had gone down in legend for joining his boats' crews and in the brutal hacking to escape the swarming gunboats that always came out to contest such spying.

It rarely happened but there could be, as now, a combina-tion favouring a ship to enter – nothing more than a light frigate, but no gunboats would dare approach her broadside.

Any variation in the weather could quickly spiral into disaster. It had to be a wind from the north: from the east, would be dead foul; from the west would embay and trap the intruder; and from the south would bring opposing frig-ates out from the port. And the timing of the tide was crucial:

if the winds were slight an ingoing tide would set up an adverse current to the south-east while the ebb would see it press to the north-west.

It was an enterprise never encouraged by admirals as the sight of a helpless frigate being taken would shake morale considerably – quite apart from the loss of strength to the fleet – and at the same time greatly raise that of the enemy. Only the most daring of captains would even consider it, but Kydd believed an accurate and timely account of all the assets facing them was worth the risk.

'Wind's turned fluky,' muttered the sailing master, eyeing the masthead vane. Without the steady north-north-easterly to rely on, they could find themselves perilously clawing their way out.

'A few more minutes only, Mr Kendall,' Kydd said, the big signal telescope steadied over a midshipman's shoulder as he, like all the officers, took careful note of what they could see on the inside of the peninsula, the great port complex of Puerto Cádiz. It was not only numbers they were after – they counted above thirty ships of size – but their readiness for sea. Sail bent on to the yard was a sure sign that a sally to seaward was in contemplation.

Midshipmen Clinch and Willock, too, were eagerly recording the observations.

'I make it eighteen o' the vermin,' Curzon rapped, his eyes on the gathering swarm at Rota, opposite. Each gunboat had a single cannon in the bows: taken together, enough fire-power to seriously challenge a frigate.

'They wouldn't dare!' grunted Kydd. Dillon, at his side, faithfully noted down everything of consequence that was said, whether he understood it or not.

'We'll be headed if'n the wind backs a point further, sir,'

Kendall said, more strongly. The leading edge of every sail was now fluttering; if the wind got past the board-hard canvas it would instantly slap it flat aback and they'd be dead in the water or, worse, a dismasted hulk.

'Sir, I must protest!' he blurted. 'We're at the five-fathom line and I can't answer should we have to stay about.'

'Very well. We shall wear ship. Now.'

'Sir, that'll put us damned close to the Vista Hermosa forts,' Curzon spluttered.

He was ignored.

'Hands to stations to wear ship!'

Agility was all. If the treacherous winds backed further they would be in serious trouble.

The order was given. The men on the helm spun the wheel. Others raced down the deck with the lines that swung the big yards in time with their falling off the wind, and going about the long way to take up on the other tack – a manoeuvre that needed much more sea-room than tacking through the eye of the wind.

It brought them within range of the forts.

A heavy thudding began, like the far-off slamming of giant doors. These were big guns in stone emplacements – and they had been sighted in properly along their firing sector.

The tearing sound of shot overhead was nerve-shredding.

The shocking passage of an invisible ball across the quarterdeck left the officers staggering with the buffeting. Others in the salvo ended in great white plumes around them, some skipping into the distance.

'Rather good practice that, the brutes,' said Bowden, rubbing his deafened ears.

But they were now headed for the safety of the open sea and the next shots were wide.

'Ease her, no need to risk our sticks.'

They won into clear water and Kydd shaped course for the anchorage to note up his findings.

Before he could go below there was a signal. 'Sir – Flag, our pennant.'

Was the captain of *L'Aurore* to be chastised for hazarding his ship?

'Heave to in her lee, away my barge.'

The admiral was not at the ship's side to greet him and he followed the flag-lieutenant down to Collingwood's day cabin.

He was deep in murmured discussion with his flag-captain and Kydd waited apprehensively, rehearsing his defence.

'Thank you, we'll talk more about it later,' Collingwood told the officer, who left. He put the papers together slowly, his face careworn and lined.

'Sir Thomas, I would have you prepare your frigate for immediate service.'

'Aye aye, sir.' So it was nothing to do with his escapade.

'There's a deal of trouble brewing in the eastern Med and I need you to undertake a mission of quite some importance.'

'Sir?'

'I've disquieting intelligence that suggests the Turks are not as neutrally inclined as they should be, given their position. They've been listening to some French agitators and seem ready to shift sides. Arbuthnot, our ambassador in the Sublime Porte – that's what they call their Turkish court – seems to think it will come to a sorry situation imminently and he's crying to be taken off.

'I don't myself believe it will come to that, an evacuation, but he's a privy councillor, in thick with Wellesley and similar, and I don't want to be thought uncaring.

'You're the swiftest sail I have, Kydd. I want you to carry

136

my instructions to Admiral Louis in Malta to do what he can to seem helpful.'

Malta had memories for Kydd. It was here that he had taken up his first command, the lovely little sloop *Teazer*, and the midshipman who alone had been present at her commissioning was here on this very quarterdeck as his second lieutenant – Bowden.

There were the massive forts so well remembered, St Elmo, Fort Tigné, and then it was Grand Harbour and the anchorage, but he couldn't delay: the situation was urgent.

They passed within, all due honours paid, but apart from a pair of sloops in Rinella, there was no squadron in port.

Kydd lost no time in taking boat for the Lascaris Steps: if he didn't find the squadron soon, Collingwood's urgent instructions could not be delivered.

Then he was hurrying over the familiar black basalt slabs of the Grand Master's Palace and up the elliptical staircase to meet the governor.

Alexander Ball had been captain of his namesake *Alexander* before the great battle of the Nile, and his daring and dogged rescue of the dismasted *Vanguard* and Nelson, which Kydd had witnessed, had been a turning point of history. There was no question – if the fabled admiral had been lost at that point, there would have been no clash of fleets and Bonaparte would now be standing astride the world.

'Then how might I be of service, Sir Thomas?' Ball opened, clearly interested in what brought a dashing frigate to the more remote eastern Mediterranean.

'I've urgent instructions for Admiral Louis, sir,' Kydd said. 'Do you have knowledge of his movements at all?'

'Pray do not alarm yourself, Captain. In this part of the

world things seldom happen with any degree of rapidity. Have you any notion of what those instructions might contain?'

This was a senior naval officer and a civil governor who had every right to know what was happening. Kydd clutched to himself the gratifying knowledge that he was no longer a dutiful messenger carrying sealed dispatches. He was at a rank and respected enough to be a player in the wider drama, trusted with inside knowledge.

'Lord Collingwood was good enough to inform me, yes, sir. And they are . . .'

He briefly told of the worsening situation in the Turkish capital and the desperate plea of the ambassador to be taken off.

'I had no idea it had got to such a pass – but I can't help you much to find Admiral Louis's squadron. Let's get out the charts and take a look at the rendezvous positions he's used in the last few months.'

It was an impossibly large area to cover: from Egypt in the south to the Aegean in the north, the ancient sea held so much of significance and threat that no single place thrust itself out over the others.

'If he's got wind of how things are deteriorating, he may wish to place himself athwart the only seaway to Constantinople. This is the strait of the Dardanelles and is damned narrow and chancy navigating. The rendezvous for that is here, at the island of Tenedos, just south of the entrance. I'd start there, if I were you.'

Standing south to avoid a blustering gregale, *L'Aurore* rounded Greece and headed for the northern Aegean.

It was sailing of the kind that Kydd disliked most:

uncertainty, aimless searching, yet all to be done at breakneck speed with no promise of a happy ending. From daybreak to darkness, doubled lookouts, relieved every half-hour, and the same intensely fatiguing duty at night, straining for lights in the blackness.

They reached the Dardanelles and the island of Tenedos. Bare, straggling and all of five miles across, it lay just off the coast of Anatolia, providing a useful haven.

But it was empty of anything that flew a British flag.

Kydd brought his ship to anchor and retired to his cabin, tired and dismayed. A crisis was brewing and the ambassador thought it so bad he was apparently abandoning his post. The longer the delay, the worse things would get, and only *L'Aurore*'s precious instructions would start in train a powerful squadron to the rescue.

He had to find Louis! *L'Aurore* was in the far north of the Aegean. If they were not here, by definition the squadron was in the south. Or in the west off the Morea, Greece. Or even, damn it all, south-west off north Africa. He could go mad just thinking of the alternatives.

One of which was – do nothing. Stay at anchor until the squadron came upon them on its constant ranging around the eastern regions.

His nature shied from inactivity as a course of action, but what else could he do?

He threw down his pencilled notes in frustration and went on deck.

He gazed on Turkish Anatolia opposite – a dry, scrubby and nondescript coastline, looking as old as time. A light breeze blew from the land, darkling the sea in delicate feather-like fans.

He was not the only one staring at the shore: Dillon stood

over the two new midshipmen, one of whom had a small telescope up.

Oh, to be as carefree as those two! Presumably this would not be their view . . .

On impulse he drew nearer.

Dillon was treating his duties as schoolmaster seriously. He had taken to carrying a rattan cane borrowed from the boatswain's mate and frowning at his charges on all possible occasions, which had raised a smile from more than one onlooker.

Kydd had let him loose on harmless paperwork after a week's apprenticeship under the ship's clerk, Goffin, and he had proved effortlessly able, even suggesting a novel system of filing. But it would inevitably be some time before he could be trusted with confidences.

For all that, the young man was keen and hadn't been dismayed by his small taste of action. Was he seeing the far parts of the world that he'd yearned for?

'Now mark this, Mr Willock,' Dillon said, in gruff tones. 'If I inform you that the river you see to the left is the Scamander, what does this tell you?'

Kydd gave a small smile: Dillon must have sighted the ship's charts to know that.

'Oh, it's a long one?' one boy hazarded.

Even in the small weeks they had been at sea, the pair had bloomed, due in most part to his inspired idea to have that hardened old reprobate but first-class seaman Doud on hand as their 'sea-daddy' just as, so long ago, the seamed old Bowyer had taken him under his wing.

Doud had found them both in his watch and was at first disdainful and short, but their childish desire to deserve well of *L'Aurore* had melted him, and now there was none on the gun-deck who would dare make sport of his lads.

To watch him teach the youngsters fine sennit or an intricately worked west-country whipping would have softened the hardest heart. His big, blunt seaman's fingers would carefully tease the twine and rope, and the result would always be a perfection of neatness that challenged their little fingers. He would softly encourage, allow them to make their mistakes and never let impatience show.

The result had been a rising confidence, a willingness to try more and a disarming glee at what they had accomplished, which was on occasion brought before their captain for grave praise.

Before long he would allow Doud to get them aloft.

'No, no, Mr Willock,' the schoolmaster said reprovingly. He pointed the cane sternly at the bare hillocks. 'Regard! That . . . is the Troy of Helen and Paris, Achilles and Hector, is it not?'

'It is?'

Curzon turning to listen, raised his eyebrows in surprise.

Ignoring him, Dillon glared at the hapless boy. 'Scoundrel! You have not attended to your histories. In the dog-watch you'll write out for me two hundred times: "διχθαδίας κῆρας φερέμεν θανάτοιο τέλος δέ".'

'Oh, sir! Do I have to?'

'Which being meanly translated from the Homer is, "I carry two sorts of destiny towards the day of my death." You may choose which tongue it is you inscribe.'

With new-found respect Curzon came over, too.

'And now, Mr Clinch. You have the advantage, you know where we are. Pray tell us, then, what of this island, that we anchor in its shelter?'

'Oh, well, it has a temple of sacrifices and similar?' the lad said hopefully.

141

'For not knowing that this is the very island behind which the Greeks hid their ships while the Trojans hauled their wooden horse inside the city, you are under the same penalty, sir.'

Kydd grinned. 'I do believe we're not to be spared an education even as Mr Renzi has left us, Mr Curzon.'

In much improved humour he returned to his dilemma – and quite suddenly had the answer. Just as the Greeks had cut through an insoluble stalemate at Troy with a bold stroke, so would he.

'Ask Mr Kendall to step down,' he said, and put his thoughts in order.

'Sir?'

'We've an urgent situation as won't allow us to wait in idleness for Admiral Louis to join us. I've a mind to do something about it.'

'Send out boats, sir?'

'Not at all. I intend that *L'Aurore* shall pierce the Dardanelles and go to the rescue of the ambassador directly on our own.'

'To Constantinople?' The master tried to hide his anxieties. 'We've nary a chart as takes us past the Sigeum, and I've heard the currents inside are a sore trial. And as well—'

'We find a pilot.'

'Sir?' Pilots had legal obligations, duties of care, and in England were closely examined for competency by Trinity House. If there was an equivalent here, where the devil . . . ?

'Mr Curzon will take a boat away and find one who knows his Dardanelles in the first town of size he comes to.'

The first lieutenant was hesitant. 'If the capital is in an uproar then what'll we meet? No one who's about to cross the grand sultan by conning a British man-o'-war up the strait.'

'Constantinople is far away and they owe it nothing but taxes. You'll offer honest silver, and I'd find it singular should any in these parts refuse coin for a simple passage up the strait.'

'Not wishing to cry coward, Sir Thomas, but there's one objection I feel I do have to voice.'

'And what's that, pray?'

'I've not a word of the Turkish. How I'm to persuade some old fellow to our way of thinking without the lingo, I'm vexed to know, sir.'

'Why, you've no need to. On board we happen to have a scholar of modern languages who I'm sure would bear you a hand.'

Dillon was more than happy to take on the role.

'Do I have to wear a cutlass?' he asked, and looked disappointed when it was explained that the entire boat's crew would be going without weapons to forestall any accusation by the Turks of an armed incursion.

'You've twenty-four hours,' Kydd told Curzon genially. 'Then we'll come and look for you.'

They were back before nightfall with not one but two gentlemen, both sporting an elaborate turban and gown to the clear satisfaction of *L'Aurore*'s crew.

'What's this, then, Mr Curzon?'

'My idea, sir,' he answered smugly. 'We have one in the bows, one on the quarterdeck. If they're in agreement on a helm order, we do it. If not, we can be sure one's up to trickery.'

'Well done, Mr Curzon. And you too, Mr Dillon. So you've studied the Turkish?'

'Not really, sir. That's a heathen tongue, by origin from Tamerlane and his ilk of Central Asia, who overran these lands not so many centuries ago.'

'Then how . . . ?'

'All in these parts know a species of barbarous Greek, which answered, Sir Thomas.'

'Good work! Then we'll not waste time any further. Hands to unmoor ship!'

Kydd clutched to himself the thought that should get them through: his brazen entry would catch any hostile elements by surprise. Their speed would ensure they were well past before orders could arrive from Constantinople to stop them.

But no captain ever relished putting his ship voluntarily into restricted waters and the Dardanelles was narrow and confined.

A cleft of sea pointing to the north-east, it ran for forty miles or so of tight navigation, at times with opposite shores being less than a mile apart, then opened up into the internal Sea of Marmora, which narrowed again to the Bosporus at Constantinople. Beyond that were the Black Sea and Russia.

It meant that any wind within three points either side of north-east would be dead foul – if this present north-westerly held, they were fair for the ancient city but if it changed, while they were deep within the passage, it would be a serious matter. Kydd's experience and sea sense told him that the flood of fresh water from the Black Sea mixing with the salt water would create complex and baffling currents, which, if strong, could prevail against anything from sails in a light breeze.

The biggest unknown was the Turkish fleet.

It consisted of ships-of-the-line, frigates and many smaller types, any or all of which Kydd could find arrayed across his path.

L'Aurore got under way for the entrance, slipping within two headlands not more than a couple of miles apart.

The coast on the left was steep and forbidding, to the right more even and low, and when they closed in on both sides, here and there a pale-walled fortress could be made out.

But wearing the colours of an ally they were not troubled and they made good time through the narrow waterway until they reached the Sea of Marmora, an open stretch of water.

After an easy overnight sail a grey coastline appeared with the morning – the fabled Constantinople, a city of the Byzantines but now the capital of the great Ottoman sultan, Selim III, with his harem and all the mystery of an Oriental court.

Kydd was well aware that he was taking his ship into a situation with not the slightest knowledge of what was going on. Should he proceed closed up at the guns in readiness or would that be construed a provocative act? Or should he play the part of a peaceable visitor and be defenceless?

His 'pilots' had not eased his mind with their insistence that both be dropped at one of the islands before Constantinople, and as the coast firmed, his anxiety grew.

Dismayingly, there was no offshore multitude of merchant shipping in this chief port between the Black Sea and the Mediterranean. Had they fled an impending calamity?

Nearer still the city took shape: sea-walls miles long were surmounted by hills thronged with white buildings, domes and lofty minarets, then the unmistakable form of the beautiful Hagia Sophia at the end of a peninsula to the left.

A mile-wide channel, the famed Bosporus leading to Russia, separated the coast of Asia to the right from Europe to the left.

Palaces and stately buildings amid parks and groves occupied most of the end of the peninsula and, with another noble grouping further along, made for one of the most dramatic and magnificent sights Kydd had ever seen.

'Sir, where . . . ?' The master seemed subdued by the spectacular panorama.

'We heave to for now, Mr Kendall. Two cables off should do it.'

'A boat, sir?' Curzon asked.

Kydd eyed the shoreline where excited activity was building at their arrival, whether in fear or outrage it was not possible to tell.

'No, I'm sending nobody ashore in this.'

'Then?'

'We wait. I've yet to come across a port without it has its swarm of meddlesome officials. We'll find out from them how the land lies.'

Bowden had his glass up. 'My, but they're in a taking over something, and I rather think it's us, sir.'

Kydd borrowed it. Along the seafront he saw waving fists, odd triangular flags and crowds coming together.

They were safe for now and, without an anchor cast, if any hostile sail appeared it was the work of minutes to loose canvas and be under way again.

'Boat, sir,' Calloway called, pointing.

An odd-looking craft was heading their way. A wide-gutted galley of at least fifteen oars a side, it flew an enormous two-tailed crimson and gold pennant and proceeded to the beat of a heavy drum.

'Man the side,' Kydd ordered.

They welcomed a visitor in embroidered robe and magnificent turban.

'His Excellency Kaptan Pasha,' an interpreter announced, his hands respectfully prayerful, his accent colourful. 'He in charge the harbour and ship of Constantinople.'

The pasha gave a sketchy Oriental bow, hand on heart,

which Kydd tried to return, then without change of expression gave out with a barrage of Turkish.

'He say, what are your business in the port, sirs?'

'Tell him we come to attend on our ambassador.'

It was relayed but produced only a contemptuous snort and another declamation.

'Kaptan Pasha is not please, you at imperial anchorage. You move to Seraglio Point, is better. There you wait your ambassador *bey.*'

'Ask him . . . ask him if there is trouble on the land, the people stirred up against us.'

This evoked a sharp look and a snapped retort.

'He say, why you ask? English are ally with Turkey, nothing to worry.'

'We are seeing the people on the shore. They're disturbed, shouting.'

'Their business, nothing you worry. He say I will take you to Seraglio Point, you go now.'

Despite his anxieties Kydd was enchanted by the prospect as they slowly sailed the mile or so to the point, past the white beauty of Hagia Sophia and the splendour of the Topkapi Palace. The anchorage was just around the promontory, well situated at the entrance to the fabulous Golden Horn, the trading and shipping heart of an empire.

And, sharing their holding ground, were three Turkish ships-of-the-line.

'Anchor, Cap'ten, they leave you alone.'

Kydd soon saw they were going to be no threat: their topmasts were struck and, with no flags flying, they were in no fit condition for sea.

'Can you inform our ambassador we're here?' he asked, as the man lowered himself into a boat.

'He see,' he answered, and pointed up to where *L'Aurore*'s ensign floated free.

In a short time a crowded boat put out from the opposite shore, a large Union flag in its bows.

Kydd went forward to greet the man who stepped aboard.

Spare, thin-faced and with a haughty air, he ignored Kydd's outstretched hand and gave a short bow. 'Charles Arbuthnot, His Britannic Majesty's ambassador and plenipotentiary to the Ottoman Empire.'

'Sir Thomas Kydd, captain of His Majesty's Frigate *L'Aurore*.'

'You took your time, Captain,' the man said acidly. 'Is not your commander aware of the grave developments that have taken place here?'

His eyes strayed seaward. 'And where are the others? I was particularly firm in my communications that a force of size be dispatched. Pray where is this fleet, sir?'

'I am in advance of it, sir,' Kydd said flatly. He sincerely hoped this would be the case but as its instructions from Collingwood were still in his cabin this might be problematical.

Arbuthnot gave him a withering look. 'You're not to know of it but His Majesty's interests in the Sublime Porte have been greatly injured. Only a gesture of undoubted martial strength will go towards restoring our position there.'

'Sir, this is not a matter within my ability to command. You may, however, suggest any course that you desire, and if it is in my power to effect it, I will do so.'

There was a pause. The ambassador seemed to make up his mind. 'Captain, my position in Constantinople is now untenable and, further, I go daily under fear of my life. My

148

decision therefore is that I seek refuge in your ship. That will be possible, I trust?'

'Certainly, sir.' It would mean yielding up his own bed-place and cabin but a diplomat had every right to demand this of a king's ship.

'Together with my immediate staff, if you please, twelve in all.'

This was stretching things but he was not going to abandon fellow countrymen to be condemned ashore to some appalling eastern fate.

Fortunately the same north-westerly that had brought them would be fair for a rapid departure.

'Very well, Your Excellency. I should like to point out that the winds are not always favourable in these parts and—'

'What is that to me, sir?'

'If the evacuation is to get away safely, then—'

'What? You have a wrong impression, sir. I am not evacuating, Captain, I am merely taking a prudent sanctuary in your vessel. Now, if you would be so good as to provide a species of cabin with a modicum of space I shall set up my office.'

It soon became clear to Kydd what Arbuthnot was doing. From his assumed safety afloat he was going to bombard the sultan and his government with strong-worded notes, carrying on his diplomatic war with the French from Kydd's own cabin. Whatever the tumult and confusion in the city and from whatever cause, the man was taking *L'Aurore* as a little piece of England from which he could shake his fist at his enemies.

His was not to complain, but didn't the ambassador realise how illusory was his refuge?

They were anchored within a stone's throw of three 74s,

149

which, however stood down, could still be manned and their guns turned on *L'Aurore* to reduce her to splintered wreckage in minutes. And, with the waters here restricted to a bare mile wide, their escape route to the open sea could be sealed off by just a few elements of the Turkish Navy.

And what if his angry words inflamed the population? So close to the shore, they would be overwhelmed by scores of boats well before they could weigh and set sail.

'I beg you to reconsider, sir,' Kydd tried. 'We are at hazard here. If the Turks wish to offer us violence, there's little we can do. And I'm persuaded that even if we sail now, if they are minded to, there are forts in the Dardanelles that could sink us within a very short time. It would be best should we leave while we can, reach safety and then—'

'No. Kindly do as I desire, sir, and remain here.'

In the evening, dining alone with Arbuthnot, Kydd pressed for details of what was going on in the city.

'That is not your concern as a frigate captain, sir. Yet I'll tell you that I'm deeply angry and mortified that the rascally Sultan Selim sees fit to continue to entertain the scheming French, who have intrigued to reach positions of power and influence with him. It is nothing less than scandalous. They have perjured themselves to spread vile rumours about our intentions and to denigrate our military effectiveness and I'm grieved to note they have been all too successful.'

Did he mean he had been outclassed in intrigue by the wily French?

'There's only one way to redress this deplorable state of affairs. A display of military might before their very gates as will bring them to their senses. With Bonaparte's troops flaunting themselves as near as Dalmatia, nothing else will persuade the perfidious Selim to offer us the respect that is our due.'

'Sir,' Kydd said, with all the conviction he could muster, 'I was fortunate in having surprise on my side when I came here. Should the Turks wish to contest the passage of a fleet I've no doubt they could do so in the confines of the waters I've seen leading here. Do you not feel that an unfortunate reverse in our attempt to force the Dardanelles would have the opposite effect to what you'd wish?'

'I'm surprised at your tone, Captain. The very appearance of Nelson's fleet alone will strike awe and terror in the breasts of these benighted heathen. This is why – and I tell you in the strictest confidence – I have gone over the head of your commander-in-chief to Whitehall and the prime minister, demanding that a showing off Constantinople be made. I expect a positive reply daily, sir.'

This madman, if he got his way, would condemn Collingwood's fleet to a desperate fight point-blank against forts and the Turkish Navy, almost certainly to end in wreck and retreat, and to what clear purpose? England's precious blockading fleet decimated and humiliated – it didn't bear thinking about.

Surely even a land-bound government like Grenville's would see the risks and futility of it, find some other way of offsetting the French influence – and replace this haughty fool.

At eleven the next morning everything changed. Suddenly bursting into view rounding the point a massive two-decker ship-of-the-line appeared – *Canopus*, the 80-gun flagship of Rear Admiral Louis's squadron.

The rest of the squadron would no doubt be waiting hove to in the open water before the peninsula. Arbuthnot had his military might.

Kydd lost no time in taking boat to make his report and hand over Collingwood's instructions.

He'd last seen this ship as the French *Franklin* at the Nile, fighting bravely in the darkness of that infernal night – and his own ship, *Tenacious*, had been her chief antagonist.

But this was going to be a less glorious occasion unless he could persuade the admiral to deny the ambassador his ambition.

'Sir Thomas, is it, then?' Louis had a high-pitched wheeze that made him hard to follow.

'Sir,' Kydd acknowledged. Louis's baronetcy had been for his role in the San Domingo fleet action in the West Indies under Duckworth.

Handing him the instructions, Kydd waited politely. Louis put the packet aside. 'I'll take 'em up later. Do tell me what you've been about, will you, old chap?'

'New-joined to Admiral Collingwood's blockade fleet, sir. He received disturbing news from the ambassador here concerning unrest and threats to British interests. He desired me to lose no time to find yourself, sir, and give you these instructions.'

'And so you have. But don't tell me – unable to find me you took it upon yourself to come here to see what assistance you could be to the ambassador.'

'This is why I'm here, yes, sir.'

'Quite right. Then what did you find, pray?'

Kydd told briefly of the disturbances seen ashore, Arbuthnot's arrival and installation in *L'Aurore*. Delicately he explained his reservations about the ambassador's desire to raise the stakes by threatening undisclosed action with an overwhelming naval force.

'And so your appearance here with your squadron is very welcome to him,' he concluded.

'Not so, not so.' Louis coughed, banging his chest. 'I'm alone, the flagship only. My squadron lies at anchor at the mouth of the Dardanelles.'

He went on, 'A single ship by way of being no provocation was my thinking. He's to be disappointed, it seems. Does he wish to be taken off?'

'Sir, I believe he would wish to discuss such with you,' Kydd said cautiously.

'I'd better take on board what's being said here before I see him.' He picked up the instructions. 'Excuse me,' he muttered.

'Ah. In so many words I'm to make reconnaissance of these waters and afford what assistance I can to his excellency. I don't consider forcing the Dardanelles with a squadron a reconnaissance, do you?'

Arbuthnot was bitter and scathing at the admiral's attitude and insisted on a grand council in *Canopus* for the following morning.

'Let me put it to you as plainly as I can,' he said. 'I'm here on the spot. You're not. I know the Turk. You do not. And what I'm saying is that they're a backward, decayed people who understand only the language of strong and weak. At the moment, since the successes of the Corsican in Europe, they do admire him and listen to his siren words.

'Yet the greatness of Nelson is known even here, to which we certainly owe the treaty of amity the French are seeking to overthrow. Gentlemen, what I'm asking only is that the hero's own navy does flourish itself in all its glory before the walls of Constantinople. The artful Selim will instantly see it in his best interest to eject the French and receive us as brothers.'

Louis heard him out, then put his hands flat on the table and wheezed, 'No. No! I cannot counsel nor lend my name or ships to such a foolhardy gesture. Sir, I'm instructed to aid you in so far as it lies in my power – and subverting a reconnaissance into an armed provocation is not—'

A sudden knocking on the door interrupted him. A breathless lieutenant flew in and blurted, 'Sir, my apologies – you're desired on deck this minute, if you please.'

They were met with a chilling sight: smoke rising ominously from several places inland and figures running along the seafront pursued by an ugly crowd. Several stumbled and were hacked down by those following. Cries of terror and rage came floating out.

'I rather think events have overtaken us,' Louis said.

More emerged from the streets and between buildings; it was obvious that they were making for the jetties on the waterfront. Several boats were lying off and came in, firing upwards to deter pursuers. The frantic victims tumbled in. A few stragglers were too late and were mercilessly dispatched on the quayside or flung themselves into the water.

'The mob's turned against us, then.'

'So it would seem,' said Arbuthnot, without emotion.

There was no possibility of intervention as any show of force would trigger an incident that could place the situation beyond retrieving.

The boats were all headed towards the looming bulk of *Canopus*, her ensign proclaiming her a haven of peace and sanity in a world turned mad.

'Your directions, sir?' Louis asked, his features set.

'One moment. Lend me that,' Arbuthnot said to a lieutenant, and took his telescope. 'As I thought – that's Italinski.'

'Sir?'

'They're not ours. They're Russians, although what the devil set the Turks off, Heaven only knows.' He handed back the glass and folded his arms, waiting for the first boats.

The Russian ambassador, a big man, was helped over the bulwark, puffing like a whale. He saw Arbuthnot and lumbered across to him.

'T'ank the God you here,' he bellowed, then remembered a bow. 'They mad, like beast.'

'My dear Italinski, you have my sincere sympathy.' He glanced at the wild-eyed Russians scrambling over the side. 'In course you shall have sanctuary in any ship of His Britannic Majesty's Navy.'

'Ze bigger ze better, Charles. Zis vill do for now.' His bushy black eyebrows worked with emotion.

'Might I enquire just what stirred the populace to riot and slaughter against your people all of a sudden?' Arbuthnot asked.

'Don' they always?'

'Just this particular time, if you would humour me, Andrei.'

'Not'ing!'

'Nothing?'

'Well, some fool move by St Petersburg. They order troop into Moldavia, 'at's all.'

'Ah. Now I understand. You Russians, it seems, have taken Ottoman possessions in the Balkans by force, expecting no reaction from Constantinople to a rather pointed expansion of the Tsar's empire at their expense. It seems they've been rather forgetful in omitting to inform you of their intentions.'

Italinski glowered, then pointedly turned to bark orders at some uniformed flunkeys.

'My cabin?' Louis suggested smoothly, to Arbuthnot, leaving the Russians to sort themselves out.

155

Kydd hesitated, then went with them.

'Now, sir, we have a problem,' Louis said immediately. 'If we're seen to be sheltering these Russians it will only inflame the mob and I would not reject the possibility that it becomes a focus for their anger, which will then be directed at us.'

'Do you think I have not thought of this?' Arbuthnot said scornfully. 'The solution is obvious.'

'Sir?'

'You will set sail immediately with the Russians on board.'

'A wise course,' Louis said in relief. 'Captain Kydd, are you ready to sail?'

'The frigate is not involved. It will not sail.'

'Not . . . sail? It's your decision, Ambassador, but in all frankness I cannot—'

'In your profession you're not expected to understand the finer points of diplomacy, Admiral. This is a capital opportunity to remonstrate with the Sublime Porte in a strongly worded note to the effect that this unrest only points to an urgent need for a realignment of interests and so forth.'

He drew himself up. 'And it may have slipped your mind that there are British residents, merchants, commercial agents, those who so loyally assist in the Black Sea trade, all gazing upon us in trust that we will not desert them. I will not, sir!'

Kydd picked up a certain shrillness in the tone. If this man was misreading the signs, they were all in the most deadly peril.

Canopus sailed under cover of dark, and in the morning *L'Aurore* lay alone to her moorings.

A pale sun revealed sullen knots of people ashore, the flicker of a fire here and there indicating their intent to stay.

Set against the backdrop of the Oriental splendour of grand palaces and domes, the air of menace was unnerving.

Arbuthnot kept to his cabin until the afternoon, when he appeared with an elaborately sealed document. 'I desire this be landed at the Topkapi Steps and signed for by the grand vizier.'

'You're asking I risk a boat's crew to—'

'They will not be troubled by the palace functionaries there, Captain. Please do as I request,' he snapped.

An eerie unreality hung about the anchorage but at least the mob was beginning to break up and disperse, either through boredom or a cooling.

Night came. Kydd was taking no chances and posted double lookouts and hung lanthorns in the rigging.

The hours passed.

A little before midnight there was a faint cry in the darkness. Alerted, the watch-on-deck stood to and saw a boat come into the pool of light from the lanthorns. A man stood up in the thwarts and asked in a quavering voice if the ambassador was still aboard.

'Wake Mr Arbuthnot,' Kydd said, when he was told. 'There's something afoot.'

They reached the deck together. 'One to come aboard, Mr Curzon.'

A bent figure painfully made his way up the side.

'Why, it's Mr Dunn,' Arbuthnot said, in astonishment. 'This is very irregular! What brings you here?'

'Oh, Your Excellency, sir, dire news.'

'Go on.'

'My man – whom I trust with my life – comes to me with dreadful tidings.' The merchant's hands writhed together as he tried to find the words.

'He knows of a dreadful plot, Excellency, one that chills my blood, so it does!'

'Please be more specific if you will, Mr Dunn.'

'Sultan Selim plans to take all Englishmen hostage at once against what he's been told by the Frenchmen is a return of Nelson's fleet to take revenge upon their dishonouring.'

'What are you talking about, "dishonouring"?'

The whites of the man's eyes stood out in the half-light.

'I beg your excellency's pardon, but your retiring to this ship was cried up by the French as fear and − and faintness, this being what they say, not me.'

'And?'

'They say your big ship ran away from just a few Turkish ruffians and—'

'Enough! This is insupportable. That craven Sébastiani and his devilish plots touch on my honour. I will not allow that by any wight.'

Dunn continued, 'Excellency, my people are fearful of their fate. If the sultan seizes them they may well suffer the same as the Wallachian *hospodar*. Hostage, and put to torture to bring a quick yielding by others.'

Arbuthnot snorted with contempt and shot an angry glance at Kydd. 'You see, Captain? If you'd shown more backbone when . . .' He stopped, breathing hard. 'I'm feeling ill. I'm going to my cabin.'

Kydd was left standing with an astonished Dunn.

'What shall we do?' he stammered. 'Your common Turk is not nice in his manners when roused.'

'Sir, to be truthful I cannot think what to advise.'

The boat disappeared into the night, leaving Kydd to try to make sense of what was happening.

One thing was certain: it were better that *L'Aurore* prepared herself for any eventuality.

She went to single anchor, and sail was held to a spun-yarn for a rapid move to sea. Guns were awkwardly loaded inboard out of sight but not run out – every second one with canister. Lieutenant Clinton posted his marines in two watches the length of the vessel, and arms chests were brought up for use in repelling boarders.

Apart from this, there was little else he could do, given that the dangers they faced were all but unknown.

The first of the terrified refugees began arriving within an hour or two of Dunn's departure. They babbled of wild rumours, troops marching in the streets, looting of warehouses and desperate panic as fear spread.

Before daybreak it had turned to a flood – merchants, clerks, families, hapless servants, all turning to the only safety they could see: *L'Aurore*.

It was hopeless. The gun-deck was crowded with sobbing, desperate humanity; there could be no working the guns, no defences. More climbed up until every clear space was crammed with people – there had to be an end to it.

As dawn turned to morning the tide of incomers had ebbed but Kydd was left with few options.

'Wake the ambassador and tell him we've a decision to make.'

The midshipman quickly returned with a message that Arbuthnot was too ill to consider discussions. He refused the offer of a naval surgeon to attend on him.

Kydd knew very well what that meant, but it was a release: he could make the decisions alone.

If even half of what was being rumoured was true they were in mortal danger. He had no right to risk his ship and

159

all aboard simply to maintain the fiction of a British deterrent. If it meant that watchers ashore would take it as a fleeing, so be it.

'Hands to unmoor ship! Get us under way, Mr Kendall.'

Bowden pointed at the moored ships-of-the-line. 'Sir . . .'

There were crew running down the decks and disappearing below and other activity at the capstans. Manning the guns and warping around? It could be quite innocent – or the first step in a coup.

L'Aurore's anchor cable was coming in slowly, impeded by the crowded decks. 'Mr Curzon, get those lubbers flatting in at the jib. I mean to cut the cable and cast to starboard.'

It was the last degradation but *L'Aurore* had to make the open sea before the cataclysm closed in. The carpenter took his broad-axe forward and, with several blows, parted the anchor cable, which plashed with a finality into the Bosporus.

'Let loose!'

With a fair wind *L'Aurore* stood away for the Dardanelles and freedom.

Chapter 6

'You wanted to see me, m' lord.'

Jago stood warily before the Earl of Farndon in the library, his expression blank.

'I did. We're due to have a little talk together, I believe . . .'

'If'n it pleases you, m' lord.'

In the past Renzi had been deeply involved with the Duc d'Auvergne and his secret network of spies, and himself had gone out on clandestine exploits; he'd immediately recognised in Jago a touch of the night.

'. . . about your future here with me.'

There was no response, the dark eyes watchful.

'I know that my father was not as . . . how shall I put it? Not altogether open in his affairs. In fact there would be many who would say there were secrets he would rather he kept to himself, confidences that, if revealed, would prove . . . embarrassing.'

He played with his pen, letting the words hang.

'It is without doubt that he would need a well-trusted . . . assistant in this, one who would be certain to be discreet, effective and reliable. Mr Jago, I believe you must have served him satisfactorily to have stayed in your post for so long, don't you feel?'

'M' lord.' He was going to give nothing away.

'And I like that. You've been loyal and discreet – I've heard sordid tales of servants blackmailing their masters in a like position.'

There was no change in the man's features, so Renzi went on, 'I think we understand each other, Jago. Should your loyalty continue with me, then I see your future will be bright at Eskdale Hall.'

'Thank you, m' lord.'

There was a slight flicker of expression but otherwise no display of emotion. It showed control and Renzi knew he had not misjudged the man.

'Now, I would have you know that I'm not always to reside at Eskdale. There will be times I desire to go abroad. Are you of a mind to accompany me? There is no requirement on you, but if you should go, it will be in the capacity of *chargé d'affaires*, as it were, to take control of my entourage and answerable only to me. Naturally your recompense will be proportionate. How do you say?'

'I'll go, if your lordship needs me. I've accompanied the last earl on more'n a few of his own trips.'

'Splendid! Well, as it happens, I've a journey to the Levant in mind for very soon. As head of staff, you will have your ideas on who should be with us. Would you give it some thought and let me know?'

The tea things were spread in a pleasing display of delicate porcelain in the orangery, Cecilia pouring daintily for Renzi and the dowager.

'Nicholas, your wife tells me you are to desert her for foreign parts. Can this be true?'

'Mama, it distresses me to say so but it seems I have little alternative.'

'Oh. I'm interested in what it is that takes a man from a loving wife so soon after their wedding.'

'It will be only for a short while. I've just received urgent word that a tumulus reputed to be that of King Midas himself has been found in Gordion, which is in Asia Minor. A princely find for scholarship but all for nothing if we cannot establish an interest before the French.'

'And it has to be you, Nicholas?' she said sorrowfully, laying her hand on his.

'That I am familiar with the region and am no stranger to travel is known at the Royal Society, who have pressed me most ardently.'

'Well, you will be careful, won't you, dear? You have responsibilities now, remember.'

'Yes, Mama.'

Cecilia leaned across and kissed him lightly. 'You will take care, darling – for us both?'

Chapter 7

The large, square, unsprung coach lurched and rattled as it approached the Ottoman capital. It was a hired carriage of the best that could be mustered for an English lord but was sadly lacking the refinements to be expected at Eskdale and smelt dank, of old leather and ancient grime.

Behind, a covered wagon followed with the impedimenta of the expedition, then the bulk of the entourage clutching the side of a large cart of exotic appearance, and a few on horseback. In front trotted their hired escort, a troop of Turkish cavalry. It had been pressed on them by the Pasha of Murath, horrified that an English noble crossing his territory was in danger of being robbed with consequences to himself if the Porte got to hear of it.

Renzi rode in stately isolation but for Ackworth, his secretary. He had chosen the man himself: a petty, shrewish and self-important individual, he would be oblivious to the implications of what was going on around him and have no curiosity about it either. Ideal for what he was about to do.

Jago had understood what was wanted in the other staff.

It was the minimum required: the quiet Golding was his valet, assisted by Miller, a strong young man acting as general servant and footman; his cook was Henri, a second-generation Lincolnshire man with absurd claims to French ancestry.

As was the custom, local hirelings were taken on for domestics; Lord Farndon, of course, was not to be troubled in this matter. Jago, with his talent for communication and the smoothing of cultural difficulties, ably took charge.

It had worked well and a camaraderie of Englishmen together in foreign parts had grown.

Renzi had his support retinue. The rest was up to him.

At Bayrampaşa, the city walls came into view. The fabulous and mythical Constantinople lay ahead. They stopped at a last *han*, a roadside hostelry.

It was time to set the mission in motion. To achieve a foothold in the city, Renzi knew he had to make a presence in the shortest possible time. A galloper from the Turkish troop was sent bearing a courteous note to inform Arbuthnot, the ambassador, that Constantinople was about to host an English earl.

Renzi settled down to await events, changing from his plain but serviceable travelling clothes to the rich coat and breeches expected of a noble visitor.

When the messenger returned he was accompanied by a dignified Turk, with a lined face and neatly trimmed black beard. His jewelled turban proclaimed him someone of consequence.

Miller held his horse while he dismounted. After a low bow in the European fashion, the man stood before Renzi.

'My name is Doruk Zorlu, lord,' he said, in good English. 'And I am first secretary to his excellency.'

'Lord Farndon of Eskdale Hall. I'm here to—'

'Fahn'ton Pasha. I have to tell you that his excellency cannot entertain you. He is . . . is no longer in Constantinople.'

'Rest assured, I am in no hurry, Mr Zorlu.'

The man took a step closer and said, in a troubled voice, 'Pasha, it is not safe for you here. I must ask you to go back. There is feeling against the English, a rising up of the people against them.'

'I will take that risk. Thank you for telling me.'

'No! You must not stay!'

Renzi felt a prick of unease. 'Pray why not?'

'Pasha, the ambassador and all the English have this day left Constantinople in a ship. They fear that they'll be taken hostage by the sultan for security against an attack by the British.'

'What? This is madness! We are allies, friends of the sultan.'

'It is a rumour only, but the people are listening to anything. You must go.'

Renzi froze. This meant that in the war of influence the French had all but succeeded. With a clear field and the sultan's ear it would be only a matter of time and they would complete Bonaparte's plan.

Was there anything he could do to stop it happening? Was it too late?

His duty, however, was plain. In view of the colossal stakes, his safety was of secondary importance; he had to make the attempt.

'Oh dear. This is dreadful news,' he said sorrowfully. 'Dreadful. And I was so looking forward to my travels in Asia Minor. There is a service I'd greatly appreciate, Mr Zorlu. I'm so very fatigued after my journey and must rest. Have you knowledge of an inn of repute where I might stay in safety?'

Zorlu looked at him steadily. 'You plan to remain in Constantinople then, Fahn'ton Pasha.'

'For a short while. Until this little unpleasantness is over.'

'Very well. Then there is a suggestion I have that I'm sure would be what the ambassador would wish. Pasha, there is a guest suite within the embassy in Pera. You and your retinue shall be accommodated there.'

'That is most kind in you, Mr Zorlu. I accept with thanks.'

Renzi eased down in the vast marble bath with weariness. A hesitant Golding waited with towels but the burly attendants, stripped to the waist, were having none of it. He was helped to a nearby slab and the pair set about pummelling and slapping until his aches had dissolved in a flood of pleasure.

It took an effort of will to resist the temptation to let anxieties and concerns recede and resign himself to rest, but he couldn't. Not with matters reaching a climax as they were.

He dressed and asked Zorlu to join him in the guest-suite reception room.

Pleasantries were exchanged, then Zorlu asked, 'Pasha, your unworthy servant begs forgiveness for his impertinence in asking your reasons for visiting us.'

He lowered his head politely and Renzi could see no hint of the import of his question in his eyes. But he had made up his mind to trust no one.

'I flatter myself that I am a scholar of some merit and, having heard of the discoveries at Gordion, I have a desire to see them at the first hand.'

'I understand, lord. If there is any office I may provide it would be my honour to serve you.'

Was that an edge of deeper understanding, an intimation of complicity?

Renzi was not sure but his mission was not to be risked in a misplaced trust. Yet the man was still loyal to his English employers, evidenced by his remaining in post where many would have fled. His account of the situation might well be worth hearing.

Renzi motioned him to a chair.

The French, it seemed, had for many years desired influence at the court of the Ottoman sultan, Selim III, and to this end had lavished gifts and attention on him. It had all counted for nothing: in 1798 Bonaparte had invaded Ottoman Egypt, bent on conquest and empire, destroying years of intrigue. Offended, the Sublime Porte had appealed to the British and the result had been a treaty of friendship and alliance that still existed – just.

At the peace of Amiens in 1802 Bonaparte had industriously set about restoring relations. This time it was not merely presents but military advisers, training battalions, even cannon. The sultan had formed a new branch of his army, trained in the latest methods by the French, and was looking to build on it a new and reformed military. He therefore had every interest in cultivating a close relationship and was known to admire Napoleon the Conqueror.

The most formidable of these was the energetic and capable French ambassador. A serving general and favourite of Bonaparte, Horace Sébastiani was young, intelligent, wily and ruthless in his furthering of French influence. He had captured the attention of Selim and was feared and admired by those in his court. His thrust and resolution in acting for what he desired made him a deadly opponent.

Renzi nodded. This was valuable to know, even if it showed

just what titanic obstacles he himself faced. However there must be an entry point into the situation – the French were not yet in control.

The central figure in the whole drama had to be Selim III himself.

From their conquest of the old Byzantine Empire in 1453 onwards, the Ottoman sultans had reigned supreme and unchallenged. And with absolute power, in a manner that had not changed in centuries.

The sultan ruled from his palace through the Divan, a parliament of advisers, headed by the grand vizier. His religious advisers were the Ulema, a body of scholars; the military were dominated by the Janissaries, an elite corps of household troops and bodyguards whose origins were lost in time but whose power and jealously guarded privileges had steadily increased.

The outside world barely touched the existence of the sultan for he remained securely within the magnificence of the great Topkapi Palace where all the instruments of rule were concentrated, with the imperial domestics – from vast kitchens to the mysteries of the seraglio.

And within the grand edifice seethed plots and counter-plots, treachery and guile beyond anything seen in Europe since medieval times. Yet if Renzi was going to counter the French success he had to penetrate to the very heart of it all.

'Mr Zorlu.'

'Zorlu Bey,' the man said, with a short bow.

'Zorlu Bey. This has been a most gratifying discussion. Your powers of summary do you credit and—'

They were interrupted by a footman, who whispered briefly to Zorlu. There was a tone of unease in his voice as he told

Renzi, 'A gentleman of the palace, Mustafa Tayyar Efendi, has arrived and craves audience with you. Will you see him?'

'What do you counsel?'

'I know him well. The man is of the Reis-ül Kuttab, which you will know as the foreign ministry under the grand vizier. Undoubtedly he comes to see with his own eyes an Englishman who dares to remain in Constantinople at this time. I cannot advise other than not to say anything you do not want to be made instantly known throughout the palace.'

He was an imposing figure, with a ridiculously tall white hat, gold-embroidered robe, ceremonial staff and upturned slippers twinkling with jewels.

His voice was deep and commanding, speaking directly to Renzi.

'He introduces himself, lord.'

'Pray tell him my name and style.'

It was received with an elegant Oriental bow and an immediate reply.

'He asks in the name of Sultan Selim your business in Constantinople,' Zorlu smoothly relayed.

'I rest for a space before I venture to Gordion to admire the new-found tumulus of Midas the king.'

'He confesses he has not heard of this and wonders how such can engage the attention of a noble lord in far England.'

'Do explain that I am a species of scholar sent by the Royal Society to uncover new knowledge of man and his works. I would be much gratified if while I'm here he should effect an introduction of me to any learned philosopher or antiquarian who might assist in this important work.'

'He asks if you are aware that the English have fled Turkey since the threat of their fleet on our shores has been repulsed.'

'I am sorry to hear of it. This is a tiresome distraction but

I shall remain here until this distasteful affair passes, as it most assuredly will, before I venture further into the country.'

'He wishes you well of your quest and offers his assistance if required.

'By this, Fahn'ton Pasha, we can know that Mustafa Tayyar Efendi is satisfied with your explanation.'

If the palace knew of his presence then it must be assumed that the French, namely Sébastiani, would, too.

Their response would depend on what they perceived in him. As sons of the revolution, their estimate of him as a nobleman would hopefully be as a despised and leeching fop, no threat to anyone. If not, then his small reputation as a dilettante scholar might pass muster as reason for his presence. If neither . . .

Renzi felt the creeping insidiousness of personal danger steal into his bowels.

The game had started: there was no going back now.

The next move must be to make himself known to the sultan. That would not only deter the French from a crude 'disappearance' but he would have a foot in the door, a first step in redressing the insanely unfair odds against him.

But how?

Nothing suggested itself immediately but a day later Zorlu came to him with an ornate missive and a smile. 'Lord, you have been invited to meet the sultan at the Gate of Felicity in the Palace of Topkapi.'

'What does this mean, do you think?' Renzi asked, thunderstruck at the sudden turn of events. Why would Sultan Selim take notice of him at this early point – and grant him a hearing?

Zorlu was not perturbed. 'It is politeness only. As a personage of rank you have a right to be among those others who tender their respects to His Imperial Majesty at this time. You should go – your absence would be remarked, Fahn'ton Pasha.'

'Others?'

'You will be one of scores of dignitaries, only some of whom will be noticed. This is the occasion when Sultan Selim makes audience with foreigners. Nothing is expected of outlanders other than they show due respect to the person of the sultan.'

It was therefore nothing personal: he would be one among many.

'There is one matter, Fahn'ton Pasha, that requires you decide first.'

'Which is?'

'It is customary in Constantinople for all those at an eminence, whether in commerce, diplomacy or at a rank in society, to appoint a dragoman. This gentleman is more than a reliable translator, he is an adviser on matters cultural and procedural for his patron. Yet it is my duty to you to point out that by his position he will necessarily know your business confidences and movements and speak what he will to the other. Your trust in him therefore must be absolute.'

This was advice that could not be ignored. Setting aside all other concerns he was effectively at the mercy of whatever the dragoman said. And if ever he was miraculously able to speak freely to the sultan then it would always be through this man. Who would have the potential to spy, blackmail or betray him.

'You are quite right, of course, Zorlu Bey. Is it possible that you'd perform this service for myself at all?'

'Pasha, I am desolated to inform you that I cannot see how I can accept. As principal aide to his excellency, the continued business of the embassy in his absence must be my main concern. I do hope you will understand.'

And the paltry affairs of a passing lord were not of importance.

Decisions were being rushed on him and he didn't like it – but there was no alternative.

'This places me in a difficult situation, Zorlu Bey. It forces me to decide whether or not to—'

'Whether . . . to tell me why you are really here.'

He paused. The man was both intelligent and penetrating – too much so?

'Why should I trust you, Zorlu?'

'Because my father would honour you for it.'

'Your father?'

'Unhappily now deceased, lord. He admired the nobility above all things and would greatly wish I could be judged worthy of the confidences of an earl.'

'Go on.'

'He was a merchant factor from Oldham in Lancashire, who, sent as agent here, fell in love with a Persian slave-girl. I have been three times to England to see his family and to London as well. It may be truly said that I . . . love your country.'

It was an admission that could have him decapitated or worse – but it explained his excellent English, his patience with a feckless noble and his continued loyalty to an ambassador who had fled his duty.

Renzi made up his mind that he would trust the man – quite literally – with his life.

Trying not to be overawed by the sheer scale of the palace, surrounded by walls miles long, Lord Farndon was ushered into a vast courtyard, shaded by trees and with pleasant paths leading through landscaped grasslands to groups of buildings.

'The first courtyard,' murmured Zorlu.

It was lined with soldiers in turbans of different kinds and flamboyant uniforms of exotic colours, each with an ornamented hewing knife thrust into a gold-threaded sash. Their eyes followed the visitors, arrogant and cruel.

'Janissaries. The most feared warriors in the land.'

Ahead lay a rectangular inner walled structure, from what Renzi could see of it, at least a quarter of a mile long. A gate with two pointed towers led inside.

'The main palace. And just on your right, Fahn'ton Pasha, over there . . .' He pointed to a modest square tower with a small fountain at its base. 'It is where the executioner washes his hands and sword after a decapitation.'

The Gate of Salutation led into the second courtyard, grassed and planted with trees, too, but with strutting peacocks and small deer. At a distance was a second gate, set out from colonnades and greatly ornamented with a broad canopy and dome. It was thronged with people.

'Fahn'ton Pasha. This is now the Bab-üs Saadet, the Gate of Felicity, where the sultan will see us. Beyond is the third courtyard, which is forbidden to all – even the grand vizier must seek permission to go further. It contains the sultan's private walks, the treasury and Grand Throne Room, with its audience chamber. Further still is the fourth courtyard and the harem, and as well the Privy Chamber with the sacred relics.'

At the Gate of Felicity were a number of courtiers as well as soldiers. Renzi instantly noted a tight grouping of foreigners, from their dress French. His mouth dried as he saw them break off their conversations but he affected not to notice them and turned to admire the buildings to the left. 'Which are they?' he asked Zorlu.

'That is the Imperial Council Hall where the Divan meets under the offices of the grand vizier, lord.'

He glanced at the French once more. They were still watching him but there was movement along the colonnaded passage and they turned to face the new arrivals, more Janissaries, who formed a large hollow square around the front of the gate canopy. Oddly none seemed armed.

Inside the square, courtiers began assembling in solemn conclave, the grand vizier tall and imperious with his staff of office. Under the canopy a thick green carpet was unrolled and a golden throne positioned on it.

'These are the viziers,' Zorlu said quietly. 'Come to make report after our audience. If it is good they leave with rich gifts. If not, the sultan will ask his eunuchs to strangle them. It concentrates their minds wonderfully.'

Almost without warning, there was a sudden scattering of courtiers and grandees and a figure appeared from the recesses of the inner courtyard. Bejewelled with gold and pearls beyond counting, he wore a crimson robe edged with ermine and a snow-white turban.

Looking to the right and left, his robes tended by page-boys, he moved into view, acknowledging with slight nods the deep obeisance on all sides.

This was Selim III, sultan and absolute ruler of the Ottoman Empire – and Renzi's only chance of checking French ambitions.

He assumed the throne, a slender, mild-faced but dark-bearded man of some sensitivity. He looked around – the grand vizier approached, genuflected and addressed him elaborately. On cue, the entire assembly made obeisance while a quavering chanting carried on and on.

Then all rose and the first foreign dignitary was brought forward by two viziers. A central European, in voluminous Oriental trousers and short, highly ornamented waistcoat, he bowed every few yards until he dropped to his knees before the sultan.

Renzi was too far away to take in all the details of the etiquette but he decided he would treat the sultan as he would his own sovereign.

Another was placed before Selim, a dark-featured central Asian.

As Renzi watched he became aware of two courtiers appearing at either side of him. Zorlu spoke sharply to them until they fell back slightly. They had been summoned.

With the utmost grace and courtliness Renzi stepped forward, gave a studied and elegant bow and raised his eyes to meet the sultan's.

He was regarded with mild interest but the entire court was still and watchful. He felt the flanking courtiers grasp his wrists firmly – did they think he would run away?

The sultan spoke in a pleasant baritone.

'His Majesty is pleased to see an Englishman once again, they having lately deserted his realm,' Zorlu translated. 'And one at some eminence. He desires to know what it is that has led you to Constantinople at this time.'

Renzi allowed a touch of wonder and gratification to show as he bowed an acknowledgement. 'Tell him that as an English lord I am sensible of the honour he is according me.'

It was relayed on and was rewarded with a civil nod.

'Say to him I am a scholar of mean repute, but when the discovery of the tumulus of King Midas was announced, our

Royal Society saw fit to dispatch me without delay to Gordion to make report.'

There was a flicker of interest. 'His Majesty was not aware of any learned gentleman visiting his domains. As an admirer of culture and erudition and a dabbler in composing and literature himself, he wonders how long your visit to Constantinople will be.'

'Having reached Turkey overland, I am a little fatigued and must rest but then intend to cross to Asia Minor and Gordion.'

A gracious inclination of the head.

'He prays that Allah will reward your scholarly diligence.'

The audience was at an end and, with every courtly elegance, Renzi retired.

'How was it?' he whispered to Zorlu, when they had regained the anonymity of the press of people.

'Tolerably well, lord. It is not impossible that you will be given a gift of worthy antiquarian volumes or other, but you have succeeded in the first imperative: he's noticed you and we may now say you exist.'

'Why did they hold my arms?'

'To prevent you seizing a concealed dagger and falling upon the person of the sultan.'

'And if—'

Their path was barred by three French dignitaries, each wearing a sword. The one in the centre swept down in an elegant leg.

'*Je suis désolé pour cette intrusion*, and I would consider it a privilege to know your name, Monsieur.'

'Oh, er, *je suis le comte de Farndon, d'Angleterre. Et vous?*' Renzi said hesitantly, realising he must already be known.

'I am Horace François Bastien Sébastiani de la Porta and I have the honour to be the ambassador of the French Empire to the Sublime Porte.' The reply came in exquisite tones. 'And these my secretary Florimond de Fay la Tour Maubourg and my aide Louis Gustave le Doulcet, at your service, milord.'

Renzi bowed to each, confusion and embarrassment on his features as he let it be seen that, as an Englishman, he wondered what was to be expected of him on confronting an enemy of his king.

Sébastiani said smoothly, 'Do you not think it iniquitous that we should feel boorish in the presence of another with whose country we have a difference? Are there so few civilised Europeans in Turkey that we must scorn each other's company?'

'Quite so, Monsieur l'Ambassadeur.'

'So you are a scholar, milord. Are you then known in learned circles, perhaps?'

This was the inquisition: if he showed himself as anything more than a bumbling amateur it was all over.

'My paper on ethnical responses to economic challenge was well received. Count Rumford himself sponsoring its presenting.' He smiled modestly. 'Once even I was in your Institut, guest of the formidable Pierre Laplace.' That he was at the time in Paris spiriting away an American submarine inventor need not be mentioned.

'How singular. He is a friend of mine and now a count of the French Empire, regrettably taking against the English since tricked by an agent of sorts in Paris.'

Renzi gave an embarrassed smile. 'There is no accounting for the wickedness of those who would promote war as a remedy for all ills.'

'Yes. Are you finding your visit to Turkey an enlightening experience? For myself the Orient is an eternally fascinating quarter of the world.'

'Why, to a certain degree. Although I have my personal suite, I find some of the practices to which I'm exposed disagreeable, and I'm dreading conditions to be found in Asia Minor. Not at all that to which I'm accustomed, you'll understand.'

If that didn't confirm him as a fop and aristocrat . . .

'I do so sympathise,' Sébastiani replied, with oily charm. 'We must keep in touch, have dinner together perhaps. So, milord, *à bientôt*.'

Two objectives met in as many days! The sultan knew of him, and now the French, he was sure, had him down as a harmless fool.

But he was a long way from what had to be achieved. Sébastiani was as cold and ruthless as he'd imagined, and if there was a breath of suspicion, the Frenchman would move promptly and efficiently.

Time was not on his side. He had to find a way to get to Selim. Speak to him, find honeyed words that could match those Sébastiani was pouring into his ears. His optimism receded at the near impossibility of getting access, let alone offering counter-arguments – and at the same time preserving his character as a dabbling bookworm.

But he had not long to wait before Zorlu took him aside. 'I congratulate you, Fahn'ton Pasha. You underestimate your powers, I believe. I have been approached by the palace on the matter of the sultan's invitation for you to be his guest.'

'His guest!'

'It is not unprecedented for a foreigner to be so honoured, lord. For those who interest the sultan . . . and for those he would keep in a velvet cage.'

The game had changed: it was getting deeper, but was this his chance?

Their quarters were discreetly inside the walls within the first courtyard, set back from the path they had taken before. They were commodious, richly decorated with intricate blue and white tiling, marble columns and Arabic texts girdling every room. Gold-leafed filigree adorned arched passageways and the rooms were spread with fabulous carpets; it was as something from Sinbad and *One Thousand and One Nights*.

'Does it meet with your approval, Jago?' Renzi asked, trying not to be impressed.

'It will do, m' lord,' the man answered stolidly, as he supervised the household transfer. It was diverting to see him handle the delicacies of delegating duties among the palace servants and his own staff. A young lad with some English was among those assigned from the palace, and harmony was preserved, Golding continuing as personal valet to his lordship and the cook, Henri, mollified with access to his own kitchen area.

There was adjacent accommodation for a dragoman. Renzi was hesitant to offer it again to Zorlu, but the man had already settled himself in before he could broach the subject.

It was now certain that in some way or another he would have the ear of the sultan. Whatever the occasion there would be a meeting. What would he say?

Myriad thoughts crowded in and he began sorting them into logical groupings. First there was—

'Pasha, I hesitate to interrupt your thinking but you should know you will be expected at a feast tonight. For the foreign envoys. It is the expected thing in an Ottoman court.'

'But I'm not an envoy, Zorlu.'

If he was being treated as such, it destroyed in one the trust his independence from state diplomacy brought.

'The feast is not at a high level, lord. To me it appears that Selim uses the occasion of entertaining the envoys as a convenient means to meet you more intimately. Whether from curiosity or . . . deeper reasons we cannot know.'

'The French will be there.'

'Not necessarily, lord. There are sixty-nine ambassadors now in Constantinople and the choice of invitations is his.'

'Then we must prepare. You will tell me how to behave, Zorlu Bey.'

Even though a lesser affair, the spectacle was grand. As the evening drew in, hundreds of courtiers, dignitaries and clerics, arrayed in sumptuous clothing, began lining the courtyard paths. By the gate the Janissaries formed up, the thunder of their giant drums and cymbals pierced with the sharp notes of reed instruments sounding barbaric and elemental.

In an anteroom the envoys met together. Exotically dressed notables from the inner Balkans mingled with those in Arabic headdress and central Asian gold-threaded tunics. It was Renzi, dressed as a European in silk stockings and breeches, who was the stranger in this part of the world.

He looked about for Sébastiani and the French but did not see them and conversed happily in broken Greek with a genial Turk from the Morea. Zorlu brought up an Egyptian Copt with a pressing desire to meet an Englishman, and Renzi smiled pleasantly in incomprehension at an earnest little man in a colourful waistcoat and swirling trousers.

But just what approach should he take with Selim? Through Zorlu, anything would be measured facts, opinions, not charged with mind-changing revelation of feelings or the subtlety of give and take.

Out of sight trumpets brayed insolently. There was a sudden hush: movement could be heard in the inner room, then several Janissaries in tall white hats appeared at the door and snapped orders.

Renzi went in with the others, and saw Sébastiani – close to Selim.

It was a disaster. He had been humiliated by the French, forced to answer the sultan's potent questions with weak generalisations. It was unlikely he would be asked again – or even meet him on another occasion. In the game of manoeuvre and guile with which he had been entrusted by his country, he had failed dismally.

At any point, and without warning, it could all end with the French finally wooing the sultan into their camp and bringing Bonaparte's plans to success.

Arriving back at his quarters in the darkest of moods, Renzi was quite taken aback by Jago's polite announcement that the sultan's gifts were ready for inspection.

They were princely. A kaftan, with richly embroidered patterning in yellow and red, threaded with gold. A stylish white turban, with delicate feathers spraying out from a single emerald. And a pair of spangled red velvet slippers with upturned tips.

A note was attached: Zorlu translated the elegant Persian flourishes as an invitation to spare himself the discomfort of European attire for the more sensible dress of the Turk.

Included, too, was a series of embossed volumes on the history of the Osmanli, the Ottoman house, by an Italian monk. As well, a learned treatise by a Turk on the felicities of Islam translated into unreadable hieratic Greek, and a slim volume, densely ornamented, that had Zorlu draw in his breath sharply.

'This is *teşbib*, lord,' he said reverently, stroking the little book. 'It is Divan poetry, the highest and most ancient form in the land. Even the Seljuk Turks revered its beauty.'

Renzi scanned it quickly. It meant nothing, the Persian script lovingly scribed in flowing swirls and finials, yet it was certainly a thing of exquisite execution.

'What is it about?'

'Fahn'ton Pasha, it tells of the transcendent allure of nature as an expression of the ethereal.

'I will read you some.'

He did, and the sophisticated and ingenious conceits in the flowering of culture moved Renzi.

'Pray tell me, what do these gifts mean?'

'By this we can say that you are placed in a position of respect. A kaftan is usually awarded to viziers and courtiers deemed worthy of reward, but the books – I have not heard of foreigners being so favoured. It can only be he believes that, as a scholar, you will appreciate them.'

'Ah. Is it expected that I will return the princely favour with a gift of my own?'

'That is generally the case, lord.'

A diplomatic envoy would have taken precautions to bring suitable presents – he had nothing.

'If I have no gifts, would it be taken amiss?'

'Formally speaking, it would be seen as disdain, an affront, a rejection of friendliness, but as you are not an envoy, perhaps . . .'

Renzi racked his brain feverishly. But all he had was paltry indeed after this.

Something . . .

A little later he handed Zorlu a small packet, tied with a single ribbon. 'See that this goes to the sultan with my sincere respects and so forth.'

It had been a sacrifice, but too much was at stake to consider personal feelings and it might even produce a result.

In the early-morning light Renzi struggled to wakefulness.

'M' lord, do pardon the liberty.'

'Yes, Jago?'

'A summons, m' lord. From the sultan himself – now.'

A peremptory demand for his presence at this hour? It could mean anything.

'No, not that, Golding. The Turkish costume, I think.'

It felt outlandish and theatrical when he drew it on but it was undeniably comfortable and easy on the body. Even the turban was little hindrance. Passing his totally blank-faced staff, he strode confidently outside, with an approving Zorlu, to the waiting Janissary guards.

But there seemed to be some difficulty. He waited patiently for Zorlu to deal with it.

'Lord, they have orders for your own self, no others. They will not let me go with you.'

There was no arguing with the captain of the guard and, not a little apprehensive, Renzi allowed himself to be escorted away.

They passed through the Gate of Salutation into the second courtyard, deserted so early in the morning, and continued towards the hallowed third courtyard and the sultan's private spaces. Then through the Gate of Felicity with the Grand Throne Room ahead, specifically placed to hide all sight of what lay within.

Renzi was led along a marble walkway to an impressively

colonnaded building, fronted by a grassy expanse with a fountain.

And there, waiting for him, was Sultan Selim. And he was quite alone.

The Janissaries retired.

Hesitantly, Renzi bowed politely in the Turkish way, hand on heart with an inclination of the head, and, at a loss at how he should continue, bade him good morning in English.

'Allah has presented us with a new day,' Selim said, in mellifluous French. 'Is it not beautiful?'

In his hands he held the gift, Renzi's own precious little book, its leather binding so frayed and dark.

'I confess to being consumed with curiosity at your favour, Fahn'ton Pasha. I'm accustomed to rich endowments, jewels, silks, marvels – but you have given me just this. I'm therefore persuaded it has a value far above its appearance and I beg you will tell me more of it.'

'Seigneur, this is my most beloved possession. It is the work of the English poet Wordsworth, and each night I seek solace in its beauty before I sleep. Sir, I could not think of anything more valuable to give in return to the one who presented me with the *teşbih*, which I will treasure for all my days.'

'You know what it contains?'

'Sire, from Zorlu Bey I have heard its first words in adoration of nature – and was so taken with its delicacy and charm that I was immediately put in mind of my Wordsworth.'

'Really? Then I desire you should read a piece to me.'

Renzi took the book and opened it as they started walking together.

> *'In that sweet mood when pleasant thoughts*
> *Bring sad thoughts to the mind*

To her fair works did Nature link
The human soul that through me ran;
And much it grieved my heart to think
What man has made of man.'

Selim remained silent as he reflected on the words, then turned to face Renzi.

'You are a deeper soul than your manners suggest, Fahn'ton Pasha. You are a thinking man, which is rare in a world of doers, and I warm to you.'

'I'm touched, Seigneur.'

They passed the fountain, its tumbling water just beginning to glitter in the strengthening sun.

'You conceive that I, the sultan, am the possessor of all things, am omnipotent in my domains. Do you not?' he asked, with the ghost of a smile on his sensitive features.

'It is hard to think otherwise, sir – except that not all things in this world are for a mortal's commanding.'

'Indeed. It is a paradox I have long contemplated – that I do indeed have all power concentrated in my hands. At a word I may have a man's head struck from his shoulders and none may question why. Yet by that very act I unleash forces in a way perfectly unforeseeable before the event.

'When I must act on a larger stage, where the world is convulsed in tides of conflict and greed, exactly the same paradox applies.'

Renzi remained silent.

'Take my country. My rule is absolute: it cannot be put aside. Yet a wrong word from me can cast it into a tumult of rivalry and strife. For instance, it is apparent to me and, no doubt, to yourself, Fahn'ton Pasha, that unless my people

186

modernise, advance in science and industry, we shall be left to moulder on the dung-heap of history.

'I have tried to introduce reforms. The Grand Mufti Haji Samatar approves without reservation. Mehmed Ataullah Efendi, leader of the Islamic Ulema, is strongly against. Each has his followers so if I support one it will be at the cost of the other's enmity. Yet this is not the question – that must be not what satisfies them but what is the right and proper course for Ottoman Turkey. My heart says I must press for reform, but should it be at the cost of – of disorder in the realm?'

The unspoken conclusion could only be that indecision, doing nothing, was the same as denying reform. It was an impossible quandary and he felt for the man.

'Seigneur, why do you tell me this?' he said carefully.

'Why? You cannot guess? Let us then move to the largest stage of all – a world that is locked in war while Turkey sleeps, dreaming of the centuries. This war is like no other for it is one of world empires pitted one against another, and every part of the civilised globe is drawn into their struggle whether they wish it or no. The same dilemma arises: when nations demand it, which is the right side to take for my country?'

Renzi fought down excitement. It was everything he could have prayed for: the ear of the sultan alone and the very subject raised that he wanted. But he clamped an icy control on himself: any rash or unguarded comment could destroy his position.

'There are no English left in Constantinople,' Selim continued quietly. 'All I have are the French, who tell me what they will. What of the other side?'

'Sir, I am but a subject of the Crown of England, not a diplomat, still less an accredited envoy. This is beyond my powers to tell.'

'That is well said, but you have confessed to the heart of

187

the matter – you are English and may be relied on to offer to me an English view of how any matter might be perceived by your countrymen. And at your eminence I dare to say by your king and fellow nobles.'

'If I can be of service in this way to you, Seigneur, it would be my honour to provide it. Is there any question at hand that presses?'

'Since you ask it, Fahn'ton Pasha, my people are at this time in fear and trembling that the English are offended and that the great fleet of Nelson Bey will be sent against us to destroy Constantinople. Is it in your conceiving that the affront is of such a gravity that this will happen?'

Renzi inwardly exulted. It was almost too easy – but he steadied himself, slowing in his walk as if giving it grave thought.

It was ludicrous, of course, to think that the Admiralty would lift the blockade of Cádiz simply to send the warships to Constantinople to teach it a lesson for some trivial slight. But an Oriental people would not see things in the same way, their conception of honour and insult being at quite another remove.

How to put this across without offending Selim?

'Seigneur, while I am not privy to the affairs of state at a high level, as you'll understand, it would seem to me that in Parliament it would be thought that the present troubles with France would make it inadvisable to send the fleet away. It is probable that they would frown on any slight but would let it pass and be forgotten in the press of concerns nearer home.'

'You would advise then, that this will not happen.'

'Sir, tell your people to sleep easier in their beds. Nelson's fleet will not trouble them.'

Chapter 8

HMS *L'Aurore* lay at anchor in the fleet rendezvous at Tenedos. The burden of fleeing people had made working the ship through the narrows of the Dardanelles the stuff of nightmares but eventually they had all been safely landed ashore. Except the English ambassador, who still lay ailing in Kydd's cabin.

On arrival Kydd had been quick to advise Admiral Louis of events. He had orders for the Aegean and eastern Mediterranean in general, but no instructions touching on the situation they found themselves in – that the British had been summarily excluded from Constantinople and its strategic vicinity.

'I'll send dispatches, of course, but all we can do is resume our cruise north,' Louis decided. 'You've two days to get your vessel in shape before we sail.'

But then the situation changed completely.

Coming into view around the headland a crowd of sail quickly resolved into a full-scale battle fleet led by a massive three-decker flying the pennant of a senior admiral. As it came to for mooring, sharp eyes noted that the flagship was *Royal George*, a 100-gun first rate in the same class as *Victory*. She was followed in line by another three-decker and a host of other battleships.

At the sound of the gun salutes, men tumbled up from below and stared at the apparition. Their lordships at the Admiralty did not send massive assets such as these on jaunts – it must be to some purpose. Officers and men speculated: an invasion of Naples to forestall a French move against Sicily was the favourite, followed by the dark suspicion that the Tsar of Russia had turned again and was now allied with Bonaparte, who had offered Malta to seal the compact.

Rear Admiral Louis was on his way to the great flagship without delay, and while everyone waited for what would come of the visit, there were even wilder conjectures: the Toulon blockade had been broken and a frantic search for the French fleet was under way, or conceivably the Greeks had risen in rebellion and this fleet was sent in support or to suppress it.

When the signal was hung out on *Royal George* – 'All captains' – Kydd wasted no time in making his way there.

He was met at the entry-port and taken down to the great cabin where, along with the other captains, he was introduced to the fleet commander, Vice Admiral of the White Sir John Duckworth, victor of Santo Domingo and second in command under Collingwood of the Mediterranean fleet. With him was Rear Admiral Sir Sidney Smith.

Kydd knew both men: Duckworth had been a commodore in the taking of Menorca when he had been a junior lieutenant on a signalling mission ashore and he knew him to be bluff, ambitious but cautious. He had missed Trafalgar but gone on to personal glory in the fleet action at San Domingo against the French that had led to their withdrawal from the Caribbean, and was known now to covet Collingwood's own command.

The other could not have been more different. Kydd had first met Smith in the dramatic defence of Acre, when he had been with a motley band of British seamen and Arab irregulars under his command that had stood against a siege by Napoleon Bonaparte face to face, to send him back to France in complete defeat, even to the extent of abandoning his army.

Smith was clever, ingenious and restless, but had a knack for irritating his superiors. Yet his courage was undoubted – the Swedish king had knighted him for his role in a titanic battle against the Russians that had cost them sixty-four ships and many thousands of lives. Once he had even been captured as a spy and taken to a Paris fortress but had then escaped in dramatic circumstances.

Kydd had been in his first command, the brig-sloop *Teazer*, when he had last seen Smith in Alexandria and where he had experienced his jealousy and glory-seeking at first-hand. He wondered what the man was doing in Duckworth's command, then recalled the rumour that he had been the lover of Princess Caroline of Brunswick, the consort of the Prince of Wales; there had been talk of a child. It was more than likely he had been packed off out of the country.

He knew one other of the dozen commanders seated around the vast polished table – the captain of *Ajax*, a legendary 74-gun ship-of-the-line. This was Nelson's Blackwood, the dour frigate captain whom Kydd had served under at Trafalgar and who had first brought the news of the French at Cádiz to Merton. He ventured a smile across the cabin and was rewarded with a slight easing of a frown

– but that was Blackwood's way, and Kydd determined to make a visit when he could, to talk over times still fresh for them both.

'Shall we come to order, gentlemen?' Duckworth's booming voice cut across the conversations. 'There's much to do, and time presses.'

He was more portly than Kydd remembered, a heavy face and a ready scowl. He wore his full-dress admiral's uniform, a mass of gold lace, stars and ribbons.

'As of this date, the detached squadron of Rear Admiral Louis is dissolved, its ships to come under my direct command. This is for a particular service for which I have my orders.'

He had their full attention and looked around the table.

'Gentlemen, we are to force the Dardanelles and lie before Constantinople.'

There were gasps of incredulity but Duckworth ignored them. 'The government has had word of French intrigue and treachery in the court of the Sultan of Turkey that threatens to gain for Bonaparte what he lost at the Nile and this cannot be tolerated. My task is to reverse that state of affairs in our favour, by force, if necessary.'

'Sir, when you say force, do you mean—'

'My orders are clear. We lie off the city with guns run out. Our demands are simple: the Turk is to eject the chief French troublemaker, one M'sieur Sébastiani, and his crew to us or alternatively yield up their entire navy, ships and stores to prevent their falling into the hands of the French. Failing that, we bombard the city of Constantinople and lay it in ruins.'

'Good God! This is madness!' Smith stuttered, his face reddening. 'The work of a lunatic! We can't just—'

'Admiral Smith!' rapped Duckworth, 'Kindly keep yourself

under control. These orders are not mine – they're not even those of the commander-in-chief. They originate in London at the highest – I say, the highest – level. Do you understand what I'm saying?'

Smith subsided, his fists bunched.

'I'm further instructed to take advice from the ambassador on this matter. His assessments regarding this grave confrontation are trusted by Whitehall and are, no doubt, the reason why we're here. Where is the fellow, by the way?'

'He lies indisposed in my ship, Sir John,' Kydd answered quickly.

'Well, see he gets the best treatments. He's much to be consulted.'

'There seems to be a conundrum at large,' Louis came in.

'What do you mean, sir?'

'Are not the Turks our allies? A penetration of the Dardanelles by force must be in breach of our treaty of friendship of 1798, surely.'

'We come in peace,' there was a muffled guffaw from Smith, 'so if they open fire, it is the Turk who is in default. Never underestimate the wily Oriental, sir! They know full well what they're about and it's up to us to bring them to their senses. That is why we've been dispatched on this mission.'

He sniffed disdainfully, then said, 'And, for your information, the Russian Navy in Corfu, under their Admiral Senyavin, has offered to send us ships-of-the-line in the common cause. Naturally I shall not avail myself of this, considering our present armament sufficient against the Navy of the Ottomans.'

There was quiet for a space as the import of what had been said sank in. Then Smith said coldly, 'Sir, I have met Sultan Selim, my brother having been the previous ambassador. He's no fool but has problems with his own people and takes to dithering between two courses of action when pressured. He's close to the French now but can be swayed back just as easily. In all charity, can we not move forward by diplomacy instead of bludgeoning our way—'

'Your objections are noted, sir. My orders are explicit. I can see no reason to delay. We sail against Constantinople.'

'Very good, sir,' Smith said icily. 'That leaves only the question of what to say when we fail.'

'Your attitude borders on the mutinous, sir. Explain yourself!'

'Certainly. I know these waters well – are you aware there are thirty-eight forts and batteries on the shores of the Dardanelles before ever the Sea of Marmora is reached? In a passage a mile or so wide this is hard enough to bear, I would have thought. A single ship is no threat and may pass unmolested, but a fleet such as ours will be an intolerable provocation.'

Duckworth looked as though he was going to say something but stayed quiet.

'Then there are the elements. The strait is long and narrow and there are currents and winds that can set the fairest vessel at a stand – I give you what the Turk calls the *meltemi*, a remorseless nor'-easterly that can blow for days and, of course, is dead foul for passage through.'

There were nods about the table. A ponderous line-of-battle ship could sail no closer than six points off the wind's eye and it didn't take a lot of imagination to picture a scene of back-winded ships milling helplessly before the guns of a Turkish fortress.

'And did I say currents? There are some swifter than a man may run, many that will stem a ship motionless in a tops'l breeze. Sir, *you* may be confident of our first armed incursion into the strait since the Crusaders, but *I* am not.'

Duckworth glowered. 'Why wasn't I told of this in more detail? Don't we have pilots as will preserve us through the hazards?'

'You'll trust a Turk to conn us safely through to fall upon his countrymen?'

'Humph. A good point, o' course. Thirty-eight fortifications, you say. This will not be easy – to reduce them one by one will take time.'

'And given the narrow width of the channel we cannot concentrate our fire-power at once,' Louis added. 'It requires we brave the enemy's shot ship by ship instead.'

'Quite,' Duckworth said, the frown now permanent. 'In view of what I've heard on fortresses, winds, restricted waters and currents, I'm minded to delay the expedition until we have a clearer plan in hand. It seems obvious to me now that their lordships were never in possession of all the facts when they drew up their orders.'

'Sir,' Kydd intervened, 'as I'm new returned from Constantinople, I've seen how fast things are happening there. If we're indeed to make an impression on the Porte then we should move now, before the French can establish themselves further.'

'Port? What does he mean?'

'The Sublime Porte,' Smith said sharply. 'The government of Turkey, named for the gateway where they meet the infidel. And he's right. If we go through with this madness, better we do it before they get word and set up a resistance.'

'I will be the judge of when we sail. And I say we wait until we can look further into the obstacles that face us. That is my decision.'

An uncomfortable silence was broken by some kind of disturbance outside the cabin. The door opened and the flag-lieutenant poked his head in. 'Sorry to interrupt, sir, but the ambassador, Mr Arbuthnot, is here and demands entry to any discussion concerning Constantinople.'

'Very well. Send him in.'

Arbuthnot showed no sign of any ailment. He bustled in, eyes a-gleam, seized a chair and sat close to Duckworth.

'I've just heard of your arrival, Admiral. How splendid!' he spluttered. 'Excellent! London has been listening to what I've been saying these last months. A show of force! Nelson's fleet!'

'I'm happy to see you've made a full recovery from your indisposition, sir.'

'Yes, yes, I'm quite ready to play my part, Admiral. Now, how then are we to proceed on our great expedition?'

'My orders are to lie off Constantinople and demand the persons of the French delegation. Failing that, to demand the handing over of the entire Ottoman fleet and stores to prevent their falling into French hands.'

'And if they won't comply?'

'We are to bombard the city until it lies in ruins.'

'Splendid! Our standing among the Turks – who invariably connect power with prestige – will never be higher.'

'Or any other acts as you shall from time to time recommend,' Duckworth said heavily. 'And are within my power to undertake.'

'It may not come to that, Admiral. So when might we start our chastising?'

'Sir, I'm not altogether of the opinion that you have a proper regard for the difficulties we are facing.'

'Difficulties?' Arbuthnot said, with surprise. 'With a grand fleet such as this? They'll run like rats at the first sight of it.'

'No, sir. I'm more referring to our forcing of a passage through the Dardanelles. Have you ever given thought to the fact that no hostile armada has ever gone through unopposed since before Drake's time? There is a reason for that. Fortresses, currents – I won't weary you with details, sir. Suffice it to say that it is my inviolable decision to delay any sailing until we have thoroughly considered the elements.'

'Delay? I thought I was talking to the fearless hero of Santo Domingo, sir.'

Duckworth smouldered. 'It is not your career that is in jeopardy, Mr Arbuthnot, it is mine. To lose a fleet to the Turk would damn me for ever.'

'You are forgetting something, Admiral.'

'What is that, sir?' Duckworth said stiffly.

'Your orders, sir,' Arbuthnot replied silkily. 'Which place my wishes to the fore. And these are that we waste no time in responding to our shameful ejection by the Ottomans by appearing before Constantinople at once. At once, sir!'

'I must first await the arrival of reinforcements from the Russian Navy under Admiral Senyavin before ever I can proceed, sir.'

'Admiral. I write my dispatches at the outset of this expedition tonight. Should you wish me to include the fact that we are lying idle at anchor indefinitely here while our high admiral waits for things to turn more in his favour?'

'I take note of your opinion, Mr Ambassador. Know that I also shall be writing dispatches – to lay before my commander-in-chief the grave professional difficulties we are under.'

'Do so, Admiral. As long as we're on our way. The triumph will be yours too, never fear.'

'Very well. We get under way tomorrow.'

Smith, who had been listening to the exchange with a lazy smile and with his hands folded behind his head, declared confidently, 'I rather think not.'

'What the devil do you mean, sir?'

'Has no one noticed? The wind's in the north and veering. We'll be headed by a dead foul wind in the morning – we're going nowhere.'

As the captains waited for their boats on the spacious quarterdeck of the battleship, Blackwood came up to Kydd. 'A pleasure to see you again, old fellow – oh, I do beg your pardon, Sir Thomas.'

'The pleasure is mine also, sir.'

'A trying time, this afternoon. Would you wish to take dinner with me tonight, at all? I've some capital lamb cutlets just come aboard that I'd like your opinion of – and perhaps we'll remember the more uplifting times we've had together.'

It was just what he needed to raise his spirits.

Ajax was an old friend. He had seen her first in Alexandria, setting ashore Abercromby's army that had finished the French in Egypt while he had been a junior commander in *Teazer*. And then it was Trafalgar – from the deck of his frigate he had seen her take on the bigger French flagship *Bucentaure* and then the even bigger *Santissima Trinidad* in an epic fight, nearly invisible in the boiling gun-smoke of the cannonading going on all around her.

Now for the first time he trod her decks – and as a guest.

'Welcome to my ship, Sir Thomas.' Blackwood greeted him warmly, shaking his hand in pleasure. 'Shall we go below?'

The evening was settling in, the last dog-watchmen on deck, lanthorns being rigged.

Blackwood's cabin was as austere as the man: a single

polished table set squarely in the middle of the deck, a lamp on gimbals at either side and a candelabrum at the geometric centre. There were few domestic touches, a chaste, almost puritanical feel about it reflecting the personality of the man Kydd remembered.

'I so deplore it when our leaders fall out,' Blackwood murmured, over sherry. 'I remember not so long ago the elevated spirit in every heart when Lord Nelson was still with us, every captain burning to do his utmost for the man and his country.'

'When orders were hardly necessary, each knowing his duty and the greater plan,' agreed Kydd.

Blackwood nodded sadly. 'Just between you and me, Kydd, I have the gravest reservations about this mission. It's one as is ill conceived by an interfering Admiralty acting under political pressure and not knowing the facts of the matter.'

These were near treasonable sentiments and Kydd knew that only the worst fears would have driven the loyal Blackwood to utter them.

'Here we have Admiral Duckworth arriving afire for action, and in a day backing and filling with caution when he should be boldly standing on. You know what this implies?'

'That Duckworth is not confiding in his subordinates – he's had weeks to consult Sir Sidney Smith, who knows these waters and could have warned him of conditions?'

'Just so. I rather think we have an ambitious man over-reaching himself, who now sees that, far from a glorious opportunity for fame and distinction, this is threatening to descend into failure and ignominy. Hardly a leader to inspire.'

'And his orders are to defer to the ambassador in both strategy and tactics – a divided command, I believe.'

'Yes, indeed. I'm particularly exercised in how he'll rein in

Sir Sidney. Our Swedish knight is not known for either his tact or strict obedience to orders.'

'His courage is undoubted.'

'As will be tested when we attempt the Dardanelles, of course, but this is not the prime requisite in our case. We shall see.'

More sherry was poured. 'You've done well, indeed, Sir Thomas,' Blackwood said respectfully. 'Since first shipping your swab, Trafalgar within a few months in a new frigate command and then . . . what was it next? The Cape?'

The dinner passed agreeably, the lamb cutlets superbly cooked and accompanied by a very passable claret.

'Do you miss *Euryalus*?' Kydd asked.

Blackwood's frigate had played a central role in Trafalgar even after the battle, acting as flagship for Collingwood, towing the *Royal Sovereign* to safety in the great storm that followed, and under a flag of truce going into Cádiz to parley for prisoners.

'To be frank, I do. She was only a year or two old and I had her set to rights just as I wanted her. But a frigate . . . Well, they're a young man's command and a ship-of-the-line is a next step to one's flag, so as of last year, here I have *Ajax*.'

'A fine command, even so,' Kydd said, with sincere admiration. 'I saw her in action at Trafalgar.'

'Of course you did. And did you know it was Lieutenant Pinfold, her first lieutenant, who commanded? Lechmere was called away to a court-martial and the young fellow found himself pitched in without warning.'

'And served nobly, as what I witnessed.'

'I heard he was made post directly and given a frigate command.'

The two men sat back reflectively. It was not so long ago but already it seemed another age, a time for heroes, fighting for survival against fearful odds and the end always in doubt. Now it was the slow but sure acquisition of empire and—

There was a muffled crash that seemed to come from under their feet, perhaps in the wardroom or midshipman's berth.

Blackwood frowned.

Another. Then the thump of running feet.

Blackwood jumped up, lunging to open the door. He was met by the heart-stopping sight of billowing dark smoke and the stink of burning.

A tearing cry of 'Fire!' was taken up, urgently spreading forward and an unseen stampede began.

'If I can do anything . . .'

But Blackwood was off into the roiling murk, fighting to reach his quarterdeck.

Kydd had a primitive fear of fire and his heart pounded as he thrust after him. In seconds he was staggering in the choking darkness, nearly knocked off his feet by running figures. Bellowed orders and cries of panic rang out.

How had the 'tween decks filled with smoke so fast?

Kydd dimly saw it was puffing up the main-hatch out into the gun-deck – which suggested it had taken hold below first.

It was near impossible to see to manoeuvre a fire-engine in the darkness or even get some idea of where the core of the blaze was. And to get water down to the bowels of the vessel in quantity meant a long and near useless bucket chain, or opening the bilge cocks and risking the ship sinking with no guarantee that the water flooding in could be diverted for fire-fighting.

He hesitated – his every fibre screamed at him to get out of the claustrophobia to the open air; this was not his ship, or the men his to command, and he had no reason to get in the way of those who were trying to stem the rampaging advance of the fire. He heard a lieutenant's hoarse urging – and stumbled guiltily, eyes streaming, to the ladder and the blessedly clear night air.

The smoke was soon thick and billowing on deck as well, streaming up through the gratings of the main-hatch, a choking hindrance to those trying to rig fire appliances. As yet there were no open flames.

Kydd went to the knot of men he could just see on the quarterdeck. Blackwood was in the centre with a lace kerchief over his mouth and nose, the only officer – the others, no doubt, were below rallying the men. Those about him were the master and boatswain; the carpenter was away knocking down bulkheads to get at the fire.

'If there's any—'

But Blackwood just looked through him at the extremity of distraction.

'I sent my first luff below to discover the fire but he's not returned,' he said eventually. 'I've no idea what's to do down there.'

In a surge of sympathy Kydd's hand went out, but it fell away in hopelessness at trying to convey his feelings.

It was one thing to have command and responsibility, quite another to have no knowledge at all on which to base decisions and orders.

An inhuman shriek came clear above the pandemonium and then another – things of horror were happening and they could do nothing.

'All boats in the water,' Blackwood ordered, in not much more than a croak.

The boatswain left, bellowing for hands to muster at the

boat skids forward. These would have to be hoisted out by block and tackle at the yardarm, a task normally needing hundreds of men and there was not that number on deck. The smoke was getting worse, now with an acrid edge that made it a choking, suffocating trial. An increasingly impenetrable murkiness hid everything: what it must be like between decks for the heroes at the bucket chains and pumps could not be imagined.

A sudden bright orange light flickered through at the main-hatch. The blaze was now flaring up from the bowels of the ship, hopelessly afire below.

Blackwood hesitated for only a moment. 'Abandon ship!' he said, breaking off in a paroxysm of coughing. 'Get the men out, every one – abandon ship!'

As if to add point to the inevitability the flames shot up in a sudden blaze amid a hellish chorus of shrieks. The end was not far off – but how could word be spread below? Those it reached might make the safety of the upper deck but many, fighting for the life of their ship, would never hear it.

The smoke was near invisible in the dark so it came as a shock to the other ships at anchor to see flames stabbing up. A gun banged out into the night from forward, *Ajax*'s anguished cry for help. More cracked out, vivid flashes just piercing the sullen smoke clouds rolling about the deck.

It would take time for boats from the ships to be launched and reach them.

Men stumbled up from below, retching and pitiable. Some took a few breaths and fought their way back down to pass the word and help up shipmates blinded by smoke. Kydd's heart went out to them.

The main-hatch was turning into an inferno, the sails on

the lower yards smouldering and taking fire. Such was its ferocity, Kydd realised, with sick dismay, that in a very short time the after end of the ship would be a death-trap.

He seized Blackwood's arm and gasped urgently, above the chaos, 'We have to get forrard.'

It was a desperate journey: the roaring blaze blinding them with its light in the blackness, the conflagration's heat and roar beating on them as they passed, paralysing Kydd's mind with the stark terror of elemental fire, wild and berserk.

On the far side were the long gangways leading over the waist of the ship and past the boats, still on their skids, to the fore-deck. There were scores of men at the ship's side, broken and gasping, staring at the flaring blaze taking pitiless hold aft, then looking down into the inky blackness of the water. Very few could swim and in the blackness their struggles would be invisible, their cries unheard against the crackling din. Every man now faced a stark choice – to be incinerated or drowned.

'They're not coming,' Blackwood said, in a low voice, gesturing to the other ships.

The few boats that had been launched were hanging back, fearful of what must come. They knew that when the fires reached the grand magazine of the great guns *Ajax* would cease to be.

'We've got to go,' Kydd urged, but he, too, was held in deadly thrall by the still, dark waters.

Blackwood drew himself up. In strong, solemn tones, he told his men, 'There's no hope for it, I'm sorry to say. Cast yourselves over-side is your only chance. God bless you and keep you.'

Several plunged into the sea but many more held back in eye-bulging terror.

Unexpectedly, Blackwood touched Kydd's arm. 'Dear chap. I hesitate to ask it, but if you'd help me, I'd be much obliged to you.'

In the wildness of the night his calmness reached out to Kydd. 'Of course. How might I . . . ?'

It was the act of a brave and intelligent man. Blackwood knew that his ship was destined for destruction but he realised that the rest of those in the anchorage could not escape in time and would be caught up in the holocaust. He had noticed that they were all riding to their anchors facing into the slight night breeze so he was asking Kydd to help him cut the cable of *Ajax* to let her drift through the fleet and away before the cataclysm.

They stumbled down the fore-hatchway in near pitch dark, the smoke choking, blinding, while they fumbled about for the riding bitts where the anchor cable was belayed, feeling their way in a howling chaos of panic and death. And all the time the fire was raging out of control. The final blast could happen at any moment; the actual time would depend on where the fire had started. If above the level of the magazine, then the rising heat of the blaze would consume the upper part of the vessel before it ate its way down. If not, then the next second could be their last.

They found the massive square bitts. Grabbing a fire-axe from each side of the fore-mast they threw off their coats and, coughing helplessly, eyes streaming, by turns swung in savage hits at the six-inch thick cable.

Obstinately the cable remained iron-hard and unyielding — the thousands of tons of battleship at her anchor tautening it.

In the confined space they couldn't take a vertical swing or be sure to strike in the same place and, in despair, Kydd saw that their efforts were only stranding the massive rope.

Nearly blinded now with sweat and tears he swung and hit mechanically, on and on, until suddenly the rope parted with a bang and slithered and bumped away out of the hawse.

'Let's be out!' Kydd gasped, and they made for the broad ladder to the fore-deck.

He saw by the other ships starkly illuminated in the outer blackness that they had begun imperceptibly to slip away sternwards.

'Shall we go?' he said, hesitating with his leg over the side-rail.

'I'll – I'll be along presently,' Blackwood said, his eyes fixed on the raging fire now turning the whole after end of the ship into a white-hot furnace.

Kydd crossed to him quickly, tugging at his sleeve. 'We have to go now – she'll blow any second!'

Blackwood turned slowly to him with a sad smile. 'You see, I can't swim, old chap.'

Kydd ran to one of the boats and pulled out an oar. 'Clap hold of this when you're in the water until they find you.'

He pushed him to the beakhead, the closer for Blackwood to drop into the water. The man swung down on to the small grating above the bowsprit and, hesitating only a little, grabbed a line and lowered himself down, dropping the last few feet into the blackness. Kydd saw him, frantically splashing about, and quickly let the oar go to float near him. Blackwood grabbed it, giving a shamefaced wave.

With a last glance at the terrible scene Kydd peered down at the dark waters to check they were clear, and let go. A half-second of weightlessness and then shocking cold. He spluttered and kicked until he was head above water and looked around.

On one side was the immense bulk of the battleship, on the other the fleet, its boats hanging back in fear and impossibly far off. The cold was ferocious, clamping in and forcing his inner core of warmth smaller and smaller. He knew that when it was finally extinguished he would be dead.

There were men in the water here and there, some splashing and shouting, others ominously still, but no sign of Blackwood.

He stroked clumsily to a piece of wreckage. It turned out to be a chicken coop, drowned fowls still inside and a body slumped half across it. There was no sign of life, its eyes stared sightlessly up. He gently pushed it off and tried to pull himself up. It was a mistake – out of water the wind cut into him cruelly and, reluctantly, he slid back into it.

The burning hulk of *Ajax* retreated into the distance and the boats finally moved in.

At the last extremity of bitter cold Kydd was dragged out of the water and a rough blanket wrapped tenderly about him. He joined two or three others bundled on the bottom boards. Shuddering uncontrollably he took a gulp from the flask of rum offered, then lay down, letting the fire of the spirit spread through his body.

It was now only a matter of enduring.

'I think I speak for all of us,' Duckworth declared ponderously, 'when I say how in sympathy we are for Captain Blackwood on the loss of his ship.'

'And her company,' muttered Smith.

'And at such tragic cost,' he added, glaring at his junior.

'So we think it in the region of some, two – three hundred perished?' Smith remarked drily.

'By muster, two hundred and fifty-two,' snapped Blackwood, looking haggard and drained. 'All good men. Most fought and survived at Trafalgar, poor souls.'

'Then we must think it one of the worst disasters the Navy has suffered in these wars,' Smith came back smoothly.

Kydd felt a rush of anger. Petty bickering to make points when the burial parties had not yet returned from Tenedos. *Ajax* had drifted as planned, taking the ground on the island to detonate in a thunderous cataclysm in the early hours of the morning.

Duckworth shifted uncomfortably. 'Gentlemen, gentlemen, I won't have any further talk on the loss of *Ajax* before the court of inquiry sits. We are in the presence of the enemy as well you know and have decisions to make.'

'Then you have reconsidered this venture, sir?' Smith asked innocently.

Duckworth fiddled with a pencil. 'We must reflect on our position, I believe. That no one in modern times has forced the Dardanelles bears hard on our hopes that we might be an exception. And with the wind still foul . . .'

'As is a delay enabling the Turk to be forewarned and bring up his navy,' Smith said.

'Admiral Smith! I am annoyed and wearied by your attitude. Your duty as a senior officer is to support His Majesty's arms in any operation ordered by their lordships. You'll be more positive and helpful in your remarks *or, by God, I'll have you relieved of your command, sir*!'

Smith gave a half-smile and looked down.

'Now! The ambassador requires we should proceed in this enterprise. We have no option in the matter.' He tugged at his collar irritably.

'Admiral Smith, do you care to outline the military situation that confronts us?'

'Why, that's simple enough,' Smith answered easily, as if nothing had happened. 'The forts are paired along the strait, one on the north, European, shore and another on the Asiatic side. The chief ones are at the entrance, then the outer castles at Sedil Bahr, where it narrows to a couple of miles. Some nine miles further on we have the inner castles at Chanak Kaleh, where the entire width of the Dardanelles is less than three-quarters of a mile. More defences under Point Pesquies, but if we get past those we've clear sailing for a space – until the worst is to be met with at Gallipoli.'

'A hard tale,' Boyles of *Windsor Castle* remarked softly. 'And after Gallipoli what must we face?'

'Afterwards? Nothing. We enter the Sea of Marmora with naught but the open waters between us and Constantinople.'

'Except the Ottoman Navy,' Duckworth said darkly. 'My information is that their order of battle includes ships-of-the-line and frigates by the score.'

'I rather fancy these will be in the north, arrayed against the Russians whom they are not fond of, but I could be wrong,' Smith said languidly.

Duckworth glowered, then gave a thin smile. 'You are ready enough with your opinions, sir. Now, tell me, is it in your conceiving that the forces opposing us are too formidable to contemplate an attempt on the Dardanelles?'

Smith paused, and Kydd knew why. He was being asked either to hand Duckworth the excuse he needed to call off the operation, or to hazard his reputation on predicting a successful outcome.

'These forces are daunting indeed, yet I believe it will be the fortunes of war that will as ever determine the issue,' he answered.

'Ah! So you see before us no immediate impediment to the expedition?'

'Beyond those I have mentioned, no.'

'Thank you,' Duckworth said. 'And with that assurance from you we shall advance the operation.'

So Smith was to be implicated in the event of a failure. It would not stand up in a court-martial but might perhaps colour the findings.

Duckworth leaned back. 'My orders are this. If, and only if, a fair wind is squarely in our favour, we shall proceed. You, Admiral Smith, will form one division in the rear, comprising *Pompée*, *Thunderer*, *Standard*, *L'Aurore* and the two bomb-ketches, while I shall command from *Royal George* in the van with the heavier class of ships. We shall enter in line-of-battle and engage the forts hotly as we pass.'

There was more: detail on signals, towing and other matters, but it added up to just one thing. The British fleet would penetrate into the Dardanelles. They would go in single line ahead and trust to their fire-power to silence the forts on the way.

There was much to think about as Kydd returned to *L'Aurore*. A pall was hanging over the whole operation and it wasn't just from the so-recent distressing scenes of *Ajax*'s immolation. A divided command, not just politically but in personalities – it cast the worst of omens before them.

He was in Smith's squadron. While Duckworth's heavies would stay dutifully together, the restless Smith would take any opportunity for action, however far it strayed from the main mission, if only to prove how active he was compared to his senior.

Why did such a gifted and intelligent man have to be so damned contrary? And was it really so necessary to flatten the ancient city, the beautiful Hagia Sophia and all? It probably wouldn't happen – the odds were very much against them ever getting past all of thirty-eight fortresses with their hundreds of guns.

In a black mood he took to his cabin and sat by the stern windows, automatically leaving 'Renzi's seat' vacant. But Renzi was part of the past. He was alone now and had to make the best of it. He'd have the old chair struck down in the hold and be damned to it all.

Tysoe appeared, like magic, with a whisky and water and left quickly. How the devil did the villain know?

He sipped appreciatively and let his thoughts wander. It was now more probable than not that some day he would be an admiral himself. How would he have dealt with a junior like Smith? And such a situation with the civil power telling him what he had to do. Well, he wasn't an admiral yet and therefore didn't have to find an answer. He began to feel better.

Then his eyes strayed to the work he'd taken out ready from his locked escritoire and his sour mood returned. It was his dispatches to Collingwood, following his return from Constantinople, and they were pressing: a cutter would leave shortly with those from all captains, including Arbuthnot's, and his weren't ready.

He swore out loud. It wasn't the communication itself that took the time – it was a plain enough tale – but the ciphering afterwards. A tedious but important task that, until now, Renzi had quietly relieved him of. Some captains told off one of the officers for the duty but he would never do that. First, it involved taking the officer off the watch bill, understand-ably unpopular with his fellows, but more importantly, he would no longer have the assurance that the captain alone knew the content of the dispatch.

God damn, but he missed Renzi!

He rose reluctantly – then had a thought. He employed a confidential secretary. Why shouldn't he make use of him?

Admiralty regulations gave no hard and fast rules over who should do the ciphering, merely that the captain must be in a position to assure himself of their strict confidentiality. Renzi, previously a naval officer, had had impeccable credentials. Did Dillon?

He quashed the retort that he could never be another Renzi, for no one could. He had to be taken on his own terms or not at all.

The young man was willing enough, but his romantic leanings were out of place in a man-o'-war. Apparently he wrote poetry, had declaimed into his first Mediterranean sunset and had grown soulful over the distant sight of Lesbos – much as Renzi had, Kydd was forced to admit.

Then again he'd seen him dress for a gun-room dinner in a blue velvet jacket and artistically *déshabillé* neck-cloth, his hair unclubbed and long. The rig of a trusted and discreet amanuensis?

With his easy manner Dillon had found acceptance there, a character in his own right. That he didn't know his nauticals was no bar to fellowship for he'd made it plain that this was not his calling. At the first-night dinner, when Curzon had cattily put him right over the meaning of 'martingale' as applied to a bowsprit, he had innocently asked him to explain the word itself. At Curzon's reluctance, Dillon had lightly mused on its horse-coping usage and then, to the delight of the others, had gone on to trace its probable Middle English origins back to Chaucer and Piers Plowman.

Kydd sighed. If he didn't trust the man he had no right to engage him as a secretary. He'd served in *L'Aurore* now for some time and never shown himself unfit for the position or slack in stays as regards diligence – and if he couldn't bring the man on he would have to do the work himself indefinitely.

It was being forced on him but there was little choice. He'd do it – perhaps with the proviso that Dillon swore himself to confidentiality.

This last idea pleased him, and it led to another. If he was being entrusted with codes, vital national secrets, then surely he was to be trusted with his personal matters. Kydd was a martyr to paperwork, loathing its passive nature, tedium and need for form and correctness, but had not felt able to turn it over to Dillon because it felt a violation of privacy. His humble origins as a wig-maker and pressed man were now behind him, but if he gave access to his papers, his financial details and so on, Dillon would know everything.

He didn't recall who had said it but the old saw 'No man can be a hero to his valet' came to mind.

'Desire Mr Dillon to attend on me,' he ordered at the door, and returned to his chair to consider his decision.

'Sir Thomas?'

As usual he stood loosely, features composed and respectful.

'Ah, Dillon. A word with you,' Kydd harrumphed.

'Sir?'

'I think it time for you to earn your keep. I desire that you assume duties of a more confidential nature.'

'Of course, sir. I'd be delighted.' There was an animation that seemed to show he had been waiting for just this moment – a release from the mundane?

'Then you'll be instructed in ciphering, for you will be transcribing my dispatches from this point forward.'

'I understand, Sir Thomas. About the grave nature of being privy to such secrets, I mean.'

'Good. I shall, of course, require you swear that you will keep them and so forth. Have you any objection?'

'None, Sir Thomas.'

'Very well. And, further, you are to undertake the care and upkeep of my personal correspondence and papers.'

'I'm honoured by your trust, sir.'

'Yes. Well, that's decided, then. How are you settling in – the gun-room mess, that is?'

'Happily, thank you, Sir Thomas. In large part I'm obliged to Lieutenant Bowden for his amiable manners and patience, which have enabled me to take my place in such august and hearty company.'

It appeared the young man was succeeding well in fitting in and finding fulfilment in their fellowship.

Kydd continued, 'I see you are keeping the young gentlemen to their studies. Are they progressing well?'

'Both in their way, sir. But, you see, there is . . .'

'Yes?'

'My grasp of mathematicals is slender, I do confess, and their navigation studies require that . . .'

'Well. Perhaps we shall leave that side to the sailing master.' It was oddly gratifying that he'd discovered a weakness in the young man.

'Thank you, Sir Thomas.'

'I should mention that your confidential work will be carried out in this cabin. You may use the escritoire, for which I have the key, and . . . and should you have need of good daylight, do feel free to use . . . that chair.' Renzi's accustomed seat.

'Right. Well, we'll begin this afternoon at three bells. Good day to you, Dillon.'

But the next day the winds relented, veering to a playful

southerly. Almost as soon as it was light enough to see, *Royal George* ran up a signal: 'prepare to weigh'.

Kydd felt a lurch of unreality. Against all reason it was going ahead: the British fleet was on its way to force the Dardanelles and level Constantinople to the ground.

Chapter 9

From the Dardanelles shore it was a grim sight: a long line of battleship after battleship, with their rows of guns, frigates, others, all under full sail – and flying from each the feared ensign of Admiral Nelson. Now there could be no longer any doubt of British intentions.

Smith held his squadron at the rear in a tight line; his orders to them were simple – clap eyes on his flag and no other, obey signals on the instant, and be prepared for anything. From the sudden appearance of the Ottoman Navy to the rescue of a stricken first-rate hammered to destruction by the forts, mused Kydd.

Each ship towed its boats astern for if the worst happened – a hopeless tangle of trapped vessels under fire – there would be no time to launch them.

It was eerily quiet as they entered the strait.

The first side to fire would break the treaty between Turkey and Great Britain and be responsible for whatever followed. Yet what they were doing was an act of war in itself, an intolerable provocation in sending a battle-fleet against the capital.

The fortifications across the entrance remained silent as the ships passed, their colours flapping lazily in the light breeze.

They must have been seen – were they going to get away with it?

The British fleet were all at quarters, guns loaded, but not run out. The gun-ports remained firmly closed. If the Turks opened fire it would be on warships ostensibly about their peaceful occasions.

The sides of the passage began closing in. Kydd knew that not so far ahead were more fortresses, the 'outer castles', and these were massive – at a particularly constricted point.

Still the deathly quiet.

He looked ahead to the van of the line. *Canopus* was leading *Repulse* and the two three-deckers into the narrows, the wind fair but light. They seemed to be favouring the north bank – deeper water and away from the bigger fortress.

Nearer and nearer . . . Then both citadels erupted in smoke and gun-flash. These were shotted and *Canopus* was quickly straddled, *Repulse* next. But there was no return fire – Duckworth was going to play it out as the injured party.

There was no holding back from the shore. Each ship was targeted as they passed . . . still with no reply. And these were heavy-calibre weapons, sending up plumes to the main-yards – sixty-pounders was the best guess, vastly out-gunning anything the fleet mounted.

The line moved on agonisingly slowly as the guns played on them. The three-deckers were clearly the focus of anger but still their gun-ports remained obstinately shut.

Kydd's face set hard. The point had been made: the Turks had definitely opened fire first. Why didn't the admiral unleash the combined broadsides of the fleet?

The leading ships passed beyond range and into a bend to

the left, the following ships now coming under fire. Harvey's *Standard* lost a spar and then it was *L'Aurore*'s turn to face the fortresses' spite. With shot so big coming in, it was useless to take cover. Kydd slowly paced his quarterdeck as the tension grew.

But it seemed the Turkish gunners were growing fatigued, manhandling the huge guns: only a few shots came their way – and then they were through.

Unexpectedly, behind them the little bomb-ketches suddenly fired their thirteen-inch mortars – just two rounds in reply to all the punishment the fleet had taken.

Now the inner castles had to be penetrated. These were double the size and fully alerted – Duckworth must surely respond!

There wasn't long to wait. His signal was made: gun-ports flew open at the rush and the fleet showed its teeth.

The channel was getting perilously narrow: if any of the line-of-battle took a crippling hit it would cause a disastrous obstruction. Sailing before the wind there was no chance for the rest to turn and retreat.

The fortifications opened up with a deep thunder of heavy guns. Instantly *Canopus* got off her broadside in a mighty roar of stabbing flame and towering gun-smoke. It was well-aimed, the shot-strike around the redoubt leaping and battering and throwing up dark, whirling chunks. Its fire petered out rapidly – the Turks manning it could never have experienced such a holocaust before.

The fort opposite was quickly battered by another broad-side but a weakness showed: in the interval of reloading in the ships the gun-smoke receded, the forts recovered and the firing resumed. *Repulse* and the following battleships took the lesson and kept up a rippling fire that dismayed the shore gunners, and in a continuous roar of cannonading the ships slipped past, one by one.

The most dangerous part lay ahead: they could not retreat against the wind so their only course was to continue. Kydd remembered only too well the succession of redoubts, forts and strongholds of the legendary Dardanelles defences he had seen along the strait.

Looming over all was the dread prospect of the Ottoman fleet descending on them and a pitched fleet action in the impossible confines of these waters. It would be a slaughterhouse fight of ship laid alongside ship until the issue was decided.

Kydd raised his glass. The head of the line was coming up to a point that stood out from the Asiatic shore, hiding the strait, which led on around it in a bend to the right. On its tip was a fortification, Point Pesquies, which had to be passed to reach the relative safety of the slightly broadening strait further on.

Canopus fired early and the fort was nearly hidden in flying debris and its own powder smoke, the duel continuing as the big sail-of-the-line moved slowly on.

The other battleships crashed out their anger at the fort as they shaped course to round the low point. *L'Aurore* followed in their wake. Then came a chilling sight.

Too late, the line-of-battle had passed beyond the point. Suddenly revealed, tucked in its lee, was the Ottoman fleet.

It was cunningly positioned: the big ships passing could not turn back and engage, and now the Turks were upwind and in a dominating position for attack.

Duckworth, with no room to manoeuvre, immediately anchored in an impregnable line and awaited the onslaught.

Smith, however, had sighted the masts above the low point and had his signal for close action soaring up. With his division tightly astern, he swept around the headland to fall on the Turks.

Beside Kydd, Dillon stood clutching his notebook, waiting. It would be hardest on him, intelligent and imaginative but with no fighting role to discharge tension and fear, in his first big action.

Kydd took in the rest of the quarterdeck group, grave and confident as they waited for orders; the men, stripped to the waist at the guns, loose-limbed and fearless; the boatswain on his rounds, checking preventer tackles, the becketing of stoppers in their place, a gruff word to his mates. Kydd had trusted each one in the greatest battle of the age and he trusted them now. He knew what to expect and what to do – but Dillon would have none of this comfort.

He spared him a quick glance. To his surprise, the man had a look of exaltation and returned him a serene smile. Kydd was taken aback: did he think it was in some way romantic to go into battle against an enemy? If so, his education was about to be considerably advanced.

They completed rounding the point and Kydd saw the foe, the flagship in the centre and the rest at anchor in formal array about it not a half-mile distant.

In disbelief he blinked and looked again.

The fleet the Turks had brought against them was contemptible, derisory. Not much more than a single 64 as flag and a motley collection of frigates, corvettes, with a brig, gunboats – against the might of British battleships.

Surely Duckworth would sail on, confident that the Ottoman admiral would fall back in awe at the crushing superiority of numbers and weight of metal, leaving them untouched.

Their commander, though, was not going to let them pass without a show of defiance, and opened fire.

Like a vengeful tiger, Smith led his squadron around and into the midst of the Turks. A storm of destruction followed: broadsides from port and starboard into the mass of motionless ships filled the little bay with smoke and gunfire.

Cables were cut to escape the punishment but one by one ships drove aground in their terror, their crews scrambling for the shore. One frigate, managing to claw out of the maelstrom, was set upon by *Active* and fled but was overhauled and, under the terrible gun-fire into her stern, slewed and grounded on the opposite shore.

In minutes the Ottoman fleet had been transformed into a dozen scattered wrecks. Signals flew up *Pompée*'s mizzen: boats were to be manned and sent to board the derelict warships and burn them under menace of the squadron's guns.

Pompée was first away, her launch and cutter making for the flagship, forlornly at an angle on the shoreline. Others took their cue, and soon boats were frantically criss-crossing on their mission to destroy.

Kydd sent Curzon and Calloway in the launch to board the beached 38-gun frigate opposite and the cutter with Bowden to deal with a brig.

But as the gun-smoke over the anchorage dissipated Kydd saw, close to the foreshore, a long, squat fortification of some size. It had a clear field of fire and its heavy guns began to speak.

'Mr Oakley – kedge fore 'n' aft,' Kydd bellowed, above the noise. He snapped to Kendall, 'Take her in.'

As the one with the least draught, he was best placed to do what was necessary.

A leadsman hastily took post in the fore-chains and began his chant. As the water shallowed under her keel, she dropped a kedge on short stay forward, and when she swung under the impetus the other was cast aft. Now they had cables they could haul on to train the ship's entire battery.

They didn't waste time. After the first broadside her twelve-pounders were fired in successive aimed shots at the redoubt's embrasures and its deadly fire ceased. The sight of *L'Aurore* close in with a regiment's worth of artillery devoted just to them caused the soldiers to flee for their lives.

The mission to burn and destroy continued.

The Turkish flagship was first afire, then smoke was issuing from a frigate's fore end. It was the same in other stranded ships – it was a rout.

Lieutenant Clinton drew Kydd's attention. 'Sir, may I make a suggestion?'

'Why, certainly.'

'It crosses my mind that we shall be this way again on our return. It might well be of service should we land and spike the guns of that redoubt. Might I . . . ?'

'A good idea, Mr Clinton. Get your men together with the gunner's mate and his tools.' Stirk would take great satisfaction in the job and they still had one boat.

Brice stepped up. 'Sir – you're sending a party ashore against the fort?' His uniform was stained and his eyes masked with the grey smudging of powder-smoke.

'I am. Why do you ask?'

'Sir. I want to lead them.'

Kydd hesitated. It would leave him without a single officer on board and Clinton possessed a cool head, but they were landing on enemy soil where so many had fled and had every reason to return to take revenge. He nodded to Brice and saw the party off.

They landed and made speed up to the redoubt, then disappeared inside. Kydd's attention returned to the mayhem.

Curzon returned from his mission, ecstatic. 'My God, you should have seen it! Ran like rabbits and we had the barky ablaze in a brace o' shakes. Then when we—'

'Trouble, sir,' the master interrupted, pointing ashore.

Beyond the redoubt a seething mass of horsemen was assembling at the skyline.

'To the guns, tell 'em to shift aim to the Turk cavalry!' Kydd rapped, but within minutes he heard back that they were out of effective range of their twelve-pounders.

The fate of their courageous band didn't bear thinking about, and Kydd's blood ran cold at the image of Stirk's sturdy loyalty ending under an Ottoman scimitar.

All eyes turned to him – but the matter was taken out of his hands when, like the vengeful thunder of Jove, the powerful thirty-two-pounders of *Pompée* opened up past them and the horsemen were swept from sight.

Come on! Kydd mentally urged the strike ashore. They seemed to be taking their time. But, then, to disable fifty or so great guns would be a considerable task and—

'Flag, sir. Signal to retire.'

Kydd swung to face *Pompée*.

'No, sir. *Royal George*.'

Duckworth was pulling out Smith's squadron. All around the anchorage ships were on fire but the enemy flagship was blazing so furiously that sparks were ascending above its masthead. This was threatening a cataclysm that could turn victory into disaster in a blinding flash.

'Get in the after kedge, shorten cable forrard,' Kydd ordered, willing on the brave souls ashore.

Smith had the grace to wait and cover the scene until running figures suddenly appeared and *L'Aurore*'s boat put off.

Showing sail aft, *L'Aurore* slowly pivoted around her anchor until she was before the wind once more and the boat had thrown a line. Then, with *Pompée*, they sailed away in relief from the scene of devastation.

Against all the odds, and despite prophecies of doom, they had broken through.

They had some hours of quiet sailing before they reached the great fortresses of Gallipoli. Smith's division took position at the rear in the line-of-battle and the fleet sailed on. If only the wind held . . .

Kendall spotted that *Royal George* was shortening sail and the entire battle line therefore was slowing. For a moment Kydd did not realise what was going on.

Then he had it. 'As he wishes to transit the Gallipoli forts under cover of dark, a bold notion, don't you think?'

It also gave a chance for the tired men to be fed and take their grog.

As planned, the fleet reached the closing point at the far end of the Dardanelles, Gallipoli, in darkness. Unlike passing the outer and inner castles, which involved two bends nearly at right angles and impossible to navigate at night, here the narrows were straight and uncomplicated. It might just work.

Under a press of sail the fleet swept on by the Gallipoli fortresses. Wild firing tore apart the night but a brisk breeze saw them past unscathed and into the Sea of Marmora beyond.

It was miraculous. They had penetrated the famed Dardanelles, and all their number, save *Ajax*, still with them.

There was nothing between the powerful battle-fleet and Constantinople but the open sea.

Chapter *10*

Renzi allowed himself to be draped with a napkin and accepted a quite decent claret, apparently from the Balkans. He was fussed over by a possessive Jago, who took it upon himself to keep the heathen Turkish servants at bay.

In the warm light of the oil-lamps Zorlu sat decorously opposite – they would talk together only after they were left alone.

Renzi was under no delusions: Selim was using him. The shrewd sultan wanted to hear from all sources, not just the French, before he made up his mind, and an English lord's presence was a very convenient situation. Renzi allowed himself a touch of optimism. If he could exploit this further, perhaps by—

But something was happening. Out beyond the palace walls, shouts and disorder.

Zorlu's eyes caught his in alarm.

More noises – Zorlu excused himself. He was back quickly, his face lined. 'They're shouting something about Nelson's fleet returning to take its vengeance – I couldn't make out more.'

They must mean the frigate that had taken off the ambassador just before he'd arrived. But why would it come back, knowing it would inflame the population? Taking vengeance was nonsense, of course: no captain would be mad enough to think to restore honour by beginning a shooting war against an ally.

'It'll settle down.' Renzi tried to sound confident but he was aware that only a single gate separated them from a gathering mob.

They continued eating but the unrest grew louder, more strident.

'I don't like it, my lord,' Zorlu muttered. 'They're—'

At the outside door there was a fierce knocking.

A frightened Miller answered but was pushed aside roughly by a Janissary. The man glowered, then pointed at Renzi, unmistakably ordering him outside.

Zorlu got up, protesting. A scimitar hissed out, and he stopped in his tracks.

'Stay, Zorlu Bey. I'll be back when—'

The Janissary shouted at him, gesturing angrily.

In the outer darkness Renzi could see at least a hundred of the elaborately plumed soldiers, the steely gleam of their weapons caught in the moonlight.

At an ill-tempered command he was jostled into the centre of the group, which closed around him and stepped off quickly.

Out of the courtyard, then on to the inner second one, advancing right across to a long domed and arched edifice, shadowed, but in parts lit luridly by torches. Waiting for him was a smaller party of men in tall white hats and gold-edged robes. He was handed over: his wrists were bound and a hood placed over his head. Then he was marched away.

After a succession of turns they finally came to a halt. Renzi heard a door being unlocked and he was pushed inside. His hands were untied and his hood removed. The door crashed shut, leaving him alone in a room lit only by a small lamp on a side table. There was a low, plain bed and a form of dresser with a water-jug.

He sat on the bed and calmed his racing heart. He was a hated Englishman of the tribe that was bringing their ship against the capital. It could all be over quickly when the frigate captain came to his senses and left . . . or just as easily the crowd could bawl for his head as a token of defiance.

In the deathly quiet he tried to think. Would he ever see dear Cecilia again? He crushed the thought.

The door suddenly rattled and a tall dark man in the same white robes he'd seen before stepped in. He bowed without a word, then beckoned Renzi to follow.

They passed down a narrow passage into a small room, richly ornamented with intricate gilded fretwork.

Sultan Selim rose from a divan. He was alone.

'You will appreciate, my dear Fahn'ton Pasha, that this is for your own protection.'

With a courtly bow, Renzi murmured an acknowledgement and added, 'My household, Sire?'

'They will be protected, never fear. Do you know why you are here?'

'Seigneur, I heard an English warship lies close.'

'Not one. Many! There is a fleet of great ships now at anchor by the Princes Islands, not eight miles from us here. Some with three lines of guns, many with two. And others.'

It took Renzi's breath away. This was no stray frigate – with first-rate battleships it was a squadron of a size equipped to engage in a fleet action. What in Hades was a major asset like this, so sorely needed out on the Atlantic blockade, doing here?

There was no sense in any of it and he tried to blink away his confusion.

'What do you think they mean by it, Fahn'ton Pasha,' Selim said quietly, 'that they so terrify my people by their presence?'

'I – I cannot think it has any meaning to me, not a military man, sir.' What was Whitehall contemplating – to reduce French influence by a flourish, by force? If so, it was madness!

'Then I must put my own construction upon it. I believe you English wish me to gaze upon your might that I may stop my ears to the French whispering. That you desire me to follow your path, not theirs. Am I right?'

'This I cannot possibly answer, sir.'

'I understand.' He looked away, his expression unreadable.

After a few moments the sultan said softly, 'All Constantinople now believes you to be taken, to have disappeared into the Topkapi Palace, as so many have done, never to be seen again. And they will approve. But I can see how it may be to our mutual advantage.

'You are safe here. But in return you will give me your counsel, your opinions, which I greatly value.'

'If you wish it, Sire.'

'And perhaps there will be time for you to read to me from your poetry, to plumb its depths of meaning for me.'

Renzi felt a jet of sympathy for the man: with the seething currents of plotting and power struggles all about him, was he groping for something like friendship?

'It will be my honour.'

'Do advise me now, my friend. What do the English want? The people are frantic – I must tell them something.'

Renzi concentrated savagely. The fleet commander would have his orders; any assessment he gave had a chance of frustrating their intent. Yet he had to come up with some sage counsel that would satisfy or he was finished.

Damn to hell the unknown politicals who had dreamed up whatever hare-brained scheme this was, without either telling him or giving his mission a chance to succeed, as it was certainly beginning to.

'Sire, the character of an Englishman is one who cherishes fair play above all else. There will be no precipitate falling upon you, no invasion, no firing on your great city, not until a formal note is communicated to you specifying any grievance.'

Any admiral would be committing professional suicide to open fire without the due formalities recognised by civilised nations.

'Therefore, Sire, my advice is to wait calmly for the demand and then, knowing what is asked, let enlightened diplomacy relieve the situation. Meanwhile, your people are in no danger and must wait patiently, as we are all obliged to do.'

'You are sure of this?'

'Quite certain, sir.'

'I was not wrong. Your counsel is most wise, Fahn'ton Pasha.'

He hesitated, then asked, 'Therefore it would be prudent of me to have you aware of other advice given, that you might be in a position to comment upon it.'

Did he mean . . . ?

'Shortly I will be in audience with General Sébastiani who will advise me on the situation. I desire you shall hear him.'

'Sir! How can I—'

'No one knows your exact whereabouts here. This must remain so. Nevertheless I conceive that there is a way for you to be able to overhear what passes between us. I shall meet him in the Mabeyn, a hall that is the most privileged and secure of my receiving chambers. It is at the edge of my harem, and when one of my wives is consumed with curiosity by a guest she is enabled to satisfy herself by passing up a secret staircase and hearing all that goes on from behind a privy screen. This you shall do.'

Selim clapped his hands. The tall dark man entered, bowing with hands widespread.

'This is Mahmut. He is chief of the eunuchs and I trust him more than any, for he is mute. He cannot speak to betray my secrets. He will conduct you by the secret stairway when there is need of you.'

Renzi could hardly believe his good fortune. To listen in on the machinations of Sébastiani was a priceless boon, and all unknown to the French.

'It is only fair to tell you, Fahn'ton Pasha, that if you are discovered in this place, by the laws of the sultanate your life is forfeit. Even I will not be able to save you. Shall you proceed?'

With that opportunity? Of course!

'For the sake of our friendship, Sire, I will.'

Mahmut appeared noiselessly and they left the cell. The beautiful arabesque corridor stretched away in the soft illumination of elaborate sconces but just a few paces further on they came to a discreet door, which Mahmut opened.

By the light of a small taper Renzi could see steps leading down. At the bottom they walked along for a space and, after a sharp turn, climbed up again.

Ahead was a patterning of light from a fretwork panelling.

Through its slits and holes Renzi found himself looking into a room that gleamed with the splendour of gold, enamel and intricate ornamenting that had no equal in Paris or London.

Sprawled in an elaborately carved chair and looking moodily at the scarlet divan under a gold-tasselled canopy, Sébastiani was in full dress uniform and decorations.

The space held an elusive, eastern fragrance, and Renzi remembered that he was to all intents and purposes in the harem of the sultan.

He pressed forward in his eagerness to see but Mahmut drew him back with patient gestures, away from the light that might give away his presence.

In rising excitement he peered at the officer, careful to stay in the darkness. Young, energetic and formidably intelligent, this was the man he must beat.

He studied him intently. Was he imagining it or was he trying to conceal nervousness – a lack of confidence perhaps?

If so, there could be only one reason. Nelson's long shadow was reaching out and touching him – the legend of invincibility at sea that the Royal Navy had won for itself was now a confronting reality. If Selim was swayed by its appearance he could well be handed over, a prisoner of the English, within the day.

Renzi's eyes glowed. This was working better than he'd hoped. If only he knew the unknown admiral's orders . . . Still, their massive presence might be all that would be required for him to turn the tables on the French.

There was movement outside and Sébastiani shot to his feet with a broad smile.

'Why, General, you are already here, I see,' Selim said,

accepting Sébastiani's ostentatious court bow with an airy flourish of his hands.

'I believed my Turkish seigneur would be appreciative of my military counsel at this grave time.'

'Very well, General. The English are here for a purpose. What is your advice?'

'Sire, we know full well why they're here.'

'Oh?'

'It is simple,' he began smoothly. 'They are allied to the Russians. Tsar Alexander is ambitious and, as we have so recently seen, expands his empire into Turkish lands, which is scandalous. If you were the King of England would you rather favour this European monarch with friends, or will it be an Oriental sultan with none?'

'General, it is a mighty fleet, that of the ever-victorious Nelson himself. We cannot possibly prevail over them.'

'We cannot know this, Sire. My counsel from the heart to you, at this time of the greatest peril, is to delay. Obstruct and procrastinate until the situation is known. Only then can plans and decisions be made. It is the wisest course.'

'Very well. I thank you for your sagacious words and bid you goodnight.'

Renzi was taken back to his cell.

The Frenchman was good – very good. The advice to delay was what he would have given in the circumstances, and talk of the Russians was a neat ploy even if completely fallacious. The British would never take sides one against the other, not for any noble reason but because the risk of backing the wrong horse was too great when no commitment was being demanded.

It was disturbing that Selim did not visit afterwards. Not that he had anything to say: only when the true reason for the fleet's presence was known would it be possible to bring to bear rational deliberation.

He was awake at break of day. If there was to be a note of demands it would be delivered promptly. He could only wait.

The morning wore on in hours of tedium.

The situation was unreadable: with the fleet at anchor only eight miles away, there could be no difficulty in getting a message ashore under flag of truce. What was holding them up?

In a fever of impatience he waited. Mid-morning a silent Mahmut arrived to take him to the eyrie. Renzi looked on as Sébastiani was brought in.

'General. We have our demands.'

'You will delay, Seigneur, of course.'

'We have done so. Our water guard refused to recognise the boat's flag of truce. It was put ashore by a trick, however.'

'May I know its contents, sir?'

'My dragoman will read it to us both.'

So that Renzi could know it, too. In his hiding-place he smiled his appreciation.

A portly man was ushered in. Selim handed him the paper.

'Ah, from the English Admiral Duckworth to the Reis-ül Kuttab.'

'Our foreign minister, as you'll remember, General.'

'Yes, Sire. And . . . ?'

Even in the courtly French the demand was baldly stated and brief.

The British viewed the growing influence of the French at the Sublime Porte as intolerable to their existing treaty of alliance. It was demanded that the French agitator

233

Sébastiani and his associates be yielded up under pain of further action.

Sébastiani gave a superior smile, as if throwing off a triviality. Renzi was forced to admire his control and waited with interest for his reaction.

'I have to confess I'm not certain I'm flattered, Sire.'

'Why so, General?'

'This great fleet – to lay hands on my person? I rather think not. It is to a larger purpose – that of removing the only one standing in the way of dismantling your defences against their Russian allies. And I'm determined that you shall not be left at their mercy.'

'How can you say this, sir?'

'Sire, when before I said you had no friends, this may be true in the formal sense. Yet even without an alliance, the august Emperor Napoleon wishes me to do all in my power to assist you, and has empowered me to offer the resources of the empire to resist this insult and safeguard your throne. I will do so.'

'Against the fleet at our gates this very hour?'

'It can be done.'

'Forgive me, General, I cannot see how.'

'Sire, let me bring to your recollection the unbroken string of victories our illustrious emperor has won on the continent of Europe against the most dreadful of foes. The contemptible English successes pale against our laurels. True, they have prevailed in several battles out at sea, but who cares what happens on waters distant from the homeland?'

'Continue, sir.'

'They have foolishly sent their precious fleet to do the work of an army. What can it do? Fire cannon at us, make a lot of frightening noise, but then they must sail away. Without they have an army to land to enforce their demands, it is nonsense and I see no transports with them.'

The dragoman intervened: 'I have not yet finished my translation, Great Lord.'

'What else, then?'

It was an alternative demand. If reluctant to yield up the person of Sébastiani to his enemy, the entire Ottoman Navy should be neutralised by the simple device of handing it and its stores over to Admiral Duckworth forthwith. Failing that, the consequences would be very grave – the fleet would close with the city, and Constantinople would be bombarded by the great guns of the battleships until it was entirely levelled to the ground.

'And it concludes by allowing the Sublime Porte half an hour to reply.'

There was a horrified silence.

Sébastiani asked abruptly, 'When was this written?'

'At seven this morning.'

'Ha! At least three hours ago – does this seem the act of one determined on action? He would have moved into position by now, Sire.'

But Selim had paled and his hands twisted around a tasselled silk belt. 'What can we do? This is a calamity for the Ottoman dynasty beyond believing.'

Sébastiani gave a grim smile, and rapped, 'Give me leave to see to our defences, Sire! I will throw a ring of iron about Constantinople that will stand against anything the barbarians can mount against us. All I need is time.'

'But we have no time. The fleet will come and blow us to ruins!'

'Better you stand a hero in the ruins than cravenly surrender to the infidel,' Sébastiani spat. 'Your enemies would never stand for it.'

Selim shot a hopeless glance directly at the screen and Renzi instinctively recoiled.

Then he twitched up his robe, as though a decision had been made. 'Delay, you said delay. That is what I shall do.'

'Bravely said, Sire. Just a little time is all I'll need.'

The sultan was still white with shock when he swept into Renzi's cell.

'Is this the action of a civilised nation? Tell me, Fahn'ton Pasha – will they do it?'

So much hung on what he said next.

Renzi shook his head sorrowfully. 'I rather fear Admiral Duckworth will, Sire. He is under orders and dare not disobey his king. Your clear course is to surrender up the Frenchmen and save yourselves and the city from destruction.'

Would this be his crowning moment? Was his persuasion the equal of Sébastiani?

'I'll – I'll think on it, Fahn'ton Pasha. It is too great a matter to decide at this time.'

Renzi felt he was teetering on the brink of complete success in his mission – the ejecting of the French and the ruination of Bonaparte's plans. It was nail-biting but if Duckworth moved quickly and sailed his fleet across in a grand martial display before the famous waterfront of Constantinople the pressure on Selim might do the trick.

If he moved fast.

But another message arrived: it threatened instant destruction – but only if no favourable reply was received by sunset.

Renzi could hardly believe it: Duckworth was throwing

away his best chance of bringing everything to a successful conclusion by conceding, for no real reason, a relaxing of terms, and Sébastiani leaped at the opportunity.

Like a demon, he was everywhere setting about the defences, sending out parties to locate every cannon that existed and wheeling them with donkeys and mules through the streets to line up along the shoreline, his promised ring of iron.

Selim hesitated: if the English admiral could see through his telescope to what use the Turks were putting their period of grace he might become enraged and carry out his threat. Was it not better to appease the commander of such an overwhelming force?

Sébastiani was having none of it. With a cunning worthy of his master, he worked on Selim's fears that a capitulation to demands without a fight implied he was on the side of the infidels, that he was no longer fit to be sultan in the long and illustrious line of the Ottoman dynasty and everyone knew what happened to such creatures.

Renzi's advice was the same as before, but this time he also tried to paint Selim going down in history as the sultan who had destroyed Constantinople.

It hit home. 'The cup of unhappiness has never left my lips, my friend. What am I to do? Where is my duty?'

'Your friends are the English, with whom you have an alliance. Not the French, who betrayed you by offering peace but invading Egypt. You owe it to—'

'Fahn'ton Pasha. I ask you this. If I bow to your English demands, can you save me from the wrath of my shamed people? Where is your promise?'

There was still a chance. If by some means he could get word to Duckworth, he could demand he open the sealed orders he knew all flagships carried with the authorisation for him to act as he saw fit. He could thus instruct the admiral to make a convincing display and land marines sufficient to reassure Selim to take the final step.

But hope died quickly. Any attempt to contact the fleet would be proof positive he was a British spy and his end would be unpleasant. Ironically, he had not even set eyes on the armada that was causing such pandemonium.

'Seigneur, I'm desolated that I can find no further words of comfort in your time of trial. The decision must be yours.'

Even as he said it, he knew what Selim had decided: quite simply . . . not to decide.

At an hour or so before sunset Sébastiani came up with another master-stroke.

They would send an emissary to the admiral to negotiate. There could be no bombardment while negotiations were under way and he selected his man well. Isaac Bey was a wily and dignified figure from another age, revered for his early adventures in the Balkans and close to the centre of power.

He left quickly and, as predicted, the day ended without the threatened cataclysm.

Renzi suffered agonies of frustration. Time was slipping by while Sébastiani was energetically performing miracles, galvanising the soldiery and putting heart into the citizenry with his show of cannon.

Isaac Bey returned after midnight. He had done what he could and was very tired.

And the next day the British fleet still lay quietly at anchor.

It couldn't last.

At ten, signal flags broke out at the masthead of the flagship.

Spyglasses turned on the dread sight revealed on every ship

men racing up from below, crew taking position on the fore-deck as capstans were manned and gun-ports opened one by one. The fleet was on the move.

Renzi sighed with relief at the news. Even now it was not too late to bring the overwhelming weight of a battle-fleet to bear on the situation.

Wearily he reached for patience, sitting on the bed with his head in his hands . . . and waiting.

Hours later, too wrought up to take the refreshment Mahmut brought, he tried yet again to put a construction on what was happening.

He vaguely remembered Commodore Duckworth in Menorca, a heavy-faced, ponderous-mannered individual unlikely to be described as imaginative or bold. Yet he had led his ships to a decisive victory at Santo Domingo only the year before.

Couldn't he see his way forward, for God's sake?

In the early afternoon, the fleet still poised at anchor, a note was sent. It was from Duckworth, a long, confusing and senseless missive that complained the Turks were taking unfair advantage of the truce period to strengthen their defences and, 'if they wished to save their capital from the dreadful calamities that are ready to burst upon it, the thought of which is shocking to our feelings of humanity, you will be sent here very early tomorrow morning with full powers to conclude with me this work of peace . . .'

Renzi listened to the diatribe in despair, hearing Sébastiani snort with derision at yet another postponing of the day of reckoning.

His counsel was not sought. When Isaac Bey was roused and sent with instructions, he knew nothing of it until after-wards, when he returned.

What he came back with gratified Sébastiani immensely. An acceptance of the previous offer to negotiate, and on the following day.

It was child's play for the clever Frenchman to turn this into an interminable delay: where would the parley take place, there being no neutral ground? Who was there on both sides to be invested with plenipotentiary powers to conclude a peace? What precautions would be needed to guarantee the safety of both parties?

Renzi lay in his cell, more helpless and frustrated than he'd felt in his life before. He'd racked his brains, trying to conceive of a line of argument, a ruse even, that would repair the damage. But there was not a thing he could think to do.

The morning came and, with it, more hours of insufferable tedium in the little cell.

And then, a little before midday, Selim visited.

He was a different man. Calm, dignified and completely in possession of himself, he thought it only right to tell Renzi that, first, he had been informed the winds had changed and an assault by the British fleet was now foreseeably impossible. Then, in neutral tones, he allowed that at that very moment English captives from the fleet were being paraded through the streets before incarceration.

Renzi's mind reeled. Did this mean there had been an action and a British ship had hauled down its colours?

In dumb incomprehension, he heard further that Sébastiani had clandestinely landed troops and cannon on the main island overlooking the fleet and now was menacing the ships at their anchorage.

Selim looked at him kindly. 'I rather think this unpleasant business will soon be over, Fahn'ton Pasha. We will keep you here, perhaps until the ships are all gone, and then consult the circumstances to see if it be wise to restore you to your residence.'

'I thank you, Sire,' he muttered. 'You have been always most amiable towards me and I am truly grateful.'

The sultan's face softened. Then, hesitantly, he offered his hand. Just in time Renzi caught himself, and touched it to his forehead.

'I would that we could meet in more tranquil times, my friend.'

'There's much I would know about your great country and its ways, Seigneur. On a different occasion, perhaps.'

Renzi spent a miserable night. The worst of it was that he was in a fog of ignorance. He had been comprehensively outflanked by the brilliant Sébastiani.

But when morning dawned everything changed.

Voices sounded outside and the sultan burst in, his face contorted with anxiety.

'The wind, it has shifted. Fahn'ton Pasha – the fleet of Nelson, it has up its anchor, it sails to here!'

'You are saying the ships are heading for Constantinople?' he said in amazement.

'Yes, yes! What will happen? You must tell me!'

Throwing off the dull tiredness of his night, Renzi flogged his mind.

'Sire, it is very difficult for me to say from my place here. Cannot a way be found that I can see them for myself that I can better advise?'

Selim gave him a hunted look, then shot a volley of instructions at the chief eunuch. 'The morning prayers are not yet started. Go with Mahmut. He will take you high into the minaret where you may see them. But – this is a sacrilege. If you are discovered it will be death to you.'

'I go now, Sire.'

The steps up the slender minaret were a giddy torment but eventually he reached the tiny gallery at the top.

His eyes blinked at the strength of the morning sun. He stared out – and saw, in line-of-battle, the sails of Royal Navy battleships stretching away, one after the other into the distance.

In perfect station, there was no mistaking their course. Close to the wind at the northern point of the peninsula, they would then put helm down to fall before the wind, to come triumphantly down with starboard broadsides run out.

It was going to happen: Duckworth had finally lost patience and Constantinople was about to be cannonaded to a ruin.

Chapter 11

The voyage across the Sea of Marmora from Gallipoli was uneventful and, as intended, the fleet reached its anchorage as dusk was drawing in.

Kydd stood down *L'Aurore* but lingered on deck, the moment intense with the knowledge that he was part of an expedition that had as its objective the razing to the ground of ancient Byzantium. The Constantinople of the last Roman emperor. The glory of the Turks for a century or more before Shakespeare's time.

The war against Bonaparte was reaching new depths of ruthlessness, and who knew what else he would be called upon to wreak on the civilised world?

If his old friend Renzi could see this warlike array, what would he think? He would, no doubt, hear later of it in England, read of the part his former shipmate had played and shake his head sorrowfully.

The doomed city could not be seen from the deck but was in plain view from the tops. Several men had climbed up to look across the water of the Bosporus to the sight so enchanting in the early evening. In the morning those same domes and minarets would know the anger of their guns.

Depressed, Kydd left the deck for the solitude of his cabin. Dillon was still working there but gathered his papers and rose respectfully. If this had been Renzi there would most certainly have been a lively discussion in promise.

Impulsively Kydd asked, 'Tomorrow we destroy Constantinople. Does it not trouble you, Dillon?'

'We all have our duty, Sir Thomas,' he replied neutrally.

'That's not what I asked.'

'Sir, it's not my place to have views on the operations of this ship, whatever the outcome.'

'Not even when it involves the destruction of a great and noble city?'

'Sir.'

'And if I give you leave to say your mind?'

It was unfair to press the issue but Kydd felt a stubborn need to.

'Sir?'

'Say away, Mr Dillon.'

'Then, sir, I'd be obliged to reflect that it will stand on its own as a peerless act of barbarity, and under the flag of England. Will that be all, Sir Thomas?'

Kydd nodded sadly.

In the last of the light *Royal George* hung out the signal for all captains. Kydd's barge quickly pushed off to join the others that converged on the flagship.

Admiral Duckworth was at the entry-port in welcome and took them to his day cabin. It was of prodigious size compared to *L'Aurore*'s modest appointments and easily accommodated the dozen or so captains, seated around the broad table in strict order of seniority.

The admiral assumed his seat at one end, Arbuthnot at the other, looking peevish and ill-at-ease. Kydd sat next to Moubray of *Active*, another frigate, and opposite Blackwood, now a supernumerary in the flagship.

'Gentlemen, gentlemen,' Duckworth said genially, looking about. 'It's my pleasant duty to congratulate us on our success in penetrating the Dardanelles under arms, as we have, with virtually no loss. This stands as an achievement without parallel in history. Well done, all of you.'

There was a polite murmuring but every face was guarded.

'So, Mr Arbuthnot, what do you say to that, sir? We have fulfilled our mission and lie at the gates of Constantinople, as you have desired us. And tomorrow we are ready for the final sanction.'

He frowned at the ambassador's sour expression. 'Are you not content, sir? So ardent in your martial encouragements, I would have thought—'

'Spare me your comradely cheer, Admiral, if you would,' came the acid reply. 'And let us hear your plans for the morrow. I fancy it will be a long day.'

'Which we will endeavour to bear,' Duckworth said, with a sarcasm that appeared lost on him. 'So now I address myself to my captains.'

He picked up a paper. 'It will be a straightforward enough procedure, I'm persuaded, gentlemen. I have in my hand a note for the Sublime Porte, which will be delivered at first light. It contains a demand laid out in the strongest terms that the French will be ejected forthwith or they shall suffer the consequences.'

'Are these spelled out?'

'They are indeed,' Duckworth grunted. 'Failing they hand over Sébastiani and his scurvy crew, they then have the choice of surrendering their entire navy to me – or suffer a bombardment of half a thousand great guns that will leave their precious capital in ruin.'

'A hard chastising for a small enough thing,' Moubray murmured.

'Captain,' Duckworth said, in a tone that suggested a heavy irony, 'if you knew what Bonaparte plans in these parts you would be far warmer in your support. As it is, pray leave it that your superiors believe it to be the most devilish plot this age. Do you not agree, Ambassador?'

'I suppose so,' muttered Arbuthnot.

Swallowing his annoyance, Duckworth added huffily, 'And I've given them one half an hour to reply, after which we sail against them.'

A brooding silence was broken by Smith. 'As it doesn't have to be this way,' he said to no one in particular.

'What is it, Sir Sidney?' Duckworth said irritably. 'We're limited in our manoeuvring by our instructions from Whitehall, I'll remind you.'

'Which state objectives to be attained, the chief of which is the banishment of the French. Is not this the case?'

'Certainly. And I'd be exercised how else it shall be done, sir!'

'One quick way. I know Selim, he knows me, the wily coot. I whisper sweet reason to him and, with a battle fleet at my back, he cannot fail but to see the error in his ways. Let me go ashore and—'

'Damn it! Who's in command here? If anyone is to go it will be me, and I've no intention whatsoever of putting myself in the power of that Oriental despot. Let him hear the music of our guns and he'll come around, depend upon it.'

There was no more opposition: the fate of Constantinople was sealed.

'Very well. We being all of the same mind, let us get down to detail.

L'Aurore frigate will close with Constantinople at dawn and deliver the note. She will wait for the stipulated half an hour and if no reply, or an unsatisfactory response, is received will report the fact to me immediately.

'The fleet will then weigh and proceed to Seraglio Point, wearing in succession to assume line-of-battle southward. *Canopus* will be in the van and will refrain from opening fire until all vessels are in position opposite the Topkapi Palace and other such. Targeting will be easy enough. The Turk is obliging to have all his major edifices within close gunshot of inshore waters.

'Bombardment will be continuous until all the grander buildings are brought down. No sense in leaving any standing – the beggars will believe it's because we're not capable enough, and in any event firing will carry on until a cease-fire is signalled by me. The fleet will then return to this anchorage to await terms.

'Any questions? No? Then my order pack with signals and so on will be waiting for you after we have taken dinner together.'

In the early morning *L'Aurore* prepared for her duty. As if picking up on Kydd's mood her seamen moved sombrely as her anchor was brought to her bows and sail was spread abroad.

'I mislike this breeze, sir,' Kendall said, pursing his lips as he looked aloft. The upper sails were catching the slight wind steadily enough but the courses on all three masts were fitfully bellying and collapsing. 'Unless it picks up we'll be hard put t' cross the strait.'

The north-easter was fair for Constantinople but looking too scant to think to challenge the strong Black Sea current that surged through the narrow strait of the Bosporus.

'Keep us with it,' Kydd told the sailing master. 'There's much depends on *L'Aurore.*'

The anchorage was on the Asian side among offshore islands; once they rounded the point ahead they would be in the main stream and not two miles from the city across the other side.

But as they reached it Kydd felt the tug of the current across their bows, the give-away sagging off course to leeward.

'We'll not make it, sir,' Kendall muttered. 'It'll be a sad spectacle afore long.'

It was imperative that the note be delivered: the whole operation was now under way and the first act was Kydd's to perform. It couldn't be allowed to fail before it started, in a defeat by the winds and current.

To larboard was the open expanse of the Sea of Marmora, to starboard the continuous low coast of Anatolia a bare mile or so distant.

'I'll put into the bay beyond the point and anchor, send a boat.' It would be less impressive but better than seeing the frigate carried off helpless in the grip of the current.

It took an exaggerated tacking of nearly an hour to make the bay but they found good holding there and ignored the little fort, which in turn decided to take no heed of them.

'Mr Curzon. Away my barge under the largest flag of truce you can find to the steps of the palace and hand over the note, ensuring you have a signature and recording the time it was done.' The first lieutenant took the sealed packet, so innocent-looking, so deadly.

Kydd watched the boat make off under sail. Its fore and aft rig allowed it to point higher and he saw it reach the far shore. When sail was lowered it could no longer be seen but Kydd remained on deck anxious for its return.

It was more than an hour before Bowden's sharp eyes picked up the boat's sails hoisted once more.

Soon it was alongside and Curzon came aboard, spluttering with indignation. 'Unable to get it delivered, sir, the rogues!'

Kydd couldn't believe his ears. 'You mean they refused to take it?'

'Not even that. That rogue Kaptan Pasha in his fancy galley kept us off and when I went in anyway he fired on us.'

'With a white flag up? They can't have seen it.'

'I gave it more'n a few tries, sir,' Curzon said stubbornly.

'Well, rig two flags and lie to until they let you go in. They've got to get that note.'

Well into the morning, he was back.

'No damned luck, sir. Lets me sit there until I make a move in and then they fire away.'

Kydd cursed under his breath. Curzon was not to blame and there was no future in sacrificing a boat's crew in a gesture, but now he had to explain himself to the admiral.

'You – you've not even handed over the note?' Duckworth spluttered. 'After wasting all this time and they've not got our demands?'

He went red with frustration and the other captains pointedly looked away.

'I'm disappointed in you, Kydd, and I don't care who hears it. If you'd only—'

'He's not to know.'

'Wh-what did you say, sir?' Duckworth gobbled.

Sidney Smith languidly raised his eyebrows. 'Those who've been in the Levant more than a dog-watch have learned that a white flag means nothing to your Turk. They probably thought it an impertinence, with that colour topping it the sultan's flunkey to get on shore.'

'Damn it, Smith, I'll not hear of such tomfoolery. We're English, that's our tradition and they know it. This is a ridiculous state of affairs and I won't stand for it.'

He smouldered, then rounded on Kydd. 'Captain, I desire you to return and, by any means you choose, get that note in the hands of the Ottomans or you'll answer to me for it. Understood?'

On the way back to his ship Kydd reviewed his options. Force was out of the question; a boat of marines to fire back would only start a war. To capture a native craft and smuggle the note in was not possible: there was nothing prepared to be on the water, which was as clear as a swept board.

Then he remembered the supercilious Kaptan Pasha and his enormous turban – and before he had reached *L'Aurore* he had a plan.

'Lay 'em out, Tysoe – as quick as you may.'

In minutes he was ready and the weary boat's crew set out again for the shore, this time with their captain himself in the sternsheets looking grim and unforgiving.

The galley of Kaptan Pasha swept out and muskets were flourished.

'Keep on,' Kydd growled.

There were faint shouts and then the pop of musket fire.

The boat's crew fearfully ducked below the gunwale but Kydd made his way to the prow of the boat and stood up, dignified and erect.

It was an impressive sight. He was in formal full dress uniform with every star, decoration, length of gold lace and medal he had been able to find, glittering and imposing. It was foolhardy – but it worked.

The musket fire died away at the vision. Was this a great admiral pasha come to parley? A panjandrum of fearsome power demanding the sultan's presence? It would be folly to fire upon such, inevitably to answer later to the grand vizier for their rash act.

It was enough. The boat hastened to the Topkapi Steps and Kydd lordly stepped ashore. Too late, Kaptan Pasha hurried after him.

Kydd bowed and, with great ceremony, handed the packet to an unsuspecting minion, who unthinkingly presented it to the fuming official. It was then just a matter for Kydd to declaim, 'Sir, I have sufficient witnesses to state that this note to the Sublime Porte from my commander has been duly accepted by you.'

'They have it, sir.'

'Thank God for that. Now we'll see some action. I'd wager the whole palace is in a right commotion now, don't you think so?'

Arbuthnot got up abruptly and left the cabin.

'Odd fellow,' mused Duckworth, with just a hint of malice.

'We wait, sir?'

'For a space – let them stew.'

The wind was now brisk and fair. The moment the admiral

gave the word, in the same hour the entire fleet would have Constantinople under its guns.

After some time the flag-captain diffidently pointed out that the half-hour was well past but was met with a withering blast from Duckworth. 'I know that, damn it! Do you want the world to hear I ordered a bombardment without I wait for a reply?'

He glowered at the unfortunate man, then snapped, 'They don't seem to have any notion of what they're facing. I'll have to spell it out for them, the useless shabs.'

Within the hour he was back. 'Take this, Kydd. Make sure they sign for it or some such.'

'Aye aye, sir,' he replied, only too glad to get away from the tensions and boredom of inactivity.

There were no problems in delivery, and he was able to report its acceptance, even if by blank-faced functionaries.

After midday Duckworth took to his quarterdeck, pacing fiercely up and down. At two he threw his cocked hat to the deck. 'Good God! I've given those villains every chance but they've tried my patience too long. Mr Arbuthnot, we can't waste this northerly. I'm sailing against them in one hour. How does that please you?'

The ambassador looked uncomfortable. 'I'd rather we had our reply, Admiral. Give them a little longer, I beg.'

Duckworth glanced at him with irritation. 'Sir, you were the one on fire to bring the Turks to their senses. Why should we indulge 'em any further?'

'I'd be happier if we did.' The steel in his voice was unconcealed.

'Very well. But at four I move – a few hours of daylight is all I need to bring that damned place to a ruin.'

* * *

A little short of the deadline the officer-of-the-watch handed his telescope to Duckworth. 'Sir – I see a boat under sail come around the point, heading towards us.'

The admiral grunted. 'Odd-looking, but has some sort of colours up.'

It drew closer. Kydd recognised the vessel type from a past voyage to Smyrna: a small *tekne*. It flew a triangular red flag with a moon and stars in white. A dignified gentleman, with a long beard, wearing a large turban, was sitting in its after part.

'Hale him aboard, if you please,' Duckworth ordered, and went down to the entry-port to meet him.

Two stepped on deck, the other plainly a dragoman.

'Great lord, may I present the noble Isaac Bey of Roumelia. He has been charged by the Reis-ül Kuttab to treat with you in this grave matter.'

Duckworth gave a short bow. The old man approached, then waited with glittering black eyes.

'Give him your hand,' hissed Smith, from behind.

'Oh, yes. Pleased to meet you, sir.' He extended his hand – but when Isaac Bey took it, he brought it to his forehead and lowered his head.

In the uncompromising martial simplicity of the ship it was a touching gesture and Duckworth was taken aback.

The man looked up and spoke flowery phrases in a reedy, high-pitched voice. It seemed he was flattered and honoured to be addressing one of Nelson's great commanders and knew he would be listened to with gracious respect.

'Ah, invite him down into my cabin and pass the word for the ambassador.'

Seated at the polished mahogany expanse of the vast table, where war maps were more likely to be found, their visitor seemed diminutive and vulnerable. His dragoman respectfully drew up a chair, then Arbuthnot entered the cabin.

He saw the old man and started. 'Isaac Bey!'

'You know him?' Duckworth asked.

'He is a much-respected man in Constantinople, a childhood friend of the sultan and with a record of service second to none. You may understand him to be the most trustworthy of emissaries, Admiral.'

Pompously, Duckworth told the dragoman, 'Tell him that I also am honoured at the presence of such a name in my ship.'

'He is grateful for the opportunity to lay before you the dolorous condition in which the Porte finds itself.'

'Have him go on.' There was undisguised triumph on Duckworth's features.

He told of widespread fear and anguish in the population at their imminent destruction. Chaos and disorder on a scale that had made proper diplomatic dealings impossible. Worse, even, the helplessness of the Sublime Porte to placate the foreigners, to retain honour in the face of a naked threat to the sultan's authority, meant that a rising – a revolution by the lower orders – was no longer impossible. Sultan Selim might well be overthrown.

Arbuthnot got up, bent close to the admiral's ear and whispered, 'This is a catastrophic result, Admiral. If Selim goes, the French will step straight into the vacuum – recollect, Marshal Marmont's veterans are in Dalmatia with artillery and . . .'

'You bring grave news indeed, Isaac Bey, and I can see why you've come out to us with your dilemma. We must discuss this as a matter of urgency.'

It was midnight before the envoy left.

Duckworth wiped his brow in fatigue. There had been no

conclusion to the negotiations and he was tired, frustrated and angry.

'The man's as slippery as an eel,' he spat at Arbuthnot. 'Why you humour him so escapes me, sir.'

'For the reason he's trusted and respected on both sides, sir. Now if you'll excuse me, I'm to bed before I drop of mortal tiredness.'

'The man's playing with us, can't you see it? Wasting time, hoping we'll sail away.'

'Admiral, can't this wait until the morning? I'm—'

'Well, I wouldn't put it past the blackguards to be hard at it, throwing up defences and similar while we're wasting time with the old man.'

'There's nothing you or I can do about it now, in the middle of the night. For God's sake – let's get some sleep.'

Kydd awoke muzzily to Curzon's anxious pleading.

'Sir! It's first light and the flagship has a signal hung out. Sorry to wake you but—'

'Which?'

'Sir, "Fleet prepare to weigh".'

Kydd swung out of his cot. 'Damn! It's on – turn up the hands and—'

'I've piped "stations to unmoor" this minute, Sir Thomas.'

'I'll be on deck presently, Mr Curzon. I shall expect it to be completed when I am.'

He was damned if he was going up without a shave. An imperturbable Tysoe had razor and strop at the ready.

'Clear for action, sir?'

'No. We're not in the line-of-battle and, besides, I want the men to get a proper breakfast first.'

He, too, snatched a quick meal and hurried back up. Around him the big battleships were preparing for sea, fo'c'slemen at the cat-head with the fish tackle to secure the anchor when it came aboard, others at the braces in the waist trimming the heavy yards for a starboard tack when sail was set. A scene of seaman-like expectation.

At five minutes to eight the signal to weigh was hoisted, with the preparative flag, indicating that the manoeuvre would be executed the instant this was jerked down.

'Fo'c'slemen ready?' Kydd checked. Curzon responded with an injured look and turned back to watch the flagship.

The capstan was manned, the messenger secured to the cable. Joe Martin, *L'Aurore*'s best fiddler, sat on the capstan head waiting for the word. Aloft, the topmen were ready to lay out along the yard to loose sail to the wind.

Eight bells sounded out from the belfry forward, and from every ship in a discordant chorus.

The men stood expectantly at their stations, gazing across at the flagship for the signal.

After ten minutes there was baffled murmuring on the quarterdeck.

'A mort less than smart in their motions, Mr Curzon.'

'*We're* ready, sir.'

'I'm glad to hear it.'

More minutes passed and then, at a full hour later, Kydd stood the men down at their stations.

It was incomprehensible. A fleet at a split-yarn's readiness to sail and the preparative still close up? If the manoeuvre was cancelled, both flags would be struck – as it stood, the signification was that they could expect to proceed to sea at a moment's notice.

Another hour went by.

By now the men were lying on deck, telling yarns, taking a nap, laughing at well-worn mess-deck dits. If it lasted for much longer there would be real unrest, resentment at the imposition on their off-watch time.

Time stretched on interminably – at eleven another signal was made from *Royal George*.

'Our pennant, "Captain to repair on board".'

Kydd hastened to obey, as much out of consuming curiosity as duty.

He was not met at the entry-port by Duckworth, and a tight-lipped flag captain hurriedly escorted him to the admiral.

Admiral Duckworth was alone. 'Captain Kydd. I'll not have you misled in this. There has been . . . That is to say, there is a difference of opinion between myself and Ambassador Arbuthnot that leaves me unable to continue in a productive relationship with the fool.'

'Sir, may I know—'

'He's tacked right about and now thinks an armed descent on Constantinople a mistake. A mistake! He the one who stirred up Whitehall to get an expedition mounted in the first place, he the one badgering Collingwood for ships and guns – and now he's gone tepid on the whole idea. So what does he expect me to do with a first-class fighting squadron? Sit about and wait?'

He fumed and retorted, 'That's not my way, Kydd. I've done with this pettifogging diplomacy. You'll take my note of instant destruction by sunset if there's no favourable reply before that time. The only way to deal with the beggars.'

'Aye aye, sir.'

'And do go down and see Arbuthnot, there's a good fellow. He's in a sulk and insists his note goes along with mine.'

'Sir.'

The ambassador had taken over the first lieutenant's cabin with its private stern window looking out over the drab anchorage. It was at a gratifying separation from the admiral's quarters and was away from the noise and fuss of the higher levels.

Kydd knocked quietly on the door. 'Ambassador?'

Arbuthnot was seated at the little desk, papers untidily in front of him. He swivelled round.

'Ah, Captain. You'll be on your way with the admiral's note, then.'

His eyes were bloodshot, his voice unsteady, and he didn't hold Kydd's gaze.

'I am, sir. It was mentioned you had a note as well, sir.'

'I – I have. Which is to say, there will be one shortly. I've had a hard time drafting it, you see.'

'Sir. All the same, Admiral Duckworth wishes his note to be delivered forthwith.'

'May I ask you something, Captain?'

'Of course,' Kydd answered warily.

'These several days I've been haunted by a vision. One that I . . . cannot shake off.'

'A vision, sir?'

'Yes.' He played with his pen, then looked up and said, 'How would *you* like to go down in history, Captain? I would think as a brave and resourceful warrior of your sea world.'

'Why, yes.'

'So how would you feel, Sir Thomas, to be known down the ages as the man who destroyed Byzantium, the Hagia Sophia, a thousand and a half years of civilisation? Captain, I'll be for ever cursed by history. Every school child will learn of Arbuthnot the barbarian and—'

'Sir, in war there are many evil acts we're called upon to

do in the line of duty. But you know better than I the terrible consequences to us of Bonaparte gaining access to India and the world. If this act is the only way we can put a stop to French influence then we have to do it. No matter how we feel.'

That he was needed to put backbone into a state envoy was a sorry state of affairs.

'Then you're the same as all the others,' Arbuthnot said, with venom. 'More concerned to make distinction in the field in place of finer feelings. Do, then, glory in your destruction, Captain.'

Kydd stiffened. 'I'll wait a half-hour on the quarterdeck for your note, sir. After that, I leave. Good day to you, sir.'

Out in the open air under the eyes of the curious watch-on-deck he paced up and down, moodily reflecting on the idiocies he had been witness to. Now Duckworth was going ahead with the bombardment without support and agreement from the civil power.

'You're still here, Kydd?'

He wheeled around at the admiral's voice. 'The ambassador hasn't finished his note, sir. I told him I'd wait half an hour before I—'

'Damn his hide. He's to have it up here in ten minutes or not at all. What's he said to you?'

Kydd hesitated, but saw no reason to conceal his revelation. 'Sir, he feels he'll be cursed by history if he colludes in the bombarding of Constantinople.'

Duckworth recoiled in disbelief. 'The man's demented! Doesn't he understand what we're up against, damn it? God only knows what he's put in his note but if it crosses mine I'll see him in Hell.'

*   *   *

259

Just as he was about to leave, the ambassador's note came up and Kydd added it to the other in his dispatch satchel. He was piped down the side, glad to be quit of the flagship.

Light winds on the way to the Topkapi Steps made for a frustrating passage but the notes were finally delivered and he returned to his ship.

In the short time remaining before sunset a boat put out from the shore. In it was Isaac Bey once more heading straight for *Royal George*.

Kydd waited for a summons but none came.

And in the morning all options, all alternatives and all opportunities were made null. The light wind had backed into a gentle westerly. Dead foul for Constantinople.

The fleet was as helpless as if it were in a blockaded port. It was going nowhere. The initiative had passed out of their hands.

God only knew when the breeze would relent and give them a chance, but for now there was nothing but to stand down from sea routines and set about seeing to the ship with the never-ending tally of little tasks that could be done only while idle.

Around ten the purser came with a suggestion. 'We're low on green stuff as usual, sir. What do you say we make visit to one of these islands and bargain for some?'

Kydd agreed. As a light frigate *L'Aurore* had a limited hold stowage and always came to the end of her victuals well before the others.

'Mr Calloway, take away the cutter and a crew of trusties and land at Prota, that big island over there. Mr Owen will tell you what he wants in the way of supplies.'

As an afterthought, he added, 'And take along Midshipmen Clinch and Willock. They'll relish the jaunt.'

'And I, sir?' Dillon asked hopefully.

'Not this time.' Kydd had other plans. Without interruptions the day could be turned to advantage by the handing over of his private papers. It was the last stage of trust, but if he'd misjudged Dillon's character . . .

It was not as hard as he'd feared. The young man accepted politely and without question his origins and lack of an estate. Efficiently, and with a pleasing confidence, he set about organising things to best effect, separating ship business from personal matters and quickly finding his way around Kydd's life.

By mid-morning Kydd was happy to leave him to it. There were people in this world born to organise paperwork, had a gift for it.

He turned his attention to other concerns. The expedition would be over one way or the other in the not too distant future and the ships detached for it would be dispersed. Probably to Cádiz for *L'Aurore*. Already low on provisions he would need to think about storing and victualling for a transit of the Mediterranean. That meant Malta and—

'Sir?' A grave-looking Bowden popped his head around the door. 'I rather think you're needed on deck.'

Kydd gathered up his papers, passed them to Dillon, then followed him up.

A pale-faced Calloway was standing with Brice.

'Trouble, sir,' the third lieutenant said, seeing Kydd.

'Yes?'

'Calloway has returned from his provisions run.'

'And?'

'He reports four men missing.'

Calloway faced Kydd nervously. 'It's like this, sir. Poulden, Cumby and the two reefers went off to the market—'

'What were you doing?'

'Ah, stayed with the boat-keeper, sir. No taste for galli-vanting, like.'

No doubt they had shared a flask of something congenial while the others were away.

'Carry on.'

'When they didn't come back, as I told 'em, I got worried, went off to see what they was up to. The market was not a good place t' be, they all hard-faced an' all. No sign of our people so I went back to the boat, and that's when we saw 'em.'

'Who, damn it?'

'Up on the sides o' the hill. In uniform, coming down, and I swear they has muskets!'

'And?'

'Well, we didn't like the look of 'em, too many for us, so I lies off in the boat, hoping Poulden would come, but he doesn't. Then someone takes a pop at us like – the ball nearly takes Jevons, sir.'

'You were under fire?'

'Well, a few times. It weren't like regular soldiers.'

'And you saw uniforms.'

'My oath on it, sir.'

There had been a precautionary sweep of the islands when the fleet had come to anchor. Where had these come from?

'You were right to come back, Mr Calloway.'

It was not like an old hand such as Poulden to stray; the midshipmen were, in the Navy way, nominally in charge but would recognise the coxswain's moral authority and the steadying influence of the older boatswain's mate, Cumby.

'Mr Brice, away the cutter, Mr Saxton in charge,' he threw at the officer-of-the-watch.

'We're going back, Mr Calloway. Get hold of Stirk, ask him for four men, arm them and meet me in ten minutes.'

'Aye aye, sir.'

Kydd went down to his cabin to find his secretary.

'We're missing four men ashore, Dillon. I've no right to ask it, but it would be obliging of you to come with us when we look for them, to ask the villagers questions.'

'Sir Thomas, of course I'd be glad to – but the Turkish lingo is like no other. It originates in the great steppe lands and—'

'I'm sure you'll do your best. Now, I can't be certain we won't face a mort of pother. Are you up for it at all?'

'Certainly, sir.' The young man's eyes shone at the talk of danger.

A grim-faced Stirk and the men were waiting, fingering cutlasses and with a brace of pistols each in their belts. 'Shaky dos, sir, L'Aurores gone straggling in among all them Turks.'

Dillon saw the weapons and his eyes widened. 'Sir Thomas, you can't expect me to go on the land unarmed. May I?' He pointed to the lethal grey steel of a cutlass.

'Find Mr Dillon a slasher, if you please.'

The young man was delighted, and even more so when he was also handed a baldric and scabbard to fit over his plain black secretarial clothes.

'Mr Curzon, the ship's yours. If I'm not back in an hour or two send word to Admiral Duckworth. And no rescue parties – clear?'

'Sir.'

The boat put off and scudded in to the little jetty.

They looked around watchfully, ready for any hostile move. There was nothing – but Kydd could feel tension in the air. One or two villagers stopped to stare, their features defensive, while others walked hurriedly away.

'Where's the market?'

'Up the street t' the left, sir,' Calloway said uneasily.

They strode up the steep incline in a tight group, under orders not to draw weapons unless threatened.

The houses on either side were of nameless antiquity, poor with peeling shutters. The market was on level ground, still in full swing, noisy and crowded, but when the party came into view the babble fell away.

Kydd went to the nearest merchant, an onion-seller in a grubby turban with a seamed face. 'Dillon, ask him if he's seen anything of our friends.'

The man's beady eyes never left Kydd's as he listened. Then he spread his hands and shrugged.

Dillon took out a notebook and wrote some words in Greek. The man glanced at them, then drew back and spat on the ground. A murmuring began in the crowd gathering behind him.

Kydd gave a wry smile. 'We'll get nothing out of them. Can't spy any uniforms here – Calloway, where did you see them?'

He pointed up the steep street where the houses ended and the road continued up the hill.

Kydd knew it unlikely in the extreme that Poulden would lead the lads into temptation in some tavern or worse – had they gone into hiding at the sight of the uniforms?

'Stirk – give 'em a pipe.'

The gunner's mate pulled out his boatswain's call. The harsh shrieking of 'hands to muster' echoed from building to building across the other side, stopping conversations in the square.

'Again.'

The expressions on the crowd went from astonishment to curiosity, then to suspicion. But no shame-faced L'Aurores emerged.

Kydd faced a dilemma. It could never be justified later that he, a distinguished and valuable post-captain, had gone ashore to rescue stragglers, even with the excuse that on the strength of a vague report of uniforms on the island he had gone to take a look.

But if he gave up on them now and sailed away, the Navy would then consider the men deserters. An accusing 'R', for 'run', would appear next to their name on the ship's books and on recapture they would face a court-martial and the lash.

And if they were somewhere else? How far should he search in an increasingly hostile island? 'Calloway, when you spotted your uniforms, what direction were they going?' he snapped urgently.

'Like I said, sir. From over that hill and down this side, and—'

'I see. Back to the boat then,' Kydd ordered crisply.

They stood out to sea, ostensibly returning to *L'Aurore*, but then altered as if to report to the flagship and carried on to mingle with the usual ship-to-ship boat traffic.

'We're not looking any more, Sir Thomas?' Dillon asked.

'We're not returning on board, are we?' Kydd said, with an arch expression, and nodded to Stirk. He thrust down the tiller, put the cutter about and they stretched out through the passage between Prota and the next island, but as they passed close to the southern end Kydd growled orders that saw them heading for a tiny sandy cove.

They scrambled ashore, leaving the bows on a kedge out

to seaward. The boat's crew, under Saxton, the senior master's mate, readied the gear for hoisting in preparation for a rapid departure, if need be.

Where the diminutive beach ended to the right, a point of land jutted out. A tumble of brown rocks and scrub hid what was beyond.

Stirk was sent ahead, slipping and sliding up to the ragged crest of the point. He inched his head up – then ducked and beckoned furiously, a finger to his lips.

There were no paths and the pebble shale was loose and dusty, Kydd scurried as fast as he could to Stirk's side. He raised his head cautiously.

Anchored offshore was an inoffensive merchantman, brig-rigged, the usual maid-of-all-work around the Mediterranean, but it was off-loading field guns on to rafts for the short trip inshore. The Turks were using the delay to secretly land weapons to mount on the summit of the island to menace the British fleet.

Every instinct urged Kydd to get back to his frigate and fall on them but there were larger considerations. If troops and guns were already ashore, destroying the supply ship would do little to lessen the threat to the fleet.

He scanned the side of the hill above and spotted a monastery of the sort so common in these parts, but there was something odd about it: the windows were narrow and vertical. Loopholes! As he gazed at it he saw a line of men coming up from the landing cove, too far away to make out in detail but certainly on their way to it, and they all wore red and grey uniforms.

His duty was to alert Duckworth that his fleet was now under grave threat.

He turned to go – but there was a faint tap of a musket.

He looked back: high on the hillside the tell-tale white puff lazily drifted away. Some hawk-eyed individual with a view over the point had seen them.

Kydd snapped, 'Back to the boat!' but even as he said it, he saw a craft under sail put about and head their way. It was full of uniformed men and would get to their cutter before they could.

Heart thudding, he looked about desperately. 'Follow me!'

He scrambled up the slope, around the side of the hill. After a few minutes they were above the boat and he signalled frantically to them. Saxton caught on and had the cutter under way as the other came around the point.

The officer in command chose to chase the boat instead of landing his soldiers to go after those ashore. They had a chance.

It was brutal going, struggling along the stony hillside, ankles twisting, legs burning with effort.

Then they crashed through thorny scrub, cutlasses swinging, down into a gully, heaving and gasping.

They found themselves on the bare slopes above the little village. It was what Kydd had been hoping to see: beyond the huts, the fleet was anchored majestically in line across his vision.

'We're safe!' he gasped.

No Turk in his right mind with a boat full of soldiers would come into view of the fleet.

Breathless and hot, they ran on to the jetty and, with perfect timing, Saxton brought the cutter curving in.

'The damned rascals!' roared Duckworth. 'They've broken the terms of the cease-fire!'

He paced the cabin and stopped. 'They can't be allowed

to get away with it. Flags — orders. To *Canopus*: "Land strong reconnaissance party of marines and report".'

To Kydd, he said gruffly, 'Thank you for bringing this villainy to notice, sir. Leave this to me and get back to your ship. There'll be hot work to do before long, I believe.'

'Sir?'

'This is the last straw. I'm going against Constantinople as soon as there's a wind fair for that blasted place.'

'Will Mr Arbuthnot agree, do you think?'

'Ha! Mr Ambassador has just taken ill again and begs to be excused any further involvement. We're on our own at last, Kydd.'

As soon as he was decently able, Kydd returned to the sanity of *L'Aurore*. He had done what he could for his missing men. A strong body of marines was going to land on Prota; hopefully, they would sort it out.

Now, however, the last check on Duckworth was gone. What lunatic scheme would he dream up to salvage his reputation?

Shortly after midday signs of battle could be seen arising beyond the hill-crest on Prota.

Kydd guessed they were coming up to the monastery on the other side. It raged on — they must be in a stiff fight. A little later one of the landing boats left the jetty and made for the flagship under a press of sail.

'"Ships to send reinforcements",' a signal midshipman reported. 'Pennants include ours, sir.'

L'Aurore's contribution mustered in the waist. Twenty Royal Marines with accoutrements in impeccable order. Kydd went down to inspect them, taking a quivering salute from Lieutenant Clinton. He passed down the two ranks slowly, and at the end turned to him and said loudly, 'Take care of these men while you're on shore, Lieutenant. They're the finest we have.'

He watched as they landed and formed up on the jetty, heading off smartly in a spirited display of scarlet and white. But it failed to lift his heart. Were they marching to disaster, trusting in their superiors to make winning plans and decisions? In his bones he knew they would fail – and good men would pay with their lives.

From Whitehall's interference to Duckworth's irresolution in the face of the ambassador's conflicting advice, he had seen the all-too-human side of high command.

He chased Dillon out of his cabin and took up his favoured chair by the stern windows.

In the past Renzi had sat in his place on the other side with a quizzical smile as Kydd shared his doubts and hopes.

But now came the dawning realisation that he no longer had need of advice, comforting reassurance, the logical perspective. If he felt the necessity for any of them, he would find it within himself. As was right and proper for a leader of men.

The afternoon wore on with no news, but as the shadows lengthened the boats began returning. One of them *L'Aurore*'s.

In it, a bandaged figure lay full length. Kydd didn't need to be told. It was Clinton.

He was hoisted aboard, those near hearing him moan softly at the pain as he was taken below to the surgeon. There were other wounded – and Kydd counted only seventeen in the party.

Later he had the lieutenant brought to the coach and placed in an officer's cot.

Kydd sat with him but it was well after dark before he

came back to consciousness and some time before he could recognise his captain.

'How goes it for you, William?' Kydd asked.

'S-sir, what . . . am I doing here?'

'Never mind. Ship's company at their grog, too noisy for a sufferer,' he answered gruffly.

The field guns Kydd had seen landed had been turned on the British and a six-pounder ball impacting near Clinton had driven shards of rock into his body and caused a concussion.

The marine had stood at Kydd's side in the climactic last days of siege in Buenos Aires and other adventures too numerous to recall. His heart wrung with pity at the thought of the young officer leaving his bones to rot here – and for what grand cause?

'Surgeon thinks you've a good chance, William.' It wasn't quite what had been said.

'My r-report, sir.' The voice was weak and slurred but piteously determined.

'Not now, dear fellow,' Kydd said.

But Clinton was going to do his duty. It came out painfully, with pauses to gather his strength.

The first to land had not known the extent of the enemy infiltration until they had rounded the hill and come under fire from concealed gun emplacements protected by the fortified monastery.

They had held their ground until the reinforcements from the fleet had reached them. Jointly it was decided that the guns were too big a threat to be ignored. Mounted on the crest overlooking the fleet, they could place it under a pitiless onslaught of steady, aimed fire.

The problem was that any advance on the gun-pits would

be dominated by musket fire from the loopholes of the monastery. One course would have been to land their own guns for an artillery duel but that would take time.

It had to be a frontal assault with no wavering and this had been bravely accomplished. The monastery was taken, the guns spiked and the enemy in full retreat. But before it had ended Clinton had lost three men killed and much of his detachment wounded.

Then orders had come to return on board.

Without knowledge of events on the island Duckworth had obliged them to break off and leave it to the Turks.

'Thank you for your report, Lieutenant,' Kydd said softly. 'You have done your duty most nobly, sir.'

Dawn came, and with it, what Kydd had been most dreading. The wind had veered during the night and now was fitfully blowing from the north-east. A broad reach to Constantinople in one board.

It was fair at last for the bombarding of the ancient city.

Like the tragic conclusion of a Greek drama, each of the main players stepped through their parts to the inevitable climax.

A signal mounted in the flagship's halliards: 'Weigh and proceed as previously ordered'. Obediently the warships of the squadron raised anchor and ensigns rose in the ships as they manoeuvred into line-of-battle.

In the delicate early light, the terrifying majesty of the spectacle was made poignant by the knowledge of what was to come. The Ottomans had broken the cease-fire and must now endure the consequences. That morning there would be scenes of destruction that would resound around the world.

L'Aurore took her position to starboard of the line. With

the other frigate, her duty was to keep watch to seaward as the battleships did their work. At least Kydd's ship would have no direct part in the ruin of the city.

The wind strengthened; sails caught and bellied, speeding the ships on to their destiny. Very soon magnificent buildings, olive groves and the splendour of the imperial palace spread out ahead, firming from a blue haze.

Within the hour they would . . .

Kydd grabbed a glass.

Stretching all along the seafront were moored warships, large and small, a ringing of the peninsula with a continuous line of guns. Kydd steadied his telescope further in – on the cannon manned and waiting, an unbroken chain of artillery that encircled the capital.

A monstrous gathering of strength, an insuperable barrier that even a battle-fleet could not batter down.

They were too late.

Duckworth signalled the fleet to reverse its course in succession. It did so, carefully out of range. The shore guns remained silent.

Another signal – 'wear and advance'.

Tacking and veering in front of Constantinople, the admiral flaunted his might at the Turks in the hope of luring them to sea and a confrontation. Again and again, up and down, but the Turks never stirred from their unassailable positions.

It was useless, humiliating, and could have only one ending. Before the close of the day the British fleet had retreated: spread sail and set course southward for the Dardanelles and the wider world.

As they sailed into the darkness there was little cheer in *L'Aurore*. It was clear to the humblest crew member that the expedition, bigger by far than had taken Cape Town and Buenos Aires, comparable in scale to anything seen in the Mediterranean since Trafalgar, had completely failed.

To Kydd, it now seemed plain that, with their helplessness so vividly demonstrated, French influence could only increase to the point at which Bonaparte might at long last look to bursting out of his European confines.

And there was now no conceivable hope that anything could stop the inevitable slide from influence to power, from there to domination and rule, just as it had in so many countries. Would Bonaparte insist that the next sultan be a brother or cousin, crowned and loyal to France only? He would then have his royal road to India and the world.

It was an utterly depressing thought, made worse by their very helplessness.

That night the gun-room invited him to dinner. He was grateful, for a black mood had clamped in – not only at their dismal failure but at the news that Poulden, Cumby and the midshipmen had not been found in the monastery. He was leaving them behind to their fate in a Turkish prison.

'Cádiz will be a sad let-down after this,' Bowden offered.

'A pox on that,' retorted Curzon. 'Any station that offers me a trifle of sport at the Frogs' expense will do.'

'Afore there's talk o' going back,' Redmond, the gunner rumbled, 'there's a little matter should give us pause.'

'What's that, then?'

'Yez saw how quick-smart your Turk was, gettin' the defences as they were, in only a few days? Now, if they's as nimble in the Dardanelles, we're in for a right mauling as we sails down past them forts.'

'Wasn't so bad coming up, Thad,' Oakley said. 'All a mort pitiful, them Turks as had a try at us.'

'Ah — that's because they weren't expectin'. I'll give youse a guinea to a shilling that they, knowin' we has to go back the same way, has somethin' in the way of a farewell salute in mind.'

'How piquant.'

Everyone looked suspiciously at the surgeon Peyton, who rarely spoke at gun-room gatherings.

'What do y' mean, Doc?'

'Why, can't you see? The French are the enemies of Turkey and have been since 'ninety-eight when they invaded their territory in Egypt. We're their allies from the same date. So who's firing at whom?'

'All a bit murky f'r an old shellback like me,' the boatswain growled. 'I'd be beholden to the cap'n to give us a steer.' In the recent past the question would have been directed at Renzi.

'Not so hard to fathom. I'm grieved to say it, but we're seeing yet another country drop into Napoleon's bony hands. Unless we can come up with some sort of stratagem, I fear we're witness to yet one more conquest.'

'Stratagem? You mean land an army or some such, sir?'

'Well, something — anything as sees Johnny Crapaud put to embarrassment, is all I can say.'

'No chance o' that now, I'm thinking. We're scuttling off like frightened rabbits, no glory in that a-tall.'

The evening tailed off, none of the usual jollity — well polished yarns, songs, sly digs and honest laughter. How could it be otherwise, with the pitiful burden of pain and suffering in the coach above and every mile they sailed into the night separating them from their chubby-faced midshipmen and honest British tars in some Turkish dungeon?

* * *

The next day the fleet was informed it was Duckworth's decision that, as they had intention of making the straightforward passage of Gallipoli at night, they would anchor at Marmora Island, thirty miles from the northern entrance of the Dardanelles and there they would water.

Kydd had his reservations. Would not this give warning of the British re-passing? Nevertheless a chance to re-stow with fresh water was always welcome.

The anchors went down in the lee of the island, off a tiny fishing village nestling snugly beneath bare mountains. The watering place near the tip of the sharp headland could accommodate only a few boats at a time and several took the opportunity to land in the port to bargain for fish and vegetables.

'Go with 'em, Dillon. You never know what you might hear.'

After the loss of their shipmates on another island they were taking no chances, and the launch with its water leaguers was accompanied by a full section of armed marines.

They arrived back some hours later and Dillon hurried to Kydd. 'Sir Thomas, I've disturbing news that I'm not sure you'll want to hear.'

'I'll be the judge of that.'

It was an extraordinary tale. An old fisherman, an ethnic Greek, had approached Brice with information to offer. His broken English could not easily be made out and Dillon was brought across. With a mix of makeshift modern Greek, a little English and much signing, the essence was learned.

After the first forcing of the Dardanelles the Turks had been enraged. Knowing they must return the same way, this time there would be a nasty surprise for the insolent British at its narrowest part. Monster guns would be put in place to smash the helpless ships to splinters. The very ones that the great Sultan Mehmet had used many centuries before to batter his way into Constantinople and bring down the Byzantine Empire and the last Roman Caesar.

The old man had seen them pass with his own eyes and had asked the marching gunners about them. He was told they were the biggest guns in the world, firing marble shot of immense size, each weighing as much as four men. No ship could pass them and live.

He had begged the English admiral to think again about going back through.

'I had no reason to disbelieve him, Sir Thomas. He had little to gain by telling us a fabrication.'

There was nothing for it but to go to Duckworth with the information.

'Monster guns? I'd believe eighty-pounders – we saw some great shot thrown at us on our way up, but more than that, I doubt it. I think your man's been practised upon – how the devil would they load the piece if they can't lift the ball? And what sort of charge would you need to . . . No, it's just not possible.'

'There may be some truth behind it, sir.'

'Dragging out an old museum piece to frighten us? Where would they get the ammunition, hey? No, Kydd. We'll be having a warm time of it at Pesquies but not like that. I'm surprised at you, upsetting your people with wild rumours from damned foreigners.'

At dusk they weighed for the Dardanelles.

As before, they made the transit of Gallipoli in pitch darkness. This time the night was split apart by gun-flash in a frenzy of violence but they sailed on untouched. In the morning they were well down the passage and nearing the awkward dog-leg about Point Pesquies and Abydos, which had to be navigated in daylight.

At full alert the fleet stole on, gun-ports open, ready for what must come in the narrows. Battleships in line ahead, frigates on either side.

There was an eerie quiet as the head of the line closed with the same point of land where Smith's division had over-whelmed the Turkish force. The many wrecks were still there and the sour stink of destruction lingered.

The first ships rounded the point – and first one, then another titanic blast of sound erupted, like an earthquake sending shock-waves through the ground and water.

Almost too quick to register, Kydd saw a brief blur that transformed a seaman into a hanging red mist and flung his shipmates into a huddle of bodies. Then, with a violent crash, the ball went on to send the main-mast of *Windsor Castle* teetering and falling like a great tree in a forest.

Another fearful roar of sound, now accompanied by a tempest of other cannon-fire. It stunned the senses but Kydd reasoned the mammoth guns would not be wasting their gargantuan shot on mere frigates: they would be going after the big three-deckers.

'Shiver the tops'ls,' he bellowed. *L'Aurore* slowed until she could slip in astern, out of the line of fire. Towering pyramids of smoke ashore drifted over, masking targets for her own gunners, but under the furious storm of shot the only essential was to get off a convincing reply.

The noise was indescribable. Could they survive the holocaust?

He watched helplessly as, ahead of them, *Windsor Castle* grappled with their damage. She was under topsails but the loss of her biggest mast with its staysails badly unbalanced the ship.

An out-of-control battleship would effectively block the escape of others behind.

Kydd looked in dread past her to *Repulse* as one of the massive shots struck and sent up a spray of black specks – how much more could they take?

The firing reached a mind-numbing crescendo – but then he saw how they had a chance. The wind was not only fair but now from dead astern, urging them on without the need for *Windsor Castle* and others to risk sail manoeuvres. And the monster guns might have been giant in calibre but this brought with it a fatal disadvantage – a paralysingly slow rate of fire.

They had only to win through the narrows and they would be in the open sea.

The furious cannonade became ragged and gradually died, the gun-smoke clearing. There had been devastation and casualties but the fleet was still together, every ship under way in a blessed release.

There were a few desultory shots from Cape Janissary and then they were free of the Dardanelles.

Tenedos was the fleet rendezvous. The anchors had barely gone down when a demand was signalled for a damage survey and casualties report. *L'Aurore* had escaped lightly: a scored yard, rigging parted, two small shot-holes. And one seaman killed with three lying moaning in their hammocks. Clinton was now fully conscious and showed every sign of being on the mend.

It was a different matter for some of the others. The gigantic stone ball strike Kydd had seen had smashed through

Repulse's poop, splintering the deck, carrying away her wheel and nearly severing her mizzen-mast. As it did so, it had killed both quartermasters, five seamen and three marines, and wounded many more in a single blow.

Standard had been cruelly mauled but steady work had seen her taken in hand just as *Thunderer* and others came under fire from the opposite shore.

Canopus had been pierced through and seen her helm dissolve into splinters; *Royal George* had suffered shrouds carried away and masts injured. One of the immense marble shot had not gone completely through the massive 100-gun first rate and was lodged below.

The reporting captains went down to inspect the monstrous object – an obscenely huge, pale sphere stuck in the fore-peak timbers. The carpenter was summoned to take a measure of the beast and reported it as more than six feet around; quick calculation revealed it as being near five men in weight. The old fisherman had not exaggerated.

The roll of dead and injured was long, but not as grievous as the searing experience had foreshadowed. At thirty killed and 138 wounded, the fleet had escaped lightly for its temerity in challenging the Ottoman Turks.

Duckworth made it plain he was not about to waste time in recrimination and the captains returned to their ships. After immediate repairs the fleet was to sail in three days, away from the scene of their humiliation.

But just before anchors were weighed, the Russians arrived: six ships-of-the-line and five frigates in immaculate order. Allies of the British and in a stroke doubling their force. This was now a legion capable of a major fleet action and therefore things had changed radically.

While elaborate salutes were exchanged, Kydd looked with

279

interest at the ships. Virtually the same as their own, even down to the Nelson chequer, the only real difference from the outside was the colours: the double-headed black eagle on a yellow banner of the Romanovs.

Their seamanship was capable enough, coming to a moor opposite as if to demonstrate how it was to be done.

It was not long before a ceremonial barge put out from the Russian flagship to make its way to *Royal George*, the dash of colour in the sternsheets contrasting with the plain grey of the boat's crew.

The sound of the Russian admiral piped aboard carried clear across the water and Kydd saw him go up the side steps and disappear into the entry-port. What happened in the next hour was going to determine the fate of so many.

Surprisingly quickly, the Russian emerged and his boat returned to his own ship.

This first meeting was probably only preliminary, Kydd reasoned, setting a time for lengthier deliberations on how the allies would co-operate.

Soon after, Kydd was summoned to *Royal George*.

'That was Admiral Senyavin,' Duckworth grunted dismissively. 'Seems to think if we joined forces we'd have a better chance against the Turk. I told him it was nonsense – if the Royal Navy couldn't achieve anything then adding an odd few Russians won't change things.'

'So he's leaving, sir?'

'No, Kydd. We leave, he stays. That is why I sent for you. Don't forget the Russians are in a state of war with Turkey. He's under orders from his tsar to attack them and dare not disobey. What I want you to do is just stay here, see what happens. They'll fail, of course, but we need to know the details. Shouldn't take long.'

'Sir.'

'No need to get involved, no heroics, just observe is all.'

'Aye aye, sir.'

Kydd watched the British fleet sail away, the feeling of unworthy failure lifting with their departure, and he settled to observe the Russians.

It felt odd, *L'Aurore* anchored within plain sight, watching them at their domestics. An occasional flash on the quarter-deck of their ships showed it was not altogether a one-way thing.

He wondered whether it would be a politeness to call on Admiral Senyavin but decided not. There was every chance they would give up and leave very soon, in which case he would be released.

The following day, however, at eight in the morning the L'Aurores were treated to the sight of bands on each ship coming to life and flags rising in a stream in the rigging. The Russians were dressing ship for some occasion.

A little later a boat put off, heading directly for *L'Aurore*. In the sternsheets sat a young officer in full ceremonials. The boat came smartly alongside and the officer stiffly boarded, his bearing impeccable. With a bow and a click of the heels, he handed Kydd a sealed letter.

It was formally addressed to the captain of *L'Aurore* frigate in proper naval terms and in English. The young man waited: an answer was clearly expected.

Kydd opened it. 'An invitation to join the admiral and officers of the *Tverdyi* on the occasion of the anniversary of the accession of Tsar Alexander I of Russia.'

'Well, now, and do you remember the Ivans in the Adriatic before Trafalgar at all?' Curzon rubbed his hands in glee. 'I've a yen to see 'em again, a pretty notion of entertaining as I remember.'

'Shall I take a notebook, Sir Thomas?' Dillon said lightly. 'No knowing what will be said.'

'It will be full-fig uniform and swords, I'd imagine,' Bowden said, buffing his lace absent-mindedly.

'And if y' requires more stout hands—'

Kendall's barely disguised plea was cut off. 'I shall have need of only the first and second lieutenant and my secretary. Mr Brice to remain in command.'

They were welcomed over the side of the 74 with full ceremony and escorted to the wardroom, where solemn toasts were proclaimed.

When Kydd left to talk with Admiral Senyavin in his great cabin, the wardroom was well advanced in merriment, drunken cheers and off-key bass voices. Curzon had mimed an old navy wardroom turn, and Bowden's light baritone was delivering 'Sweet Lass of Richmond Hill' to a bemused audience of burly sons of the steppes.

Kydd had vivid memories of vodka and had to plead his stomach to avoid the many refills thrust on him. He wanted to remain clear-headed. From what Duckworth had said, Senyavin had some crucial decisions to make and needed information. And what better source than one who had just returned from the field?

The Russians were at war with Turkey, and for the usual reason. The Black Sea had the only ports in Russia that were free of ice year round. A major part of their trade plied from there, grain and timber from the Crimea and the vast interior, imports from the greater world flooding inward. Yet there was a fatal weakness in its situation: access was by only one route – the Dardanelles. Any disagreements with Turkey, and it was instantly closed to Russian ships, an intolerable provocation.

Was Senyavin really thinking of striking at the Ottomans? Now aroused and heavily defended?

'Perhaps a little cognac – it will be easier on the stomach.' Senyavin's English was good; it was rumoured he had spent some time with the Royal Navy.

'That's kind in you, Admiral,' Kydd answered politely.

'Please, "Dmitry" while we are alone, sir.' He was a small man but with a controlled intensity and neat manners.

The great cabin was sparse and dark-timbered, small portraits and Russian country scenes the only concession to domesticity. A large, frowning Tsar Alexander dominated one side and the few pieces of furniture were sombre and heavy.

The cognac was excellent and Kydd allowed himself to be seated in a chair by the stern windows.

'You have passed through the Dardanelles under fire, Captain. My congratulations – it is something we've never been able to achieve.'

'Thank you, Dmitry. It has to be said, the giant guns at Point Pesquies gave us pause.'

Freedom of the seas was second nature to the Royal Navy; he tried to see things from the Russian's point of view.

To get here, with the Dardanelles closed to him, Senyavin would have had to sail his squadron the thousands of miles from Kronstadt, in the deep Baltic around Scandinavia, through the Channel, past hostile France and Spain, then the whole length of the Mediterranean. Yet only at the opposite end of this same strait, past Constantinople, there lay the Black Sea Russian fleet at Sebastopol no more than a couple of days' sail away.

And he was being ordered by his tsar to strike at the Turks

and free their stranglehold. Duckworth's refusal to join with them must have been a bitter blow.

'I've heard that you were before Constantinople threatening a bombardment.' The tone was cautious but respectful.

'The winds failed us in the end,' Kydd replied. 'Without brisk airs we couldn't cross the current, and when we did the French had strengthened defences to the point at which we couldn't contemplate a confrontation.'

Senyavin, even if he didn't already know it, would hear all this later anyway.

'Ah, the French. Such a great pity we could not have gone forward together to bundle the vermin out of Constantinople.'

'Well, yes.' He was not going to commit himself to commenting on Duckworth's strategics.

The admiral sighed. 'And now I'm being asked to take the war to the Ottomans. If Nelson's fleet cannot achieve a humbling, what chance is there for me?'

Was he fishing for a suggestion or just making conversation?

'We saw little of the Turk Navy as would cause us to tremble, Dmitry. Why not bring 'em to battle, sweep them from the sea? You'll then have only the guns to worry about.'

'You saw few because they were arrayed in the north against our Black Sea fleet, holding it powerless. Now it will be a different matter, but still we are outnumbered by an unacceptable margin.'

Kydd sympathised, but what could he do?

'I can give you help with currents, gun emplacements and similar,' he said. 'We noted them down, every one.'

Senyavin's face set. 'I'll be frank. It's not a risk we can take, that our ships are destroyed in the eyes of the Turks. It would give them hope and excuse for vain display at our expense and my place at Court will be compromised. Yet I must do something.'

But then there was one thing Kydd could suggest. Perhaps the most effective weapon of all against Bonaparte – why wouldn't it work here too?

'Dmitry. Your ships and trade are choked off, can't move. We ourselves have long experience of this, and we call it the blockade by which we embarrass the French in their home ports.

'Why don't you turn it on its head and pay back the Turk in his own coin? Mount a formal blockade of the Dardanelles, seal it off so no Turkish trade can exist?'

'A blockade of our own?' He rubbed his chin. 'We're not familiar with this. Unless it's effective and complete, it will be seen as an act of the weaker.'

'I will tell you how you can do it, Dmitry. First you need a base, and what better than here at Tenedos? Now, blockade is in several depths and . . .'

Kydd went on to describe the complex multi-layered organisation that he'd first learned of in *Teazer* and the Channel fleet, the small ships to intercept, the larger to threaten retaliation for a sally, the constant sea-keeping with victualling support, the vigilance and steadfastness.

Senyavin was a swift learner and saw that, with the Black Sea fleet turned active at the opposite end, the result would be the entire Dardanelles and Bosporus a dead zone for the Turks.

'I'm grateful indeed for your advice, my friend. I rather think I will do it . . .'

Chapter 12

Renzi descended slowly from the minaret, stunned. He had vaguely recognised one or two of the British ships but their war flags were unmistakable. And there had been no doubt about their course – it was direct for Constantinople. But now they were sailing away, with not a single shot fired. What in the name of all the devils in Hell were they about?

Even in the little passage heading back to his cell he could hear the shouts of jubilation, the crack and pop of muskets fired into the air, raucous drumming, full-throated yelling; he winced at the humiliation.

Mahmut closed the door quietly and left.

It was an unmitigated catastrophe. With the only effective card the British had, played so disastrously, Renzi's situation was now impossible. Before, he had had the ear of the sultan. Now . . .

He lay on the low bed, moodily staring up. The French had won by default and were now in a position to complete their grand project.

It was over.

With all options closed, there was nothing for it but to return to London and admit failure on his first mission.

At least he'd be quit of this place of menace and ignominy.

The evening gloom closed in with no lessening of the racket outside and time passed drearily.

A rattling at the door disturbed his melancholy. But it was only Mahmut, bringing leftovers from some celebration feast.

Renzi picked at it: lamb *yahni* and pomegranate sherbet. He knew he wouldn't be allowed to depart without getting leave from Selim who, significantly, had not visited to discuss these final developments. Unease pricked him. On one hand he stood to be quietly forgotten as an embarrassment, to be done away with at a convenient time; on the other, if the French got to hear of him, it would be in Selim's interest to hand him over to General Sébastiani.

The next day the sultan appeared in the afternoon without warning.

'Seigneur, how kind in you.' Renzi bowed.

Selim wore a magnificent turquoise and crimson gown with a large turban and pearls, clearly just returned from some grand occasion. Renzi, in his clothes of some days, and unshaven, tried to keep a lordly countenance.

'Fahn'ton Pasha, I've come to release you from this unfitting confinement.'

'Liberty is most precious to the human soul when it is absent, Sire.'

'Ah, perhaps not liberty.'

Renzi felt a stab of alarm. 'I had hoped to—'

'It would be foolish for an Englishman to venture abroad at this time. I have thus arranged accommodation for you at a remove from this, but perhaps not to your accustomed degree of comfort. However, you will be safe there.'

'Thank you, Sire. It would be of some gratification to me to know what has transpired since I . . . was brought here. I have had no news.'

'Certainly. Things are much clearer to me now.' He gave a tight smile. 'Even you can see that the British are powerless, for this is a contest on land, not on the sea where they are at their strongest. Our own borders are far from the sea, to the very Danube, and there the Russians are intriguing in the hope of expanding their empire at our cost. What we need are strong friends who can help us stand against them – armies, not navies.'

'And you believe the French will offer you this?'

'They have already done so, and I'm minded to accept.'

'Their price a formal alliance.'

Selim looked at him thoughtfully. 'You are astute, indeed, for a simple scholar, Fahn'ton Pasha.'

'Seigneur, I thank you for the compliment, but confess to you that it is only what is readily to be observed in any country that falls under the sway of Napoleon Bonaparte. First the sweet words, then the formalities, and after, domination at the highest levels, which leaves the nation subservient to the wishes of the French. Finally there is placed on the throne yet another of Bonaparte's family. Shall I rehearse to you the countries of Europe that have been served so? It is—'

'Thank you, no,' the sultan said sharply. 'Recollect to whom you are speaking, sir!'

'My humble apologies, Your Majesty,' Renzi said, with a deep bow. 'It is only my regard for your person and the dignity of the great Ottoman Empire that obliges me to speak in such manner.'

288

Selim's expression did not change, but he went on quietly, 'Nevertheless, I shall give your words careful thought before the alliance is signed, for it would grieve me deeply to make an enemy of your people, as no doubt I shall be required to do.'

Renzi knew that feeling against the English was running high: was Selim just exercising a degree of discretion in not revealing one in protection within the Topkapi Palace? There could be more sinister motives: the retaining of a high-value hostage for the inevitable confrontation with Britain, when their treaty was abrogated and interests aligned with the French.

Mahmut came for him after dark to take him to his new quarters.

The location was brilliantly conceived. He would be concealed in plain view – and in perfect safety.

In the second courtyard was the tallest structure in the palace. The Adalet Kulesi, the Tower of Justice, symbolised the eternal vigilance of the sultan against oppression. His people from far and near could look upon it and be reassured.

There were three storeys, and Renzi's was to be the uppermost, the bare floor area cunningly set out with silk tents in imitation of a pasha's field camp.

He was greeted in the middle storey by his wide-eyed staff and Zorlu, to one side.

'You have been here long?'

'Not so long, m' lord,' Jago replied imperturbably. 'As we was taken up when you went to . . . to where you went. Been here since, m' lord.'

It would have been good to know they were secure while he had been distracted in his cell.

Zorlu listened intently to his experiences. 'I rather fear your anxieties are not misplaced, my lord. The sooner we are gone . . .'

Renzi saw that the tower had some useful features. It was for the sole use of the sultan and therefore entrance was only from the harem. At the top there was a grilled observation port for Selim's viewing pleasure and in its lower part the 'Golden Window', a means of secretly listening to the deliberations of the grand vizier's Divan, the Imperial Council, which was adjacent.

There was a sense of order and normality; Jago had not been flustered at being spirited away into these singular surroundings, and the basics of a household were in place.

'A bath, and then a shave,' he decided.

'Certainly, m' lord.'

Ablutions completed, and wearing a fresh-smelling kaftan, Renzi explored their little world. The viewing port on his floor allowed a fine sight of the Gate of Felicity and the area in front of the Imperial Council Hall, as well as providing a lookout over the whole city.

The mechanics of supporting the little group were simple. At set times Jago, with his Turkish interpreter, would meet one of the eunuchs at the ground floor and their needs would be explained. These, with meals and fresh water, would appear and be carried up by Golding and the others and routine would be observed.

The Lord Farndon would not want for comforts, it seemed.

That night Renzi lay in an opulent fur-spread bed in his 'tent' and tried to make sense of events.

The French were about to become effective rulers. Did he not then have a duty to remain and see what happened? Yet there was little point if he could not report and he had no way to communicate with the outside world.

His central mission was to bring about the ejection of the French from their position of influence. Nothing else mattered.

He forced his mind to an icy calm.

The key to it all was Selim. Only he had the authority to bring it about. But he had chosen to go with the French. They offered the only security against the Russians and English, had armies in the Balkans that could be called upon, and since the Nile, Bonaparte had gone out of his way to woo him, above all with military advisers who had done much to reform the Turkish Army.

The French were identified now with national security and the new world order. The sultan would be a fool to turn his back on them.

Renzi's thoughts darkened as he considered every alternative, irrespective of honour or morality. It chilled him for he found his logic hardening into a conclusion that was as inexorable as it was cold-blooded.

If Selim was leading Turkey into this alliance, he had to be stopped, removed from the equation.

A Russian invasion would do it, but there was little chance of that in the near future. The alternative was appalling to contemplate. Assassination. Presumably by himself.

There was excellent opportunity, for they always met alone and he was trusted above most. It wouldn't be difficult.

Renzi's very being was revolted at the treachery but his merciless logic asked if he had a more effective answer.

He didn't. The consequences he must put aside: it would probably end with his unpleasant demise – better he took a pistol to himself first.

An image of Cecilia thrust itself unbearably into his mind. All he had to do was to wait it out and he would eventually be back in her arms in the opulence of Eskdale Hall and . . .

He crushed the thought and focused on the present. How much did he believe in his mission? An assassination would achieve its object – there would be no alliance, no road to India and empire for Bonaparte. Almost certainly an immeasurable adversity to his country would have been forestalled and it was in his power to do it.

It was not too late – for if he drew back, didn't go through with it, no one would ever know.

But he would have to live with the failure for the rest of his life.

At some time in the early hours another possibility emerged. A slender, much less certain alternative, but it would mean Selim need not die.

He had heard the sultan himself admit he had adversaries among those who opposed reform. Was there any chance of an uprising? A revolution of sorts that would strip Selim of his powers, go against his friends the French?

He had no idea, and in any case, the thought of his playing a part in something like that was laughable.

Or was it?

A tiny shoot of a stratagem sprang into existence. Yes, it might be possible.

He knew nothing of the factions that seethed in the Ottoman capital – but Zorlu did.

This was now at a different plane of danger entirely. If any suspected what he was plotting it would be a cruel and barbarous death in prospect. He would be putting his life and cause into the hands of one man.

Zorlu had professed a love of England, but it was not his

native land. Would he give his support to a rising against his sovereign lord, Sultan Selim? Quite apart from the personal danger, would he see the cause as more important than the inevitable anarchy and bloodshed? It was asking a lot of the man, and if Renzi had misjudged him it would be all over for himself.

Yet if he didn't attempt to win over Zorlu, he must fall back on the first sanction.

In the morning came news. The Russians, barred from the Dardanelles, had hit on an ingenious solution. They in turn were blockading the same strait to Turkish shipping, cutting off Constantinople from the outer world and its trade, at a stroke touching the lives of every inhabitant in the land.

As it began to bite, there would be unrest and ugly scenes: the scenario any zealous anarchist could wish for. Renzi had to make his move soon.

'Zorlu. A word, if I may?'

He started by sorrowing for the destiny of Turkey at the hands of France, the inevitable taking over of every position of power: if Bonaparte were to retain his longed-for route to glory, he would not leave anything to chance in this price-less strategic asset. The fate of the people, their traditions, their freedom.

Carefully he brought the subject around to Selim, a sultan who had probably made the wrong decision and very shortly would go ahead with it – if he was not stopped.

Zorlu listened without comment.

Renzi then went on innocently to enquire if there was any likelihood that he would be overthrown by a faction, say, one opposed to reform.

'Lord, let me tell you something of the situation, remembering

293

that false-hearted viziers never show their true fidelity until circumstances dictate.'

'I understand, Zorlu. Please go on.'

'On the one hand we have those who crave reform and entry to the modern world, and are Sultan Selim's most ardent followers. Chief of these, you may say, is the grand vizier, İbrahim Hilmi Pasha, and the grand mufti, Haji Samatar, is loud in his support. There are others, but these two are the ones he may count upon.

'In those against his reforms we may especially note the Janissaries, who have ancient privileges and much power, but they are held in check by the rising new army trained by the French, the Nizam-i Cedid, which has modern weapons and discipline and is hated by them.'

'So there's no central figure who might be considered a focus for the discontented?'

'Lord, that is difficult to say. No man dare tell the world he stands against the sultan, but I have heard the leader of the Ulema, Mehmed Ataullah, utter words unbecoming.'

'The Ulema?'

'The highest body of Muslim legal scholars, making him a powerful man.'

'So no one of stature in the Army, say?'

'There are many, but none openly declared to be in opposition. A personage of note, however, and a sly, treacherous fox, is the deputy grand vizier, one Köse Musa, who I'm certain harbours secret desires of his own.'

'Then, as far as you know, there are none actively plotting against Sultan Selim?'

'They dare not move while the forces are balanced so.'

'Is there not a crown prince of sorts they may push forward to replace Selim?'

'If you mean Prince Mustafa, although he stands to inherit the Osman Sultanate, they will have a weak enough reed to rest their hopes on – he has since birth been reared and confined within the harem, dissipating his life in pleasures of the flesh. It is said he has never once set foot outside the palace.'

Zorlu looked at Renzi intently, his eyes troubled. 'Fahn'ton Pasha, why are you asking me these things?'

'Zorlu, please bear with me. I have one final question: in your opinion, if the disaffected saw a chance to rise up by reason of a favourable external circumstance, would they at all?'

'I will tell you directly. There is much hatred of the sultan's reforms and the situation is volatile. But it will never happen while the grand vizier reigns and the Nizam-i Cedid remains loyal, as it most assuredly will.'

Renzi had his answer. There would be no revolt. That left only one course and he must do it. He knew of no other who would.

It had to be the knife. His heart cringed at the vision of his assassin's blade ending the existence of one who had befriended and trusted him, but there was no other way. Possibly, if it happened at night in his third-floor apartment, he could open the grilled window wide and thrust the body through. Later it would be found at the base of the tower.

He was checked in his thoughts. Where was the morality, the pity in him? How could he contemplate cold-blooded murder so dispassionately?

It was his logic. The merciless outworking of that part of him that had always kept him aloof from the world and its perplexities.

* * *

Securing a knife was no problem. He extravagantly admired a curved, ornamented dagger worn by one of the eunuchs and offered to buy it as a souvenir to take back to England. A working weapon for those entrusted with guarding the harem, its exotically fashioned hilt was in complete contrast to the lightly blued wicked blade.

He concealed it behind a tent's draperies and prepared himself. There was no knowing when Selim would appear so he put it about that he valued his privacy and wished to be left alone.

The blockade was taking its toll and there were noisy disturbances out on the streets. Renzi gave a half-smile – it was turning into a naval war after all. The French had been wrong about that but could do nothing to counter it and therefore Selim had much to concern himself with.

When his supper was brought, he heard word had come from Roumelia, at the Wallachia border along the Danube. The Russians were massing. Orders were given, and the grand vizier left with his best troops to confront them.

The decision was also made that the Russian blockade had to be broken. The Turkish Navy was concentrated together in a battle squadron and sailed to meet the Russians.

This was now a different matter. The Navy was obligated to Selim for his reforms, which had brought it into the modern world, and fiercely loyal – but now the entire fleet was sailing south and was out of reach.

With the grand vizier leaving for Roumelia, Selim had few supporters. However, he still had the loyalty of the Nizam-i Cedid, which safely outnumbered even the Janissaries and all of the others in Constantinople.

But they were quartered in Levend Chiftlik, across the water, in recognition of their controversial presence.

The duplicitous deputy grand vizier, Musa, had assumed plenary powers and was now Selim's prime minister, with the leader of the Ulema, Ataullah, as his right-hand man.

Was it time to consider his other course? Renzi could see there would be no better moment to make his move to spark a revolt.

But if he went this way and Zorlu or others turned on him, the other plan would be made impossible and Selim would go on to make the fatal alliance.

One way was certain; this other had the potential to fail.

He wrestled with the elements and decided it would not be the assassin's knife.

Fighting down the protests from his logical self that he was shying away from the act, he weighed his chances.

Zorlu was the only one who could put him into contact with the players. If he backed him, with his spark of a scheme, there was a chance he could pull off his revolt and Selim's life would not be forfeit.

But if Zorlu turned against him, Renzi would be forced to use his knife on him then and there to preserve the first sanction.

In the deathly quiet of the deserted floor, draped all about with Oriental silks and tassels, Renzi set out his plan to Zorlu, who listened politely, his features drawn.

Then he spoke slowly, bleakly. 'Lord – I understand more than you can know. It must be done. What should I do?'

Relief flooded Renzi.

It was quickly followed by warmth towards one who was wrestling his demons without complaint and who was about to be placed in deadly danger as he approached the most powerful men in the caliphate with a plot against the sultan.

'Our object is to place so much pressure on Selim that he dare not go ahead with the alliance. The haters of reform are our target but they will not move until they feel secure. I have a plan that meets this but requires I speak to them directly. Can you . . . ?'

This was a turning point: once they went ahead the future was unknown.

Not only was Zorlu in mortal peril but by giving up the secret of their existence in the tower, Renzi, Jago and all of the others would be at their mercy.

'Fahn'ton Pasha, it is done.'

'When?'

'This very night. It has caused great interest among Selim's opponents and they desire you should lay your plans before them at the earliest possible time.'

Renzi's heart skipped a beat. There was no stopping the juggernaut now.

'Zorlu Bey, I can't tell you how much I admire your courage and fidelity. I've a notion you risked much?'

He gave a tiny smile. 'Lord, if only to reveal to you whom we march with, my fate, if it's deemed we're charlatans, is to be sewn into a sack with a dozen rats and dropped into the Bosporus.'

'I see.'

'For you, Lord, your head will decorate the Yedikule for a period not less than thirty days and nights.'

'Then we had better be sure of our little intrigue. What do you think of this?'

It was carefully arranged. There would be no face-to-face meeting. Instead they would make use of the sultan's Golden

Window. The conspirators would meet as they were entitled to in the Imperial Council Hall. Renzi would be on the other side and speak through the grille, Zorlu translating.

It did not escape Renzi that, while the Divan could claim complete innocence on their side, his actions were those of a spy. All it needed was for a eunuch to enter from the harem and it would be the end for him.

The grille was high, but a peculiar-shaped piece of furniture stood opposite that was clearly used as the sultan's clandestine surveillance platform. Fortunately it could take the two of them so Renzi and Zorlu gingerly climbed up.

Renzi peered in: the Imperial Council Hall was lit by a central lamp and beautifully figured in gold and blue, a crimson velvet bench against the walls.

But there was no sign of life.

'Do I address anyone within?' he asked. Zorlu relayed his question.

Instantly there was a hard, guttural response from close to the grille, out of their range of vision.

'There will be no discussion of names,' Zorlu said neutrally.

Muttering, then a sharp question:

'The essence of your offer, and quickly.'

'Tell them . . . tell them this.'

He was an English scholar, treasuring the old ways and valuing those traditions handed down from the past, polished by the ages. Here in Constantinople, where he'd come to discover relics of history, he had been dismayed to find Sultan Selim so quick to bring in modern, foreign fashions to displace the old and wished to assist those who cherished their past.

It brought another curt growl.

'The offer?'

Putting as much feeling into it as he could, Renzi went on

to make plain his sympathy for those wishing to stand up for their traditions but understandably reluctant for fear that Selim would quickly call in his French friends and their overwhelming armies from Dalmatia.

The answering grunt was tinged with impatience. Then came a curt demand for the name of the English scholar they were addressing.

Fahn'ton Pasha was a noble lord of England, a peer of the realm and of the court of the legendary King of England; his name and word were respected throughout the kingdom. He was offering that should there be a rising, he alone could guarantee that there would be no interference from the French.

There was a disbelieving snort.

How?

Well, the armies were in Dalmatia. Normally troops were moved quickly by sea transports and would be on the scene in a day or two. If, however, he saw a revolt begin, he would send an urgent message to Nelson's admiral of the Adriatic Sea, under his name as a close friend of the King, ordering him to intercept the transports and stop them. The admiral would not dare refuse.

To reach here, the French would be forced to march overland, weeks must pass, and by that time it would all be over. There would be no interference from the French.

This brought on much excited muttering but it was answered by savage snarls and then the harsh voice demanded something.

'How can we trust you will send this message? This may well be an evil trick to get those opposed to Selim to reveal themselves.'

Renzi was ready for that and played his trump card.

'The righteous, standing for their freedoms, will need a figure to represent them against the repressive rule of Sultan Selim. Who better than Prince Mustafa? In his innocence he will need guidance, which can safely be left in your hands.'

An immediate response showed he had hit the mark.

'The prince is in the harem, under the direct eye of the sultan, who knows too well he can be the centre of a rebellion. While he's there, confined, we cannot move.'

'There is a way,' Renzi said. 'Should he be told privily that an Englishman will hide him and he obeys, to Selim it will appear he has escaped. I am held in the tower as his pawn but he has no reason to distrust me.

'Gentlemen, your signal to rouse the people will be the disappearing of Prince Mustafa.'

It was bold to the point of madness but it was cunningly balanced. They must show their hand first but in turn he was required to act openly.

Whispering went on interminably.

Standing in the gloom on the carved furniture, Renzi knew he was very vulnerable – at any moment the little harem gate could be flung wide and they would be discovered. Yet he felt a giddy elation: this might succeed.

The murmuring suddenly stopped and the voice hissed something.

'We agree. A good plan. You will recognise the hand of justice begin its work. Then you will send your message to your great admiral pasha.'

Still trembling with reaction, Renzi lay on his bed in the shadows of night and reflected on what he'd done.

He brutally crushed any shame at the betrayal. There was no room for high morality, not with the lives at stake of the thousands who would face Bonaparte in his breakout to India. But was this a despicable justification for a tawdry attempt to seize success for his mission – or was he being swept along before forces he could no longer control?

Only one thing was morally certain in all this. He had been right to refuse Cecilia's begging to accompany him.

Dear, sweet, darling Cecilia.

His eyes pricked and a wave of helpless emotion engulfed him. But in the darkness there was no one to see the tears.

The officer stalked into the barracks in Rumeli Kavak. He was a proud, trained captain in the Nizam-i Cedid and despised these *yamak*s, low-grade Circassian and Albanian auxiliaries, but he had his orders. Unwise ones, in his opinion, but from the very highest level, requiring his command to show their loyalty to the sultan by throwing aside their colourful traditional garb and putting on the new order uniforms of the reformed army.

They wouldn't like it, but he was making sure of it by refusing to hand over their quarterly pay to any not in the new uniform.

Loudly he told them, not bothering to hide his contempt.

There was murmuring, which turned to shouts.

'Astsubay,' he roared at his sergeant. 'Show these dogs!'

But the sergeant with the uniforms held back at the ugly press of men now bunching truculently in front of him.

'Go on! Don't be afraid of such as these. They're vermin and must obey orders!'

A dangerous edge lay on the shouts now and a burly *yamak* pushed himself to the front and folded his arms defiantly. 'We don't wear those accursed infidel goat-skins!' he snarled. 'As Allah is my witness.'

The officer swaggered forward. 'You're an impudent fool. You'll take my orders or suffer.'

The big *yamak* held his eyes with a sneer. Annoyed, the officer swept back his horse crop and made to slash the man across the face, but a beefy arm seized it. Astonished, the officer tried to free it but in one movement he was yanked forward off balance and a fist took him full in the face.

He cried out in outrage and crumpled to his knees. With a savage growl the *yamak* brought his linked fists down on the officer's neck and he slumped to the ground.

'Damn him and his kind to Hell!'

It released a fury and the officer disappeared under a hail of fists and clubs. The sergeant looked on in horror and turned to flee but was tripped and fell under an onslaught of murderous battering.

'We've nothing to lose but our yokes!' the man roared. 'Let's put an end here and now to this new order blasphemy. Follow me, those who have the heart and stomach to stop the desecration of our sacred fathers' memory!'

There was a swelling uproar and *yamak*s spilled out into the night, whooping and yelling. It brought others, and the fever spread. Officers panicked and tried to flee but the soldiers knew they were untouchable, and years of degradation at the hands of the arrogant Nizam-i Cedid drove them on into open revolt.

The deputy grand vizier laid down the scribbled message with a smile. 'There. It sufficed. We have our rising.'

'As Allah allows, Köse Musa,' chided Mehmed Ataullah, leader of the Ulema, but there was an air of triumph about him. 'Now you must face Selim, of course.'

'Not yet,' Musa said smoothly. 'Let matters take their course, mature a little.'

The sultan's urgent summons came later, but he was ready.

'Great Khan, this is terrible news.'

'It is, Vizier. It has to be stopped before it spreads.' The sultan was pale and agitated.

'Yes, Sire. I've sent agents out to determine the ringleaders and await their return, but whatever else, we must not be seen to give it too much attention or we'll be thought to fear the wretches.'

'We can stop it – call out the Nizam-i Cedid.'

'I cannot approve of that, Ghazi Sultan. Craving your forgiveness, it has to be said they are not admired absolutely and their appearance may well bring on the very situation we fear. It is a delicate situation and only level-headed leadership will answer.'

'So?'

'To prevent a conflagration, the Nizam-i Cedid should receive orders to remain in their barracks in Levend Chiftlik until the rising is put down. The Janissaries here – of long and ancient loyalties – will be sufficient to safeguard the palace, Supreme Lord.'

'Are you sure that . . . ?'

'It will be sufficient, Sire.'

Jago appeared before Renzi. 'A Turk o' sorts presents you with this 'un. Didn't stay, m' lord.'

It was the polite gift of a piece of gold cloth embroidered with an elaborate calligraphic device. There was no mistaking its significance.

'Thank you, Jago. We will have a guest. Do make up a tent or such next to mine, will you?'

'Yes, m' lord.' Would nothing shake his impassive air?

Prince Mustafa was a deathly pale, willowy young man, with eyes like a frightened dove's.

'I greet Your Highness and fear my hospitality is not that to which you are accustomed.'

It seemed it would be adequate in the circumstances.

'Here is Master Jago. He is to attend to your every want, in so far as we can oblige.'

Jago's real instructions were never to leave his side and, above all, to make certain that he never showed himself.

The clock was ticking.

Musa worked energetically. To succeed, the rising must look spontaneous and widespread.

To this end he first penned, in his elegant Persian script, a *firman* from Sultan Selim himself requiring his Nizam-i Cedid to remain in their barracks and not to move out without explicit orders from himself. This was sent with all dispatch.

Next he called about him his trusted lieutenants. 'Go to the Janissaries. Tell them that at last the time has come to seize back the honour that is rightfully theirs – they have been presented by Heaven with a once only opportunity to rid their world of these ungodly reforms and so forth. Get them to join with the *yamak*s to make certain the cause is triumphant, for the Nizam-i Cedid cannot interfere.

'Tell them also that they have a champion, one to stand for them against Selim's misguided reforms. Prince Mustafa is free and in hiding now but will reveal himself when the time is right.'

That night every corner of Constantinople was alive with excitement and disquiet, rumours of Janissaries rising up, bands of *yamak*s inviting the common people under their banner – and then it began.

Musa knew it would: now with a cause, a leading figure and the hated Nizam-i Cedid on a leash there was everything to win. The people were on the march – for Constantinople and the palace of the sultan.

He sighed with satisfaction. It was proceeding far better than he had anticipated. The Army over at Levend Chiftlik had no inkling of what was going on for he had blocked access and they remained there, waiting for word from their sultan.

With the masses surging towards Constantinople there would now be an irresistible pressure on Selim to abandon his plans to join with the French and the comfortable old ways would return, but with quite a different power-sharing at the highest.

Renzi stood with Zorlu at the viewing port, looking out over the city. In place of the quiet of the night there were now lights twinkling everywhere, noise eddying up from the streets, faint shouts, and an electric atmosphere that was heavy with pent-up menace.

They didn't speak – Renzi couldn't bring himself to make conversation in the face of what was happening before his eyes.

Earlier he had watched from this lookout as search-parties of eunuchs and Janissaries hurriedly fanned out over the palace looking for the crown prince. It must have been a shock to Selim: that he held the only credible figure on whom unrest might centre was his guarantee of personal security. Now with the prince missing it was an ominous signal that something was in the wind.

There was a sudden hammering at the door below. Renzi motioned frantically to Mustafa, who disappeared into one of the tents. Then he flew down the stairs, followed by Zorlu.

If this was a search, without doubt none of them would ever see another dawn.

Heart pounding, Renzi opened the door. It was a Janissary officer, behind him others. He barked a series of commands. Then, astonishingly, he turned and left with his men.

Zorlu wiped his brow. 'We're to shut and lock our doors from now on. No one to go in or out. With Prince Mustafa unaccounted for, it's not safe to be out.'

Renzi let out a shuddering sigh. They were trusted; there would be no searches.

Then he checked himself. How did the Janissaries know there was an Englishman in the tower?

The answer came swiftly: they must be the conspirators' men, ensuring that Mustafa would not be found.

Early in the morning Renzi was woken by the sound of a crowd. It was coming from the direction of the vast open space of the Meydani beyond, once the hippodrome of the Byzantines. Somewhere there a restless multitude was gathering in the early-morning light.

They had to have come with some purpose: the Janissaries in firm control of the Topkapi Palace, they had no hope of storming it. Were they hoping to gain concessions from the sultan to tone down his reforms?

While Renzi watched from above, a delegation was allowed into the courtyard, closely escorted. They advanced to the area in front of the Imperial Council Hall – perfectly placed directly beneath his gaze.

Vizier Musa emerged from the Divan and met them, accepting a scroll. They were then escorted away.

A little later there was a flurry of activity at the Gate of Felicity, leading from the sultan's courtyard. It was Selim – in gorgeous raiment that shimmered as he processed, moving directly into the Imperial Council Hall to meet his Divan.

Inside the splendid room the mood was tense and fractious.

'Sire, this petition is outrageous. It demands you disband the Nizam-i Cedid!'

'Vizier Mehmet, your views are well known,' Selim said uncomfortably, his face troubled. 'What I need to decide at this moment is how to proceed without antagonising them further.'

Musa kept mute, watching each of the ministers reveal themselves. Already some were temporising, unwilling to be seen on the wrong side if things went against the sultan. For once time was in his favour – the longer Selim dithered, the uglier the crowd would get.

'Then, Great One, command the Nizam-i Cedid to come here. They'll make short work of the rabble and restore your authority to its full respect without delay.'

Selim hesitated. 'It does seem the time to make a firm gesture, I'll admit. Perhaps I will send them orders.'

'Sire, that would, surely, be to your eternal regret,' Ataullah Efendi snapped immediately. As the highest legal scholar of Islam in the land, he had to be heard.

'Oh?'

'This I declare unto you. There will be a bloodbath – the soldiery will be resisted and the population will turn on them. You will be known for ever more as the Ottoman sultan who took a sword to his own people.'

Tight-faced, Shakir Efendi grated, 'He needs to make a move of firmness and strength before it gets out of hand – then you'll see a bloodbath, take my word on it.'

Musa let them take their positions, allowing the venomous debate to ebb and flow without conclusion, then he spoke. 'Excellency, there is another solution.'

It brought quiet and a wary attention.

'Grand Vizier, I'd be gratified to hear it.'

'It is insupportable that a barbarous crowd issues demands to their sultan. Yet you are at the moment in a position of weakness and this is an act of extortion. Lie to them that you will disband the foreign-trained army – having got what they want they will disperse without harm to anyone. Afterwards, in your own time, you may reverse the decree.'

'Ah! It is offensive to our morals to break our word but it does have the merit of immediate effect.'

'Sire!' exploded Shakir. 'That robs you of your last defences – don't listen! You'll have none to stand at your side against—'

'Shakir Efendi, this is only a temporary shift. When things are calmer I will rescind my words.'

'The crowd is swelling. The common people are joined by traitorous Janissaries. This is madness, Sire! We should—'

'Shakir,' Musa said slyly, 'are you questioning your sultan?'

There could be no reply.

It was done.

Musa lifted his eyes to Heaven and murmured a prayer, then serenely addressed Sultan Selim: 'Sire, I go now to try to speak to the crowd, tell them of your magnanimous decision. In peril of my life, I do so in the knowledge that it is my sacred duty to my liege khan.'

'Your courage and loyalty are a lesson to us all, Köse Musa. Go with the blessings of Allah.'

'I, the leader of the Ulema, will not stand by in the hour of the caliphate's need,' intoned Ataullah. 'Come, Vizier Musa, let us face what test Allah is bringing us and speak to the congregation together.'

They left in great dignity.

Afterwards the sultan was besieged by frightened ministers who had spoken out for him. 'Sire, we're in great peril – the masses may not disband. I beg you, send for the—'

'We are in the hands of Allah the Merciful,' Selim said weakly. 'I go now to my harem.'

'Sire – Sire! We, your faithful servants – do not leave us alone with our enemies!'

The sultan stopped, troubled. 'Very well. Shakir, Mehmet – you others. You may accompany me into sanctuary.'

'They're going to speak to the crowd,' Zorlu murmured to Renzi, watching the two turbaned heads sweep off towards the outer gates. 'That's Köse Musa and with him Ataullah Efendi. It's plain to me what they'll do now.'

'Stir the people up, not pacify them.'

'Just so, my lord.'

Their attention was distracted: all over the palace, ornamental gates that had not moved for centuries ground shut and detachments of Janissaries took up lines in the first courtyard, their scimitars glittering in the morning sunlight.

'Will it be effective, do you think?'

'I do not know what was decided below us, but the plotters need to bring as much pressure on the sultan as they can muster to overcome his supreme will in the matter of reforms. We shall see.'

After an hour, a dangerous roar rose up.

The two returned later, and quickly disappeared into the Imperial Council Hall.

'There's something afoot,' Renzi murmured.

The uproar and clamour increased, a horde now at the gates of the Topkapi Palace itself, spreading as it grew. From their midst burst a horseman with a huge red triangular banner. He made for the Imperial Gate, which seemed to open of its own accord, raced through and into the courtyard.

'To ride in a palace courtyard is forbidden to all but the sultan himself,' Zorlu murmured.

The Janissaries held their ground and the horse came to a stop, gyrating nervously while the rider argued with an officer.

'Lord, I do believe this is a species of demand on the sultan. I beg we may go to a lower floor that I might listen.'

They ran down the stone stairs to Jago's realm. The staff were sitting despondently, knowing not a thing of what was going on, for the only window was out of reach high on the wall.

'We need to hear what's going on, Jago,' Renzi puffed. 'Do drag up some of this furniture to make a lookout through the window.'

'Very good, m' lord.'

Upended beds, dressers, tables, were all brought to bear.

Renzi climbed up and peered out cautiously. Their viewpoint was well placed, overlooking the space of ground between the Imperial Council Hall and the Gate of Felicity and within earshot. Zorlu took position next to him.

The horseman had been let through the Janissary lines and now galloped recklessly up to the Imperial Council Hall. Reining in, he shouted – hectoring, demanding.

'He says he comes from the people, who have lost patience with the godless foreign deviations from the true faith, who see Sultan Selim led astray by false advisers, and demand that these be handed over to them for justice.'

Zorlu turned to Renzi, disturbed. 'Lord, it seems the crowd feels its power. The French are finished now, you may be certain, but they want more – to seek revenge on those who supported Selim's reforms. The sultan would be very unwise to agree to this.'

With a defiant gesture, the horseman bellowed a final threat and, wheeling about, raced back to the outer gate.

'And by this he is given an hour only to deliver up the men who took sanctuary. A most terrible decision for him.'

Musa stood respectfully to hear Selim speak.

It mattered little what he said: the reforms were finished, the Nizam-i Cedid disbanded, and the sultan was defenceless against the horde. A pity they were overstepping it, but it handily removed any rivals in the restored Divan.

He looked pityingly at the terrified sultan. This was now the end-game for Selim.

'There is . . . no alternative, is there?'

'None, Sire.'

'To deliver them up for – for justice.'

'You must.'

'Then leave me for a space, Vizier Musa. I will call on you when I'm ready.'

Selim walked back slowly into the interior of his palace, magnificently decorated in gold and blue tiles, hanging tassels and exquisitely wrought calligraphy picked out in ebony on emerald green. These had been added to down the centuries from the first sultan, Ahmet the Conqueror, bequeathed to each sultan in turn until today they were his.

He stopped in the tulip garden of the fourth courtyard, with its tiered fountains and sublime tranquillity.

The eunuch Nezir Ağa came out and bowed.

'Summon our guests.'

One by one they came to the garden, some fearful, others trusting but apprehensive.

Selim returned their obeisance with dignity and the utmost respect. Here were men who had supported him and his efforts to reform, who had stood loyally between him and the forces of reaction and hatred and now looked to him for succour.

'Memish Efendi, Shakir, Safi, my good and loyal servants,' he said, in a low voice. 'Allah has decreed that our cause is not yet. Worse, the forces of evil and discontent are in the ascendant.'

In poignant tones he told them what had happened.

'I'm grieved to tell you that your sultan is no longer in control of his fate.'

Their shocked faces looked back at him. If the sultan was not secure in his own harem, their world was turned upside down.

'They demand that you be handed over to them. This I cannot prevent.'

His words brought gasps of disbelief.

'I can, however, render it impossible for them to torment you further.

'Dear friends, I do offer you a clean and quick exit from this sorry world, an end to your terror and striving. Rather than being torn to pieces by the rabble you may meet a swift dispatch by my blade.'

He left them, walking slowly up the garden to the fountain as they fell prostrate to their prayers.

After a decent interval he signalled to Nezir.

'Are you prepared?'

In a line, one by one, they knelt in the beautiful garden.

The eunuch lifted his gleaming scimitar.

Anxious not to leave Prince Mustafa alone for too long, Renzi returned to the eerie quiet of their tent village. He motioned to the observation port. 'Keep a watch, Zorlu. Tell me if—'

Then he went over to Prince Mustafa, who was agitated and needed calming.

'Fahn'ton Pasha. I think you must come.'

Zorlu's voice was unsteady and Renzi hurried to see. A man he recognised as Ahmed, the secretary to Selim, was emerging from the Gate of Felicity. He walked in front of a small cart. Along the sides of it were pikes. On each was impaled a head.

'Good God!' Renzi whispered. 'What does this mean?'

'He placates the crowd with the heads of those they seek.'

The lonely figure of Ahmed stepped out, heading for the gate and the baying crowd.

'There goes as brave a fellow as any I've seen,' Renzi said quietly.

Zorlu snorted. 'It should be the grand vizier.'

They waited. A mighty roar went up from the hidden crowd.

'Will they be satisfied? This is more than they can ask, surely.'

'I cannot say, lord. This is now a rabble that is out of control. If Musa does not act quickly . . .'

314

Before the hour was out they had their answer. The horseman galloped back arrogantly, carrying a bundle.

No one attempted to stop him and he reined in opposite the Imperial Council Hall. He paused significantly so it could be seen that the bundle was Ahmed's golden cloak of authority.

In a single gesture of contempt he unfurled the cloak and from it tumbled what remained of the secretary. A hideously gruesome head, the white of the skull gleaming through the blood-matted hair, part of the spinal column still attached as token of the ferocity with which he'd been torn to pieces.

Renzi turned away in sick despair.

Musa sought out Sultan Selim. He found him in his garden with Pakize, his favourite concubine.

'Sire, I have to tell you—'

'Can't you do something for your lord?' spat Pakize. 'You're grand vizier – use your power on that lawless vermin.'

'Khan of Khans, it's with the utmost sadness that I'm to tell you that the revolt is succeeding. Sire, they now ask . . . that you yield up the Bayram Throne to another.'

Selim went rigid. 'They cannot . . .'

'My humble self can only pass on what that rebellious horde is demanding, Sire.'

'I will not do it! I, of the House of Osman, my right to rule is handed down to me from Mehmet Fatih himself!'

'Great Lord, this is true but the press of rebels is such that—'

'No! I have still my faithful Janissaries of unquestioned and venerable devotion. Any who dares to approach me will be slain by them without mercy.'

'Sire, my advice—'

'Go – tell the rabble this! Tell them I will never give up my holy inheritance!'

'Very well, my lord.'

'You have gone too far, Musa. The mob howls only to be rid of the godless reformers, not His Sacred Majesty himself! You had no right to—'

'Be silent, Ataullah!' hissed the vizier. 'Think. When this dies down and order is restored, Selim will discover for himself our part in raising the rebellion for suppressing the reforms. What then is our future? The only way is to render him powerless. Put another on the throne, even if it be the witless Mustafa.'

'Depose the sultan? This is too much, Musa, even for you. In any case, it'll turn into a slaughter with the Janissaries still loyal.'

'It has to be done. And I've a notion how.'

'Tell me.'

'Is not the root cause of all the protests the same? That infidel ways and unholy alliances with unbelievers lie behind each and every one of these reforms?'

'As I am witness.'

'Then this is why I want you, Ataullah Efendi, Sheyh ul-Islam and leader of the Ulema, to issue a *fatwa* declaring it permissible – even a sacred obligation – of all to withdraw their loyalty from one who seeks to draw away from the true faith. Preach it to the Janissaries, allow that any who hold back from their greater holy calling will condemn themselves as *Zindīq*s, worthy of death.'

'Leave the piety to me, Musa. It doesn't suit your kind.'

'The *fatwa*?'

'You'll have it.'

*   *   *

In the late afternoon Renzi was drawn to the viewport by the distant harsh stridency of massed drums, cymbals, a cacophony of other instruments and tramping boots.

Into the courtyard came the brazen colour of the entire corps of Janissaries. They stamped and marched in an irresistible flood until they filled the area before the Gate of Felicity, a discordant blare of trumpets, the visceral thumping of giant drums, a vast, swirling concourse of the fearsome Turkish warrior caste.

A huge figure of a man detached from the others and went to stand in front of the ceremonial gate. He held up his hands to quiet the throng, then turned and bellowed a challenge, so loud it carried clearly up to them.

Zorlu listened. 'That is Kabakji Mustafa and he demands the sultan attend on them. He is a troublemaker.'

Apprehensively they watched as the drama unfolded.

There was an impatient pause and the challenge was given again.

Then at the gate Sultan Selim appeared.

'Kabakji Bey. What does this insolence mean? Why have you turned out my loyal Janissaries?'

'We have a *fatwa* issued by Ataullah Efendi in which you are condemned as no longer fit to rule. Deliver up your throne to us!'

'You are impertinent and treasonable. Go back to your barracks!'

'Sire, you force us to—'

'You haven't considered this, Kabakji Bey. Without me there is no sultan, the caliphate goes unruled. The crown prince has disappeared and without him you have no successor. You cannot go further.'

The man drew himself up impressively and flung out an arm. It pointed directly to the tower and held.

Renzi pulled back from the window instinctively.

'He wants us to show Prince Mustafa,' Zorlu hissed.

'No!'

'We must.'

'I – I can't do this to Selim!'

Zorlu pushed past, throwing the grille window wide and thrust Mustafa up to it.

There was an instant roar of recognition and a chant began: 'Sultan Mustafa Han! Sultan Mustafa Han!'

Drums rolled and volleyed, and wild shouts of jubilation echoed up.

Renzi went reluctantly to the window to see the entire mass in ecstatic gyrating, waving scimitars – and a single lonely figure. In his rich robes and turban, Sultan Selim gazed up, and even over the distance his look, with its terrible accusation of betrayal, pierced Renzi to his soul.

Slowly, Selim turned about and walked back into his harem.

'So, you have your triumph, Köse Musa,' Ataullah said. 'But here's something that'll give you pause.'

'Now what can that be, I wonder?' Musa said comfortably, sipping his sherbet.

'Only that the Nizam-i Cedid Army in Edirne has just learned of the rising and is marching back to restore Selim to his powers.'

Musa put down his goblet. 'That is not what I wanted to hear.'

'There's every chance they'll do it, with their new weapons and numbers.'

'They have to be stopped.'

'There is only one way.'

'If you are saying . . .'

'I am, Vizier Musa. It's the only sure cure.'

'Who will do it?'

'That's your business, is it not?' Ataullah answered silkily.

Renzi heard them. This time muted, subdued. A jingling of accoutrements, the heavy tramp of many boots.

He'd expected them to come. It was logical. An inevitable outcome of the course they had taken.

Dully he watched from the window as the last act began.

'Eunuch Mehmet! Hear me! Deliver up to us the person of Selim Osman, by strict order of the Sultan Mustafa.'

After an interval it was repeated.

'If we must enter, there will be none spared. This is our final word.'

Selim came to the gates, flanked by eunuchs, Pakize clutching him, imploring, tearful.

He saw the bared blades and tried to break free. Two men, stripped to the waist and with scimitars at the ready, darted forward but Pakize threw herself in front of her master. It didn't stop them – the first swing of the sword laid open her arm and, thrusting aside her shrieking form, Selim was cut down in a merciless hacking until his lifeless body lay still.

Renzi slumped back, stricken by what he'd brought about.

The hunt for the last loyal supporters of Selim went on throughout the city and long into the night.

'We're safest here,' Renzi told Jago, and his terrified household. He could not admit that, in view of his central part in the uprising, he was more likely to be hailed a hero by the 'winning side' than anything. He dreaded the prospect and, just as soon as he could, he would leave this beautiful and terrible place.

Sleep would not come. On the one hand there were the brutal images seared on his memory – that look of Selim's would haunt him to the end of his days.

But on the other hand he could go back to London and rightly claim that, while the English had been humiliated and banished, he had brought about the same thing for the French. Summarily ejected and identified so thoroughly with the wrong side, they would never be a threat again.

His achievement – at such cost to others – was no less than the saving of empire and the thwarting of Napoleon Bonaparte.

In the early morning a platoon of moustachioed Janissaries came for him. When Zorlu tried to intervene, he was thrown aside.

Renzi was taken to a rough, unsprung carriage, which ground off, out of the courtyard, through the Imperial Gate and into the city. At that hour the streets were deserted and the noise of their passing echoed sharply off the buildings.

He had no idea what was going on and, without Zorlu, could not find out. He tried to remain calm.

After an interminable journey along grey-glistening sea-walls they took a sharp turn inland.

Through the side window Renzi caught a glimpse of a fortress with many towers, which for some reason meant something to him. Then he had it: in his childhood he'd been taken by an illustrated account of old Constantinople. This was the famed Golden Gate, the entry point to the fabled city of the Byzantine emperors, its massive gates then gilded, with four bronze elephants at guard.

Now dour and oppressive, it loomed over him as the gates swung open and they continued on to the shadowed interior.

He was handed over without ceremony and hustled up stone steps to a guarded cell in one of the ancient towers. He was pushed in, the door crashing to behind.

Human stench wafted over him. There was a low bed on either side of the gloomy room, rushes on the floor, a single high, barred window.

A voice behind startled him. He swung around. It was Sébastiani, his arms folded and a cynical smile playing.

'Well, well. Our English lord. How the mighty have fallen.'

Renzi was instantly on guard. So the French were taken too.

How much did Sébastiani know? If his character as an amiable noble fool was penetrated, his worth to Congalton in the future – should ever he get out of here – would be little or nothing.

'These Ottoman dolts, they have no conception how to treat their guests,' Renzi said peevishly. 'And what all this means is beyond me. Obviously there's been some mistake.'

'Oh? If you're Selim's friend, it explains everything, don't you think?'

'We got along together well, I admit. A talented writer, composer – he and I rather enjoyed our few visits.'

'He did speak well of you, I remember. But do tell, when your fleet came you disappeared from mortal ken. We assumed you had been an unfortunate victim of the understandable loathing of the English at the time. Where did you go?'

'Ha!' Renzi spat. 'Those accursed Janissaries. They locked me up in some prison, said it was Selim's orders and that it was for my own protection. I was outraged! I, a noble lord, sitting for days in a cell, like a common felon.'

'It must have been a harrowing experience for you, milord,' Sébastiani soothed, but with a mischievous smile.

'Just so. I had no idea what was going on, no one to talk to and—'

'I do understand. So that is why you took against His Sacred Majesty and warmed to the idea of a revolt.'

Renzi froze. 'Why do you say that, General?'

'Why? I do have it as a fact that it was you hid the Prince Mustafa, a necessary pre-condition for any rising.'

'Well, I . . .'

'A cynic might go on to observe that, for the sacred goal of frustrating us in our legitimate relations with the Sublime Porte, a devious plot might well have been conceived by a high-placed Englishman to overthrow the friends of the French. Yes?'

Renzi allowed a look of astonishment to be quickly replaced by one of gratification. 'You really think I could do something like that, General? That's very kind in you to say. However, I'm embarrassed to admit the concealing was from quite another motive.

'You've no idea how expensive travel is in Oriental lands. Simple daily comforts come at extraordinary prices and, to be truthful about it, the delay while you warriors sorted things out between you has been ruinous to my purse. So, when an offer was made by the rebels to . . . Well, it was difficult to refuse gold in hand, and with Selim having treated me like that . . .'

'Quite so. And for your efforts you are now rewarded with this.'

'It's disgraceful! I can only think there's been some confusion and that when the new sultan discovers what has happened to a noble of England he'll be sorely angry.'

Sébastiani grunted dismissively and began pacing while Renzi smothered a sigh of relief. It appeared his secret was safe.

'So you really don't know where you are?'

'No, I do not.'

'Then allow me to enlighten you. You're in the Yedikule, Fortress of the Seven Towers, the worst hell-hole in Constantinople and reserved for foreign enemies of the state. There has been no mistake – the new order has decided. Above everything, it's declared we're both equally infidels and threatening to the old ways. Therefore our prospects are dim.'

Despite himself, Renzi felt a surge of sympathy for the man. Gifted and ruthless, he was a fine servant of his master Bonaparte and, but for Renzi's coup, would have succeeded in his glorious destiny.

Sébastiani went on moodily, 'Either they don't know what to do with us or they're taking precautionary hostages. In the first, we'll probably be an embarrassment and will be eliminated. In the second we could still be here in ten years' time.'

'We have to get out.'

'There's no chance of leaving here by our own efforts,' mused Sébastiani. 'Any release has to come from outside – influence, bribery, threat. Do you not agree?'

'Oh, well, yes, I imagine you're right.'

'Now, how are we going to do that?'

'Perhaps by a letter of sorts. To someone we know will help?'

'Very good, milord,' Sébastiani said sarcastically. 'And how—'

'Every man has his price,' Renzi said, as casually as he could. 'When our gaoler finishes work today he seeks out my steward, for he has my note of hand. It instructs the fellow to hand over a certain sum –'

'Of your thirty pieces of silver!'

'– in return for my letter. This is then sent on urgently by

323

my man. Then the world will know of my unjust sufferings in a Turkish prison.'

'Bravo!' exclaimed Sébastiani. 'You have it, I'm persuaded. Were it not for one small detail.'

'Oh dear.'

'That he carries not one but two letters. One from me. No offence intended, milord, but I've a fancy I have more friends in this part of the world than your good self.'

'Really? The *baskam* of Gordion, a formidable scholar, is hardly to be scouted as a friend.' His real letter, of course, would not be heading there.

'A good man, but I was thinking of Marshal Marmont in Dalmatia at the head of forty thousand *poilu*.'

'I see. Well, shall we agree that the first to arrive with succour will take the other?'

'Only if the other accedes to the status of internee, as it were?'

'Agreed.'

Chapter 13

Gun-smoke drifted across Kydd's view in the light winds but it didn't hide the immense triangular red pennant atop the Turkish flagship, marking the centre of their fleet stretching away northwards.

Unlike British practice, they were engaging in 'long bowls', occasionally yawing to bring guns to bear on their pursuers, firing at extreme range, then resuming their flight.

What were they about, sailing ever deeper into the Aegean and away from the Dardanelles when they could either have retreated inside or turned and brought about a deciding battle? Were the Russians being led on, and if so, into what?

A few days earlier Kydd had taken up an offer from Senyavin to join a short cruise with the Russian Navy – his price, the spinning of yarns of Trafalgar and Nelson at wardroom dinners. It was all going very agreeably until a frigate had sighted the Turks and they'd immediately set off in pursuit with no time to send Kydd back to his ship.

Kydd had squared his conscience about being away from

L'Aurore as she was safely anchored at Tenedos and, after all, it was his duty to make measure of the naval capabilities of a foreign power.

He'd taken the trouble to get around *Tverdyi*, a 74-gun ship-of-the-line that was as technically competent as a British ship – perhaps over-gunned and with her cramped hold-space not as capable of long sea voyaging but every bit as powerful.

His escort and interpreter was the amiable and intelligent Lieutenant Aleksey Ochakov, whose English had been won from a two-year voyage in a Baltic trader.

They had toured all parts of the ship, Kydd alert for differences, inadequacies, strengths.

In the matter of the Russian crew, he was left with an impression of courage but of the passive kind – endurance, able to take the worst without complaint. They were stolid, blankly obedient, never lively or spirited. In their off-watch hours they would pass their time at cards, in prayer, asleep on the hard deck – or picking fleas.

Ochakov had explained that the Baltic fleet in winter was iced in and the ship cocooned. The men dispersed ashore, becoming in effect soldiers.

They would seldom return to the same ship in spring and their few months of sea-time gave no chance to build up the bond between sailor and ship that was so much in Jack Tar's blood.

There was also a greater distance between the quarterdeck and the foc's'le than in the Royal Navy. No Russian officer would ever think to visit the men's mess-deck to inspect their living conditions. Ochakov had reluctantly agreed when Kydd had asked to see the sailors at their evening meal. Their entrance to the ill-lit gun-deck brought an instant hush to the low rumble of voices as every man looked up in astonishment at the two officers.

Most were dressed in little more than grey homespun, with long lank hair and deep-set eyes. They were eating mutton-bone gruel with their fingers from tin dishes. One by one they got to their feet, unsure and resentful.

Kydd had left quickly. Those men would fight to the finish but they lacked the initiative that came from individualism and confidence in their officers, the mark of a British seaman.

Talk over dinner with the Russian officers had revealed more divergence. There was no purser: the captain ran slops clothing and victuals and made good money out of it, appointing one of the officers to relieve him of the details. The master was a lower species, not having the respect or the qualifications of those in Royal Navy service and in effect left the captain to his own decisions. The doctor was nothing better than a barber-surgeon. Neither had a place in the wardroom.

But there was polished professional talk: that the Baltic fleet was top dog and the Black Sea fleet a poor relation, locked up, as it were, for long periods of history by the Ottomans. Poor morale, the naval dockyard at Sebastopol a disgrace, the ships in a deplorable state and—

Senyavin had subtly pointed out that such topics could not possibly interest their guest and the conversation had turned to St Petersburg and its attractions for a returned mariner.

As a ship in King George's service was said to resemble an English village afloat, with the captain as squire, traditions and customs transplanted to sea, Kydd had mused, so the Tsar's navy reflected the Russian countryside of serfdom and servility.

Now, standing a little back from the group on the

327

quarterdeck, he took in more of the scene. This was their battle and he had no role, but nothing would have kept him below decks.

Senyavin was clearly frustrated by the light winds and pounded his fist into his palm. The other officers stood respectfully by, the seamen at the guns calm and patient.

The Turks were slowly pulling away. The Russians, far from their home dockyards and with foul bottoms, were unable to close to engage.

The guns fell silent as the range grew longer and the smoke cleared to allow Kydd a fine sight of the Ottoman formation.

The fleets were evenly matched, ten ships-of-the-line on either side. Time was not on the Turkish side. They needed to break the blockade – why did they not bring about a deciding battle?

Then it became clear to Kydd what the canny Turkish admiral must be scheming.

On the far horizon a faint line of grey was lifting above the blue haze. It was a long island and the Ottoman fleet was heading for its eastern tip.

Once out of sight they could position themselves in a number of ways. If Senyavin chose to follow them, they could sail around faster and fall on his rear. If he decided on the other end, the Turks could disappear southwards to the Dardanelles and safety while Senyavin was still north of the island.

And finally, if he made the logical decision to split his forces and send half to either end to make sure, the Ottoman admiral could pounce on either outnumbered half and cripple it first before attending to the other.

It was a gamble for the Turks but in the light winds a bigger one for Senyavin.

But by this the Ottomans could achieve their deciding clash and break the stranglehold.

As Kydd watched, the sails of the Turkish fleet disappeared around the point.

Then a memory came from years ago: of a big French privateer chasing his little ship, then concealing itself in a similar manner behind an island. The Île de Batz, off Roscoff. And he had outwitted it by landing in a boat and going to the crest of the hill to spy out the hidden privateer, then sailing off in the opposite direction.

In a different way it would work here.

'Sir, a word?'

Senyavin understood instantly. Signal was made to shorten sail and slow. At his request, Kydd quickly found himself with Ochakov and two signalmen in a boat, together with an escort of half a dozen musket-wielding Russians.

It was a simple enough task. Go to the top of the island, sight the Turks and signal back with one of two flags, red or blue depending at which end the enemy were lying. *Tverdyi* in turn would have a white flag hoisted at the fore, which would instantly be lowered on satisfactorily sighting their signal.

The boat hissed into sand at the base of a small cliff. The escort tumbled out and looked cautiously about even though the island was said to be uninhabited.

The signalmen carried a long pole between them and together the party hurried up the cliff path.

At the top a gentle scrubby slope led to the bare summit with an escarpment further to the right. The island was clear of any signs of humans. Only scraggy bushes covered the rust-coloured soil and they reached their objective in minutes.

And there the Turks were! They had settled on the far end. Blue flag!

The signalmen bent it on and one went to the highest point and heaved the pole up. The flag streamed out satisfyingly.

But within moments a bullet slapped through it. Shocked, the man dropped the pole and everyone fell prone.

Kydd saw a wisp of smoke arising from a bush further down the rise but their unknown assailant would have quickly moved. How many others did the dark scrub conceal?

Ochakov snarled a command and the men with muskets spread out protectively.

'Alexsey, if we don't—' Kydd began.

'I know.' He rapped an order.

One of the signalmen heaved the pole up again and held it against the wind, the whites of his eyes showing, his head turning in fear.

A bullet took splinters out of the pole but he gripped it doggedly. Another went past low, its *whuup* clearly audible.

The soldiers fired at the origin of the shot but another took the signalman in the thigh. He staggered and clamped his eyes shut in pain but obstinately clutched the pole upright.

Kydd looked back to the flagship: her white flag was still at the fore.

He then saw that a fluke of topography had directed the wind so the flag was fluttering end on directly towards *Tverdyi* and hadn't been seen.

His eyes darted about and he spotted the thin line used to secure the landed gear. It would be enough. He slithered towards it, his back crawling as he imagined a sniper taking aim.

A ball took the signalman full in his body and he fell with a choking gasp, the flag tumbling down with him. The man writhed and groaned, then was still.

Ochakov growled a single word.

The second signalman went stolidly to take up the pole but Kydd motioned for him to get down while he secured the line to the fly of the flag.

'Now!' he told him, gesturing vigorously upwards.

The man stood and heaved the pole vertically. A bullet flew past him, then another hit the pole with a shocking judder, but Kydd was already yanking on the line and the flag was pulled sideways, bellying full like a sail.

In seconds the white flag jerked down. It was done.

Now to get away. The boat lay off, the crew alarmed but unable to do anything. And between them and it, there was a quarter-mile of treacherous scrub.

'Over there.' Kydd pointed towards the escarpment. 'There's sure to be caves.'

After a painful scramble they were behind boulders and impregnable against anything but a full-scale assault.

The firing stopped.

Hidden in the lee of the island, Senyavin's squadron raced to intercept the Turks – their gamble was called.

In their place of refuge Kydd had time to think. It made no sense to garrison an uninhabited island on the odd chance that an enemy would land. Who were their attackers?

He smiled ruefully. The Turkish admiral was smarter than he'd given him credit for. These were no more than his men doing the same as themselves – signalling the movements of Senyavin's fleet from a lookout. And when they had seen the flag atop the hill they must have realised what was going on and moved to stop it.

If that was right, then . . .

Sure enough, the Ottoman fleet was already warned and had hauled in to resume their run north. No doubt their shore party had re-embarked, but it was a different matter for themselves. They could get to their boat now but Senyavin was well past in close pursuit of the fleeing Turks.

There was nothing for it but to wait for rescue.

Kydd stepped aboard *L'Aurore* with satisfaction and relief. In the time she had lain idly at anchor, her first lieutenant had not wasted days and the ship was spotless, not a rope out of place, the decks gleaming white. He murmured in appreciation.

'An enjoyable cruise with the Ivans, sir?' Curzon asked, with ill-disguised curiosity.

'Yes, indeed. And some tolerable entertainment provided for us by the Turk.'

He sketched out what had happened. 'Admiral Senyavin was mortified that on account of light winds the Turks hauled away, but I've no doubt there'll be a reckoning before long.'

'As will release us to quit this place.'

'Just so.'

'Oh, one thing. The Russian guard ship at the entrance to the strait was approached by a disreputable Moor and thought it right to pass it on to us.'

'What do you mean?'

'Would you believe it? The fellow climbed aboard and demanded they accept a letter addressed to the nearest English man-o'-war. Had a covering note to the effect that in return for handing it over he was to receive the sum of twenty *kuruş* in gold. The captain is anxious that he be reimbursed before we sail, he said.'

'Very well. We'll take a look at this expensive piece of mail after I'm fettled.'

With remarkable speed Tysoe produced a piping hot hip-bath and a clean rig.

Refreshed, Kydd took the little packet, salt-stained and grubby, to the stern windows and sat in his favourite chair.

Was this another plea to be taken back to England at His Majesty's expense? The address, barely legible, was in impeccably correct form.

Inside, the folded paper was of very poor quality and ink had stained through it to the other side. A traveller fallen on hard times?

In a wash of disbelief Kydd could only stop and stare.

It was signed 'The Right Honourable the Lord Farndon' – and how could he ever forget the elegant, sweeping hand that he had last seen on ship's papers in this very cabin?

Renzi!

Kydd feverishly re-read the words. A prisoner of the Turks in Constantinople, Renzi calmly requested that authorities be alerted with a view to negotiations for his release.

Thoughts stampeded through Kydd's mind.

What in the name of God was Renzi doing in Constantinople? He quickly put that aside as unanswerable.

There was a more pressing question, namely, which authorities could be reached quickly?

Admiral Duckworth was somewhere near Alexandria, engaged in an opposed landing and not to be distracted. Rear Admiral Louis was at large in the Adriatic and said to be now mortally ill.

That left the civil authorities. Malta was the closest, weeks' sailing away, but it was a small station, no relations with or interest in Turkey or the Dardanelles.

In effect, there was no English representation of standing and influence in the entire Mediterranean now.

There was only Collingwood, out in the Atlantic off Cádiz,

who had any kind of power, and by the time he was reached and came to a decision, Renzi might have been . . .

Kydd shot to his feet and paced about the cabin.

Collingwood would probably see the fate of a single British subject caught up in the recent humiliation and retreat as regrettable but no reason to mount another attempt on the Sublime Porte.

Kydd's orders were to remain in the area to report on Russian operations, not leave station to go off looking for help.

It had to be faced. Renzi would probably rot in an Oriental gaol for ever . . .

But could he return to England and tell Cecilia that he had done nothing to save her husband?

Were there any possibilities, however improbable?

A return through the Dardanelles and a daring rescue? Not after the mauling they had taken escaping – and, besides, with the Russians abroad, the forts would be reinforced, well manned and alert.

Some kind of furtive undercover expedition? But without the language, the local knowledge – even finding where Renzi was held in chains – made it impossible. And then to hack his way into some fortress prison against the hordes of . . .

This was wild thinking. What was needed now was guile, not hot-blooded recklessness.

What if he . . . ?

Yes! Crazy, lunatic, even, but this would give him a chance, however slight.

He would sail to Constantinople and demand that if they didn't hand over Renzi he would call on all of Nelson's fleet, which was not far behind, to finish the job.

Something like that, anyway.

Constantinople was only a day or two away, less for a taut sailer like *L'Aurore*.

Supposing, with the experience he now had of the Dardanelles and Kendall's meticulous notes, he made passage – at night?

Timing – a fair wind, moonlight. It could be done.

He went on deck to sniff the wind and collect his thoughts, then called the master down.

'Mr Kendall, we have a duty to the hydrographer of the Navy to report on areas of possible future operations. I'd like your thoughts on how a British man-o'-war might fare, should she look to passing Point Pesquies at night under full sail.'

He stared at Kydd as though he were mad. 'At night, sir? I'd be obliged to call that an act o' desperation. Full sail – if she were t' touch bottom at speed it could send her sticks down, an' if the wind turned foul, there'd be—'

'Think again, Mr Kendall. Enough moonlight we can see, the gunners ashore not so much. Wind fair and brisk from the east-sou'-east . . .'

Rubbing his chin, the seasoned old mariner replied slowly, 'Well, I suppose it could be done. If they has m' notes, there's mention of a useful current around the point hard against the Europe shore and I've note of all seamarks as can be seen. An' if it's to be an east-sou'-easterly like now, why, that's fair for 'em all the way – and back, if'n it holds.'

Kydd held down a rush of hope. 'That seems reasonable enough, Mr Kendall. Thank you.'

This night there was a quarter-moon as well – it was as if the gods were encouraging them on.

After the master had left he eagerly went back to the charts. From Cape Janissary at the entrance to the outer castles was ten miles. To the monster guns at Point Pesquies – the inner castles – another four or five. If *L'Aurore* gave of her best they could do it.

Then objections rushed in.

He was leaving station, the gravest of crimes. He would argue that one when it came – he would be gone only a day or so, if he got through. If not, it didn't matter anyway.

Placing his command in mortal hazard? This was always a judgement of the captain's, and could not be questioned.

But there was one final hurdle: the moral dimension.

Had he the right to thrust *L'Aurore*'s company into mortal danger, just for the sake of a friend?

Given the range of what could go wrong, there was a good chance that the whole enterprise might come to a sorry end.

He strode to the door. 'The officer-of-the-watch to see me. Now!'

Bowden entered, mystified.

'Clear lower deck. I'm to address the ship's company in ten minutes. That's the lot – watch on deck, idlers, everybody.'

'Aye aye, sir.'

It was a rare occasion that brought the entire crew of the frigate on deck at the same time. Divisions, church, dress ship – but none had the power that 'clear lower deck' had. This was the order that brought every single soul up without exception: watch-keepers, cooks, men off-watch sleeping, marine sentries, the carpenter.

Word came that they were assembled. As soon as he emerged on deck the excited murmuring died, making super-fluous Oakley's furious pipe of 'still'.

Curzon touched his hat. 'Ship's company mustered as ordered, Sir Thomas.'

336

'Very good,' Kydd replied, and stepped up to the little deck space left to him, by the wheel.

'L'Aurores,' he began impressively, but at the last moment hesitated at the enormity of what he was asking of them. And what could he do if they held back?

'Ahem. I'll have you know I had a letter a little while ago. It was from an Englishman in a desperate plight in chains in some fortress in Constantinople.

'It pleads with the nearest British man-o'-war to find an authority to negotiate for his release. I have to tell you that at this stage in our political fortunes there is none.'

He let it sink in.

'This means that if we sail away, his last hope will be extinguished and he must lie there, abandoned by all.'

He raised his voice aggressively. 'I can't let that happen! While I have my honour, and an English heart that beats, I will not cease from an attempt at his liberty!'

There was a roar of tigerish approval so he went on, 'I have a plan. It will not be easy, in fact it'll be damned dangerous, but I know you'll want to be with me.'

The noise fell away – it was replaced by a muttering.

'A racing passage through the Dardanelles – at night, and under full sail. Something you'll tell your grandchildren, the day when *L'Aurore* caught the Turk on the hop and rescued a countryman, like heroes.'

There was now an unmistakable hush, then low murmuring. They were not fools and could work out the fearful dangers lying in wait.

'It's only a day's run, if our stout frigate cracks on sail, and I've got the timings as will allow us to do it before they wake up. What say you, L'Aurores? Are you with me?'

All the officers stared at him as if he was mad.

'For the sake of our people – boat's crew and the midshipmen, they'll be with him, no doubt on it.' He couldn't know, of course, whether they would be there.

This brought an agitated growling but no full-throated clamour.

He was losing them.

It was time to play his last and only card.

'What if I told you the name of this captive, this victim of Turkish treachery? It's one you know – for he's been your shipmate since *L'Aurore* was first commissioned.'

There was an astonished silence at this.

'I'll tell you who. It's Nicholas Renzi as was. Who's seen us through more than one adventure, put his life at stake for his ship, always played us true. Now, will we sail away without we even try?'

'Sir?'

'Yes?'

'What about them monster guns? We ain't got a chance agin 'em all firing at one target.'

'I'm surprised at you, Mason, a fine gunner like you. I ask you, how do we fight a night action? Always yardarm to yardarm, that way we can't miss, for at night sighting is useless. So even if they're ready for us – which they won't be – they'll not get off a shot worth the aiming.

'Martin?' Another gunner.

'Cracking on wi' a full spread o' canvas – what if we touch? It'll be all over main quickly, I'm thinking.'

'Good question. Here's the answer: we've been up and down that damned ditch enough times we're not going to be surprised by it. Most important, we've got some copper-bottomed pilot notes, thanks to Mr Kendall, which we're going to use to set up a right good steer for ourselves. We go into this with the best navigation there is.'

A hum of interest started and he caught the word 'Renzi' more than once.

Curzon came up beside him. 'Sir, you're saying that it's Lord Farndon in a Turkish clink? How can this be? We left him in England. Are you sure this is not an imposter?'

'It's him, sure enough. I'd recognise his hand anywhere – but the devil alone knows what he's doing in all this.'

'What'll ye do, sir, once we gets to Constantinople, like?' came a question from the tattooed hulk of Oakley, the boatswain.

'Ah, yes. That's when we spin our yarn as says we're scouts for the biggest fleet Nelson ever had, and if they're not relieved of our men, our admiral will be tempted to come up the same way as we did before and finish the job.'

It brought hesitant laughs, for wasn't Kydd joking? He must really have a secret plan as he always had before.

Now was probably the best time to try for the decider.

'So, maybe we'll have a crack at it. I'm not going to call for a show of hands – I'm your captain, after all – but here's my word on it: if any man feels he doesn't want to be a part of it, he's free to go ashore and wait it out with the Russians, no questions asked. And if—'

'Cap'n Kydd!' came Toby Stirk's bull roar. 'I were wi' Renzi back in the old *Royal Billy* and, be buggered to it, I'm not leavin' a messmate to die in some Turk chokey! I say what're we waitin' about for? Let's get the bastard *and* our boat's crew out an' worry about it later!'

The answering cheer said it all: they were going to Constantinople or Hell, like true British tars, for a shipmate. The adventure was on.

The master took his time studying the chart before he gravely pronounced, 'This'n is the hardest beat to wind'd of any run

339

I've heard . . . 'Cepting Cap'n Cook's night sail up the St Lawrence as fooled the Frenchies, o' course,' he added.

'What I advises is a passage plan as takes advantage of the shore seamarks, there bein' no buoyage in the Dardanelles. We're lucky the Turk has plenty o' them mosques – they're always white an' will show in the moonlight. So we has our waypoints depending on these.'

It was a sound plan: he'd noted quite a number of mosques and had taken their bearings at points along their course. What they had to do now was to come up with a best track; then at the waypoints where a change of course was necessary, transfer to the original plotted course new bearings. This would fix the point at which the helm should go over.

It was professional work in which Kendall could be expected to excel, and Kydd turned his mind to the practicalities.

The passage through would be all in one board, on the starboard tack, so sail-handling would not be a problem. The only need to touch gear was in the dog-leg between the inner castles when they would have to brace around to conform to their heading.

Firing back was out of the question – gun-flash would blind the helm and those taking sights. They would have to make the entire distance without defending themselves.

The slightest error in the bearings would be disastrous. It was crucial to be sure of the course changes, and Kydd took pains to make it so.

The passage plan waypoints were in the form of specified bearings. That was, if the seamark bore on its line of bearing at the same time as an opposite one lined up with its own, then the waypoint had been reached and the wheel would be put over.

He would have all the officers at the same task: separately

equipped with boat compasses, they would each be tracking progress on their side of the ship and call a warning when coming up to a line of bearing. At the same time the master's mates would be ahead of them, searching out and identifying the next seamark.

It was as much as they could do to prepare – but would it be enough?

Kydd was uncomfortably aware of the two things he could not control and which might in a trice render them a helpless wreck: the moon and the wind.

The quarter-moon was favourable: enough to make out their marks ashore but not so bright as to allow the fort gunners to aim accurately. But if the worst happened – clouds coming up to veil the face of the moon – then they would no longer make out their seamarks, and under full sail a quick end was inevitable.

For the moment the wind was fair: east-south-easterly. But Kydd knew now that the usual pattern in this part of the world was for the reigning winds tending to be either north-easterly or south-westerly. The master's log, taking wind direction every watch, showed their present good fortune to be only a stage in a slow but persistent backing as it shifted from south to north.

They had a bracket of time that was unknown – if it came round too swiftly they would be headed, unable in the narrow confines to make way against it, and must anchor or return. If it happened while passing through the danger zone, disaster would be complete.

They had just two hours before they must set sail.

The boatswain, accompanied by his mate, roamed the ship like a bear, becketing up loose gear and laying along stopper tackles ready to clap on to any severed line.

Dillon set about his duty: the vital task of assembling all confidential papers, codes, lists, anything of value to the enemy. He placed these in a canvas sack weighted with grape shot and securely padlocked. If the worst happened he would throw this out of the stern window to sink out of reach.

Kydd, however, had leisure to worry and endlessly go over the plan.

But two things were on their side.

Surprise! A mighty fleet might try but a lone frigate? At speed under cover of night – it would be the last thing expected.

And the Ottoman Navy. It was all somewhere in the Aegean trying for conclusions with the Russians. He therefore need not fear meeting any on the way or when they reached Constantinople.

With the sun a glowing orb behind them, *L'Aurore* weighed and proceeded.

She began under easy sail, as if on blockade searching here and there for prey. The forts at the entrance didn't bother with a shot as the last of the daylight dwindled and they took up on a slant inward.

It was time to make their move.

'Lay out 'n' loose!'

Topmen leaped into action and sail fell from the yards. Courses on fore and main, the biggest and most powerful driving sails, caught the wind with a bang and a flap before being sheeted in, the driver on the mizzen brought in and hauled in hard.

L'Aurore felt their impetus and the trot turned to a gallop.

'A whisker off twelve!' The cry from the log showed them now creaming through the water at a full four times the speed of soldiers quick-marching. Nothing could touch the flying *L'Aurore* on a bowline.

Kydd looked up anxiously. There was cloud but it was scattered in low layers and for now the moon poured its chill splendour freely upon the scene. The coastline could be made out distinctly, darker shadowing against the moonpath.

'Mark t' larboard!' sang out Saxton. His outflung arm towards the European shore had Bowden and Curzon up and sighting while on the other side Brice and Kydd waited impatiently for their call.

'Mark to starboard!' Kydd put his compass to work with its dimmed lamp and steady lubber's line, the card swimming lazily. Kendall was right: the mosque's white dome was an indisputable mark for them.

Usually all but deserted in the night watches, the deck was full of men, the tension keeping conversation short as they concentrated.

As they neared the bearings, warnings rapped out and the sailing master bent to the binnacle with its main ship's compass and waited for the right moment. 'Helm up, steer nor'-east b' north.'

Their course was now shaping more northward and the two sides of the Dardanelles began closing in on them – they would meet ahead at the outer castles and then they would know their fate.

Completely silent to any watcher, the frigate raced on, a half-acre of sail aloft, prettily illuminated by the calm moonlight. But so far there was no interest showing from the shore.

They were nearly up with the forts that Kydd remembered so well when the first alarm was given. A signal cannon from the solid mass of the fortress to starboard – and another, but no firing on them.

He smiled thinly: it would be a scene of consternation ashore, where a sleepy duty officer was being asked to decide urgently if they should open fire on what could well be one of their own fleeing from a pursuer. The hapless man could have seen no colours aloft, for *L'Aurore* was flying none, but evidently he'd thought the chances of an English ship sailing at full tilt up the narrows in the dead of night was too bizarre to contemplate and they passed through without a shot being fired.

Reaching their next waypoint precisely mid-stream, the helm was put up another point and their track was now dead north – with Point Pesquies just two miles ahead.

Their wake seethed and bubbled in a straight line astern, white and glistening in the night, like an accusing finger towards them as the dark thrust of the headland loomed.

This was the most treacherous place of all – the narrows, where the decision had to be made to stay by the north bank, away from the guns but with the greatest current set against them, or the south bank, with clearer water but closer to the guns. And at the same time there was the complication of the risky sharp turn to starboard through nearly a right angle.

Lights twinkled ashore; people there had no idea that an English ship was—

But suddenly – a monstrous gun-flash and deep concussion. Soon gunfire was general, livid flashes and thunderous booming echoing about the still night.

The flash and smoke were making it impossible to spot the passive white of the mosques.

'I've lost the mark!' Saxton burst out.

Kendall's pale face turned to Kydd. 'If I doesn't have the bearings . . .'

The custom of the sea demanded it was up to the captain to make the fateful decision.

'Lay the foreland two cables to starboard,' Kydd ordered. It was a known position and took them closer to the guns but faster around the point.

The firing was intense – but they were gloriously untouched. Closer still: distant figures of the gunners could be seen frozen in the gun-flash as they frenziedly plied their cannon, but the shots were going wild, giant splashes rearing up in the darkness, smaller skittering across the moonpath.

The point neared – a dull twanging aloft was a backstay shot through and unstranding. A thud and tremor followed: *L'Aurore* had suffered at least one ball strike to the hull.

She began the turn; they could take up their marks again once they were around and—

In an instant Kydd's world was transformed into a chaos of pain and disorientation. He found himself sprawled on deck, hearing from an infinite distance Curzon shouting orders and seeing the quartermaster looking down anxiously.

He levered himself up and noticed a still shape next to him. Kendall.

Shaking his head to clear it, he staggered to his feet.

'Sir – wind o' ball!' Bowden said anxiously.

It took long seconds to register that the path of a cannon ball that had blasted between them had knocked Kendall unconscious and thrown him down with concussion.

The sailing master – of all of them to be taken out of the fight . . .

Through the pain of a spitting headache Kydd forced himself to focus.

Point Pesquies was coming up fast and the guns were blasting out in a frenzy – but he could see that, blinded by the constant flashes, they were firing more or less at random and probably would not even know when *L'Aurore* had passed by.

345

When they lay over at last for the haul to the north-east, they left behind thundering guns in manic play on an empty sea.

They were through!

Kydd's body throbbed with pain and he squeezed away tears as he flogged his mind to concentration.

It was not over yet.

There was a stretch of twenty or more miles and then it was the Gallipoli forts. It was now well on into the early hours and sunrise could not be far off. If they didn't get past while it was still dark the gunners would have them over open sights in full daylight.

'Crack on, Mr Curzon,' he croaked. 'Every stitch o' canvas counts.'

He clutched on to one thing: *L'Aurore* was now sailing at her best. She was travelling at speeds impossible on land: no word of warning could possibly be passed – no running messenger, not even a horse at full gallop, could sustain the pace.

And Kendall's painstaking work was paying off.

Quickly picking up the seamarks again, they made good speed but there was a perceptible change now. To starboard the sky was definitely lightening.

It was a race to the finish.

When it came it was almost an anticlimax.

The craggy cliffs loomed to larboard and there was no alarm. Even as the grey chill break-of-day spread there was still no sudden activity on the land.

The sight of an anonymous frigate scudding by in the innocent dawn had taken them completely by surprise. When well past, forlorn shots rang out but it was too late. Now they were free: ahead was open sea – and Constantinople!

* * *

Kydd leaned on his elbow in his cot while the surgeon pressed on him an evil-tasting concoction, apparently a sovereign remedy for headache. After a few hours' sleep he was on the mend although his head still pounded – but he had to face that the critical time lay ahead.

They had achieved a miracle by surprise and daring but it would be all for nothing if he failed at his main task: to force the Turks to deliver up his friend.

In the rush of technical and professional preparation for the passage, he had not had time to give it much thought but now he must.

He groaned and pushed aside Tysoe's well-meant gruel.

Even supposing he could brazenly arrive under flag of truce and demand to speak with their sultan or whomever, what argument could he bring to bear?

A wave of nausea threatened to undo Peyton's good work.

'Leave me,' he gasped, but it was too late.

The surgeon wordlessly cleaned it up and left, prescribing more rest.

Kydd lay back in despair.

By the afternoon he could sit up without queasiness but his headache still thumped pitilessly.

They were hours away only . . .

Incredibly, quite soon, it came to him what he would say.

It would be: the Turks, quite unwittingly, had made a serious blunder.

It had been brought to the ear of the puissant and dread King of England that his cousin the sultan was shamefully detaining the person of the noble and worthy Lord Farndon, closely related to the royal family.

Certainly an oversight – nevertheless, if the wholly innocent aristocrat was not delivered up safely to the captain of the frigate detailed to bring him home, the King would feel it upon his honour to strip the rest of the world of his very own Royal Navy and send it – all 467 battleships – to Constantinople to effect his release.

No doubt the sultan would be pleased to comply once the mistake was known and that would be an end of the matter.

Yes!

'Mr Dillon, the carpenter and the gunner to attend on me,' he ordered firmly.

Shortly, there took place an extraordinary meeting.

The result was perfect: two boards, covered with red baize and bound like a book. On the outside of the 'cover' was fastened a gun tompion from the saluting cannon, in the form of a King George crown, suitably gilded, licked with scarlet and green and satisfyingly heavy.

On the inside was a vellum, executed in meticulous script by Dillon and detailing the King's solemn concerns. It was liberally adorned with seals and ciphers, each of which had a tail of gold lace or tassel sacrificed from Kydd's own dress uniform.

Curzon arrived and announced, 'The coast o' Turkey, nor'-west eight miles.'

It was a question, of course.

'Stand off and on until after dark, if you please. We want to arrive before dawn.'

There was little danger of being sighted. The blockade was biting and there was no point in anything being at sea when they had nowhere to go, and with their navy otherwise engaged . . .

After midnight they approached the peninsula. It slumbered in darkness but at its end city lights pointed the way.

Ghosting along under staysails and jib, the frigate would be near invisible from the shore; the moon hung low in the east. It didn't take long to reach the tip – Seraglio Point. It was a great relief to see the anchorage deserted for it confirmed that all Turkish ships were away and they could flaunt their impudence without interference.

Instead of anchoring in the long outer stretch of water they came to at the series of buoys reserved for the Ottoman Navy and picked up moorings on the first. The inboard part of the mooring cable was not belayed, but seized together with light line. If there was the slightest trouble, the boatswain at the ready could, in a slice of his knife, set them free.

At first light there was the astonishing sight for the beleaguered city of a Royal Navy frigate calmly at a buoy, the largest ensign of the King's Navy at her mizzen and a white flag firmly at the fore-masthead.

Kydd smiled grimly at the thought of what must be happening ashore.

They should be opening fire with everything they had – but it would pass belief that this bold frigate, appearing from nowhere to take up rest, was challenging their defences. Why was it here? It must have a purpose, and better for all if they find out before anything happened that they might regret later.

Sure enough, the galley of Kaptan Pasha left for *L'Aurore* without delay.

As soon as he had clambered aboard, Kydd detected the man's consternation.

The dragoman bowed hastily. 'Kaptan, he want to know, why you here?'

It seemed there were to be no subtle preliminaries so without a word Kydd pressed on with the main act.

He clapped his hands imperiously. From the main-hatch a pair of seamen bore a sea-chest draped with a Union flag. Everyone on deck snapped to attention.

They brought it forward and placed it by the main-mast.

Curzon stepped up, ceremoniously opened it, drew out the contents and held them aloft for all to see.

Kydd roared a command and at once everyone bowed deeply to it.

'Kaptan Pasha. This is from the King of England himself and it is to be placed in the hands of the sultan instantly.'

'My master, he say, what it contain?'

Kydd stared at him in apparent disbelief.

'This is a communication from one great sovereign to another and he asks what it says? I'm shocked that such a high official of the Sublime Porte is so ignorant of the ways of the immortals. Do convey it to the sultan without delay, at peril of his displeasure.'

Chapter 14

'And . . . there! In check, *mon ami*. Another three moves, I think?'

His opponent played to his image, Lord Farndon was bored with it all – with himself, the four blank and noisome walls of his cell and Sébastiani, who was taking their chess game far too seriously.

They had squares of paper with inked pictures of the pieces on them and a scrawled board on the filthy little table. Sébastiani seemed to take a ferocious pleasure in marshalling his forces in detail to crowd in on Renzi before bringing about an elaborate and inevitable defeat.

And when it became too dim to see, there was nothing for it but to lie back on the rank-smelling beds and exchange life experiences.

At least it was entertainment of a sort: Renzi took satisfaction in conjuring up a pampered world of society balls, tricky situations at Court, errant footmen and charming foolishness for Sébastiani, who, to his surprise, was always naïvely agog for more.

In return, the French general brought out wearisome campaign anecdotes, interspersed with hesitations as he reviewed what he was going to say, that it did not offer intelligence of use to an Englishman.

Nevertheless Renzi was keenly interested, for Sébastiani's service included Egypt where he himself had been on the opposing and winning side. His cellmate had been at the Court of the Holy Roman Empire in its last days, being wounded and promoted at the battle of Austerlitz.

Then it was the unutterable tedium of the night, broken only in the morning by the clanking arrival of the guard, when another day would begin.

This day they had set up their 'board' early for the general seemed to have a fierce need to break his record of six straight victories.

Another three moves? The noble lord could see it, but who cared?

'*Merde!*' Sébastiani swore, for the sound of the guard approaching and opening the door was always followed by a gusting of the paper pieces everywhere, game over.

The door rattled, but instead of the amiable old guard there was Grand Vizier Köse Musa and a phalanx of officials – and, incredibly, Zorlu, whose blank expression was an immediate warning.

Was this to be an entreaty for the noble captive to recant before trial and execution? What else could have brought the highest servant of the sultan here? Or could it be . . .

Renzi bowed politely in the English manner and was rewarded with an Oriental bow from Musa. Sébastiani was completely ignored.

A lordly statement was made; Zorlu politely relayed the platitudes.

Then came the real reason for the visit.

'We are here witness to the carrying out of the sentence handed down by Sultan Mustafa IV on the Englishman known as Fahn'ton Pasha.'

A chill of fear flooded Renzi.

Was this to be hauled out into the dingy quadrangle, there to be decapitated? His plan had failed and—

'His Greatness decrees that the said Fahn'ton Pasha be banished from his realm for ever.'

Zorlu's control was nearly perfect but Renzi saw through it.

'Wherein an English ship has been summoned to carry out the sentence forthwith.'

'The Lord Farndon accepts his fate with sorrow, but will comply.'

There was visible relief.

'Providing his household and all his servants accompany him into exile.'

'Of course.'

He turned to Sébastiani to explain his departure, but the general, staring at him with wild eyes, blurted, 'Take me with you – it was our bargain!'

So the villain had perfect English to overhear everything that had been said.

'I do remember,' Renzi replied. 'As I do our agreement that the succoured should assume the status of internee to the other. Very well. Do you wish to be gone from this place?'

'I do,' the Frenchman said, with a fierce sincerity.

'Then consider yourself a guest of the British Crown, sir.'

To Zorlu, he said, 'Tell the vizier I shall ask General Sébastiani to leave with me.'

This caused confusion and dismay.

'That is not possible. The general has yet to answer before a state trial why, when given all trust and resources, he failed to defend Constantinople against the Russians.'

For all the vainglory and boasting of the French, they had yet again been brought to their knees by the sea, the element Bonaparte would never understand.

'I'm sorry, General, so truly sorry,' Renzi said, shaking his head in compassion.

'You must help me! Please – help me, m' lord,' he whispered hoarsely.

Renzi hesitated. He owed the man nothing, but the vision of his fine mind brought to a squalid conclusion under a Turkish scimitar troubled him – and, besides, was not his mission to achieve the ejecting of the French from the Porte? Then he would ensure that very article.

'Tell the vizier I'm desolated to hear that my wishes in the matter are ignored. Do not the Turks wish all infidels gone from their door? I desire the same thing, surely.'

'This cannot be done. The general must stand trial.'

'Then, unhappily, it seems I must decline to leave.' He went over to his bed and elaborately lay down.

Zorlu gave him a worried glance but Renzi knew he was reading the situation for what it was, that whatever pressure was being applied it was overwhelming and irresistible.

Musa flashed him a murderous look, then quickly collected himself. 'Then it is granted on the understanding that, in addition, all the foreign unbelievers of the general's household are taken off our hands.'

Renzi acknowledged this with a gracious bow and got to his feet. 'Shall we go, *mon général*?'

*   *   *

The carriage stopped at the waterfront and Renzi was handed down by an imperturbable Jago. He raised his eyes and there before him was a vision beautiful beyond compare and which took away his breath in a shuddering realisation of who his saviour was.

HMS *L'Aurore*: trim, warlike and every bit as lovely as he remembered.

Come to take him home.

Her captain's barge had put off and there, in the sternsheets, was a figure. One he would always count as his closest friend.

The boat glided in, her crew slapping the loom of their oars to bring them smartly vertical.

With tears pricking, Renzi watched Kydd step ashore and advance towards him, that same masculine stride, those direct brown eyes now so creased with pleasure.

'Why, Nicholas, m' friend. Am I seeing you well?'

He stretched out his hand – but Renzi felt a tide of over-whelming feeling take him and he fell on Kydd's neck, hugging him. The two clung to each other for a long moment, then drew away, embarrassed.

'We have to sail while the wind's fair, Nicholas,' Kydd managed.

'Of course. Might I present General Horace Sébastiani de la Porta? He's to take passage with us.'

The Frenchman's eyes glittered and he bowed stiffly.

'Your household is not here to include with us, General?'

'They fled early,' Sébastiani bit off.

'Then it is only our own that comes. Mr Jago, are all present and correct?'

'They're all here, m' lord.'

Kydd intervened: 'Have you seen two midshipmen and a boat's crew b' chance?'

'No, I'm afraid not. I've heard some English were taken but I've not seen any sign of them.'

'That's a great pity but we must be away before things turn bad.'

The launch and cutter arrived ready to take Renzi's retinue.

'Mr Zorlu? You will come with us, of course.'

'Fahn'ton Pasha, I fancy there will be need for a British embassy before very long. I have therefore a duty to remain, my lord.'

'Then do so, and please believe that your services will be recognised in due course by the Crown, sir.'

Zorlu bowed wordlessly.

The two friends sat side by side in the sternsheets of the barge.

'Give way, you lubbers!' Kydd ordered happily.

L'Aurore hove to off Cape Janissary at the seaward entrance to the Dardanelles after an uneventful passage, secured for them by the large pennant they were instructed by Kaptan Pasha to fly prominently from the fore-masthead. This had now to be surrendered to the fort commander.

Kydd paced his quarterdeck slowly in satisfaction, relishing their achievement and his doughty crew, who had made it possible.

Renzi came on deck slowly, blinking in the sunshine.

'Nicholas!' he said, with pleasure. 'You're awake! You've slept more than a day, do you know that?'

'I needed it, brother. Where are we?'

'You'll see the wide Mediterranean ahead, and those two points the entry to the Dardanelles.'

'So . . .'

'Yes, m' friend, we're free at last. I'm to make my number

with Admiral Senyavin at Tenedos now, and when I get back we must see about what to do with you.'

'Please, dear fellow, don't feel that—'

'Nonsense. We have to think about getting you back by some means. I'm detained here, so heartily regret I cannot take you.'

Curzon came up. 'Boat ready, Sir Thomas.' It was amazing how formal *L'Aurore* had become simply by being the temporary bearer of a peer of the realm.

'We'll talk when I get back, Nicholas.'

As Kydd left, Renzi drew a deep, shuddering sigh. The sights, sounds and comfortable smells of the frigate he had spent so much of his life in were working their balm on his soul.

Life had been so simple then, bounded by straightforward rules of conduct, of direct pleasures and the ever-changing purity of a seascape. Compared to the moral complexities and crushing responsibilities of his new calling, it had been such a very different existence. And here he was, if only for a short time, back in that world.

He strolled forward, past the main-mast and along the gangway over the guns to the fore-deck. Grinning seamen touched their forelocks in exaggerated respect, and well-known faces stammered awkward words to their old shipmate as he passed them by.

Dillon came to offer congratulations on his escape and a marked curiosity about how he had come to be in Constantinople. He answered with the Gordion mission, which seemed to satisfy.

The young man had changed: no longer the pale-faced, studious youth he had last seen on the estate, he was now tanned, fit, and passed down the deck like a seasoned mariner.

Even as he asked, he knew the answer to his question: was Dillon desirous of returning to Eskdale Hall with him?

His charmingly evasive reply was to the effect that perhaps he would persevere for a little longer – if Captain Kydd was agreeable.

The sails slapped fretfully aback as they continued their heaving to and the bell was given two double-strikes. As if in a dream he swung up to the fore-shrouds and climbed up into the fore-top where he sat, as he had so often in the past, with his back to the mast, and closed his eyes in contentment.

All was well with the world.

A sudden raising of voices, then astonished cheering roused him and he looked over the edge of the fighting top – Kydd was returning in the boat.

Puzzled, he descended to the deck. He was just in time to see him coming over the side and a small crowd gathering.

'A glorious day!' Kydd grinned. 'But first see who we've here!'

A gaunt Poulden shepherded two wide-eyed young midshipmen over the side, the rest of *L'Aurore*'s missing boat's crew following. They arrived on deck to slaps on the back, shouts of joy and a rising babble of incredulous talk.

'They were found in irons in the Turk flagship. This was after a famous battle when Senyavin caught up and did for 'em in splendid fashion.'

Almost stumbling in a dream-walk, the lads were led below by kindly sailors.

Kydd chuckled. 'They'll not know it now, but in years to come, wardrooms around the fleet will be hearing of the time they were held captive by Turkish fiends.'

'You said a famous battle?'

'As would stand with any since Trafalgar, I'm persuaded. But don't you see, Nicholas? It's done, over. The Turks will now be seeking peace and I've no more reason to stay here in this benighted land.

'We sail for Cádiz this hour. And tonight we'll dine together – for the first time since, let me see . . . a very long time.'

That evening, as *L'Aurore* put out over the Mediterranean into a setting sun that blazed with a splendour that touched the heart, the two friends supped together.

'I haven't seen M'sieur Sébastiani,' Renzi said, reaching for yet more gilt-head bream.

'Ah. The devil was too quick for us. Just as we were passing the Gallipoli forts, rejoicing in our flag of protection, he leaped over the side and stroked out like a good 'un for the shore. Knew, o' course, he was safe – that we couldn't turn in the narrows or sail back against the blow.'

He held his Moschofilero up to the light. 'Splendid drop this, don't you think?'

There was a pause of some significance. Then Kydd put down his wine. 'I don't suppose you'll tell me why you're in these waters, Nicholas?'

'Perhaps at another time.'

Kydd sighed, his face thoughtful. 'I'm sanguine Collingwood will look kindly on your suffering. He's a considerate sort of chap and I'll wager he'll ask me to be so good as to convey such a noble martyr back to England.'

'That will be a particular pleasure, dear friend. And I'm sure I could prevail upon Cecilia to allow me to entertain you for a space at Eskdale Hall.'

Kydd grinned. 'In course there'll be such a public fuss for

L'Aurore, she having snatched a belted earl from the clutches of a sultan of the Turks and—'

'It mustn't happen!' Renzi snapped. 'I don't want it known, under any circumstances.'

'Well, well. If I didn't know you better, I'd think you a wanton noble out on a tour sporting with the native ladies.'

'No, believe me, it's much more important than that.'

Kydd smiled wickedly. 'Then I think you'd better confess to me before Cecilia gets to hear of it.'

'She already has,' Renzi whispered, his eyes filling.

Touched, Kydd said softly, 'Then what's to do, that my friend's in such a moil?'

'Do forgive me, old chap. It's been somewhat of an ordeal.'

'I'll try to understand, dear fellow, but if you don't tell me—'

'Perhaps I will. There's none in this world that I'd trust beyond your good self, Thomas. That I swear to you.'

'Thank you, Nicholas – I suspect you're now to tell me something singular.'

'I am. The year 'ninety-four. We were in *Seaflower* cutter in the Caribbean and had on board the Lord Stanhope. Then the hurricane and our open-boat voyage. Do you remember?'

'I do. A near-run thing.'

'Do you know why Lord Stanhope insisted on departing in the boat? Instead of remaining safely on the island?'

'Don't I remember you two being particularly hugger-mugger together?'

'Quite so. He told me all.

'He had intelligence of a Spanish plot and had to reach England before war was declared—'

'Ah! Now I understand. It always puzzled me why, when

360

he didn't need to, he took his life in his hands in our little boat.'

'It's because this was what he did.'

'You're not being clear, old trout.'

'Lord Stanhope was in fact a species of servant to the Crown who had no office but a calling, one of such gravity and importance that he had the respect and gratitude of the highest in the land. And for this he required the most complete discretion, the exercise of the strictest confidence, for, you see, he deployed his aristocratic lineage as a cloak to conduct activities that diplomats, soldiers and others could not.'

'Nicholas, why are you telling me this? If ever it's known . . .'

'Because Lord Stanhope – or should I say the Marquess of Bloomsbury? – has lately laid down his burden. My dear fellow, I am anointed his successor.'

'Good God!'

He hesitated, then asked, 'You said Cecilia . . . ?'

'Yes. She knows all. As did Lady Stanhope.'

'You didn't—'

'I forbade her to come on this mission, if that is your meaning.'

'I'm damned glad to hear it. But it has to be said that things didn't turn out well for you this first time.'

'On the contrary. The French are ejected from the Sublime Porte. That is all that counts.'

'You're not telling me everything, m' friend.'

'And neither should I. There was nothing you could have done, nothing I could have asked and nothing that wasn't achieved by other means than the broadside of a saucy frigate.'

'Damn it all! There's something—'

'When we're old greybeards together, perhaps we'll sit by a winter fire and tell our stories. Then you'll know. Until then it's imperative I assume the foolishness of rank. Now you can see why my daring exit – which I've yet to express my sensibility of – should not be widely known.'

'It shall be done, old friend. The L'Aurores will stay mum if I tell 'em.'

'And it goes without saying, our conversation tonight is in the highest confidence.'

'Understood, Nicholas. Will you tell Cecilia of your adventures here?'

'There can be no secrets between us,' Renzi said softly. He stopped. 'Ah, that is to say . . .'

'You said *no* secrets from Cecilia.'

'Well, there is actually . . . Can I rely on your understanding, brother? It's rather embarrassing . . .'

'Possibly.'

'It's about—'

'What are you asking me to conceal from my sister?'

'*Portrait of an Adventurer*, Il Giramondo.'

'Ah, your novel. It was published, then.'

'She must never know! I . . .' He tailed off miserably.

Kydd roared with laughter. 'So I've something over you, m' lord. Ha!'

He recovered and managed, 'Pay no mind, Nicholas, I'll keep it quiet.'

'Thank you.'

'In the meantime . . .'

'Yes?'

'If there's trouble and pestilence somewhere in this world, do I take it that not far away a certain peer of the realm might be found?'

Renzi gave a half-smile and refilled their glasses.

'My dear fellow, I couldn't possibly comment.'

Author's Note

Constantinople – or should I say Istanbul? – is one of the world's genuinely iconic locations. It is surpassingly beautiful and has a beguilingly romantic air, tinged with Oriental mystery.

It was one of my life's special moments when, on location research for this book, I stood on a balcony of Topkapi Palace on Seraglio Point and looked out over the Golden Horn, across to Asia and up through the Bosporus in the direction of the Black Sea and Russia. I urge the reader to make the pilgrimage.

There is much remaining of what is mentioned in my book: the sublimity of the Hagia Sophia still takes the breath away; Topkapi, although now without a sultan in residence, is there in its glory and mystery, and the Tower of Justice stands to this day, albeit altered from what Renzi would recognise. Even Bab-ı Ali, the Sublime Porte, still exists, now a bit sad-looking and off in a side-street.

The Dardanelles is a place of fierce currents, and the narrows funnel winds of surprising briskness. To give an idea of the respect it retains, the Admiralty Pilot of today warns that even modern ships should not attempt the strait when currents exceed six knots.

I enjoyed writing this book: that Kydd's world of salt-water seamanship intersected so centrally with such tectonic events in the history of the Levant not well known to the West was irresistible to me.

For the main part things happened much as I relate they did, and as always, although I've taken occasional liberties with elapsed time to tighten the story, I've kept the sequence of events true to history. (For example, I've brought forward by some months Selim's slaying in order to make the experience for the reader more complete.)

The fates of the historical players are interesting.

Blackwood was honourably acquitted over the *Ajax* fire: it remains one of the gravest tragedies the Royal Navy has suffered. The unsmiling Blackwood went on to become admiral but an ill-judged contretemps later with Lord Keith ended his active service.

Arbuthnot returned to a frosty reception, but as a friend of Wellington, and with his wife a lady-in-waiting to Princess Caroline of Brunswick, he escaped censure, as did the well-connected Admiral Duckworth, who went on to command the Channel fleet but died soon after the end of the war.

Senyavin, in my opinion, is a much underrated figure, to this day hardly mentioned by his own navy even though he served with great distinction before and afterwards. The battle to which I alluded in the last chapter, Athos (or Lemnos), in which he finally confronted the Ottomans, was on a scale comparable to Trafalgar. No less than twenty battleships with frigates met off the entrance to the Dardanelles and in a smashing victory Senyavin won the day, the result equally as conclusive – the Turks sued for peace two weeks later. It remains an action almost completely unknown to us in the West and, yes, two British midshipmen and a boat's crew were found in irons in the Turkish flagship and restored to their ship.

Unfortunately for Senyavin, the tide of history turned and he found himself formally at war with Collingwood's fleet. How he diplomatically avoided a clash and sailed his Baltic fleet back after two years' travail is an epic tale in itself, but once home he fell foul of the Tsar and St Petersburg politics and was retired.

Selim met a grim fate, but so did Mustafa, who replaced him, killed on the orders of his younger brother Mahmud, who went on to reinstate the reform agenda.

For Sébastiani, an ironic fate awaited. Biding his time, he returned to Constantinople, then worked tirelessly to restore French influence and Bonaparte's dream of a road to India. But the wily emperor lost interest in the project entirely when he beguiled Tsar Alexander of Russia into an alliance instead, fatally antagonising the Ottomans.

Incidentally, in a quirk of history, at the time Sébastiani was being considered for his post in Constantinople the French Directory thought him too valuable to lose and the choice fell on a lesser, also an artillery, officer. This last, however, in the weeks before he was due to depart made himself indispensable in the affair of 'the whiff of grapeshot', which put down a rebellion in Paris with cannon on the streets. Sébastiani went on to Constantinople; one N. Bonaparte remained in Paris.

The monster guns that wreaked havoc in Duckworth's fleet were real enough, and did indeed originate from the time of the fall of Constantinople and the last Roman Caesar. As far as I'm able to trace, this was their only taste of action since that time. However, as a postscript, the reforming Sultan Abdülâziz after the Crimean war gave one to Queen Victoria who, no doubt bemused, thanked him and tried to think what to do with it.

Today you can see the Great Turkish Bombard for yourself – I've stood next to and marvelled at the giant near twenty-ton bronze beast where it's stored, in Fort Nelson, above Portsmouth.

I've a lot of sympathy for Selim, a cultured and sensitive man, whose compositions are played to this day in Istanbul but whose delicacy and love of learning were no match for the titanic struggles around him.

There's something of a similarity between him and Admiral Duckworth. They both dithered in the face of a need for resolution and firm decision. General Sébastiani himself admitted in later years that if Duckworth had followed Collingwood's orders to stand by his half-hour ultimatum he would have been delivered up to the English instantly. For Selim, if the uprising had been met with immediate orders to his Nizam-i Cedid it would have been another story I'd be telling, but his temporising ways were part of the man and led directly to his death.

The salutary lesson of the Dardanelles expedition was the fatal consequence of divided command. What possessed Whitehall to go over the heads of the sage and competent Collingwood to order the bombardment of Constantinople, to subject the military decisions of the operational commander to the civil power and to second-guess events thousands of miles and months away passes my understanding.

This forcing of the Dardanelles stands alone, never having been done before or since, the last attempt being in the First

World War when it stalled at Gallipoli where the Anzacs went on to win immortality. Since then Turkey has been our ally and during the Cold War firmly kept the door locked on the Russians, whose only warm-water port could therefore be denied the Mediterranean and the outer world.

To all who assisted me in the research for this book I am deeply grateful. I would like to express my special thanks to Ziya Yerlikaya, Jason Goodwin and Tacdin Aker, for generously sharing their knowledge of Turkish history and culture.

And a large huzzah to Team Stockwin – my splendid editors at Hodder & Stoughton, Oliver Johnson and Anne Perry, and their creative art/design team; and copy editor Hazel Orme, who has brought her meticulous blue pencil to bear on the Kydd series right from the debut title. And, as always, heartfelt appreciation to my wife and literary partner Kathy – and my agent Carole Blake.

Glossary

amain	with intent of force and vigour
apoplexy	a stroke
arabesque	in the ornamental Arab style of Baghdad, Samarkand, etc.
baldric	leather sling over the shoulder to suspend the scabbard
Balkans	south-east Europe; the general geographic area lying between Italy and Turkey
barge	boat of slight and spacious construction for use of the captain or admiral
becket	small piece of rope with a knot in one end and an eye in the other to keep an item confined
belfry	ornamental shelter for the ship's bell forward
blashy	dirty weather, miserable and wet, not strong enough to be called a storm
broadside	the entire side of a ship; in gunnery, all the guns on that side
bulwark	the raised edge of the upper deck
capstan	rotating device operated with long bars to lift heavy weights
coach	a frigate captain's quarters consist of a great cabin, with a bedplace and coach where ship's administration was performed
convoy	ships sailing in company provided with an escort
corvette	flush-decked, three-masted armed vessel smaller than a frigate
cuirass	soldier's breastplate
cutter	a ship's boat, broader and deeper than a pinnace

devoir	an act of civility and respect due another
Divan	highest council of state under the sultan; courtly poetry
Dons	the Spanish
dragoman	an interpreter and adviser of Levantine languages
earnest, an	money in advance as a goodwill gesture
encomium	formal expression of warm praise for services completed
escritoire	writing desk with compartments for accessories, often highly ornamental
escutcheon	a shield or other containing armorial bearings
fo'c'sle	forecastle: upper deck above the bow section; in the merchant service the enclosed space below where seamen mess
gregale	north-easterly gale in the Mediterranean; St Paul was wrecked by one on his way to Rome
guardo	an unfair move on a landman; as in a guardship for receiving press-gang victims
gun-room	in a large ship, the gunner's abode; in a frigate, the officers' dining and mess room
hospodar	vassal Slavic ruler in the Ottoman Empire
instanter	that very moment; schoolboy Latin
Janissaries	sultan's elite household troops
kedge	an anchor light enough to be taken to a distance by a boat to allow the ship to haul itself up to it
knittles	the small clew-lines from the edge of the canvas converging in an eye for slinging the hammock
landau	graceful open carriage with facing seats
loom	the shaft of an oar
luff	the edge of the sail closer to the wind
magazines	storeplace for gunpowder
Nizam-ı Cedid	new army established following reforms of Sultan Selim III
ostler	one employed at a hostelry or stable to look after horses
Pasha, Bey, Efendi	Ottoman honorifics in descending order
Peace of Amiens	peace that separated the French Revolutionary War and the Napoleonic war that followed
pendant	a piece of rope with a block or eye at its end to operate an object at a distance
pennant	a long narrow flag; not to be confused with pendant
pilot	one with local nautical knowledge as an adviser; also an authoritative printed guide
piping the eye	crying, as in a child
poilu	term of endearment for French infantryman similar to 'Tommy'
posset	spiced drink of hot milk curdled with ale

post-chaise	fast horse-drawn closed four-wheeled carriage
posy ring	ring with inscribed words; French *poesy*
preventer tackles	rigged to prevent a spar taking charge in a blow
quarters	after the ship is cleared for action, the men close up at quarters for battle
reefer	midshipman
Reis-ül Kuttab	essentially the Ottoman foreign ministry
riband	ornate ribbon used in military decorations
scabbard	the sheath of a sword or bayonet
seraglio	strictly, the living quarters of the harem (wives and concubines), generalised to harem today
sextant	navigational instrument with a 60° arc, used for determining latitudes
shab	shabaroon; disreputable and unreliable
sky hook	mythical device for hoisting higher than the masthead
slasher	cutlass; barkers and slashers – pistols and cutlasses
spar	general term for mast, yard, boom, etc.
staysail	a triangular sail hoisted on the stays between the masts
stopper	to check or hold fast one rope by means of another
Sublime Porte	term for the state apparatus for receiving foreign envoys in the Ottoman Court
tarpaulin officer	officer who started as a common seaman
Tobias Smollett	early picaresque novelist of the sea; see *Roderick Random*
trusties	those men trusted to return to the ship if given liberty
Ulema	body of Islamic scholars in counsel to the sultan
victuals	provisions for the ship's company
weigh	weigh anchor: to raise it clear of the seabed, metaphorically to start a voyage
yamak	auxiliary soldier in the Ottoman Army
zindīq	infidel, heretic

Timeline

1773   Thomas Paine Kydd is born 20 June, in Guildford, Surrey, son of Walter and Fanny Kydd.

1789   The Storming of the Bastille, 14 July.

1793–1794   Louis XVI executed, 21 January 1793.

                 France declares war on England; Kydd, a **KYDD** wig-maker by trade, is press-ganged into the 98-gun ship of the line *Duke William*.

                 The Reign of Terror begins, 5 September **ARTEMIS** 1793–28 July 1794.

                 Transferred aboard the crack frigate *Artemis,* Kydd is now a true Jack Tar who comes to love the sea-going life.

1795   The Netherlands is invaded by France, **SEAFLOWER** 19 January, and becomes the Batavian Republic.

                 In the Caribbean, Kydd continues to grow as a prime seaman.

1797   Battle of Cape St Vincent, 14 February. Mutiny at the Nore, 17 April.

	Kydd is promoted to acting lieutenant at Battle of Camperdown, 11 October.	*MUTINY*
1798–1799	Kydd passes exam for lieutenancy; now he must become a gentleman.	*QUARTERDECK*
	From the Halifax station, Kydd and his ship are summoned to join Nelson on an urgent mission.	
	The Battle of the Nile, 1 August 1798. Britain takes Minorca as a naval base from Spain, 16 November 1798. Siege of Acre, March–May 1799.	*TENACIOUS*
1801–1802	Prime Minister Pitt resigns February 1801. Battle of Copenhagen, 2 April 1801. Kydd is made commander of brig-sloop *Teazer* but his jubilation is cut short when peace is declared and he finds himself unemployed.	
	Peace at Treaty of Amiens, 25 March 1802.	*COMMAND*
1803	War resumes 18 May, with Britain declaring war on the French.	
	Unexpectedly, Kydd finds himself back in command of his beloved *Teazer*.	*THE ADMIRAL'S DAUGHTER*
	Kydd is dismissed his ship in the Channel Islands station.	*TREACHERY*
1804	Napoleon's invasion plans are to the fore.	
	May, Pitt becomes Prime Minister again Napoleon is crowned Emperor, 2 December 1804.	*INVASION*
1805	Kydd is made post-captain of *L'Aurore*.	
	The Battle of Trafalgar, 21 October 1805.	*VICTORY*
1806	The race to empire begins in South Africa. British forces take Cape Town, 12 January.	
	A bold attack on Buenos Aires is successful, 2 July 1806.	*CONQUEST*

Effective end of The Fourth Coalition,   *BETRAYAL*
14 October 1806.

In the Caribbean, the French threat takes a new   *CARIBBEE*
and menacing form.

Now read an extract from Julian Stockwin's thrilling novel

CARIBBEE

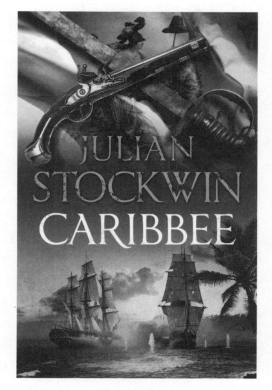

After unremitting war, a Caribbean posting seems a welcome respite for Kydd and Renzi. But, in addition to the balmy warmth and turquoise waters, they finds themselves facing a familiar threat as the French imperil Britain's vital sugar trade.

Soon Kydd and Renzi must embark on a dangerous game of espionage in order to destroy this new and terrible danger to the Empire.

Chapter 1

'S-sir! Mr Curzon's compliments, an' we've raised Barbados!' came the wide-eyed report.

The frigate *L'Aurore* had been at sea for long weeks, beating up the coast of South America in frantic haste on a mission that might well see the catastrophic situation of the British in Buenos Aires reversed. It had been a voyage of daring speed and increasing privation as provisions and water ran low under the pressing need for hurry. Reduced to short allowance, the griping of hunger was constantly with them.

Captain Thomas Kydd looked up from his desk. 'Thank you, Mr Searle.'

The ship's youngest midshipman hesitated, unsure whether to wait for a response for the second lieutenant.

Kydd laid down his pen. 'Tell Mr Curzon I'll be on deck presently.'

Apprehension stole over Kydd as he contemplated his task: to persuade a senior commander-in-chief to detach part of his fleet to go south in rescue of an unauthorised expedition that had sought to liberate South America from the Spanish.

It had all started brilliantly. Their tiny force had quickly captured the seat of the viceroyalty of the River Plate, Buenos Aires, but then the population had turned on their liberators and forced the surrender of their land forces. Commodore Popham, still at anchor off the port there, was desperately seeking support to retake the city.

From the quarterdeck Kydd gazed across an exuberant expanse of white-flecked blue sea to a distant light grey smudge, Barbados – where was to be found the Leeward Islands Squadron. There were just hours left to ensure that his arguments to its admiral for weakening the defences of the vital sugar islands by parting with his valuable assets were sound and convincing.

'A noble achievement, our voyage, sir, I'm persuaded,' Curzon offered, as they neared.

'A damned challenging one,' agreed Kydd, absently. There was murmuring that he didn't catch from the group around the wheel behind him but it wasn't hard to guess its drift. These were men who had left shipmates as prisoners to the Spaniards and they were expecting to see them freed soon by bold naval action.

Barbados was at its shimmering tropical best. After the intense blue of the deep sea, with its gaily tumbling white combers, and shoals of bonito and flying fish pursued by dolphins, there was now calm and beguiling transparent jade water above the corals. Along the shore coconut palms fringed dazzling white beaches. Neat houses on stilts with distinctive green jalousies perched above the tideline.

It was an impossibly lovely prospect for those who had voyaged so long and endured so much but, mission accomplished, they must leave and return to that grey southern madness.

By the time they had made the bluffs of South Point and left the brown and regular green of sugar fields safely to starboard, anxiety returned to steal in on Kydd. There was the possibility that the Leeward Islands Squadron was at sea, in which case it could be anywhere and would have to be found. However, his real concern was that, as a junior frigate captain, he was going to debate high strategy with a senior admiral. But there was no alternative: too many brave men depended on what he was about to say.

He was in full dress uniform well before they opened Carlisle Bay. It was soon established that the fleet was in, an imposing sight – three ships-of-the-line, escorting frigates and many others. But Kydd's eyes were on just one, the largest, which bore the flag of the commander-in-chief, Leeward Islands Squadron.

He knew little of the man: that he was a Cochrane unrelated to the one Napoleon called 'the wolf of the seas', that by reputation he was cautious and punctilious but had nevertheless distinguished himself in battle, and that he was yet another Scot who had reached flag rank in the Royal Navy. None of this was going to help.

An officious brig-sloop rounded to under their lee and, after a brief exchange of hails, *L'Aurore* was shepherded into the anchorage to take up moorings with three other frigates. It felt odd after so long under a press of canvas to be at rest with naked masts.

In his mind Kydd went over yet again the burden of what

he would argue. If successful they could be returning south within days with reinforcements and if not . . . Well, would he have to go back empty-handed?

An expressionless Coxswain Poulden kept tight discipline in the boat's crew as they approached the flagship. *Northumberland* was in immaculate order, the welcoming captain in white gloves as Kydd stepped aboard, carefully lifting his hat to the quarterdeck and waiting while the boatswain's call died away. Then he was escorted to the grand cabin of the commander-in-chief.

'Captain Kydd, is it not?' Cochrane said, in a dry Scots burr, rising from his desk.

'*L'Aurore* frigate, thirty-two guns, sir.'

'As I can see. Her reputation for speed on a bowline is known even here, Captain.'

'Sir, I've news of great importance, a matter that sorely presses, bearing as it does on our situation in the south.'

'Oh? Do carry on then, sir.'

'I'm directed by Commodore Popham, my commander, to make my number with you in respect of an urgent operational request he has to make.'

'I see.' Cochrane's manner became unexpectedly mild, almost whimsical, as if restraining a humorous confidence. 'And you are his emissary. Then do tell what this might be at all.'

'I'm not sure how much you know, sir, of our descent on Buenos Aires, which—'

'You'll take a sherry, Kydd? I favour a light manzanilla in this climate. Will you?'

'Thank you, sir. We met with some success initially, seizing the city and quantities of silver, but –'

'Do sit, Captain. I'm sure it's been something of a trial, your long voyage.'

'– but he now stands embarrassed for want of reinforcement,' Kydd went on doggedly.

'Which he begs I might furnish.'

'Sir, the matter is pressing, I believe, and—'

'And I'm therefore grieved to tell you that your mission is in vain.'

Was this a direct refusal before he'd even mentioned the details? 'Sir, I have a letter for you from the commodore that establishes the strategics at back of his request.'

Cochrane laid it on the desk, unopened. 'That won't be necessary.'

Kydd felt a flush rising. 'Sir, I do feel—'

'Captain, two weeks ago your reinforcements touched here on their way to the River Plate.'

'Why, that's—'

'Together with your commodore's replacement. He is under recall to England to answer for his conduct.'

Kydd was thunderstruck.

'So that disposes of the matter as far as you are concerned, wouldn't you say?' the admiral said, toying with his quill.

'Um, yes, it does seem, sir, that—'

'Quite. Then I suppose it would appear that you and your valiant frigate are now without purpose.'

Keyed up for a protracted confrontation, Kydd could think of nothing with which to meet this.

Cochrane leaned forward and said, with a frown, 'I presume you realise how vital – how *crucial* – these islands are to Great Britain? You do? Then you'll be as distracted as I am, not to say dismayed, when you learn that this humble fleet is all that is left to me in the great purpose of defending the same. After Trafalgar we were stripped – I say *stripped*, sir – of ships of force and value. Should the French make a descent with serious intent, I have the gravest reservations whether I'm in any kind of a position to deter them.'

'Er, I see, sir.'

'So I have it in mind that, following the stranding of *Félicité* frigate, I shall be attaching you to my station pending Admiralty approval.'

Kydd caught his breath. As a commander-in-chief, Cochrane was entitled to avail himself of the services of passing vessels, and there was little doubt that the Admiralty would be reluctant to go to the trouble of sending out a replacement when one had so fortuitously presented itself.

'A light frigate, of little consequence to operations in the south, while here I'm in great want of frigates both for the fleet and to go against French cruisers and privateers. Yes, my dear Kydd, consider yourself as of this moment under my command. Flags will find you a copy of my orders and see you entered into the fleet's signal card and so forth, and I've no doubt you'll wish to water and store while you can. We're shortly to sail on fleet manoeuvres, which will serve as a capital introduction to our ways.'

There was nothing for it: Kydd had to accept that he and *L'Aurore* were now taken up and Popham's brave little expedition was replaced by a full-scale enterprise from England that didn't need them. Their being was now to be found in the Caribbean.

Cochrane mused for a moment, then rose and extended his hand. 'Therefore I do welcome you to the Leeward Islands Squadron, Kydd – you'll find me strict, but fair.' He rang a silver handbell.

A wary lieutenant entered. 'Sir?'

'Flags, this is Captain Kydd of *L'Aurore* frigate. He's to join our little band and I leave him in your capable hands to perform the consequentials. Oh, and the residence will need to know that they'll be having another guest at the levee.'

'Aye aye, sir. Er, it does cross the mind that Captain Kydd's presence might be considered fortunate at this time . . . ?'

'What's that, Flags?'

'The court-martial, sir. You now have your five captains.'

'Ah, yes. Like to get this disagreeable business over with before we sail. Er, set it in train, will you? There's a good fellow.'

Legal proceedings could not begin in a court-martial unless five post captains could be found to sit in judgment and cases had sometimes dragged on for months while waiting for the requisite number.

It was not the most auspicious beginning to his service here.

Back aboard his ship, Kydd cleared lower deck and told her company of developments, mentioning that with powerful reinforcements on their way their shipmates would soon be set at liberty, and announcing the agreeable news that they would be exchanging the winter shoals and lowering darkness of defeat in Buenos Aires for the delights of the Caribbean. It more than made up for the trials of the voyage.

In the time-honoured way, boats had already put off from the shore to the newly arrived ship, laden to the gunwales with tempting delights for sailors long at sea – hands of bananas, moist soursops, grapefruit-tasting shaddock, fried milk, not to mention bammy bread and live chickens, all dispensed with noisy gusto by laughing black faces.

Even Gilbey, the dour first lieutenant, was borne along on the tide of excitement and, wrinkling his nose at the mauby beer, insisted on picking out half a dozen fresh coconuts for the gunroom.

THE
ADVENTURES
CONTINUE
ONLINE

Visit julianstockwin.com

Find Julian on Facebook

f /julian.stockwin

Follow Julian on Twitter

🐦 @julianstockwin